37653011558361
Main   Fiction
FIC ESTRADA
Welcome to Havana, senor
Hemingway : a novel

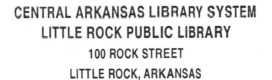

AUG   2005

CENTRAL ARKANSAS LIBRARY SYSTEM
LITTLE ROCK PUBLIC LIBRARY
100 ROCK STREET
LITTLE ROCK, ARKANSAS

WELCOME TO HAVANA, SEÑOR HEMINGWAY

ALFREDO JOSÉ ESTRADA

WELCOME TO HAVANA, SEÑOR HEMINGWAY

This is a work of fiction. While elements of the story are drawn from actual events and certain characters are based upon historical figures, they are used fictitiously and are the product of the author's imagination.

All rights reserved. No part of this book may be used or reproduced in any form whatsoever without written permission from the copyright holder except for brief passages or quotations in critical articles and reviews. For more information contact: Planeta Publishing, 2057 N.W. 87th Avenue, Miami, FL 33172.

© Alfredo José Estrada, 2005
© Planeta Publishing Corp., 2005
   2057 NW 87 Ave.
   Miami, FL 33172 (USA)

Author photograph: Mary Estrada
Cover photograph courtesy of Agualargas Editores. S. A.
Designer: Alberto Insua

First edition: June 2005

ISBN 1-933169-01-X

Printed in Colombia by Editorial Linotipia Bolívar

Para Mamaía

¡Cuba! Al fin te verás libre y pura
como el aire de luz que respiras.

José María Heredia

CENTRAL ARKANSAS LIBRARY SYSTEM
LITTLE ROCK PUBLIC LIBRARY
100 ROCK STREET
LITTLE ROCK, ARKANSAS 72201

To be Cuban is to go with Cuba everywhere.

Guillermo Cabrera Infante

My grandfather once knocked down Ernest Hemingway, or so I was told.

This quixotic legend was often recounted by my Cuban relatives at family reunions, together with stories of what they lost in the Revolution. I didn't know whether to believe them, given their tendency to exaggerate.

Still, it could have been true. My grandfather, Javier López Angulo, was a Harvard man who founded one of the largest advertising agencies in Havana. He was not one to back down from a fight, and might well have confronted the pugnacious writer. But why did they come to blows? Like much about Cuba, the reason was shrouded in mystery. My mother didn't know, nor did her brothers, since it was before their time. As for my grandmother, the mere mention of Hemingway brought out the worst in her, and she dismissed him as a *comunista* and a *come-mierda,* in that order.

But I had reached a point in my life where I was (as they say in novels) at loose ends. My collection of short stories, which I was certain would make me famous, had sunk into oblivion like a rock thrown in the ocean. Although my agent had long stopped returning my phone calls, a woman I knew in college was now the editor of a travel magazine. My rent was due, and over dinner at a Cuban Chinese restaurant on Broadway, I offered to write an article about Hemingway, who lived in Cuba for many years and wrote about it in *The Old Man and the Sea.*

9

"Somebody pitched me that last week," she said, and took another sip from her rum and coke. "Don't they have Hemingway look-alike contests in Havana?"

"That's Key West," I said. "But I know of someone who gave him a black eye."

That was when I told her about my grandfather. Perhaps she was one of the few people who liked my stories, or else it was the second rum and coke. Whatever the reason, she thought it was worth sending me to Havana for a few days at the magazine's expense. But first I needed to talk to my grandmother in Miami.

Abuela (as my cousins and I called her) was still a force of nature in her eighties. In Cuba, she had been a formidable businesswoman who ran the advertising agency after my grandfather's death, long before I was born. It was quite successful for a number of years, and is still remembered by old-timers in the business for its outlandish campaigns. During the late 1940s, at the height of the flying saucer craze, a shiny, spherical object appeared one morning at a baseball stadium in Havana. A crowd gathered in the merciless heat, and even the police were called. Suddenly, the door of the mysterious spaceship slid open, and a trio of dancing girls from the Tropicana emerged, passing out bottles of Hatuey beer to a rumba beat.

But the advertising agency folded after 1959, when Castro came to power and my family left Cuba. Since then, my grandmother had lived in the same shabby bungalow in Key Biscayne, stubbornly refusing to move despite the entreaties of my uncles, who wanted to tear it down and sell the property. In the last few years she had grown forgetful, but each morning she walked down Crandon Boulevard to the park, and sat in the shade of a coconut palm watching the children play.

"*¿Estás loco?*" asked *Abuela* when I told her about my trip. "Why do you want to go back to Cuba?"

"I've never been," I reminded her.

"You might not like what you find."

"But I've always wanted to go," I said. "And I'm writing something about Hemingway."

Abuela shook her head bitterly at the sound of the writer's name, and made that peculiar hissing noise that Cubans call "frying an egg." This confirmed her suspicion that I was insane, an opinion shared by several other members of my family, who couldn't understand what I did for a living. But in spite of everything, I was her favorite grandson. That night, while making *arroz con pollo,* she began to talk about her husband. My Spanish was terrible and my grandmother refused to speak English, so I struggled to understand her words. Stirring the cauldron of yellow rice, her raspy voice softened and she recalled he was the best-looking man at the Havana Yacht Club. Apparently, my grandfather enjoyed his rum and had a well-deserved reputation as a playboy. My mother once told me that *Abuela* was a saint to have put up with him, though that hardly seemed to matter now.

After dinner, she rummaged through her closet until she found an album of old photographs. As I had hoped, there were several pictures of my grandfather as a young man, from around the time he would have met Hemingway. One was taken on the Paseo del Prado, a broad avenue lined with Spanish laurel trees in the heart of Havana. Athletic and tall for a Cuban, he wore what must have been the height of fashion: a white linen suit, a bow tie, and a straw boater tipped at a rakish angle, like Maurice Chevalier. But despite the mocking pose, his deep-set eyes gave him a melancholy air.

Another photograph showed him with my grandmother in Paris, where they spent their honeymoon in 1934. The newlyweds stood together on the Pont Neuf, their backs to the Seine, with the dagger-like spire of the Sainte-Chapelle behind them. Their frozen smiles were for each other, not the nameless photographer, and it must have been winter since they were wearing overcoats. The wind tousled my grandfather's unruly chestnut hair, and my grandmother, still a teenager, held down her *cloche* hat with a pale hand.

There were a few brittle portraits of my grandfather's family: his parents, his sister Lydia, and his older brother Miguel, who had died just a few years before. I remembered him as a tired, broken old man who spent his last days dreaming of what he left behind in Cuba. I also found a picture of the house where my grandfather was born, an imposing Art Nouveau mansion in the suburb of El Vedado, surrounded by fig trees.

Hunting in the closet for more photographs, I had all but given up when I saw a battered hatbox above the shelf. There, together with some yellowing issues of *Bohemia*, an old Cuban magazine, I found what I was looking for. It was a grainy snapshot of my grandfather with Hemingway, not the familiar white-bearded patriarch, but a smiling man in his thirties, movie-star handsome with a clipped mustache. Torn on one edge, it had *April* 1932 scrawled on the back in faded green ink and showed them on a dock in Havana, posing beside a huge marlin. It was an unlikely threesome: my grandfather squinting in the sun, Hemingway grinning fiercely in a baseball cap, and the marlin hanging from its scythe-like tail, its sword pointed downward.

Despite her age, *Abuela's* honey-colored eyes were still sharp and she never wore spectacles. I showed her the photograph and she held it up to the light with trembling fingers.

"Ay, Dios mío," she sighed, and once more fried an egg.

As she made coffee, *Abuela* told me how my grandfather met Hemingway one afternoon at the Floridita, the bar in Havana where they claimed to have invented the daiquiri. Hemingway had arrived from Key West the night before and invited him to go marlin fishing. *Abuela* could say little about the famous fistfight that later ended their friendship, as it happened before she married my grandfather. But she remembered the name of a woman in Havana who knew them both, and I decided to look her up if she was still alive.

I left the next morning. Once in the air, the plane veered south and quickly left Miami's ragged sprawl behind. It was soon over the Florida Keys, leaving a sharp shadow on the jagged islands connected by a strip of highway. In my grand-father's day, Key West had been joined to the mainland by Flagler's railroad, which was destroyed by the great hurricane of 1935 and never rebuilt. Beyond it was the Gulf Stream, the "great blue river," as Hemingway called it. In just a few minutes, I could see Cuba. The shore was obscured by steamy clouds but I made out brownish hills crowned with palm trees and rolling fields of sugar cane.

As the wheels touched down in Havana, the passengers burst into applause. Most were exiles bringing money to rela-tives that stayed behind, or Cubans who had visited their fam-ilies in the United States and were returning with plastic bags crammed with medicine, and hampers filled with toys. One man had on three cowboy hats, one atop the other, and his wife wore a fringed buckskin jacket, like Davy Crockett. Their son sported Nike running shoes and a Miami Dolphins tee-shirt. When I descended from the plane a few steps behind them, the air hit me like a humid blast, and I broke into a sweat as I walked across the tarmac towards the gate.

"¿Usted es cubano?" asked the guard, looking me up and down.

It was a question I didn't know the answer to myself. The guard couldn't tell from my passport, since my father was American and I was born in the United States. Did I somehow look Cuban? I showed him the visa I had gotten as a journal-ist, and he waved me through with a careless shrug. It was the most characteristic of Cuban gestures—his lips pursed, his shoulders slightly hunched, his eyebrows raised. Relieved, I entered the sweltering terminal, in Cuba at last.

I took a cab to the old Hotel Nacional, where the maga-zine had booked me a room. It had been built in 1931, the year my grandfather graduated from college, and overlooked the Malecón, the once-elegant boulevard curving along the water. The hotel stood on the site of a fort which fired upon an American battleship in the Spanish American War. Now, its twin towers faced the lighthouse of El Morro at the entrance to the harbor. On the terrace, a black cannon still pointed balefully out to sea as a white-jacketed waiter served drinks.

Beneath my window, the royal palms swayed in the salty breeze. Looking out at the dark blue water, I thought again of my grandfather. Apart from his encounter with Hemingway, he had always intrigued me because he somehow justified my own failure. He dreamed of being a writer and once tried to write a novel, no doubt influenced by Hemingway himself. *Abuela* had told me that after he died, she looked for the unfinished manuscript, but he must have burned it years before. I asked her how such a man could have been happy writing advertising jingles for Hatuey beer.

"Cada uno de su chivo hace un tambor," she replied.

It was a favorite expression of hers, which like many Cuban sayings, loses much in translation. In essence, it means that we all play the cards that life deals us. But it didn't answer my question, and I wondered if I would find out in Havana.

Havana 1932

The rooms on the northeast corner of the Ambos Mundos Hotel in Havana look out, to the north, over the old cathedral, the entrance to the harbor, and the sea... If you sleep with your feet toward the east... the sun, coming up over the Casablanca side and into your open window, will shine on your face and wake you wherever you were the night before.

Ernest Hemingway, *Marlin off the Morro*

ONE

After he graduated from Harvard, Javier López Angulo would have begun the journey home by train, and I imagine him sleeping in a cozy Pullman berth as it rolled south toward Miami. Once there, he might have boarded the *Caribbean Clipper* of Pan American Airways, which lifted up like a giant pelican from Dinner Key and turned into the wind for the short flight to Havana.

It had been his father's idea to send Javier to college in the United States. Don Ramón López valued education, having had little of it himself. As a boy, he sold salt cod from a pushcart on the waterfront, but had grown wealthy in the speculative years after Cuba gained its independence. He enrolled his boys in the Jesuit school of Belén, which was then located in Habana Vieja, the old part of the city. His oldest son Miguel showed an aptitude for business, and soon left school to work with his father. But Javier had his mother's dreamy temperament, always with his nose in a book. In the afternoons, he loved to explore the maze of cobblestoned alleys around the Plaza de San Francisco, and wander down the crooked streets that led to the docks.

Even then, the tide of violence that would wash over the island in a few years had begun to mount. The university was a hotbed of politics and Don Ramón thought it prudent to keep his youngest son out of trouble for a few years by sending him north. Javier went reluctantly, since he would miss his walks in Habana Vieja and the baseball games between the

Havana Lions and the Almendares Scorpions that he watched with his friend Alberto Zayas Bazán.

At Harvard, my grandfather never grew used to the cold, and the endless winter tormented him as he sloshed through the mud to his classes in Harvard Yard. Except for the snow, everything in America thrilled him: the great factories spewing smoke, the huge bridges of iron spanning the rivers, and the skyscrapers thrusting above the teeming cities. But after the Crash, as banks closed and people waited in line at soup kitchens, Javier and his friends debated the coming revolution. Those discussions around a crackling fire in a Harvard dormitory introduced an element of doubt which tainted his enthusiasm for America. Diploma in hand, Javier returned to Cuba with no clear idea of what he wanted to do except write a novel. His father was surprised to see a slightly bewildered young man in a tweed jacket emerge from the seaplane, not the polished clubman he had expected.

To Javier, everything in Havana now seemed hopelessly backward. Along the Prado, there were cafés beneath the shady porticoes, where quaint female orchestras played *El Manisero*, the most popular song of the day. Girls in Havana thought themselves quite daring in bobbed hair and short skirts, like flappers, but Javier remembered that in Boston they had already begun to wear their hair long, and their dresses below their knees. As for the young men turned out impeccably in *jipijapa* hats and suits of crisp starched linen, what did he have in common with them?

Havana itself had changed. The new Capitolio had been finished, rivalling the one in Washington, D.C., and its dazzling white dome floated over the royal palms of the Parque Central. But the university had been closed down by President Machado and the students marched in protest. Many had been arrested by the dreaded *expertos*, the military police, and it was rumored that they were tortured in the old Spanish fortress of Atarés. A mysterious organization called the ABC had begun to fight back, and there was shooting in the streets. If things got much worse, the Americans would surely invoke the Platt Amendment and land the marines on the Malecón to restore order.

At Belén, Javier had been inseparable from Alberto, who dreamed of being a poet. Alberto had a wry sense of humor and loved to tease the self-conscious Javier. After school, they often stopped at the Acera del Louvre, the café by the Hotel Inglaterra. Here, they were joined by other students to pass the afternoon talking and sipping tiny cups of black coffee. These *tertulias* were a thing of the past and when Javier saw a group of young people sitting together, they spoke in hushed, conspiratorial tones, as though afraid to be overheard. Now, Alberto laughed bitterly when Javier suggested they see a baseball game.

"I don't have time for that," he scoffed, "and neither do you. Instead of scribbling in your notebook, you should join the fight against Machado!"

"What does that have to do with me?" shrugged Javier.

While Javier was at Harvard, his old classmate had been arrested at at a demonstration on the *escalinata*, the staircase leading up to the statue of the Alma Mater at the university, and was rumored to carry a gun. Had Alberto changed so much, or had he? Having nothing to keep him in Havana, Javier decided to go to Paris. He had read *The Sun Also Rises*, as had many of his classmates, and dreamed of living in a garret in Montparnasse and writing his novel in a café. His mother, Doña Inés Angulo, was secretly thrilled with the idea, since she had grown up speaking French, but his father contended that a year in the family business would do him good. After that, he could do whatever he pleased. Don Ramón prevailed, as he usually did, and presented his son with a graduation present, a yellow Ford Model A.

Resigned to putting off his departure, Javier started work at his father's bustling office on the esplanade facing Havana Harbor. The firm of López e Hijo had begun in an abandoned colonial palace on Muralla Street that Don Ramón's father had leased as an *almacén,* or warehouse. They had long outgrown it and now imported not just salt cod but also wine, olive oil, oranges, and countless other products from Spain to be sold throughout Cuba. The newest employee was given a desk by the window and spent his mornings poring over contracts and bills of sale. Down the hall, he could hear the commanding voices of his father and older brother above the chatter of the salesmen.

But Don Ramón soon realized that Javier's employment was counterproductive. The boy had his head in the clouds, and spent much of the afternoon gazing out the window at the boats entering the harbor, setting a bad example for the other employees. Don Ramón knew the publisher of *Bohemia*, and secured a job for him in the advertising department. Needless to say, Javier was delighted to be away from his father's stern eye. The magazine's office was located on Trocadero Street, just below the Malecón and a few blocks west of the Prado. This was the heart of the notorious *barrio* Colón, which at night came alive with burlesque shows and brothels. But during the day it was a thriving commercial district, thronged with shoppers on their way to the department stores on Galiano Street.

One afternoon, as he walked down the Prado, Javier noticed Alberto sitting with several friends at the Acera del Louvre. It had been several weeks since he had seen his friend, who sat beside an elegant older man with pomaded hair and a tiny mustache. The others, students by the look of them, appeared to hang on his every word. Javier stood hesitantly outside the café, not knowing if he would be welcome. Alberto curtly gestured for him to join them, and introduced Dr. Fernando Alvarez Leal, a law professor whose name was often in the newspaper. Javier recognized one of the students, Roberto Perez, from the Havana Yacht Club. Another, Frank Manzano, a plump young man in an incongruous plaid jacket, transferred his pipe to his left hand and offered him a firm handshake.

"You went to Harvard, didn't you?" asked Frank in English. "I'm Dartmouth, class of '30. You fellows gave us quite a pasting last year."

Javier, who had successfully managed to avoid football games, smiled noncommittally.

"Javier is writing a novel," said Alberto sardonically.

"How refreshing to hear of a writer who actually writes," said Dr. Alvarez Leal. "That isn't often the case."

"I'm afraid I haven't written much yet," said Javier, trying to hide his embarrassment.

"Could it be you lack inspiration?" asked the law professor. "Like Alberto, it was once my ambition to be a poet. Poets make excellent revolutionaries, you know. Look at José Martí."

"Then perhaps you've missed your vocation," parried Javier.

Dr. Alvarez Leal ignored this and carefully fitted a cigarette into an ebony holder, blowing the smoke out through his thin-bladed nose.

"It is truly an indulgence to discuss poetry in times such as these," he said, a sterner tone creeping into his voice. "What do they think at Harvard of our dilemma?"

"It's not something we talked much about," admitted Javier. "The *americanos* have problems of their own. President Hoover may not be re-elected this year. Many things would change, then."

"Perhaps one president is much the same as another. Do you share the same point of view?" Dr. Alvarez Leal said to Roberto, who had remained silent.

Roberto blushed and looked around himself before answering:

"Whoever is president will continue to do Wall Street's bidding. For all the *yanquis* care, Cuba can sink beneath the waves. But if it's in their interest to do so, they'll send battleships into Havana Harbor."

"Would that be such a terrible thing?" said Dr. Alvarez

Leal. "Incidentally, Cuba won't sink so easily. Did you know that our island is made of cork?"

Javier studied him carefully. Was he serious, or did he treat politics in the same playful, detached manner he reserved for poetry? Dr. Alvarez Leal was rumored to be a leader of the ABC, but he hardly seemed the type to throw a bomb into a police station.

"Surely you're joking!" blurted out Roberto. "Would you exchange one tyrant for another? Remember what Martí said: 'I have lived in the monster and I know its entrails.' Once the *yanquis* are here, how will you get them to leave?"

"It has been said that we Cubans have bad memories," said Dr. Alvarez Leal, "and that we do not profit from our mistakes. Perhaps by now we have learned."

"Most Americans don't care about Cuba," said Javier. "When we come to mind, they think only of rum, beaches, and *El Manisero*."

"*El Manisero!*" cried Dr. Alvarez Leal, throwing up his hands in mock alarm. "Will we never escape it?"

As the students burst into laughter, Javier made his excuses and stood up to leave. Alberto's handshake was cold, and his eyes shifted uncomfortably, as though he were trying to hide something. When the subject had turned to politics, it was as though a door had slammed shut between them. Javier crossed the street toward the Parque Central, and looking back he saw that the students were once again deep in discussion, the smoke from Dr. Alvarez Leal's cigarette dissipating over their heads. He had been away for so long that none of it made any difference to him. But were these would-be revolutionaries any better, with their endless arguments? A few days later, when Javier saw the arrogant law professor once again holding court beneath the green-striped awning of the café, he kept walking and hoped Alberto hadn't seen him. Shortly after that, he made a new acquaintance.

Each week, when *Bohemia* was published, it was Javier's job to personally deliver a copy to each advertiser. One Friday morning, Javier was sent to drop off the magazine to Mr. Walter Huggins, president of the Havana Trust, one of the oldest American banks on the island. Avoiding the Prado, he followed Galiano down to San Rafael, and crossed the Parque Central in the shadow of the Centro Gallego. The Havana Trust was several blocks down O'Reilly Street, on the corner of Aguacate. A corpulent guard sat in the lobby and eyed him with boozy indifference. Behind the iron grills of the cashiers were a number of desks, and Javier saw a lanky, blond-haired young man with freckles, nattily attired in a pale yellow suit, a polka-dotted tie, and two-tone shoes.

"Is Mr. Huggins here?" asked Javier.

"That's me, I guess."

Javier marveled that the president of such a large bank could be his own age. Explaining that he had come to bring a copy of the latest issue of *Bohemia*, he proudly opened it to the bank's ad, which pictured a man and his wife, obviously tourists, chatting with a cheerful bank teller. Beneath it was the caption:

Put your trust in the Havana Trust!

"Oh, you must mean my father," said the young man, realizing his mistake. "I'm Freddy Huggins. Pop's out, but I'll see that he gets it."

Freddy held the magazine up and scrutinized the ad, which had been placed opposite the weekly chess column.

"Is something wrong?" asked Javier.

"I've never liked it much," admitted Freddy. "They look like they're asking directions, '¿Dónde está el Morro?' or something like that."

"I hope they make it back to their hotel," put in Javier.

"I'm in charge of advertising, you know," said Freddy. "Why don't you buy me lunch?"

Javier could hardly refuse, and Freddy led him to a *fonda* on Villegas Street where a chinaman brought out two steaming bowls of won ton soup. Javier noticed that in the course of their conversation, Freddy had broken into Spanish, with a perfect Cuban accent. Noting his surprise, Freddy explained that he had lived in Havana nearly all his life.

"Pop sent me to college back in Texas," he said, pausing between greedy slurps. "I couldn't wait to get back."

No sooner were the huge bowls empty than Freddy looked at his watch in alarm.

"Holy mackerel!" he exclaimed. "I've got to get my lottery ticket."

Each Saturday morning, the winning lottery number was drawn by the children of the Beneficiencia, the orphanage on San Lázaro Street.

"Do you really play the lottery?" asked Javier skeptically.

"Every week."

Javier threw a few coins on the table as Freddy darted out. At a *bodega* around the corner, the lottery tickets hung from the wall, and the *billetero*, or ticket seller, waited to clip them with a pair of scissors. Freddy squinted at the numbers and then shook his head in disgust.

"Wait!" called out the *billetero*. "*El perro en la luna*, 01517!"

He pointed to the tattered image of the *Chino de la Charada* on the wall behind him. It was a comic-book mandarin, with symbols about his body, corresponding to numbers. Below the mandarin's heart was a dog (15), and at his belly was the moon (17). But Freddy scoffed and moved on.

"You've got to be careful," he said. "One time, this guy came to the bank and told us he had a ticket the same as our phone number. You can imagine what Pop said."

By then, Freddy was growing desperate, and he doubled back towards O'Reilly, with Javier a few steps behind. At the corner of San Juan de Dios, he found an old man holding a single grimy ticket in his gnarled fingers.

"That's it!" cried Freddy triumphantly. "10836. That's either a big fish and an elephant, or something else, I can't remember." He shrugged and handed the money to the *billetero*, who grinned toothlessly.

"Have you ever won?"

"Oh, no," said Freddy.

Javier began meeting Freddy after work at the Floridita, on the corner of Obispo and Monserrate streets. In the days before air-conditioning, the Floridita was open to the street, and Javier would always find his new friend in the corner to the left of the bar. Freddy introduced him to Constante Ribailagua, the Catalan *cantinero,* or bartender. His wife's family owned the Floridita, yet he insisted on tending bar himself. Invariably, he wore a neatly pressed black coat, a spotless white shirt, and a string tie.

"Un Freddy Especial," said Freddy.

"What's that?" asked Javier.

"My own invention," said Freddy proudly. "It's a daiquiri with grapefruit juice and a little maraschino. What do you think?"

Javier took a tentative sip and found it to his liking. It was tangy and sweet, and the crushed ice frosted the rim of the glass. Constante slid a plate of banana chips in their direction, and they rolled the poker dice in the heavy leather cup for the next round. As the Floridita filled up, the Trío Matancero began to play. They were three young men dressed in straw hats and red bandannas, playing a guitar, a banjo-like *tres,* and maracas. After each song, they passed their hats around the bar. There were fewer American tourists since the Crash, but occasionally, a *político* would wander in from the Capitolio across the Parque Central to see who was there, or to ascertain if anyone new had joined the ranks of the working girls at the bar. Freddy noticed Javier looking at a woman who chatted gaily with a salesman. She had mournful dark eyes and coffee-colored skin, and wore a red satin dress that hugged her generous hips.

"That's Leopoldina la Honesta," said Freddy, nudging him in the ribs.

"What an odd name," said Javier. "Is it such a dishonest profession?"

"Not at all. In her case, you truly get what you pay for. But there's someone else I want you to meet."

The following week, Freddy took him to the Teatro Alhambra on the corner of Virtudes and Consulado streets. Although the gilded plaster had started to peel from the walls, and the red velvet curtain was threadbare, the old theater remained popular. The usual burlesque show started with a rumba dance, and then featured a dialog between *negrito*, a man in blackface, and the *gallego*. The latter was a caricature of a Spaniard, with a beret and a red sash around his prominent belly. Typically, the devious *negrito* always had something up his sleeve, and succeeded in tricking the skin-flint *gallego*. That night, they vied for the affections of a gorgeous *mulata* until her jealous husband chased them off.

"Here she comes," whispered Freddy, who had seen the show many times before.

The chorus girls swept in from either side of the stage amid riotous applause, pirouetting neatly to bare their plump behinds.

"She's the one on the far right."

That was when Javier first saw Nely Chen, who arrived in Havana from Santiago de Cuba the year before. She had started out at the Zombie Club in Marianao and only recently joined the chorus line of the Alhambra. Freddy explained that Nely was also the mistress of Captain Rafael Segura.

"But he's not a jealous man," he added.

Freddy led Javier backstage, and they waited at the door of the dressing room with a bouquet of roses. Nely was delighted to see Freddy and hugged him warmly. She had taken off her sequined costume and now wore a yellow silk dressing gown. Nely had long, glossy black hair, a gift from her Chinese grandfather, with full lips and green, almond-shaped eyes, luminous as a cat's. She looked Javier up and down, appraising him professionally, but then announced they would have to leave immediately.

"Nely, I insist you have dinner with us," said Freddy, undeterred. "I've told Javier all about you."

"You're a very naughty boy," said Nely, "but you know I can't join you tonight. It's always good to see you, though. Will you come tomorrow?"

Javier smelled her perfume, a flowery scent which tickled his nostrils, and felt her small hands against his back as she pushed him out of her dressing room. He returned the following night with Freddy, but on his next visit he came alone. After the show, Nely explained that Captain Segura was often away from Havana and would be in Santa Clara for the next several days. She ducked behind the screen to change and emerged in a slinky dress that left her cinnamon-colored shoulders bare. Nely took his arm as they walked out the back entrance of the theater into the pale, sultry night. She lived in a *solar* on Zulueta Street, just a few blocks away. Once an elegant palace, its courtyard was now hung with laundry, and the smell of frying garlic wafted up the stairway. Nely was a *santera* and by her bed were five yellow candles, an offering to Oshún. There was also a bouquet of frangipani blossoms, which Javier guessed was a gift from another of her admirers, and he recognized her perfume. The next day, Javier greeted Freddy at the Floridita with an embarrassed yet triumphant smile.

"Enjoy it while it lasts," said Freddy, ordering another daiquiri.

Unfortunately, Captain Segura soon returned to Havana. When Javier and Freddy returned to the Alhambra the following week, they could not find Nely in the chorus line. From Zoila Martínez, another dancer, Freddy learned that Nely had moved out of the *solar* and Captain Segura had forbidden her to appear onstage.

"I thought he wasn't a jealous man," said Javier.

"Lucky for you he isn't," replied Freddy.

Javier was despondent, remembering the smell of frangipani, the downy curve of her neck, and Nely's achingly beautiful smile. He found that a few daiquiries after work each day helped him forget her.

One afternoon, Javier sat with Freddy at the Floridita, glumly rolling the poker dice in their usual corner. At the other end of the bar, he noticed a burly, square-jawed American with a mustache and a walnut-shaped scar over one eye. He wore a blue and white striped jersey, like a Basque fisherman, and cotton pants stained with fish blood. Holding up a towel, he waved it in front of him with a flourish, as though he were a bullfighter, demonstrating a pass with his cape to his companion, a wiry man in a beat-up yachting cap. Something was very funny and he laughed out loud, filling the bar with his booming voice. Dodging the bull's horns, he knocked over his beer, which spilled all over him.

Freddy was about to order another daiquiri when he recognized him.

"Look over there," he said to Javier, pointing across the bar. "That's Ernest Hemingway!"

By then, Hemingway was already famous, yet hardly anyone knew him in Key West.

In those days, it was a dilapidated village of wooden houses whose sloping roofs funneled rainwater into cisterns. But the wrought-iron balconies were draped with allamanda blossoms, and the pale nights smelled of rum and cigar smoke. Best of all was the fishing, whether for hog snappers at No Name Key or tarpon in the Gulf of Mexico. Only 90 miles from Havana, it was also full of tough bootleggers and trigger-happy Cuban revolutionaries, and people tended to mind their own business. Hemingway prowled the unpaved streets in moccasins, his khaki shorts held up by a length of rope. Savoring his anonymity, he told the locals to call him Papa. It was what Bumby, his son by his first wife, had called him and he liked the sound of it.

During their last trip to Paris, Hemingway had scrupulously avoided the cafés of Montparnasse, where he was much too well known. His wife Pauline was seven months pregnant, her belly uncomfortably low on her meager frame, so they went out sparingly. Yet on occasion, Americans would gawk at him and whisper to themselves, as though he were a tourist attraction like the Eiffel Tower. This had led to unpleasantness.

What's more, an imposter was at large. It appeared that someone who looked remarkably like him had been in Paris several weeks earlier, masquerading as Ernest Hemingway, telling outrageous stories about the war, autographing copies of his books, and even running up bar tabs. More than once, Hemingway encountered people who claimed to have seen him in places he had never been. This, too, had led to unpleasantness.

Pauline was anxious to have the baby in the United States, and they returned home on the *Ile-de-France* with Don Stewart, an old friend from the Pamplona days whose wife Beatrice was also noticeably *enceinte*. Their first night on board, while waiting for Pauline at the bar, Hemingway saw a tall man in white tie and tails with a willowy blond woman on his arm.

"Why, that's Grant Mason," said Stewart, putting down his drink.

As the couple approached them, Stewart remarked by way of introduction:

"He went to Yale."

"Oh, no," said Hemingway, rolling his eyes, and drained his martini.

Once introduced to Hemingway, Grant promptly ordered another round.

"I might as well say it," he said, vigorously pumping the writer's hand. "I haven't read any of your books."

"Please, darling," laughed Grant's wife, "you'll embarrass us both."

"Nonsense!" said Grant. "No sense standing on formality, here."

"I'm sure Mr. Hemingway would be happy to lend you a copy," she said.

Jane Mason was stunning in a celadon gown that plunged to the small of her back. Her hair was swept back from her forehead, framing her startling blue eyes, high cheekbones, and petulant mouth. She wore scarcely any makeup, with the exception of bright red lipstick, and her creamy complexion was set off by a string of grey pearls shaped like tiny figs. When she smiled, her lips scarcely moved, but it was easy to imagine them in a lovely pout. Turning to Hemingway, she tilted her head slightly to one side, as though to study him more carefully.

"Be careful," Stewart warned her, "he'll write about you if you don't watch out."

"Wouldn't that be lovely, to be in one of Mr. Hemingway's books?" Jane purred.

A row of martinis had appeared on the polished zinc bar. Hemingway offered a silent toast, lifting the glass by the stem and peering at her over the rim.

"Now who's embarrassing whom?" said Grant cheerily. He looked at his wristwatch and announced they were expected at the Captain's table. "Perhaps you'll join us for dinner tomorrow night," he added, more a possibility than an invitation. "By the way, I understand there's a passable squash court on board. Do you play?"

"Squash?" said Hemingway dismally.

"It's rather easy to learn, sport."

Grant grinned boyishly and led his wife into the dining room.

"You just hit the ball," said Stewart.

"*Merde*," said Hemingway, and ordered another martini.

"Grant's a big stick in Havana," explained Stewart. "I'm surprised you haven't run into them. They know absolutely everyone."

"What about her?"

Before Stewart could answer, their wives waddled in. The following night, they joined the Masons at the Captain's table, but Pauline excused herself early. When Hemingway returned to their cabin, he found her in bed, propped up by several pillows, and the game began:

"She's quite lovely, isn't she?"

"I suppose," said Hemingway vaguely.

It was a dangerous and complicated game, but Pauline played it very well:

"Oh, don't say that. I know you think she's beautiful."

"If you say so."

"For heaven's sake, Ernest," said Pauline, pressing her advantage.

"She's not my cup of tea," shrugged her husband.

"Poor child. Do you know that she tried to kill herself? Beatrice told me."

"Did she try very hard?"

"You're horrible! Don't laugh, she's very unhappy. And Grant doesn't help much."

"He seems like a nice enough sort.'"

"Oh, please," she sniffled. "Why won't you admit she's beautiful?" said Pauline.

"She's not as beautiful as little Pilar," he said, and gingerly put his ear to her womb, hoping to hear his daughter.

The next day, the sky was grey with mottled clouds. Walking on deck, Hemingway clutched the railing as it dipped toward the horizon. The Lalique chandelier tinkled ominously in the dining room, and passengers watched the water slosh in their glasses. A waiter stumbled and sent crockery flying, and a woman abruptly raced for the door. That evening, driving rain pelted the portholes of their stateroom. Somehow, their infant son Patrick slept through it, although his nanny kneeled fitfully over the commode. Pauline lay moaning, her hands on her belly, bathed in a cold sweat.

"We could order in," said Hemingway.

"How can you even think about food?" she shrieked.

Hemingway shrugged and made his way to dinner. The first seating was nearly deserted, with a disconsolate row of waiters swaying against the wall. But the band sat gamely at their places. They were six light-skinned blacks sporting nautical blue blazers, billed as the Conjunto Casablanca. Hemingway peered into the bar and saw Jane smoking a *margarita*, a dainty little cigar.

"Where's Grant?" he asked.

"He is, shall we say, indisposed. Rather a bore, isn't it? There's nothing to do on this damn boat except drink. What will you have?"

Hemingway ordered a whiskey from the bartender, who had to steady himself against the bar.

"Another manhattan for me," said Jane.

The Masons were coming home from Africa. It was Hemingway's dream to go on safari, and he felt a stab of envy when Jane told him she had bagged a lion. As she spoke, he noticed that her eyes were not really blue but a lustrous grey, set a trifle too far apart in her otherwise perfect oval face. Jane emptied her cocktail glass and took a delicate puff from her cigar. He could not help but stare at her, and when their eyes met, he realized she knew it. The awkward moment passed as an odd, lilting tune floated in from the dining room.

"It's a *conjunto de son*," said Jane brightly, and before he could protest she led him to the dance floor.

The Conjunto Casablanca, which was returning to Cuba after touring Europe, had begun to play for lack of anything better to do. It was unlike any music Hemingway had ever heard, slower than jazz with a beguiling melody. The band noticeably picked up the tempo when Jane appeared.

"Do you rumba?" she asked, gleefully tapping her stiletto heels on the parquet floor.

"Do I what?"

"As Grant would say, it's easy to learn, sport," she mimicked her husband's crisp accent, and guided Hemingway's hand around her waist. "Besides, if you visit us in Havana you'll have to dance, so you might as well learn now. First your left foot, then your right, then step forward with your left and over with your right. Got it?"

Hemingway stumbled on his bad leg and nearly stepped on her toe, but regained his balance and moved through the paces as the Conjunto Casablanca played on. Just as the song ended, the boat dipped with a sickening lurch, and that was when it hit him.

"Not you, too!" cried Jane.

"I've got to go," said Hemingway thickly.

"What about your rumba lesson?"

"It will definitely have to wait."

Nonetheless, the band began to play *El Manisero*. As Hemingway staggered out, he caught a last glimpse of Jane twirling to the music.

The following morning, the storm had passed. A weak but reassuring light filled the portholes, and the seas were calm for the remainder of the six-day cruise. Hemingway saw little of the Masons until they disembarked in New York, where the talk was all about Al Capone's trial. On the pier, Grant appeared to be directing an army of porters struggling with their voluminous baggage. Swathed in ermine, Jane embraced Pauline and made her promise to call if they ever came to Cuba.

Before the end of the year, the Hemingways were back in Key West. The new baby was not a girl, as they had hoped, but a nine-pound boy they named Gregory. Pauline's wealthy Uncle Gus had bought them a house on Whitehead Street across from an old lighthouse. It had been built before the Civil War and much needed to be done, but the carriage house could be turned into a writing studio, and the wrap-around porch let in a cool breeze at night. All winter, teams of workmen tramped through the house, plastering the peeling walls, replacing the decrepit plumbing, and sanding the creaky hardwood floors.

Hemingway had just finished his latest book, *Death in the Afternoon*, and sent it off to his publisher. Since it would be several weeks before he received the galleys to correct, he could now indulge his passion for fishing. His friend Charles Thompson told him that the best sport of all was to be had on the Gulf Stream within sight of Havana, where the billfish ran. Hemingway had never spent more than a few days in Cuba, en route to Key West, and he had yet to land a black marlin. The writer Zane Grey had once caught a monster that weighed over 1000 pounds, the world record. Not to be outdone, Hemingway decided to go on a fishing trip to Cuba for a week or so. Having suggested it, Charles could hardly object to going himself. An angular man with a soft-spoken manner, he ran the local hardware store. Hemingway's cousin Bud White, from Kansas City, agreed to come as well.

Now, all Hemingway needed was a boat. Charles had heard that Joe Russell, who ran an elbow-shaped speakeasy on Duval Street, was looking for a charter. Joe had a 34-foot cabin cruiser called the *Anita*, which he had fitted out with an icebox that ran across the stern and an extra gas tank to make the crossing from Key West to Havana. The *Anita* had a 100 horsepower Kermath engine, and trolled at 8 knots an hour. The wheel house provided protection from the sun, and it had a low-slung cabin with several bunks. Aft, there was room for two wicker fishing chairs.

The rumor was that Joe used the *Anita* to bring Hoover Gold, as he called it, from Cuba to Key West, but Hemingway didn't know whether to believe it. He had once rolled cigars for a living in Tampa before becoming a saloon keeper and party-boat captain, and his skin was leathery from years of sun and salt air. In addition, Joe had all the gear they would need: heavy bamboo rods with 24 oz. tips and Hardy reels, as well as a lighter 14 oz. rod with an old Templar reel for smaller fish.

Over a few shots of Cuban rum, Joe agreed to halve his normal rate of $20 per day, and they left that Friday morning with the tide. The *Anita* soon cleared the sandbar of the Eastern Dry Rocks, where the coral bottom dropped off, and made good time across the Florida Straits. Hemingway craned his neck over the wheel house until he could see the lights of Havana, a violet haze just above the horizon. The black water sparkled in the moonlight, and the only sound was the low growl of the engine. Before long, the crescent-shaped city spread out before them. To the left of the harbor was El Morro, built by the Spaniards to protect the city from pirates, topped with a tall stone lighthouse. Across the channel was the castle of La Punta, and beyond it the Malecón, the brilliantly-lit boulevard that skirted the seawall. As they nosed into the San Francisco Dock, there were no reporters waiting to interview him, no tourists, and no one who had read his books, just a customs official in a rat-colored uniform, who yawned as Joe presented his papers with a few dollars folded inside.

They slept the first night aboard the *Anita*, which bobbed gently in the slip, but Hemingway was up at first light. Pulling on his moccasins, he made his way out of the customs house, stepping over a bum sprawled on the pier, his head covered with a newspaper. Hemingway found the Western Union office and cabled Pauline, who would take the overnight ferry and join him in a few days. When he returned, Joe was already making coffee on the alcohol stove in the tiny galley. Charles and Bud had gone to a *bodega* on the Plaza de San Francisco and come back with sandwiches and several cases of Hatuey beer. By then, the sun had burned away the damp mist over the harbor and the lighthouse cast a shadow on the glassy water. They soon shoved off and spent the day trolling between Havana and the fishing village of Cojimar to the east. In sight of El Morro, Charles had the first strike, a white marlin that measured 8 feet, 4 inches and weighed 87 pounds. Anchoring in a cove for lunch, they started back while the sun was still high. As a soft, humid dusk descended upon the harbor, Hemingway finished the last of the Hatuey beers but decided he was still thirsty.

35

"Where can you get a drink in this town?" he asked.

"I know just the place," said Joe.

Hemingway followed Joe from the waterfront to the Plaza de Armas, an elegant square shaded by royal palms and a giant ceiba tree. Passing the American Embassy, they turned left into Obispo, a narrow street of hotels, drugstores, and cafés. It was usually clogged with automobiles, horse-drawn wagons, and pushcarts, each claiming the right of way through the sea of pedestrians, but it was Saturday and Havana was just settling down for the warm tropical night. The metal shutters of some of the stores were already shut and a radio blared from a *fonda*. A shoeshine boy watched them approach, but turned up his nose at Hemingway's moccasins. At the end of Obispo, they reached the Floridita, and ordered two more Hatueys.

"Charles is always lucky," grumbled Hemingway, who had hoped to catch the first marlin of the season.

"The Cubans have an expression," replied Joe. *"Mañana seguro."*

Drinking with his elbows on the bar, Hemingway surveyed the crowd. To his right, a plump whore with sad eyes tried to ascertain whether he was worth pursuing. In the far corner, two well-dressed young men played poker dice. One appeared Cuban, but the other was clearly American, with blond hair and freckles.

"I wish I'd come down here when Prohibition started," said Joe.

"What would a Conch like you have done in Cuba?"

"Hell, start a place like this, raise fighting cocks, and have a different *señorita* every night."

"All we need is a bullfight or two," laughed Hemingway.

He explained that bullfighting had been popular in Cuba but was prohibited by the Americans after the war. Asking the dapper bartender for a towel that hung behind the bar, he demonstrated a *verónica,* the difficult move where the matador waits until the last second to swing the cape over the bull's horns. Luckily the bull was imaginary, because Hemingway overturned the mug of beer with his elbow. The American in the corner pointed at him and whispered something to his friend.

"I think that guy recognizes you," said Joe.

Suddenly angry, Hemingway wiped his chest with the towel and turned to see that the American had left. The Cuban quickly looked away.

"What are you looking at?" Hemingway demanded.

The young man reddened but pretended not to have heard.

"I asked you a question," said Hemingway, making his way to the corner, followed reluctantly by Joe.

"I didn't realize you were speaking to me."

"Well, what do you know?" said Joe, taking off his cap and scratching his head. "He speaks English."

"Did you learn that at college?" asked Hemingway.

"Actually, I went to Harvard."

"A Hah-vahd man," said Hemingway. "Why didn't you say so? I think you owe me an apology."

"I didn't know you needed one."

Unexpectedly, the mood at the Floridita had grown tense, with the other customers looking at them anxiously.

"Perhaps you'd care to discuss the matter outside," said Hemingway.

Javier followed him out into the street, where an enthusiastic audience soon gathered. Freddy returned from the bathroom to find his friend grimly facing the broad-shouldered writer, who was throwing mock punches in the air as the shoeshine boys cheered. Beside him was a tough little sailor whom Freddy realized he would probably have to fight, if it came to that.

"I think there's been some misunderstanding here," said Freddy.

"Not at all," replied Javier, his eyes flashing. "We understand each other quite well."

"Don't get sore, Mr. Hemingway," said Freddy, "I've read all your books, or one of them, anyway, and my friend here has, too. Why don't we go back inside and you can tell us all about them?"

"I like the way you think, son," said Joe, looking over his shoulder at the crowd.

But Hemingway ignored them and continued to shadow-box as Javier took off his jacket.

"Would you like me to hold that?" said Hemingway with mock gallantry.

Out of surprise, Javier handed him the jacket, and noticed that his opponent was smiling. It was a fierce, mocking smile, like that of a wolf, stretching from one end of his broad face to the other. Hemingway faced the crowd and bowed amid great applause. Then he turned to the bewildered Javier and clapped a hand on his tense shoulders.

"Anyone willing to take a punch at me has got guts!" he said. "You're all right for a Harvard man!"

That was how my grandfather met Hemingway, or so *Abuela* told me.

If the shoeshine boys were disappointed they didn't show it because the jovial *americano* threw them a handful of coins. Freddy introduced him to a visibly relieved Constante, and ordered a round of *Freddy Especiales*. Soon, the cocktail shaker was rattling happily, and the drinks were poured into a waiting row of glasses.

"Not bad," said Hemingway, holding up the glass and smacking his lips. He drained it but upon further reflection said, "Too sweet for my taste."

As Constante archly surveyed him from across the bar, Hemingway insisted he make another one. The *cantinero* added rum and lemon juice to the shaved ice, followed by grapefruit juice and a splash of maraschino. He was about to add a scoop of powdered sugar when Hemingway said,

"Stop right there!"

Constante topped the shaker before whirling it acrobatically. His glass refilled, Hemingway sampled his handiwork, swirling it in his mouth like a fine wine.

"Perfect!" he announced, and raised his glass to Javier.

By then, Charles and Bud had found their way to the Floridita.

"Have a *Papa Especial,*" Hemingway offered.

After another round, Hemingway was hungry and Freddy suggested El Pacífico. They filed across the Parque Central past the marble statue of José Martí, who pointed sternly back toward the Floridita, as though urging them to get another daiquiri. With the illuminated dome of the Capitolio on the left, Freddy led them down San Rafael Street until they reached Chinatown. The restaurant was atop a five-story building near the Teatro Chino on Zanja Street.

"I always heard this place was an opium den," said Joe.

"That's on the third floor," said Freddy nonchalantly.

The elevator was an open metal cage operated by an emaciated chinaman in a skullcap and a tattered red robe. It stopped with a shudder at each floor, where sheets had been hung to obscure the view. Hemingway was disappointed not to get a glimpse of the activity within, and he imagined men with little axes padding down the corridors. They emerged on the roof and were greeted by a cool breeze sweeping in from the bay.

"I could eat a horse!" exclaimed Hemingway.

"You just might," said Charles, wrinkling his nose at the menu.

Javier leaned back in his chair, his head spinning from the daiquiris, and watched Hemingway shovel down his plate of food. He had been to El Pacífico many times, but coming with the *americano* somehow made it a new experience. How could he bring such enthusiasm to everything he did? Was that the secret of his writing? Between mouthfulls of spare ribs and fried rice, Hemingway described his exploits on the water, and the monstrous marlin he nearly landed that afternoon, probably a record for this time of year. After dinner, he leaned towards Javier, his breath reeking of beer and garlic, and said in a stage whisper:

"Have you ever boxed?"

"No," admitted Javier.

"Were you really going to fight me?"

"You didn't leave me much choice."

"I like you, Harvard!" Hemingway exclaimed, laying a sweaty palm on the other's knee. "I'll make you a deal: You show me around Havana while we're here, and I'll teach you how to box. What do you say?"

"I'll think about it," said Javier, smiling despite himself.

Once more they braved the elevator, and Charles announced that he was turning in for the night. But Hemingway was still full of energy, so Freddy suggested they walk over to the Havana Sport, a few blocks away on Galiano Street.

"Is that a gymnasium?" asked Hemingway.

"You'll see."

The Havana Sport, one of the largest *academias de baile*, was a dance hall on the second floor of a shoe store, overlooking one of Havana's busiest streets. Whenever the music stopped, women of all sizes and shapes and colors lined up against the wall.

"Boy howdy!" said Bud, rubbing his hands with glee.

Javier explained that for a *real* you could dance with your choice of partner.

"I can't rumba," said Hemingway.

"That doesn't matter," said Javier. "You get a free lesson."

Hemingway saw a spectacular *mulata* with honey-colored hair and caught her eye. Trotting across the dance floor, he eagerly handed her the ticket he had purchased and took her by the waist as Jane Mason had taught him on the *Ile-de-France*. She seemed unimpressed as he hopped from one foot to the other, trying to dance to the unfamiliar rumba beat.

"I think he's got the hang of it," Javier told Freddy.

Freddy spotted Zoila Martínez, who danced at the Havana Sport between shows at the Alhambra, and hurried to buy his ticket before someone else approached her. Once again, Javier thought about Nely. Zoila had said that her new apartment was on Dragones Street, but it was clear the *chinita* didn't want to see him. Or perhaps Captain Segura *was* a jealous man, after all. He wandered over to the bar as Joe and Bud clutched their tickets for the next dance. Soon, Bud was dancing with a seemingly demure girl in a Spanish shawl, and Joe attempted to get his arms around an enormous coffee-colored woman with maracas hanging from her hips. Javier suspected that Hemingway would disappear with his *mulata*, but after a while the writer joined him at the bar.

"Where to next?" he said.

Outside the Havana Sport, Freddy led the way to Sloppy Joe's, which was a block from the Prado. The bar was full of tourists and American sailors, as well as a few stray Cubans who had attended the late show at the Alhambra.

"Do they make daiquiris here too?" asked Hemingway.

"They'll make anything you want," said Freddy.

He had taken out his favorite cigar, a Rey del Mundo, and offered it to Hemingway, who took a few puffs before starting to cough.

"I haven't much use for sugar and tobacco," he admitted, "but I sure love the rum."

"You can't have one without the other," said Javier, lighting his own cigar.

"Come fishing with us tomorrow," said Hemingway, less an invitation than an order.

Freddy took a puff and watched the smoke twirl in the ceiling fan.

"I get seasick," he admitted.

"You'll be too hung over to notice, Tex," said Hemingway. "What about you, Harvard?"

Clearly, there was no point in arguing. After Hemingway and his friends returned to the waterfront, Javier decided to spend the night at Freddy's apartment on Neptuno Street, as he often did rather than risk waking his parents. Javier collapsed on the sofa, his usual spot, but no sooner had he closed his eyes than Freddy was shaking him awake. His friend stood over him wearing the blue cap of the Havana Trust Tarzans, the amateur baseball team sponsored by the bank.

"Good morning, sunshine!"

"You go and tell me about it," moaned Javier.

"Not a chance," said Freddy.

When they arrived at the Plaza de San Francisco, it was deathly still except for a mangy dog pissing in front of the fountain. A dockhand directed them to the newly-arrived *americanos* and they found Hemingway helping Charles load the icebox.

"I didn't think you'd make it!" he said, much too loudly for Sunday morning in Havana.

Meanwhile, the cobblestoned square was coming to life. Market stalls were being set up on trestles, and an old man in a black beret crossed in front of the café, pushing a handcart piled high with pastries. *"¡Chur-ros!"* he sang, rolling his r's interminably. *"¡Chur-ros!"* A fisherman pulled a load of bait towards the dock, and a horse-drawn ice wagon rumbled towards the Café de la Perla de San Francisco. The stalls were soon piled high with fruit: golden pineapples, mangoes as big as cannonballs, plantains, papayas, oranges, and mameys. A black woman wearing a red scarf on her head balanced a cast iron skillet over a fire, sizzling with pieces of fried dough. Beside her, a dentist's chair had been set up, although the dentist was away, presumably looking for customers. More *pregoneros*, or street vendors, pushed their carts over the cobblestones, selling flowers, sweets, tamales, and peanuts wrapped in paper cones.

They were soon ready to go, and when the *Anita* backed away from the pier the *brisa* was blowing out to sea, smelling fresh and clean. Anchored in front of the fortress of La Cabaña, which guarded the channel, were a row of fishing smacks, with live fish cars moored alongside. At the mouth of the harbor were the skiffs of the marlin fishermen, tiny boats with handlines trailing in the water, and silvery tarpon darted between them, shimmering just below the surface. They headed west along the Malecón, skimming over the brisk waves past the mounted statue of Antonio Maceo and the bronze eagle commemorating the sinking of the *Maine*. Suddenly, the water changed color from a pale turquoise to a dark blue, almost purple. Along the dividing line were tiny whirlpools, sucking in clumps of yellow gulfweed floating on the surface. It was the Gulf Stream, sixty miles across and a mile deep, winding past the Cuban shore like a vast serpent.

Almost as soon as they reached the open sea, Freddy lost his color and went below, only to rush back on deck with a forlorn wail and throw up over the side.

"Watch it!" said Joe. "You'll scare the fish."

Hemingway guffawed as Freddy stretched out on the bench built over the gas tank. He helped Joe toss out the teasers used to draw the marlin, two blunt wooden cylinders on twenty feet of line, one green and the other white, which bounced in the wake. They soon crossed the mouth of the Almendares River, and Javier pointed out the Havana Yacht Club where he rowed at the annual regatta. Once again Charles had the first catch of the day, a kingfish, and Bud landed a plump tuna. Then the line on the big Hardy rod jerked taut and Hemingway handed it to Javier before he could object. A wave crashed against the stern, and through the explosion of spray he saw a sailfish somersaulting over the waves.

"Not yet," said Hemingway, leaning over his shoulder.

Barely fifty yards behind the boat, the sailfish soared out of the water once again, glistening in the sunlight. It appeared to balance on its tail like a tightrope walker, but fell back against the crest of a wave.

"Now!" cried Hemingway. "Let him have it!"

Javier grasped the heavy pole with both hands and yanked it back. But the line knifed out of the water and the reel began to screech as the sailfish sounded.

"Give it some slack!" yelled Joe.

Before Javier could unscrew the drag, he felt the line give and he knew the sailfish had thrown off the hook. He reeled in frantically, hoping he had been wrong, but all he felt was the weight of the line.

"Good try, kid," said Hemingway.

A reinvigorated Freddy had stood up to watch his friend battle the sailfish, and solemnly lifted a bottle of Hatuey.

"Here's to the fish," he intoned, and handed the greenish bottle with a picture of the vanquished Siboney chieftain to Javier.

"Not even the Mahatma could have landed that bastard," said Joe.

"Why do you call him that?" asked Freddy.

In response, Joe jerked his thumb at Hemingway, who had wrapped a towel around his head, like a turban:

"See the resemblance?"

Just after Barlovento, they passed a fishing village with a sandy cove. Dropping anchor near the shore, they waded through the shallow, sparkling water to the beach. A pair of skiffs had been pulled up on the sand, and a fishing net was spread out to dry. There were a few wooden houses just beyond a clump of sea grape trees, and a *bodega* with a weathered Coca-Cola sign. Joe handed the old woman behind the counter the steaks he had cut from Bud's tuna, and she served them with rice and beans. They ate on a wooden table facing the water, and afterwards they lay on the beach, warmed by the afternoon sun. Javier had nearly dozed off when he saw Hemingway returning from the *Anita* with two pairs of boxing gloves.

"It's time for your first boxing lesson," he said.

Realizing there was no escape, Javier reluctantly got up. Hemingway showed him how to strap on the six ounce gloves, and Javier noticed how his right elbow was slightly misshapen, with an ugly-looking scar. But he was barrel-chested and his arms were muscular and bristling with black hair. They found a place on the beach were the sand was packed hard, and Hemingway shadowboxed a scraggly palm.

"Let's see what you got," he said, suddenly turning on him.

Javier held up his arms but Hemingway said, "For Pete's sake, you look like John L. Sullivan." He adjusted Javier's hands so they protected his face and then circled around him, testing his defenses with left jabs. "That's it," said Hemingway. "Keep moving!" Unexpectedly, he stepped forward and threw a right hook. Javier ducked out of the way and swung with his left. Hemingway had stumbled in the sand when his punch missed, but he regained his balance in time to block Javier's blow.

"Not bad! Maybe they taught you something at Harvard, after all."

Hemingway was sweating profusely, and with his forearm he wiped the moisture from his sunburned face. Once more, he began to circle Javier in the sand, throwing left jabs with the same dangerous smile he had worn at the Floridita. When Hemingway charged forward, Javier watched his right hand and barely saw the left cross that came at him in a blur. He turned just in time, but the glove grazed his temple. The blood rushed to his head and he swung wildly, but Hemingway neatly stepped aside and hit him in the gut. Javier's stomach muscles were still hard from rowing at the Havana Yacht Club, but it nearly knocked the wind out of him.

"Lesson number one: *Never get mad*," said Hemingway, taking off his gloves. "But you can take a punch, I'll give you that."

Hemingway's luck continued on the way back to Havana. Opposite the Hotel Nacional, he noticed a pale flash a few feet beneath the water as a marlin made for the *Anita*.

"Look at that son of a bitch," said Hemingway, eagerly strapping on the leather harness.

It flickered in and out of sight, its narrow sword breaking the water like the periscope of a submarine. The marlin was stalking them, and Hemingway was mesmerized as it abruptly shot forward and swallowed the bait whole. Joe cut the engine as the marlin shot past the boat, the leader trailing from its jaws. Hemingway let the line run out and it was soon more than one hundred yards from the *Anita*. Then he tightened the drag and the rod nearly jerked out of his clenched hands. But his grip held and he braced himself for the fight.

"Sock him!"shouted Joe.

Hemingway's muscles tensed as he slammed back the fishing pole, which was bent nearly double, and for an instant he felt the power at the other end of the line. He pumped with all his strength, until he was convinced that the hook was set, and then loosened the drag. The marlin took another hundred yards of line, and Joe chased after it, trying to cut the distance between them. Hemingway planted himself in the fishing chair and managed to jam the rod in the socket of the harness, allowing him to push back with his legs as the big fish sounded. When the marlin sailed out of the water in a graceful parabola, he leaned forward and cranked the reel, trying to gain ground.

After the 13th jump it began to tire, and Joe pulled up the piano wire leader with gloved hands. As the marlin emerged from the water, its lavender belly gleaming, Hemingway saw that the wire was wrapped around its bill. Even after Charles speared it with the curved gaff hook just behind the gills, it thrashed a few feet from the stern. Javier and Freddy looked on as Joe leaned over the gunwale and clubbed the marlin between the eyes.

When they returned to the San Francisco Dock, the *pregoneros* continued to do a brisk business but the dentist's chair was occupied by the dentist himself, who read the newspaper while smoking a cigar. Hemingway's catch measured 8 feet, 3 inches and weighed 57 pounds, not bad for early in the season but still smaller than Charles' strike of the day before. The light was still good so he borrowed the Havana Trust Tarzans baseball cap and posed for a photograph with Javier, the marlin hanging between them. They decided to give it away, even though the meat was white and fresh-smelling and could sell for as much as 10 cents a pound at the market. The dockhands stared at them slack-jawed, as that was no small amount in those days, but they were grateful when the marlin was hacked into thick steaks to be distributed among them. Best of all, Charles had only caught a kingfish, which théy wrapped in a newspaper and presented to the customs official.

"How do you like it now, gentlemen?" said Hemingway, to no one in particular.

As the crowd that had gathered around the *Anita* dispersed, the *brisa* turned cool and he offered Javier a bottle of Hatuey.

"It's been a good day," said Hemingway.

"It has," Javier admitted.

"But I've heard things are not so good in Havana. What's the true gen?"

"I think it will end like the *Fiesta de Guatao*," said Javier.

"What's that?"

"It's an old Cuban saying," put in Freddy. "It means it's going to get worse before it gets better."

"I don't care about politics," said Hemingway. "For me, the only thing that counts is friendship. I think we'll be friends."

"I think so, too, Ernesto," said Javier.

"Call me Papa."

TWO

Over lunch at the American Club, Freddy mentioned to his father that Ernest Hemingway was in Havana.

"Is that so?" said Walter Huggins, taking a sip of iced tea.

The president of the Havana Trust was a balding man with a prosperous girth, wearing wire-rimmed spectacles that rested lightly on his pink cheeks, and his pale blue eyes surveyed his son skeptically. It was often difficult to tell if Freddy was joking. Just last year, Walter had taken his family to Paris on holiday. They were having lunch at La Coupole when Freddy informed him that Pablo Picasso was walking by. Walter had looked up to see a swarthy little fellow who looked like a busboy, not the famous artist. Picasso indeed!

"Papa was at the Floridita on Saturday night," elaborated Freddy. "That's what his friends call him, you know. He took Javier and me fishing."

"Perhaps we can get him to open a checking account," said Walter with a chuckle.

His son considered this and said:

"I'll see what I can do, Pop."

Freddy then announced he had an errand to run before he returned to the bank and bounded out of the dining room. Shaking his head ruefully, his father ordered another iced tea from Cesar, the head waiter. The American Club was on the Prado at the corner of Virtudes Street, just a few blocks from the Havana Trust. It was Walter's refuge in a city that had become increasingly chaotic in recent years, and it was the only place in Havana where he could enjoy his favorite lunch of tomato soup and a pimiento cheese sandwich.

Walter ate Cuban food only when forced to, and often wondered how his Cuban employees could eat a huge lunch of *ropa vieja* (or some such concoction, with a fried egg on top) and return to work in the afternoon. Perhaps that was why the *siesta* was so prevalent, although Walter had expressly forbidden it at the Havana Trust. But even at the American Club, plush reclining chairs had been installed on the second floor, and more than one member could be seen napping after lunch.

Hemingway indeed! Freddy was a good boy, but needed supervision. Last baseball season, he had somehow gotten Hub Kendall, a left-fielder with the Washington Senators, to play three games with the Havana Trust Tarzans. Unfortunately, Hub began to deteriorate shortly after he arrived in Havana. In the first game, he was quite convivial and signed autographs, but in the second he staggered to the plate with difficulty, clearly drunk. By the third game, he had disappeared altogether. Freddy found him at a whorehouse in Marianao and put him on the ferry to Key West without further incident.

Still, there was much to be said for Freddy. It had been his idea to place an ad in *Bohemia* in an effort to attract Cuban customers. Walter himself had come up with the caption, *Put your trust in the Havana Trust!* Recently, Freddy had made friends with the son of Don Ramón López, whose business Walter had long coveted. In fact, he had invited Don Ramón to breakfast next week. The American Club served the best flapjacks in Havana and Cubans were invariably impressed.

Leaving the stolid limestone clubhouse, Walter searched for Pepe, his favorite shoeshine boy. Pepe was actually older than he was, a wizened old man wearing a dilapidated straw hat. With a stern demeanor, he motioned the banker towards his chair in the shade. A shoeshine was one of the rare indulgences Walter permitted himself, and Pepe was an artist who could make his shoes gleam. First, he deftly placed cardboard strips inside his shoes to protect his cuffs from the polish, and moved the brush with dizzying speed. Then he made a few passes with a flannel cloth, pulling it tight with a loud snap. Finally, he produced a mysterious bottle and applied a drop to each of Walter's shoes, buffing them to a high sheen. Only then did Pepe smile, revealing a mouthful of crooked yellow teeth.

Flipping him a coin, Walter steeled himself for the walk down the Prado in the blazing sun. The quaint street that once began at a belvedere on the water's edge was now a tree-lined boulevard that stretched from the Malecón to the new Capitolio. At night, the Prado was illuminated by cast-iron streetlights, and the old mansions on either side had become cafés, movie theaters, and office buildings. As for the horse-drawn buggies he remembered, they had been replaced by cars, some even driven by women. When Walter first arrived in Cuba he was in uniform, though he felt more like a tourist than a conquering hero. Havana was a city without women, then. Walking past the decaying Spanish palaces in the old part of the city, Walter would catch a glimpse of a pale face behind slatted shutters, but no decent woman would be seen on the street.

It was because of a woman that he enlisted. Walter met his future bride one afternoon when she entered his uncle's pharmacy, her long blond hair in a thick braid. Beryl Tyler was a beauty who turned many heads among the young men of Austin, Texas. To his surprise, she returned the following afternoon for another ice cream soda. Walter paid a call at the Queen Anne mansion on Enfield Street where Beryl lived, but her parents eyed him balefully, and her older brother referred to him as a soda-jerk.

The sinking of the battleship *Maine* changed everything. What better way to impress her father than go to war? Teddy

Roosevelt was recruiting at the bar of the Menger Hotel in San Antonio, and Walter was among the first to enlist. But while the famous charge up San Juan Hill took place, he waited in Tampa for the transport ship to Cuba. His sole experience of combat was guarding a half-starved group of Spanish soldiers delighted to be going home. Back in Austin, resplendent in his puttees and Sam Browne belt, he was more than welcome on Enfield Street and things proceeded rather quickly with Beryl. Within the year they were married, and he soon found himself working as a teller at her father's bank. But his days as a Rough Rider left him with a craving for adventure. When Walter heard that the island would be annexed outright, just as Texas had been taken from the Mexicans, he returned to Havana to seek his fortune.

Walter stayed at the Hotel Inglaterra, and that was where he met Mr. Gordon. As he spoke no Spanish, he was unable to order from the bewildered waiter, but at the table behind him was a jovial, red-faced man in a planter's hat. His wrinkled seersucker suit barely encased his belly, and his meaty wrists burst from his cuffs. Charles Gordon not only ordered him a steak, but also paid for it and led him to the newly-opened office of the Havana Trust. Mr. Gordon had arrived from Jamaica the year before and founded the bank with capital from a syndicate of investors in New York. Impulsively, Walter asked him for a job.

Beryl joined him a few months later, and at first they lived in a tidy wooden cottage in the new suburb of the Vedado, sleeping beneath ghostly mosquito nets. The Havana Trust thrived in the early years of the Cuban Republic, buoyed by Mr. Gordon's boundless energy. Walter wondered if there were actually two or three Mr. Gordons, since he seemed to be several places at once: meeting with Cuban officials, opening a branch in Matanzas, or placating his board in New York. A confirmed bachelor, he often spent his Sunday afternoons at Walter's new house in swank Miramar, enjoying Beryl's cooking and bouncing Freddy on his ample knee.

But in 1921 the "dance of the millions," as it was called, came to an end. When the price of sugar fell precipitously, all but a handful of Cuban banks failed. Walter, by then the bank's vice president, would never forget the last time he saw Mr. Gordon. He had seemed distracted of late, and Walter found him at his desk. Mr. Gordon claimed that a relative of his fought at Trafalgar, and he kept in his office a wooden model of the *HMS Victory*, Lord Nelson's flagship. Seemingly oblivious to Walter, he stared dreamily at the tiny pennants flying from its topmast.

"Mr. Gordon," Walter finally said, "is there something I can do?"

"So it goes, old boy," Mr. Gordon mumbled softly, as though he had cotton in his mouth. "So it goes."

The following day, the Marques de Valenzuela, whose family had owned the La Margarita sugar mill near Matanzas for generations, shot himself in the head with an antique duelling pistol. Over the years, the Havana Trust had loaned him millions of dollars in loans which were now worthless. There was a run on the bank's deposits, and if not for an infusion of cash from New York, the Havana Trust would surely have gone under. In the resulting confusion, Mr. Gordon disappeared. Over the years, he was reported to be in Bermuda, in Singapore, and even back in England, living under an assumed name.

Walter succeeded him as president of the Havana Trust. Among the bank's assets was now La Margarita, and Walter found it in shambles. The machinery was rusty and the workers lived in rat-infested shanties. Walter promptly fired the foreman, a drunken Spaniard, and replaced him with a young Cuban who had been educated at the University of Florida. Under Walter's direction, La Margarita became a trim village with a school, a church, and even a baseball diamond, surrounded by endless fields of sugar cane. Walter's growing family often visited, and Freddy and his two little sisters enjoyed the weekends in the country. Once more, the Havana

Trust prospered as Americans visited Cuba in great numbers, whether fleeing cold weather or Prohibition. Even after the Crash, new hotels such as the Hotel Nacional sprang up everywhere, and the election of President Machado brought a number of impressive public works, including the Central Highway, which made it possible to drive from one end of the island to the other for the first time.

Nonetheless, that afternoon Walter knew all was not well. Although business was slow because of the political turmoil, the bank remained profitable. He had long become inured to the indignities of Havana—the incessant noise, the strange food, and above all, the blasted heat—but something else troubled him, like a lingering toothache. What was it?

Walter turned into O'Reilly Street and passed between the reassuring Corinthian columns of the Havana Trust. Inside, it was cool and somber, as a bank lobby should be. Elmer Johnson, the guard, nodded and touched the visor of his cap, and Walter saw with approval that several customers waited in line at each window. The only sound was the delicious shuffle of dollar bills behind the iron grills. Mounting the stairs to the second floor, Walter saw with approval that no one was taking a *siesta* after lunch. Walter entered his office, where his secretary had arrayed his correspondence in neat little piles. On the bookshelf was the model of the *HMS Victory* that once belonged to Mr. Gordon, and had been left behind when he fled Cuba. Walter admired the intricate rigging and the miniature cannons bristling on either side of the hull. It was truly a thing of beauty, and he soon forgot his queer anxiety.

Later that afternoon, Edward Hopgood stopped by his office. Over the years, the bank's vice president had changed little. He was tall and stooped, with a long dyspeptic face. Hopgood's wife had left him for a salesman in Cienfuegos many years before, which accounted for his contempt for Cubans.

"There's something I forgot to mention," Hopgood said with a thin smile. "It's nothing, really. Just the other day the

54

strangest character walked into the bank. He was just off a banana boat by the look of him, and I don't suppose he'd taken a bath for weeks. Would you believe that he wanted to cash a check? Elmer was about to throw him out when I happened by and actually met him. Can you guess what he expected me to believe?"

Walter shrugged blankly.

"He said he was Ernest Hemingway!"

Hemingway soon grew tired of sleeping in the cramped cabin of the *Anita*, which smelled of brine and dirty clothes. Javier suggested the Hotel Ambos Mundos, on the corner of Obispo and Mercaderes streets. It was across from the ivy-covered walls of the Santo Domingo convent and strategically situated between the Floridita and the docks. But when Hemingway appeared at the front desk, unshaven and fresh from a day's fishing, the manager refused to let him in. Only when Javier intervened, explaining the eccentricities of the *americano*, was Hemingway shown to a corner room on the fifth floor.

It was plain though spacious, with yellowish walls, a brown and white-tiled floor, and mahogany furniture. From the window, beyond the palm trees of the Plaza de Armas, Hemingway could see the lighthouse of El Morro. The room was $2.00 a night, but when Pauline came, they charged him 50 cents more. She had arrived with Bud's wife Helen on the P&O ferry, and looked about apprehensively on the way to the hotel.

"Why couldn't we have stayed at the Hotel Nacional?" she said.

"Too far from the docks," growled her husband.

Pauline suddenly regretted she had come. When Gregory was born after their return from Paris, the doctor had told her that another pregnancy was out of the question. She had lain

55

in bed for several weeks following the delivery, and slept in the parlor so as not to climb the stairs. Before Hemingway left for Havana, she was healthy once again, but at night she lay in bed staring at the ceiling, waiting for the measured breathing that would tell her he was asleep.

"Don't worry," she whispered in his ear as he shifted restlessly. "Everything is going to be fine."

But it wasn't, and some nights he went out after dinner to Joe's speakeasy and came home smelling of whiskey, stumbling up the stairs and falling into bed while she pretended to be asleep. It had happened before, shortly after they were married, but it had gone away by itself. So she did not see it as a problem and it was far from her mind as they finished dinner that night on the rooftop of the Ambos Mundos.

"We'll need to get an early start tomorrow," announced Hemingway.

"Couldn't we sleep late, just this once?" said Pauline, looking to Helen for support.

Suddenly there was a loud report from the direction of the harbor.

"What was that?" cried Pauline in alarm. "It sounded like an explosion!"

"Nothing to worry about," chuckled Hemingway, checking his watch. "It's an old tradition. Every night at nine, they fire one of the *Doce Apóstoles*, the cannons in La Cabaña. That's when they used to close the city gates."

"As long as they don't hit us," laughed Helen, who was eager to catch a marlin.

But when he opened the shutters in the morning, Hemingway saw ugly clouds hanging over El Morro, like puffs of dark smoke, and he knew there would be no fishing that day. A damp wind was blowing from the north, and not even the fishing smacks were in the harbor.

"I thought I'd call Jane Mason," said Pauline, still in bed. "Do you remember her from that night on the *Ile-de-France?*"

"Was she a blond?" asked Hemingway.

"Oh, I know you do, because you couldn't keep your eyes off her. You and every other man on the boat. And I was out to here, broad as a barrel."

"Poor old Mama."

"I won't call if you don't want me to."

"What's the harm?"

The operator put Pauline through to Jaimanitas. Jane was delighted to hear from her and said she and Grant would love to join them for dinner.

Hemingway walked down to the pier and found Joe sitting atop an empty wooden crate. Behind him, the *Anita* pulled at the moorings with a sinister creak. They traded frowns and crossed the square to the Café de la Perla de San Francisco. The bartender was a scowling Asturian nicknamed Kaiser Guillermo because of his handlebar mustache, and he grudgingly offered them a breakfast of *café con leche* and *tostadas*. Soon, it began to rain, flooding the stalls in the market and dousing the cooking pots. A *pregonero* ran frantically for cover, his cart skidding over the slick cobblestones. The thick cold raindrops slanted into the café and they moved from their table by the door to the bar.

"No luck today, Mahatma," said Joe, lighting a Lucky Strike.

"We're well and truly *jodido,* Josie."

The rest of the day, Hemingway sat in the lobby of the Ambos Mundos playing chess. Charles was a good player and beat him easily, so after a few games they put away the pieces. Bud and Helen braved the rain to go sightseeing, and Pauline went to get her hair done on the Prado. When Charles asked about the Masons, Hemingway replied:

"Grant runs Pan American Airways here and probably the YMCA, too. His wife's a damn fine looking girl but crazy as a loon."

"Whatever you say," said Charles.

Charles had learned to accept his friend's judgements on people with a grain of salt, but just the same he decided to have dinner with Joe. The rain had stopped by the time the Masons pulled up to the Ambos Mundos. Grant came over from the passenger's side to open Jane's door, and her long, lovely legs emerged.

By way of introduction, Grant said: "We've had a devil of a time today, sport. All the flights were canceled!"

"Sorry to hear it," said Hemingway.

For a moment, the two men clenched hands with determined grins.

"It's all for the better," said Jane. "We don't want to lose any passengers, do we?"

"Don't be silly, darling," said Grant irritably.

Jane and Pauline daintily kissed on both cheeks, like in Paris, and stepped back to eye each other's shoes. Helen, *hors de combat*, remained on her husband's arm. Over a round of manhattans at the bar, Hemingway recounted his triumphant struggle with the marlin that jumped thirteen times.

"Splendid!" said Grant, and described his own boat, a 48-foot Matthews cruiser called the Pelican II. "Janie's quite a hand with a rod and reel herself."

"Hardly, Stoneface," laughed Jane, rolling her eyes. It was her special name for him.

"My biggest one so far was over eight feet long," put in Hemingway. "I could barely pull it over the transom."

"It's still early in the year," said Grant. "Just wait a few weeks. Last year, I landed one that weighed over 500 pounds, just off Cojimar."

"Which way do the marlin travel?" asked Helen.

"They always swim from east to west," said Hemingway, "against the current."

"It's actually the opposite, sport," said Grant. "The marlin travel with the Gulf Stream, but they feed in the opposite direction."

"Same difference," mumbled Hemingway.

For dinner, they strolled up Obispo to the Zaragozana Restaurant, around the corner from the Floridita, where the white-gloved captain made a great show of greeting Jane and led them to the Masons' usual table. Grant insisted on ordering for all of them, and they began with the Morro crabs. The plump claws arrived on a bed of lettuce with a dollop of mayonaise, and Pauline and Helen watched carefully as Jane expertly picked out the meat with a tiny fork and dabbed at her lips with a napkin. Hemingway had asked for a bottle of Meursault, and as the glasses were filled, he sent the waiter scurrying off for another.

"I've spent all day at the gallery," lamented Jane, "watching it rain."

"Gallery?" asked Pauline.

"It's a hobby of Janie's," said Grant. "Quite a swell little place on Tejadillo Street, not too far from here. Tell them about it, darling."

"I'm sure they don't want to hear about it," said Jane quickly.

"I'm sure they do," insisted Grant.

"I'd rather not discuss it, darling," said Jane, an odd note in her voice.

"Well, if you don't I will," said her husband. "Janie's found all sorts of funny things across the bay in Regla: carved coconuts, necklaces made of shells, voodoo beads, you know what I mean. Have I missed anything, darling?"

"Why no, you've said it all," she said, and abruptly left the table.

A pall came over them. Pauline hesitated, looked at Hemingway's blank expression, and then hurried after her.

"Now, what did I say to upset her?" said Grant, shrugging his shoulders in mock dismay. "With all due respect," he added, nodding at Helen, "I simply don't understand women at all."

Momentarily, Jane came sweeping back to the table, her perfume wafting behind her, flanked by Pauline.

"I hope I haven't missed anything," said Jane, flashing a brilliant smile.

59

"Nothing at all, darling," said Grant.

Peace was apparently restored when the waiter returned with the main course, a magnificent snapper served with tiny boiled potatoes. Pauline mentioned that they planned to go to Africa later that year. It was another gift from Uncle Gus.

"You absolutely must get Philip Percival," announced Grant. "A capital fellow. Absolutely the best white hunter in Tanganyika, no question about it. Do you know that he took Teddy Roosevelt himself on safari? Janie took quite a liking to him, I must say."

As Hemingway turned towards her, a delicate blush spread across her cheeks, but she devoted all her attention to the fish.

"If he's not available, then his partner Bror Blixen is the man for you," continued Grant. "Otherwise, watch out! Some of these white hunters are little more than crooks. And you must stay with Dick Cooper at his place on Lake Manyara. Nothing like it. Isn't that right, darling?"

Jane speared a potato with her fork.

"Ernest is very excited about the trip," Pauline put in hastily. "He's been planning it ever so long. Just like a little boy!"

Hemingway sipped his glass of white wine as dinner proceeded. He noticed that Grant had a peculiar habit of methodically cutting his food into little pieces, spreading them around his plate, and eating them one by one.

"What's happening here in Cuba?" asked Bud.

"A very difficult situation," said Grant. "Ambassador Guggenheim is our neighbor, and he admitted to me the other day that he can't make head or tails of it himself. But it seems to me that a battleship or two in the harbor would solve the problem."

"It's never worked before," said Jane.

"But it certainly has! If not for the Rough Riders, they'd still be fighting the Spaniards."

"Wouldn't the Cubans have won on their own?" asked Bud.

"Nonsense!" said Grant. "You have to understand how they think. Why, Cuba could have joined the union. Imagine that, just like Florida! But they chose not to, and we had to send in the marines twice to keep order. If not, the whole island would have gone up in flames. Take it from me, President Machado is a good chap. They elected him, you know. The problems began when he got his *político* pals to change the Cuban constitution and extend his term of office. It stirred up a real hornet's nest among the opposition. I'll grant you he's as crooked as the rest of them, but he's tough as nails. Look how he dealt with the rebels that landed at Gibara last year."

"Can he keep the students in line?" asked Hemingway.

"If he can't, then it will be up to us," said Grant.

Jane remained silent throughout dessert, smoking a *margarita*. She looked up when Pauline said: "Ernest, wouldn't it be wonderful if they came fishing with us?"

"I'm afraid we can't," said Grant. "I'm flying to Caracas tomorrow."

"You'll be awfully lonely after Pauline leaves," said Jane.

"I've got the marlin to keep me company," said Hemingway, "at least until Saturday. It's my last day on the water."

"Can we come then?" said Jane.

"Why not?" said Hemingway. "Just be at the San Francisco Dock by eight o'clock."

Back at the hotel, Hemingway asked Pauline why she invited them.

"I didn't think they'd accept," she admitted.

"It's going to be a long day on Saturday."

"Oh, Ernest, she's so sad. Don't you feel sorry for her?"

Occasionally, Don Ramón López found himself with nothing to do.

Javier's older brother Miguel now held the reins of the business, managing the firm's warehouses around the island.

This development had astounded Don Ramón's employees, who were used to him looking over their shoulders. Indeed, that was one of the many things Don Ramón had learned from his father. He remembered him saying, "*El ojo del amo engorda el caballo,*" in his stern voice. It was an old Spanish proverb, meaning that the owner of a business must always keep his eyes open. But his father, now nearing ninety, also said there was a time and place for everything.

So it was that by mid-afternoon, Don Ramón realized the day's work was done. It was a rare and unexpected gift for someone accustomed to never having enough time. When faced with this pleasant dilemma, Don Ramón enjoyed nothing better than a good *tabaco*. For many years, he had smoked Por Larrañagas, and he received an elegantly wrapped box directly from the factory once a week. It was one of his few vices, and he lovingly passed the hand-rolled, oak-brown cigar along his mustache, inhaling the aroma of the rich Vuelta Abajo tobacco. Don Ramón preferred *perfectos*, fat cigars neatly tapered at both ends.

The delicious smoke trailing behind him, Don Ramón left his office, telling his secretary that he would be out for the rest of the day. He stepped out into Empedrado Street, and drank in the view that had enchanted him as a boy, and that he would never tire of. At the end of the esplanade was the mounted statue of Máximo Gómez, and the battlements of La Punta from which a chain was stretched across the harbor to keep out pirates. Behind it was the dizzying expanse of ocean.

At the end of the day, Don Ramón's father would bring him to the waterfront to watch ships of every description enter Havana, from tall-masted freighters to solemn warships. The old *gallego* had been conscripted into the army and sent to Cuba during the first war of independence. When it ended, he remained in Havana, and soon sent for his wife and son. He was too old to fight when the Cubans once again took up arms, but by then his sympathies had changed. Angered by the atrocities committed by his countrymen, he smuggled arms for the rebels and swore never to return to Spain.

In the years following the war, when American soldiers occupied La Cabaña, the business prospered and they grew wealthy. Each summer, Don Ramón took his family to Spain, and urged his widowed father to accompany them. After all, the war was long forgotten, and many Spaniards were returning to Cuba. What good would it do to keep a vow he had made to himself so many years ago? The old man refused. Alone at night, he dreamed of the tiny walled village of Betanzos where he had been born, amid the rocky streams and cool pine forests of Galicia. But to his son, he declared he would die in Cuba.

That was one promise he had yet to keep, Don Ramón often laughed to himself. His father began each day with a glass of brandy, and was strong as an ox. On most mornings, he still went to the abandoned *almacén* on Muralla Street and spent the day staring at the red-tiled rooftops of Habana Vieja, or else playing dominoes with Father Saralegui, a Basque priest from the nearby church of Espíritu Santo.

From the waterfront, it was only a few steps to the Plaza de la Catedral, and Don Ramón passed the weathered baroque towers of the cathedral and emerged onto Monserrate Street. Across the Parque Central rose the Centro Gallego, its white marble towers dwarfing even the Hotel Inglaterra. Built in 1918, its opening had been celebrated with a command performance of *Aida*, and it was here that Don Ramón repaired to on those rare occasions when he had nothing to do.

A splinter of irritation penetrated his complacent mood as his cigar petered out. Don Ramón continued on his way, knowing the bartender at the Centro Gallego kept a box of Por Larrañagas for just such an emergency. His refuge was the mahogany-paneled lounge on the second floor, overlooking the statue of José Martí in the Parque Central. He maneuvered into his favorite leather armchair, and ordered a brandy to accompany his *perfecto*. Soon, he was puffing away contentedly, contemplating the rest of the afternoon.

A familiar voice roused him, and he welcomed his old friend Ignacio Irazurri to the neighboring armchair. Irazurri was the president of the Banco de Galicia, and had no sons to take over his business, but rather three daughters. María, the youngest, was married to Miguel.

"I have the most amazing thing to tell you," began Don Ramón. "Your rival, Mr. Walter Huggins of the Havana Trust, invited me to breakfast!"

"You don't say," chuckled Irazurri. "I hear the food is terrible."

"Have you ever eaten pancakes?" said Don Ramón. "I can't say I recommend them. The strangest thing of all was that he never told me what he wanted."

"Your money, of course."

"*Por supuesto*. But you can never be sure with the *americanos*."

"I wouldn't be surprised if he invited you to play golf."

"How did you know?" asked Don Ramón.

"I have a story to tell you as well."

Irazurri had heard that Emilio Aragon was spotted playing golf at the Havana Country Club. Tears nearly came to his eyes as he recounted how Aragon had worn an absurd tam o'shanter and almost fainted from the heat. When Don Ramón had first encountered him, Aragon was a lowly clerk in the Ayuntamiento. During the first turbulent years of the new republic, he somehow amassed a fortune, and when the banks collapsed, he bought a vast central near Matanzas and sold it to the Cuban Sugar Cane Company, of which he became president. With the election of Machado, an old crony of his from Santa Clara, his star continued to rise, and he became one of the wealthiest men in Cuba. It came as no surprise that he was learning to play golf, since he was building a gaudy mansion just off the ninth hole of the Havana Country Club.

After their laughter died down, the two men savored their cigars in silence. Don Ramón's thoughts turned to his younger son, so unlike Miguel. Javier was more an impractical Angulo than a hard-headed López. It had been on a trip to Trinidad, a colonial city in the shadow of the Escambray mountains, that Don Ramón saw Inés Angulo stepping out of a carriage. Her father had opposed the marriage on two counts: he was a tradesman and what's worse, a Spaniard. But Don Ramón had pursued her affections as methodically as he ran his business, and they were married a year later. Still, he always scorned her aristocratic family. Their once grand estates had been ravaged during the war, and all that remained was a crumbling sugar mill. The often unreasonable Angulo pride would do Javier little good in the business world, where one had to deal with men like Walter Huggins and Emilio Aragon. And yet, there was a certain strength in his younger son that Miguel lacked. Did that come from Inés as well?

But Javier had no ambition to speak of. What on earth did he learn at Harvard? Don Ramón bitterly cursed the day he sent him to study in the United States. Since his return, he had done little more than carouse with his American friends. He had also been seen in the company of a caramel-colored girl with Chinese eyes, a dancer at the Alhambra. This did not bother Don Ramón, since Javier was less likely to join his friend Alberto at a barricade. As a man of the world, he knew that such temporary attachments were quite common. Even Miguel had once kept a *negrita*. And he himself fondly remembered a freckled, red-haired Frenchwoman he met in Matanzas, so many years ago. Where was she now? Javier was still young. He would outgrow these things, just as he had outgrown short pants as a boy.

Last Sunday, Don Ramón had ushered Javier into his study. The boy sat stiffly in the high-backed chair facing his father's desk, no doubt expecting a reprimand for some excess, but Don Ramón offered him a Por Larrañaga.

"I spoke recently with Dr. Eduardo Heydrich," he began carefully. "He sends you his warmest regards."

Javier lit his *perfecto*, remembering the absent-minded doctor, one of his father's oldest friends. When he was a boy, they would spend Christmas in Trinidad, and once they stopped at the Heydrich's house in Matanzas on the way.

"Surely you remember his oldest daughter, Adelaida—"

Javier recalled that Adelaida was a plump, ill-tempered girl with thick eyebrows, reportedly a chess prodigy.

"—who's grown up into a real beauty. Eduardo and I, we thought that perhaps... Do I make myself clear?"

Suddenly, Javier's throat burned and he began to cough.

"Are you all right?" asked his father.

Even now, sitting in his favorite armchair at the Centro Gallego, as the afternoon light slanted through the high window, Don Ramón remembered the ominous silence that followed. He had never defied *his* father like that. Don Ramón did not bring the subject up again and informed Dr. Heydrich that the time was not right to put their long-cherished plan into motion.

His Por Larrañaga had burned down to a damp stub but he was reluctant to give it up. Turning to Irazurri, he saw with amusement that the greying banker had nodded off. Perhaps he had nothing to do, either.

Later that week, Joe hired an old fisherman named Carlos Gutíerrez as first mate. During the winter he captained a fishing sloop, and his dour face reflected a lifetime spent on the waves. Carlos was slender and stooped, with watery dark eyes, and as the *Anita* left the San Francisco Dock he said:

"The marlin will be hungry today, Don Ernesto."

"How can you tell?" asked Hemingway.

"They like to feed when the moon is full."

"He can smell them," said Joe with a wink.

"I can smell Carlos," said Charles.

Carlos baited the hook *por derecho*, as he called it, passing the barb through the mouth of a whole bonito and bringing it out the gill. Then he cut a slit in the fish to conceal the shank, and wrapped the line around its mouth to keep it from spinning in the water. No sooner did Hemingway cast the line than he noticed a marlin playfully trailing behind the bait.

"¡Aguja!" cried Carlos.

It was dark blue with a faint lavender stripe, and swam easily against the current. Skimming just beneath the waves, the marlin tapped the bait with its bill, its pectoral fins close by its sides.

"He cannot make up his mind, Don Ernesto," said Carlos. "When he spreads his wings, he will strike."

Carlos stowed the teasers and Hemingway flicked back the line, as though the baitfish were trying to escape. As the Cuban had predicted, the marlin's fins swung out and it swooped down on the bait like a great bird of prey. Hemingway knew that the big fish would be spooked if he tried to set the hook too early, but he kept his finger on the spool as it stayed even with the boat. As the marlin veered broadside, Hemingway screwed down the drag. The pull on the line bent the fishing pole like a bow, and Hemingway leaned back in the fishing chair, using the muscles of his back for leverage.

"El pan de mis hijos," Carlos said solemnly. [Bread for my children.]

The marlin pirouetted in the air, its curved tail clean out of the water. It had a bluntly rounded body with a long sword, and Hemingway could see its dark, saucer-like eyes. Satisfied that the hook was set, he let it run out the line as it headed for the open sea.

"I think she's playing hard to get," said Hemingway.

"The marlin is a *macho*," said Carlos.

"How can you tell?"

"They are all *machos*," insisted Carlos.

"Perhaps this one is a *maricón*."

As it leaped once again, Hemingway decided he would not be returning to Key West just yet. When the marlin was cut open at the dock, one of the fishermen excitedly pointed out the roe, glistening like jewels in the bloody entrails.

"What did I tell you, you stubborn Cuban!" said Hemingway triumphantly.

"That is very unusual, Don Ernesto," said Carlos, slowly shaking his head.

As he helped Joe empty the icebox, Carlos related the story of an old fisherman who went out in a skiff and hooked a huge fish with a handline. It was a hoary grandfather of a black marlin, weighing well over 50 *arrobas* [1250 pounds] and it towed him far out to sea. Somehow, he managed to harpoon him. A cargo ship picked him up two days later, nearly sixty miles away, and all that remained of the giant marlin was the head. The sharks were still circling the boat, and the old man was sobbing with grief.

"*Se volvió loco*," concluded Carlos. [He went crazy.]

Hemingway wrote it all down on the book of Western Union cable blanks that he used as the ship's log. That afternoon, he wired Pauline, who had returned home with Bud and Helen, and told her that he would stay in Havana another few days, though Charles was needed at the hardware store and took the ferry back. On Saturday, Javier brought several bottles of Rioja from his father's wine cellar as a going-away present.

"I'm not going anywhere, Harvard," said Hemingway.

"Then we shall have to drink all this today, Ernesto," replied Javier.

They were untying the bowline when the Mason's car appeared on the waterfront, the horn blowing a shave and a haircut.

"*Mierda,*"said Hemingway, remembering that Jane had asked to join him on what was to have been his last day.

She waved gaily as she skipped down the peer, wearing a scarf and dark glasses.

Carlos let out a low whistle, the bowline slack in his hand.

"Forgive me for being late," said Jane, as Hemingway helped her aboard. "You wouldn't have gone without me, would you?"

Jane kissed Hemingway on the cheek and extended her hand to Javier, tilting her head slightly to one side.

It was a bright morning with snowy clouds moving briskly ahead of the breeze. In the channel, a fisherman in a rowboat pulled up his net, and the *machuelos* fell at his feet like silver coins. Above the ravelined walls of La Cabaña, the seagulls patrolled in ever-narrowing circles.

"Where's Grant?" asked Hemingway.

"He's still in Caracas."

At the mouth of the harbor, a garbage scow dumped its load in the water: rotten fruit and vegetables, animal carcasses, bottles, condoms, and old newspapers. A small dinghy followed in its wake, and a man poled through the garbage looking for something of value. Joe cut the engine for fear that the propeller would snag, and they drifted until the current swept the refuse away.

Hemingway took out a few beers from the icebox and Jane happily drained hers. Carlos said he knew of a secluded *cayo* west of Havana, so they kept the teasers out of the water as Joe opened up the throttle and headed west.

"Why, we'll be in Jaimanitas soon," said Jane.

It was a fishing village of brightly painted wooden houses along a sandy beach. Jane pointed out her house on a bluff above the water, a rose-colored villa encircled by flame trees, and Hemingway smelled the lemony tang of her perfume in the sea air.

"Grant's dying to have you over for cocktails," continued Jane, her eyes flickering over to Javier, as though including him in the invitation.

"I can hardly wait," said Hemingway drily.

Joe pulled away from the shore. The seagulls that had followed them hovered playfully over the waves, and Carlos dropped a line for bait. Almost immediately, he pulled out two small fish hooked on the same line and baited a rod for Jane. She deftly landed a dolphin, which Carlos scooped up with a net. The sail of a fishing smack out of Mariel appeared to starboard, but then dipped below the horizon. They were alone until a covey of black-winged flying fish raced up from under the bow and spurted out of the water, diving only to shoot up with fresh impetus. After an hour, Carlos pointed out the *cayo*, a golden strip of sand with a single palm and a fisherman's hut. Javier scanned the horizon for billfish, eager to impress Hemingway after the other day, but all he saw were the waves, stretching before him like endless rows of wheat. Jane sat down on the fishing chair beside him.

"It's so calm out here," she said, brushing a strand of blond hair from her forehead. "It's hard to believe."

"Why is that?"

Jane told Javier how the other day she had been driving up Galiano when she saw several *expertos* in their jackboots and jodhpurs blocking the entrance to Virtudes Street. Just a few minutes earlier, a man had been shot from a passing car, but the police had killed the students inside with a hail of bullets.

"What do you suppose they died for?" she asked. "Was it worth it?"

"Maybe to them."

"What difference can that make now? My husband says that Machado is no worse than the rest of them."

"Machado is an *asno con garras*," hissed Javier.

"That's rather funny, isn't it? A donkey with claws."

Jane looked at him for a moment and then laid her fingers on his arm.

"I've insulted you, haven't I?"

Their eyes met, and Javier started to say something, but Joe cut the engine and Hemingway announced it was time for lunch. They anchored off the *cayo* and waded ashore as Joe stood guard with the shotgun, watching for sharks. The Rioja was cooling in the water as Carlos went to work inside the tiny galley. His skillet was soon sizzling with the steaks he had cut from Jane's dolphin, and they ate in the meager shade of the palm tree, cleaning their plates with a chunk of bread. For dessert, Carlos produced a huge red mango, which he sliced into quarters with the tip of his machete.

After lunch, Javier went for a swim, diving off the bow, and Hemingway lay in the sand beside Jane.

"I'm afraid your friend doesn't like me very much," she said.

"Why is that?" said Hemingway, who remembered Javier eyeing her on the pier.

"I said something I shouldn't have," said Jane. "Now I've made a hash of things."

"Don't be silly."

Jane pulled out the bottle from the wet sand and refilled her glass.

"You think I'm crazy, don't you?"

"Why do you say that?" he replied uneasily.

"I know what people say about me. It becomes a game, after a while. Jane said this, or Jane did that. Sometimes, I do things so as not to disappoint them. Maybe I am crazy."

"You'll never be that way," said Hemingway.

Jane kneeled in the sand, close enough for him to kiss her, and he remembered how beautiful she was the first time he saw her, on the arm of her husband aboard the *Ile-de-France*. At that moment, Joe called out that if they wanted to get any fishing done that afternoon, they should start back.

The sun was in their faces as the *cayo* dropped below the horizon. Hemingway's head buzzed pleasantly from the wine, and he leaned back in the fishing chair. Jane was sunning herself in the bow and Javier was taking a nap in the cabin. As Joe smoked a cigarette, Carlos softly sang a *lamento*. Hemingway tried to make out the words, but they blended with the rumble of the engine and the occasional cry of a seagull. He yawned and placed the rod on his lap, securing the butt under one leg as the line trailed in the water. Without warning, it whipped against the gunwale, and the fishing chair tipped over backwards. Hemingway scrambled to his feet, but before he could grab the pole it flew out of the boat and disappeared under the water.

As Carlos looked on wide-eyed, Joe raced back to the stern.

"Let's call it a day," he said, spitting over the side.

"I'll pay for it, goddam it," said Hemingway through clenched teeth.

Shaking with rage, he slammed his fist against the side of the boat and began cursing, at first perfunctorily but then bitterly and imaginatively. Having exhausted his vocabulary in English, he switched to French, Spanish, and finally Turkish, the most satisfying of all. His tirade brought a startled Javier up on deck and Jane peered over the wheel house.

"It's just a fishing pole," she said.

Hemingway lowered his voice with difficulty.

"That's not it," he spat out. "That's not it at all."

The trip back to Havana passed uneventfully. Jane chatted with Joe in the cockpit, and Javier watched Carlos whittle a piece of wood he'd taken from the beach. Hemingway brooded in the cabin as they entered the slip, and the waiting dockhands dispersed forlornly. When Hemingway emerged, he saw that Jane had already left.

"Can I buy you a drink, Ernesto?" asked Javier uncertainly.

"Maybe two or three."

They found Freddy at the Floridita.

"Papa!" he cried, delighted to see him with Javier.

Hemingway muttered a greeting and nodded to Constante, who began to make a round of daiquiris.

"No *azúcar*," he reminded him.

Hemingway drained his first *Papa Especial* of the night, and only then could he shake hands.

"*Estás hecho leña*," said Freddy.

"What the hell does that mean?"

"It's an old Cuban expression that says you've had a long day," put in Javier.

Hemingway frowned and ordered another round. The Trío Matancero was playing a *guaracha* in the dining room, and he tapped his foot to the beat. With each daiquiri, he thought less and less of the lost fishing rod.

"Who holds the record for daiquiris?" asked Hemingway.

"I do," replied Freddy, "but I lost count."

"Too bad," said Hemingway, who was soon up to number five.

The regulars at the Floridita began to take notice, and even Leopoldina la Honesta momentarily stopped negotiating her fee with a tourist to see him triumphantly down number six.

"It's going to be a long night," whispered Javier to Freddy.

"The worst thing you can do, gentlemen," said Hemingway, "is to go fishing with a woman. You can't exactly throw her overboard. Promise me you'll never go fishing with a woman."

"I promise," said Freddy.

"*Uno más, Constante.*"

As Javier finished his own drink, he noticed a huge, disheveled man staring at Hemingway from across the room. He wore a rumpled plaid suit with his tie loosened, and his lank blond hair had fallen over his forehead. Engulfing his highball glass in a sweaty palm, he drank it in one gulp and slammed it on the bar.

"Another whiskey!" he demanded.

"Who is that guy?" said Javier, nudging Hemingway. "I think he knows you."

"I never saw him before in my life," shrugged Hemingway, and ordered another *Papa Especial*.

Javier watched as the man tossed back his second drink, the whiskey dribbling down his chin. Wiping it with his sleeve, he made his way towards them, elbowing a tourist out of the way.

"What does he want?" asked Javier.

"Definitely not an autograph," said Freddy.

The crowd parted to let him pass. He was nearly half a head taller than Hemingway, and he thrust his broad chest only a few inches away from the writer. "You cocksucker!" he yelled, shaking with fury.

Unconcerned, Hemingway sipped the daiquiri and swirled it in his mouth. Then he nodded to the terrified *cantinero* and calmly drained his glass.

As the man cocked his fist, Hemingway turned and hit him hard in the stomach, so that the air came out of him with a *whoosh*. He toppled slowly, like a felled tree, and Hemingway landed a left hook to his head on the way down.

"No one has the right to interrupt a man while he's drinking," said Hemingway, smiling at last.

Freddy signaled to several of the shoeshine boys who had followed the fight. With difficulty, they dragged the unconscious *americano* out and stuffed him into the back of a cab, one leg sticking precariously out the window. Then Freddy tossed a coin to the driver and gave him the address of the whorehouse in Marianao where he had found Hub Kendall, the errant left-fielder of the Washington Senators.

"*Uno más, Constante,*" said Hemingway.

THREE

Pauline Hemingway returned to Havana for the weekend and brought the galleys of *Death in the Afternoon*. Although Hemingway had attempted to distill everything he knew about bullfighting into words, something was missing and much remained to be done before it could be published. But he was far away from the dust and stench of the *corrida*, and yearned to be out on the Gulf Stream once again.

That night, Hemingway told his wife that he intended to remain in Cuba until the end of the month. The striped marlin were just starting to run, and it would be a shame to leave so soon. Pauline took the news calmly, as she always did. Since the early years of her marriage, she had found that it did no good to argue with him once he made up his mind. She had grown to detest Havana, especially the waterfront—everything was so dirty, and smelled like rotting fish. Worst of all were Cuban men. Walking along the Prado, she felt their hungry stares following her every step of the way. With the exception of the Masons, she had met no one worth talking to.

As she left the Ambos Mundos to catch the ferry home, she glared at the hotel manager, who responded with his most unctuous smile. Jane had given them two flamingoes as an anniversary present, and they wailed piteously on the pier, waiting to be loaded into the hold. Pauline kissed her husband goodbye and watched from the railing as the ferry pulled away from the Arsenal Dock, beneath the fortress of Atarés. Hemingway waved until she was out of sight and then turned on his heel, hurrying back to the Plaza de San Francisco.

Aboard the *Anita*, Carlos was baiting the rods, including the new Hardy #4 bamboo pole Hemingway bought to replace the one that went over the side. The old fisherman remarked that they were now equipped *con todos los hierros*. By the end of May, Hemingway had caught 19 marlin, which he meticulously documented in his log. It pained Carlos to give away the day's catch to the crowd that eagerly awaited the *Anita* at the dock, but he usually went home with a tuna under his arm for his wife and eight children. As for Joe, he had been delighted to stay longer in Havana, since he had no other charters and times were tough in Key West. He renewed his 45 day permit from the port authorities, although he said he might have to return home for a few days. Hemingway had seen him talking to some shady characters in the Perla, and wondered what he was up to:

"Can I ask you a question, Josie?"

"No harm in asking."

"Are you going to bring back any Hoover Gold?" asked Hemingway.

Joe's expression didn't change but the knowing lines at the corners of his eyes deepened:

"Now, why would I do that?"

"Come on, Josie," protested Hemingway. "I can't write about something I don't know. What if a fellow—a character in a novel, say—wanted to smuggle some booze into Key West. How would he go about it?"

"Pretty easily," said Joe. "Havana's wide open. This fellow of yours could buy a bottle of cognac for 40 cents, and sell it stateside for $3.50. You figure it out."

"What about the police?"

"They don't mind, not if you grease the right palm. You can take anything you want off this island: rum, guns, chinamen."

"You're not going to tell me, are you?"

"You'll have to use your imagination, Mahatma."

It was no use. Even if Joe *was* a bootlegger, he was unlikely to admit it.

Most evenings, Hemingway met Javier and Freddy at the Floridita. One of the shoeshine boys would see him sauntering up Obispo, and run ahead shouting *"¡El Hemingway!"* to alert Constante, who would then have the first of many daiquiris waiting at the bar. Especially on days when the marlin wisely avoided his bait, that first daiquiri drew him back to port as effectively as the lighthouse of El Morro. He held the stem of the cocktail glass between his thumb and forefinger and took his first, long-awaited sip.

His record of six daiquiris from that woozy, violent afternoon still stood, and he approached the figure reverentially. The first *Papa Especial* merely served to quench his thirst, and the second was dispatched as a matter of course. The third involved some reflection, and the fourth was by no means taken lightly. The fifth put up some resistance, but was dealt with harshly, and the sixth was a worthy opponent.

"You are the Kid Chocolate of daiquiris," remarked Javier.

The celebrated Cuban boxer would soon be defending his title against Mike Sarko in Madison Square Garden.

"I am simply *tomando con calma*," said Hemingway. "By the way, I have a question. What is a *choteo*?"

"Where did you hear that?" asked Freddy.

"Carlos was arguing with someone at the dock."

"It's a joke," said Javier, "like a *relajo*."

"What's the difference between a *choteo* and a *relajo*?"

"A *choteo* can be a *relajo*, but not vice-versa. If taken to its logical conclusion, a *relajo* can become a *fracaso*, which is very bad."

"As bad as a *Fiesta de Guatao*?"

"That's a very bad *fracaso*," put in Freddy.

"Very well, Tex," said Hemingway, draining his daiquiri, "perhaps you can explain what a *piropo* is."

"A *piropo* is as Cuban as baseball," said Freddy. "In fact, it's like a pitch."

"This will require some research in the field," said Javier.

Hemingway settled their tab and they walked across the Parque Central to San Rafael Street. At the corner of Galiano was Woolworth's, where a diverse group of men waited, some elegantly dressed in *dril cien* suits and straw boaters, and others with frayed *guayaberas*. They were all there for the same reason, since at six o'clock the girls who worked behind the counter got off work. The first woman to take her chances was a shapely *mulata* who walked with a sensuous, maddeningly slow gait.

"*Ay mi santa,*" went the first pitch, "*¿todo eso es tuyo?*" [Is all that yours?]

She sniffed contemptuously, not deigning to reply, and continued on her way.

"Not a very good showing," commented Freddy.

The second to leave was a petite blonde who stepped out tentatively and flashed a dazzling smile at a young man who stepped out of the line to offer her his arm.

"Why didn't she rate a *piropo?*" asked Hemingway.

"Her boyfriend would have had to defend her honor, and his," explained Javier.

"I'll have to write all this down," said Hemingway.

Occasionally, after the Floridita they went to the Ambos Mundos for a boxing lesson. Hemingway cleared away the furniture in his room and produced the boxing gloves. Stripping to the waist, he loosened up while Javier hung his jacket in the closet. Armed with a stopwatch, Freddy timed the three minute rounds as the fighters circled each other.

Javier remembered that Hemingway had tremendous power in his long, muscular arms. The writer liked to jab with his left, testing his defenses, and then lunge with a deadly right hook. In contrast to his broad torso, his legs were thin and he often stumbled, perhaps because of his bad knee. But when he charged, bellowing like a bull, there was little Javier could do to avoid being backed up against the wall.

Hemingway rarely pulled his punches, and Javier's arms grew numb from fending off blows.

Javier soon realized that Hemingway was virtually blind in his left eye, which made him vulnerable to a right hook. If he could get in close, he just might be able to land a punch. As Hemingway approached, Javier backed away in a crouch, dropping his right hand, and then swung hard. But Hemingway easily dodged the blow, and hit Javier in the ribs before the younger man could regain his balance.

"Lesson number two," said Hemingway, breathing hard, the hairs on his chest matted with sweat. *"Never let the other guy see your cards."*

Hemingway's younger sister, Carol, who was attending Rollins College, came to visit for several days. She was a tall, cheerful girl with her brother's brown eyes, and took a liking to Freddy. On the Prado, she noticed the all-female orchestras that played in the cafés along the boulevard. Freddy's favorite was the Orquesta Anacaona, composed of Chinese *mulatas*, which usually played at the Café el Dorado.

"Can you imagine them in Oak Park?" she asked.

"Not likely, Beefy," said Hemingway.

Carol also liked the long-sleeved, white linen *guayaberas*, and decided she wanted to buy one for her brother. Javier suggested La Tijera on Monet Street, where his older brother Miguel had his shirts made, and Hemingway dutifully appeared for a fitting. The tailor measured his arms and wrapped a tape around his chest, and it was ready the next day. Javier bought him a string tie to go with it.

"Now, you're a Cuban," said Freddy.

"I hope I don't get a *piropo*," smirked Hemingway.

After Carol returned to Key West, a squall caught them off Cojimar, pelting the *Anita* with stinging rain. They made it back to the harbor with difficulty as the waves crashed into the black rocks below El Morro, sending torrents of spray shooting up against the walls. Trapped in his hotel room, Hemingway resigned himself to working on the galleys, but after an hour his eyes stung and he paced back and forth like a caged animal. Although he had told his publisher that he would send them back by the end of the month, he realized he needed more time. When the rain slackened, he returned to the waterfront, but Joe was nowhere to be found. The Perla was empty, and he sourly retraced his steps up Obispo. By the time Javier arrived at the Floridita, Hemingway had already finished his sixth daiquiri and had begun his seventh.

"How about another boxing lesson?"

"Not today, Ernesto."

Javier saw that Hemingway was in an ugly mood. The writer stood in the corner, his back to the wall, and looked about him with a scowl. His face was flushed, and the scar above his eye was livid.

"Why don't you ever call me Papa?" he said.

Javier was surprised by his belligerent tone of voice, but the tension was broken when Freddy joined them.

"Hello, Papa," said Freddy.

"Howdy, Tex."

Number eight went down without a struggle, and Hemingway embarked on number nine. Then he glanced at the far end of the bar and said:

"Do you know him?"

"Who?" asked Javier, surveying the room.

Hemingway pointed out a hard-faced man in a fedora, standing at the bar smoking a cigarette.

"What's his name?" asked Freddy.

"I don't know, but he looks suspicious."

"Why do you say that?" asked Javier.

Looking suspiciously around him, Hemingway slurped down what remained of his daiquiri and wiped the ice from his mustache with the back of his hand.

"I'm going to tell you a secret," he said in a hoarse whisper. "Somebody has been impersonating me. It started in Paris last year. A fellow I'd never seen before said I owed him money. Then it happened in New York and Madrid. Even in

St. Louis! Maybe there are more than one. Who knows? Now I think he's in Cuba. You've got to help me catch him."

"But why would anyone want to impersonate you?" asked Javier.

"How should I know why anyone would want to be Ernest Hemingway," he laughed bitterly. "If only they knew!"

Putting down his glass, he lurched toward the man, nearly colliding with a waiter, but somehow keeping his balance.

"This is very bad," said Freddy.

Rocking back and forth, Hemingway raised a blunt forefinger and asked:

"Have you seen me before?"

Without waiting for an answer, Hemingway stepped forward to throw a punch, but slipped and banged his head against the edge of the bar before crashing to the floor.

"Some right hook you got there, pal," said the man, putting out his cigarette before dropping a coin on the counter and stepping over him.

Javier and Freddy each grabbed an arm and they dragged Hemingway out into the street. An old chinaman stood nearby with an empty three-wheeled cart, having sold all of his oranges, and they laid the unconscious writer on top of it and rolled him down Obispo. The manager of the Ambos Mundos took one look and surrendered his room key with a sigh. Rolling the cart across the lobby, they managed to stuff him into the elevator cage and frog-march him to his room. No sooner had they taken his shoes off than he started snoring.

"Was that nine or ten?" asked Javier.

"I lost count," admitted Freddy.

That night, the wind died down and the next morning was sunny and clear. Hemingway's head throbbed from the liquor and the bump on his skull, but the *brisa* revived him and he caught a swordfish with the new rod off Boca de Jaruco. At the end of the day, he arrived at the Floridita freshly shaven and smelling of Bay Rum, resplendent in his new *guayabera*, and bought a round for everyone at the bar.

"Here we go again," whispered Javier to Freddy.

Constante reluctantly began to line up the daiquiris but Hemingway was in a splendid mood and surveyed the row of empty glasses.

"How many?" asked Freddy.

"Nine," said Hemingway. *"Uno más, Constante."*

After number ten, they walked over to Zanja Street, and rode the precarious elevator to the rooftop of El Pacífico. An awning had been stretched over the tables and it flapped gently in the breeze. Below them, the lights of Havana winked on in the violet dusk.

"This is truly a beautiful city," said Hemingway. "If Havana were a woman, she would be a very beautiful woman."

"A sad and beautiful woman," said Javier.

"I still don't understand this place. When I do, I'll write about it."

"Perhaps I will write a novel about Havana as well."

"I'd like to read your novel."

"Someday, I hope to write something that I would be proud to show you, Ernesto."

"I've known many bad writers, having been one myself for many years. Whatever you do, don't become a bad writer."

"I'll try my best," said Javier.

Nearby, there was a party in progress, and Javier saw Nely. She was the only woman at the table, happily surrounded by army officers, and her musical laughter rippled among their deep voices. Nely wore a high-necked, yellow satin Shanghai dress with a frangipani blossom behind one ear.

"Who is that woman?" asked Hemingway.

Javier pretended not to have seen her, but Freddy said: "Why, it's Nely Chen."

"Ask her to join us."

"That's not a good idea," said Freddy.

But Hemingway immediately sent over a bottle of champagne, with his compliments. The officers stopped their conversation as the waiter hesitantly approached their table, and there was a brief discussion as they learned who had ordered it. Freddy expected the worst, but Captain Segura stood up to toast the writer.

"It is an honor," he announced in his parade ground voice, "to drink with such an illustrious citizen of the world as Ernest Hemingway."

Freddy breathed a deep sigh of relief as the officers invited them to join their party. The waiters hurriedly moved a family to the other side of the restaurant to enlarge the table, and Captain Segura confessed that he had enjoyed *A Farewell to Arms* very much. As he gave the writer an *abrazo*, Javier recognized the same voracious, mocking smile, like that of a wolf.

Then Colonel Segura announced that he had to be in Matanzas early the next day and excused himself after whispering something to Nely. The other officers trooped out after him, leaving Nely alone. When she had seen Javier, her heart gave a little flutter. But he turned away and she guessed that by now he had found a pampered girl from the Havana Yacht Club, who wouldn't be caught dead in the Alhambra. Nely shrugged and chatted gaily with Freddy, whom she hadn't seen for several months. Others soon joined their party, including several tourists. One lady even asked for an autograph.

"What should I write?" Hemingway asked Nely.

Nely only spoke a few words of English and couldn't think of anything to say, but Hemingway thought for a moment and then wrote on a napkin:

From Cuba, with love.
Papa

With a flourish, he handed it to the tourist.

"My goodness!" she laughed, and showed the napkin to her husband.

Much later, Nely looked around the table and noticed that both Freddy and Javier were gone. Hemingway appeared to be showing the tourists how to hold a fishing rod. The waiter had brought one of the poles used to hold up the awning, and Hemingway dangled it over the railing, as though he had hooked a giant marlin far below.

Nely found herself beside him in the elevator as they finally left the restaurant. Outside, even Chinatown was still. A car sped down Zanja Street, and a busboy closed the steel shutter of a *fonda*, preparing to go home. Hemingway had seemed sober as he wrestled with his imaginary marlin, but now he stumbled as he followed behind her like a little dog.

"I'm thirsty," he said.

"But you drank all the champagne!" she protested.

In response, he peed against a lamp post.

"Can you make a daiquiri?" he asked, catching up with her.

Hemingway steadied himself on her arm and burped loudly as they entered her apartment. It belonged to a rich friend of Captain Segura's and she had taken nothing from the *solar* except for the five yellow candles which she lit for Oshún. Nely steered Hemingway to the couch but he refused to sit and rummaged through the cabinet until he found a cocktail shaker.

"The most important thing," he explained, "is not to add any sugar."

Hemingway soon made a mess of things. Nely pulled him out of the kitchen and undressed him as she would a little boy. The *guayabera* was damp with sweat and rum, and Nely peeled it off and laid it on a chair. He moaned and roughly embraced her, but she slipped away only to force him back on the bed, her small hands on the furry mat of his chest. Nely wriggled on top of him, sliding his pants down his ankles with her toes, and ran her tongue along the bridge of his sunburned nose.

"You're very salty, Señor Hemingway," she giggled.

"Call me Papa," he said, and promptly fell asleep.

Nely sighed and rolled off him as he began to snore. Captain Segura had blithely left her at El Pacífico, and to

84

spite him she had gone with the handsome *americano*. But it was too late to worry about that, or anything else. Nely pulled off his boxer shorts and covered him with the sheet. When she awoke, the sunlight poured in through the window but he was still asleep. Nely made *café con leche* in the kitchen, which still smelled of stale rum. Returning to the bedroom, she inspected her catch of the night before. One never knew with an *americano*. Unlike a marlin, he could not be hacked into pieces and hauled off to market.

Hemingway's eyes fluttered open. Propping himself up on his elbows, he first looked around in alarm, and then bewilderment. Soon, he remembered, and noticed the tentpole rising from his sheets.

"Did you make coffee?" he grinned.

Each morning, Walter Huggins read the *Havana Post*, the leading newspaper for the American colony. It was his favorite moment of the day, the only time he truly had to himself. While his wife padded through the bedroom in her slippers and the girls prepared for school, Walter perused the front page. Sadly, there was nothing new about the Lindbergh case, except that Al Capone had offered to help find the killers. The heinous kidnapping remained the talk of Havana, and hysterical Cuban mothers refused to leave their children alone.

What was the world coming to? It was only a few years ago that Lindbergh himself had come to Havana to celebrate the opening of the Key West-Havana route for Pan American Airways. Walter remembered that he posed for a picture with young Grant Mason and his beautiful bride Jane, and even took President Machado for a ride in his airplane.

The financial news was equally dismal. Good Republican that he was, Walter supported President Hoover, but more banks had closed, and his shares of United Steel had fallen from over 250 in 1929 to just under 25 the last time he dared look. As for Cuba, nearly a third of the men were unemployed and the price of sugar had plunged to 1/2 cent per pound. The violence had intensified in recent weeks, and hardly a day went by without another attack by the ABC. No one knew what the letters stood for, or who the leaders were, or even their objectives, other than forcing Machado from office. It made no sense, but few things did anymore.

Last week at the Havana Country Club, Walter had seen Emilio Aragon and asked him what to make of the revolutionaries. The wealthy Cuban was from Santa Clara, the president's home town, and rumored to be Machado's silent partner in a number of real estate deals.

"They are bandits," he replied in his deep, reassuring voice, "nothing more than that."

Walter's mood lightened as Olga brought him breakfast. It had taken years of trial and error for her to cook American food, and only recently had she mastered Beryl's tuna noodle casserole. A continuing dilemma was her batter, which stubbornly refused to rise. But this morning, he saw that Olga's pancakes were impeccably fluffy, almost like those at the American Club, and she beamed at his happy demeanor.

Walter's plate was nearly clean when Beryl joined him, still in her bathrobe. She was rarely at her best in the morning, her eyes puffy as though from liquor, although she rarely drank anything stronger than Coca-Cola. Despite this, she was still an attractive woman. Her waist had thickened but she still attracted a *piropo* or two on the Prado, and her legs were long and shapely, with slim ankles.

Soon after, the twins came down. Betty and Barbara would turn thirteen next year, and were plump and round-faced in the crisp white and green uniforms of the American-run Cathedral School. Walter had noticed that in the fresh air of the tropics, young girls blossomed at an astoundingly early age. Luckily, that was not the case with his daughters, although he once caught them going to school with a touch of rouge on their cheeks. Beryl seemed unconcerned.

"What do you expect?" she had said. "They live in Havana!"

"I hardly see what that has to do with anything," said Walter in the same imperious tone of voice he used at the bank.

Beryl had merely shrugged and resumed buttering her toast. Thereafter, Walter scrupulously scanned his daughter's freckled faces for traces of makeup.

That morning, he saw that their cheeks were scrubbed clean. As the girls tucked into their plates of oatmeal, Beryl lit a cigarette.

"Good morning, dear," Walter said cheerily.

"I suppose it is," she yawned.

Putting aside his newspaper, Walter finished his pancakes, which brought to mind his recent encounter with Don Ramón López. Walter knew that he had married his oldest son to Don Ignacio Irazurri's homely daughter, so he was a customer of the Banco de Galicia. But if López wanted to expand into the United States, he would need the services of an American bank like the Havana Trust. His secretary telephoned Don Ramón's office to invite him to breakfast at the American Club.

When Cesar the head waiter placed the breakfast menu before him, Don Ramón squinted at it uncertainly. Walter suggested pancakes, and the Cuban shrugged as if to say, "Why not?" Walter then described La Margarita and suggested that he and Señora López would be welcome there in the near future. Don Ramón was unimpressed and remarked that his wife's family had a *central* near Trinidad. Hearing this, Walter wondered if he had made a blunder. Had his wife's estate gone belly-up, as had so many others? But Don Ramón merely reached for his cup of watery American coffee. Wincing, he asked Cesar to bring him a *café con leche*.

Walter's next gambit was to invite him to play golf at the Havana Country Club. Somehow, Don Ramón found this very amusing.

"At my age, Huggins, I have better things to do than stand in the sun and hit a little white ball," he said.

Walter didn't know how to take this, but at that moment, breakfast arrived. Although he was starving, Walter waited while Don Ramón skeptically poked his stack of pancakes.

"Have some maple syrup," he ventured.

"What for?" replied the Cuban.

Walter gave up as Don Ramón signalled for Cesar to bring him a *tostada*. Somehow, he found his guest unusually difficult to talk to. It was impossible to know what he thought of anything, since he typically answered a question with a question. Walter delicately steered the conversation to the political crisis, but rather than give his opinion, Don Ramón smiled and said:

"But what do you think, Huggins?"

Don Ramón appeared to be in no hurry. Having ungraciously abandoned his pancakes, he leisurely dunked his bread in his *café con leche*. Finally, he looked Walter in the eye and said:

"Huggins, did you go to Harvard?"

Walter shook his head bleakly.

"That's good," said Don Ramón.

As Walter left the American Club, he judged the meeting a disaster. What was this about Harvard? Walter had never gone to college, much less Harvard. But he had heard that Don Ramón wasn't exactly a Yale man, either. Though Walter's Spanish was good (if heavily accented) perhaps he had said something to insult his guest. One could never tell with Cubans. The truth was that for all his years in Havana, Walter knew hardly any of them apart from his employees. There were few Cubans if any at the Havana Country Club except for Emilio Aragon.

Now, Walter kissed Beryl and the girls good-bye and put on his jacket. On some mornings, the heat struck him like a howitzer, but now a pleasant breeze was blowing, rustling the plump *barrigona* palms in the driveway. The Huggins lived in a colonial-style house with dark green shutters on the high windows and a sweeping verandah shaded by a mango tree. The white stucco walls were dazzling in the sunlight, and he shielded his eyes as he strode briskly to the car. Standing smartly by the Buick was his chauffeur Felix, a *mulato* with a pockmarked face who had once been a boxer.

Walter gazed out the window as they drove along the sculpted banyan trees on Fifth Avenue and past the belltower at the entrance to Miramar. Normally, there was little traffic, but as they crossed the Avenida de los Presidentes, they came to a stop. The chauffeur tried to swing the Buick around but there were several cars behind them. Walter could hear a siren and saw flashing lights. At the intersection were several police motorcycles and an olive green military truck, and a crowd gawked at the smoldering wreck of an overturned car.

"What is it?" said Walter.

Felix craned his neck out the window but all he could see were the plumes of thick black smoke.

Two soldiers in mustard-yellow uniforms moved along the line of cars, stopping to question the drivers. They carried carbines, and when they came to the Buick, they asked Felix to step out of the car.

"What's going on?" said Walter irritably.

He could not follow the conversation above the klaxons and the shouts of the crowd, but the soldier gestured toward the wreck and Felix pointed frantically back at Walter.

"All right," said Walter, stepping out of the car. "What's the problem here?"

The soldier talking to Felix ignored him, but the other casually pointed the barrel of the carbine at Walter's belly. Walter swallowed hard, resisting the impulse to raise his hands, like Edward G. Robinson in a gangster movie. The smoke stung his eyes and he lowered himself back into the car.

Soon, the argument was settled and Felix got behind the wheel. The soldiers continued moving past the stalled traffic and a policeman waved the other cars on. Once past the flaming wreck, they turned into the Malecón, leaving behind the acrid smell of burning tires.

"What was it?"

"Another *bombazo*," said Felix.

Walter took a deep breath as several drops of sweat dribbled down his neck. It was not even eight o'clock, and already his day was ruined.

Hemingway sat back contentedly in the fishing chair as the *Anita* made its way back to Havana Harbor. The day's fishing was done, and that morning he had landed his largest marlin yet, well over three hundred pounds. Without warning, he had exploded out of the water to crash the bait, and jumped 21 times before being brought to gaff off Boca Ciega. Afterwards, Carlos rubbed him down with alcohol, and his muscles ached pleasantly, which made the beer taste all the better.

That afternoon, Javier and Freddy were at their usual corner of the Floridita. Hemingway nodded to Constante, who soon had the first *Papa Especial* standing at attention on the bar. Feinting with his right and jabbing at Javier's arm, Hemingway described his epic battle with the giant marlin, but Javier continued to stare dispiritedly into his daiquiri.

"What's eating you, Harvard?" asked Hemingway.

"*Tiene un chino en el camino*," explained Freddy. [He has a chinaman in his path.] "Or in this case, *una chinita*."

"I can't possibly keep all these expressions straight."

"By the way," said Freddy, "Pop wants you to have lunch with us at the American Club. We'd like to get you to open an account at the Havana Trust."

"Nuts," laughed Hemingway as he ambled out, "I'll never step foot in there again!"

"It was worth a try," said Freddy. "Where's he going?"

"I wonder," said Javier sourly.

Hemingway could not get the sly, lilting melody of *El Manisero* out of his head, and he hummed it to himself as he walked along the Capitolio to Dragones Street. Nely had told him that Captain Segura was in Santa Clara, but that it would be better if they met at her apartment rather than the Floridita.

Ironically, he liked Captain Segura. One afternoon he had stopped by the Ambos Mundos, and Hemingway had kept him waiting a few minutes. When he saw him in the lobby, impatiently slapping a riding crop against his gleaming boots, Hemingway squared his shoulders defiantly, but the Cuban officer merely wanted to buy him a drink. Hemingway invited him to go fishing, and he appeared at the dock precisely on time. His bodyguard glared at the dockhands, who made themselves scarce, and Carlos nearly cut his hand baiting a hook, though after a swig of rum he settled down. Hemingway introduced Captain Segura to Jane, and they spent a pleasant morning aboard the *Anita*. Not a word was spoken about the evening at El Pacífico.

So what if he knows, thought Hemingway as he knocked on Nely's door.

He preferred to make love before dinner and chased her around the apartment. Nely squealed as he finally caught her in the bedroom, but pushed him away so as to take off the brightly colored beads which she wore around her neck. The sight of her bending over to slide the necklace over her radiant dark hair sent a jolt of electricity through him. Nely unbuttoned his fly, but skipped away as he lunged for her.

"You'll have to do better than that, Señor Hemingway," she taunted him.

He frantically wriggled out of his trousers and kicked off his moccasins, but Nely had come up behind him and nibbled his ear. He whirled around to grab her waist, but she leaped on the mattress and bounced to the other side.

"Now what?" she said.

Hemingway pulled his sweaty striped jersey over his head and dove across the bed before she could escape.

"Now you tell me," he said.

Afterwards, he soaked in a hot bath, his spent sex floating in the water like a shriveled flower. The wallpaper in the bathroom was yellow, and she once told him it was the favorite color of her *orisha*.

"What's that?" asked Hemingway.

"You would not understand," said Nely, and refused to say anything more.

Now, he could hear her singing softly in a language he couldn't understand. As she passed the half-open door, he caught a glimpse of her legs, brown and creamy like *café con leche*.

"I'm hungry, daughter," he announced.

"I noticed."

Nely, too, had a healthy appetite and she led him up Galiano to the Café de la Isla, across from Woolworth's.

"This is where Freddy and Javier practice their *piropos*," said Hemingway.

"They don't need any practice."

The Café de la Isla was famous for it *reservados*, booths at the back of the restaurant with high wooden walls so couples could dine discreetly. There was a bell to summon the waiter, who never failed to knock before entering.

"Havana is a very wicked city," said Hemingway approvingly.

"I think it is the *americanos* who are wicked," said Nely. "Or perhaps they are wicked when they come to Havana. Are they always that way?"

"Only in Havana. Paris too, I think."

"Tell me about Paris," said Nely.

"It is a wonderful city to be young in," he mused.

"Isn't Havana the same?"

"I think I'd rather grow old in Havana."

They left by a back door so as not to pass through the crowded restaurant, and walked down the darkened street, her small, delicate hand lost in his. As they neared Dragones, she placed a finger on his lips and said:

"*Adiós, mi amor.*"

Hemingway watched her flit through the shadows. As he walked past the Hotel New York, he smelled her perfume on his fingertips, the scent of frangipani blossoms. Poking his head into the Floridita, he saw that Constante had already gone home and he didn't trust the other bartender to make a *Papa Especial*. Whistling softly to himself, he returned to the Ambos Mundos.

The next day, Pauline arrived from Key West, and the manager at the Ambos Mundos presented her with a box of chocolates. He viewed her as a salutory influence upon the *americano*, who often staggered in drunk and had to be carried to bed by several bellboys. While her husband fished, she went to the beauty salon and shopped at El Encanto, the department store on Galiano Street. When he returned at the end of the day, she twirled around and showed off her new permanent.

"Jane says I should get it cut even shorter," said Pauline. "Would you like that?"

"I like you just the way you are," said her husband diplomatically.

Pauline coquettishly tried on her smart new rumba hat. Secretly, she was delighted that her husband had decided to put off the safari to Africa for a year. Even though it was Uncle Gus who would pay for it, she had grown weary of endless discussions about white hunters, elephant rifles, and kudus.

At dinner with the Masons, it was all they talked about. Grant and Jane had met them for drinks at the bar of the Hotel Nacional. On the terrace, royal palms rustled above the gloomy Spanish cannon guarding the Malecón.

"Blix swears by the .450 No. 2 Express rifle," said Grant, "but to stop lions, Philip uses the .256 Mannlicher."

"Do you shoot lions from the car?" asked Pauline politely as Jane sipped her manhattan.

"Oh, no," explained Grant, cutting his steak into little pieces. "That would be illegal. Not very sporting, either. Jane killed a lion with a Springfield 30.06. Quite a shot, wasn't it, darling?"

"Really, Stoneface. Blix told me to shoot, so I did. Nothing to brag about, I'm afraid."

Hemingway nodded approvingly, but Pauline looked at her wide-eyed.

"What happens if you don't get along with the white hunter?" she queried. "It could be rather a bore."

"They do it for a living," explained Grant, "so they're paid to like you. But they have an expression, 'We're still drinking their whiskey.' If the safari goes to hell, there's still that."

"I'll have to remember that," said Hemingway, and wrote it down on a napkin.

After dinner, they went to the Casino Nacional. Jane played nines at the roulette table, losing heavily until Grant pulled her away, and after another round of drinks they drove towards Marianao. Freddy had recommended a place called the Rumba Palace, where El Chori played, but after driving up and down the unpaved streets, they were unable to find it and settled on the Chateau Madrid. Grant fox-trotted with Pauline, while Hemingway drank champagne with Jane.

"Did you really shoot a lion?" he asked.

"Of course," she smiled. "The poor dear never had a chance."

They arrived in Jaimanitas as the sky began to lighten. Jane took off her high heels and handed them to Grant before tiptoeing into the house.

"Shhh!" Grant whispered, pointing to the nursery where Tony, the little boy he and Jane had adopted, lay sleeping.

Hemingway stumbled over the Talavera umbrella stand in the foyer, nearly shattering it. Jane collapsed into shrill laughter, and even Pauline smiled at the look on her husband's face. Grant insisted on making breakfast, and they watched the sunrise from the terrace. It was late morning by the time they reached the Ambos Mundos. Hemingway went straight to the *Anita*, where Joe was submerged in the engine pit. Still in his tuxedo, Hemingway looked on as Joe tightened the grease cups and called for Carlos to start the engine. It sputtered and appeared to miss on one of the cylinders.

"Cracked plug," said Joe bitterly.

For once, Hemingway was glad to stay ashore and slept all afternoon, to Pauline's great relief. She viewed marlin fishing in Cuba much as she had bullfighting in Spain, as a necessary evil. She had gamely hooked a slender white marlin, but the grip of the pole had chafed her hands and she had broken a nail reeling it in. But the next morning, Hemingway was already slipping on his moccasins before it was light out. The days Pauline spent in Havana were uniformly sunny, with tiny white clouds drifting overhead. Occcasionally, they went shooting at the club Cazadores del Cerro, an exclusive gun club in the hills above the Luyano River that the Masons belonged to. Jane was a crack shot, and Hemingway never tired of congratulating her. She often accompanied them aboard the *Anita* while Grant was at work, and even helped Carlos bait the hooks.

"Jane's rather good at everything, isn't she?" said Pauline.

Hemingway could hardly hope to win the game, and knew it was best to humor her.

"It must be swell to be perfect," Pauline continued.

"Poor old Mama," said her husband.

Pauline's sour mood vanished at the thought of leaving Havana. On her last night, Grant wanted to invite them to El Pacífico, but Hemingway claimed that it was an opium den.

"Really?" said Grant. "I thought that was just a story for tourists."

Jane suggested the Café de la Isla, but for some reason Hemingway didn't want to go there, either.

"You're getting very difficult to please," teased Jane.

Hemingway finally settled for the dining room at the Sevilla-Biltmore Hotel. The Masons were in an extraordinarily festive mood. Jane wore a shimmering, gold-lamé gown with her favorite string of Japanese pearls, and after dinner she drank pink champagne.

"How long will you stay in Havana?" she asked.

Pauline looked away but Hemingway replied:

"Until the end of June."

"Then you must come to my birthday party!" said Jane.

Grant ordered another bottle of champagne and asked Pauline how she was returning home.

"The ferry," she replied.

"Why not fly?" said Grant. "The *Caribbean Clipper* leaves at nine o'clock."

"Oh, no."

"Really, darling," said Jane. "It's ever so much fun."

Pauline looked helplessly at Hemingway, who merely raised his champagne glass in a mock toast.

"Unless you're afraid, that is," teased Jane.

The next morning, Pauline walked grimly down the pier, trailed by her husband and the porter carrying her suitcase, to where the seaplane bobbed perilously on the water. It had been dubbed the "flying submarine" by the Cubans because the hull rode low in the water beneath the broad wing. Grant awaited them at the gate.

"There's nothing to it!" he grinned.

A steward in a white jumpsuit helped her through the hatch and she sat next to a porthole. It was just above the waterline, and the brackish water gurgled against the glass. The cabin was insufferably hot, and one of the other passengers made the sign of the cross. With a shudder, the seaplane pulled away from the dock, and slowly picked up speed. Strapped into her seat, she nervously clasped her hands on her lap, deafened by the roar of the engine. Suddenly, she was bathed in light. To her utter amazement, she saw the lighthouse of El Morro falling away beneath her, small as a child's toy.

Hemingway waited with Grant on the pier as the seaplane gained altitude.

"Nice day to be on the water, sport."

"Say, Grant, do you box?" asked Hemingway.

"I haven't put on gloves since college," laughed Grant. "But why don't we play a few rounds of golf at the Havana Country Club?"

"I don't play golf," said Hemingway forlornly.

There was a silence as the two men realized they had nothing more to say to each other. They awkwardly shook hands and Hemingway hurried off to the San Francisco Dock.

High above the bay, the *Caribbean Clipper* headed north. Pauline tried to spot the *Anita,* but saw only the seaplane's frail shadow on the vast carpet of blue.

That was the year that Javier's younger sister Lydia and her best friend Mirta Rivero discovered the tango. Even as the rumba caused a sensation in New York and Paris, the tango took Havana by storm, and girls soon lost count of how many times they saw *Tango de Buenos Aires*, starring Carlos Gardel. Each Saturday morning they boarded the streetcar that took them to the Prado. Oddly enough, the trolleys had been imported from Japan. The hard straw seats occasionally harbored ticks, and the conductor winked at them lasciviously, but that was of little consequence as they alighted and walked to the Teatro Fausto on Colón Street. After the movie, they emerged humming *milongas,* and happily tangoed back up the Prado, between the laurel trees.

Doña Inés judged these outings to be sufficiently innocent so as not to warrant the presence of her sister Clara. After the death of her importunate, womanizing husband, Clara lived with them in Havana, and normally served as the chaperone.

Doña Inés did find it odd that her daughter began peppering her Spanish with bits of Argentine slang, and practicing dance steps in the hallway, but this latest *mania* seemed harmless enough. Before Carlos Gardel it had been Maurice Chevalier, and the two girls had crooned to each other in French.

But her mother was more vigilant when it came to Lydia's weekly *paseo*. There was a park just a few blocks from their house in the Vedado, with gracious almond trees surrounding a wooden pergola. Each Sunday evening, the girls strolled arm in arm, while the boys paraded in the opposite direction. Their movements were as regular as the hands of a clock, so that they would pass each other at one end of the pergola, and not see each other until they reached the other side. On comfortable benches at the perimeter sat Aunt Clara and her counterparts, keeping a sharp eye out for any irregularities.

One night, so intent was Lydia on the tango that she didn't notice Roberto Perez standing by the gate as she rounded the pergola. He was a bookish young man with curly dark hair and the beginnings of a mustache. Instead of joining the *paseo,* he stood awkwardly beside his friend Frank Manzano.

"Don't look!" whispered Mirta, furtively pointing in his direction.

Lydia blushed and swatted away her finger. Despite this, she changed places with her friend, so that she could steal a peek. By the time they reached the pergola, he had gone.

Their next encounter, equally misbegotten, came at the Havana Yacht Club. During the week, the girls would occasionally spend the afternoons by the pool sipping *mamey* milk shakes. Once again, it was Mirta who spotted Roberto as he emerged from the water, his pale arms poking out of his swimming trunks. As he approached, Lydia steeled herself and Mirta darted away for another shake. But Roberto's courage failed him and he carefully made his way around her without speaking.

Fortuitously, there was a dance at the Centro Gallego the following week. It was here that Roberto finally made his move, writing his name on her dance card. When the orchestra played, they danced a *pasodoble*. Roberto was not an accomplished dancer, and nearly stepped on her feet once or twice, but his hand resting lightly on her bare back made her skin tingle.

These developments were not lost on Aunt Clara, and Doña Inés was soon *au courant*. There followed a series of events which bewildered the male members of the family, particularly Don Ramón. He began to notice whispered conversations between his wife and daughter and sister-in-law, hastily adjourned when he approached. More than once they ended with Lydia in tears. Clara was equally affected. The Havana summers were her undoing, and she took to bed with a plaintive moan. Doña Inés kept her head, and soon ascertained that Roberto Perez was the son of a wealthy doctor and a fine catch. These deliberations having been concluded, she informed her husband that Roberto would be joining them on Sunday.

Roberto himself slept little the night before, and went so far as to attend church that morning with his parents, asking for divine intervention. Nonetheless, the short walk through the Vedado seemed endless. Most of the houses had been built at the turn of the century, with modest porticos of columns facing the leafy streets. But Lydia lived in an formidable mansion of cream-colored stone in the Catalan style, with fig trees drooping over the high walls. To the left was a high, square tower with overhanging eaves, which he knew was her father's study, and above the entrance was a second story terrace with a delicate marble balustrade. Lydia had told him that her mother loved flowers, and the window boxes overflowed with pink bougainvillea blossoms.

Luncheon on Sunday was an elaborate ritual in the López household. After a few pleasantries were exchanged, and

Roberto presented Doña Inés with a pale yellow orchid, he was led past a delicate *mampara* into the vast dining room, which overlooked the garden. At the head of the long mahogany table sat Don Ramón himself, and Doña Inés, and to the right was Miguel. His wife María fussed over their two little boys, José and Ignacio, dressed in matching sailor suits. At the other end was Abuelo López, staring dimly at the wall, and near him Father Saralegui. Close to his grandfather sat Javier, who stared moodily at his plate. Clara had risen from her torpor in time to join them, and wearily fanned herself. There were also some cousins from Sancti Spiritus, and Dr. Diaz and his wife Gemma, and someone else whom Roberto forgot as soon as he was introduced. And in the middle of the table, like the pearl within the oyster, was Lydia herself, who refused to look at him.

Roberto found himself seated next to Father Saralegui, who began to say grace as a huge kettle of *arroz con pollo* made its appearance. Hastily bringing it to a close, he tucked a napkin under his Roman collar as his plate was piled high. Roberto noticed that Javier's grandfather had taken out a wood-handled clasp knife, which apparently he intended to use despite the polished silverware before him. He was not particularly hungry, but he realized that all eyes were upon him, and he bravely set out to finish his plate as one of the little boys amused himself by throwing grains of yellow rice at him. Roberto looked beseechingly at the other end of the table, and Lydia finally offered him a shy smile that illuminated her features like the sun shining through grey clouds.

Having passed with flying colors, Roberto was now permitted to call upon Lydia. He suggested a movie, since not much conversation would be involved. Clara had once more taken to her bed and Doña Inés pressed Javier into service. Other chaperones were readily available, and Clara herself could have been revived if need be, but she liked the idea of Javier spending time with Mirta, whose father was a wealthy *político*.

Javier thus accompanied his sister, Mirta, and Roberto to the Teatro Fausto one evening. He grew quickly bored with the movie, which had something to do with a tango dancer in Buenos Aires. As he understood it, the role of the chaperone was to safeguard the girl's honor but that hardly seemed necessary with the timid Roberto. Mirta was enraptured by the movie, and appeared to be mouthing the words spoken by the actors. Glancing at her prettily made up face in the flickering light, he surmised it would be easy to turn her chin towards him with his finger, and plant a kiss on her plum-colored lips. But there would be hell to pay and he would probably find himself having lunch at the Rivero's one Sunday.

After the movie, they strolled down the Prado for ice cream at the Café de Europa. The music from a female orchestra floated over the noise of traffic and the laughter of passers-by in the warm musky night. Where was Freddy? Probably drinking with Hemingway and his mob. It would soon be time to take the girls home, he calculated, and perhaps he could make it back in time to catch them.

Over the next few days, Lydia and Mirta conferred regularly. Lydia confessed that she had fallen irrevocably in love with Roberto, but could not recall the exact moment when this occurred. It certainly was not in the park or the Havana Yacht Club or the Centro Gallego. Perhaps it was during the calamitous Sunday luncheon when he haplessly tried to start a conversation with Father Saralegui, who was interested only in his *arroz con pollo.* Mirta, on the other hand, was angry at Javier for ignoring her and being in such a hurry to rejoin his friends.

"What do you expect?" shrugged Lydia. Like the rest of the family, she had her doubts about Javier. "He's very *pesado.*"

On Saturday, Roberto invited her to join his friends for an outing to the Tropical beer garden in Marianao. Near the baseball stadium, it had tiled Moorish pavilions with elaborate columns shaped like tree trunks, where *conjuntos de son* played long into the night. Javier agreed to go only after his mother warned him in no uncertain terms to be nice to Mirta.

At the beer garden, they met Frank, whom Javier remembered from the *tertulia*, and a girl named Leticia Rodriguez, whom Mirta took an instant dislike to because she kept mentioning her recent trip to New York with her mother. Also with them was a young married couple named Raúl and Vivian Esnard. Vivian was a bright, pretty girl who had been attending medical school when the university shut down. By then, she was engaged to Raúl, a law student who had been a classmate of Frank's at LaSalle, and they were married soon after.

It was a festive afternoon and the young men wore striped straw boaters. Frank brought a tray of frothy beer mugs to the wooden table where they sat, and Vivian passed the tray of *empanadas* she had made.

"How is Alberto?" asked Javier.

"I don't see much of him these days," admitted Frank, sucking reflectively on his pipe.

Raúl frowned at the mention of Alberto's name, and Javier gathered that there had been some disagreement, perhaps about politics, like everything else these days. Raúl and his friends were active in the Directorio, the student group that had demonstrated against Machado since 1927. The leaders of the Directorio denounced the violence that had plagued Havana in recent months, although many of them were rumored to be *abecedarios*, members of the ABC. But Javier could not imagine these earnest young idealists plotting to kill policemen. As for Alberto, he could not be sure.

"Alberto is impatient," said Raúl. "He thinks the problem can be resolved with a single stroke."

"The stroke of a pen?" smiled Javier.

"Hardly," said Raúl, and made a brief chopping motion with his hand. "Machado is not the cause of the problem, but merely a symptom of the disease. If you cut off one head, even more will grow back. Alberto doesn't understand that, or doesn't want to. It's time to get to the root of the problem."

"Which is?"

"That Cuba must be free, once and for all," said Raúl.

"I've heard that before," chuckled Frank. "Like a lawyer with a weak case, Raúl hopes that if he makes the same argument, again and again, he will finally convince someone. But I'm not fooled. Why pretend the *yanquis* don't exist? Look around you!"

"You, too, see what you want to see," said Raúl.

"Must we talk about politics?" protested Leticia. "You're all so boring when you have these discussions."

"It's what they do best," put in Vivian, and patted her husband's shoulder. "If they didn't argue, what would they do all day?"

She offered Javier an *empanada*, and as he nibbled on it, Frank turned towards him and said:

"What do you think?"

"I haven't made up my mind yet about anything," Javier admitted.

Raúl looked at him for a moment and said:

"The time for indecision is past."

Across the table, Roberto was horrified at the direction the conversation had taken. Raúl and Frank were eager to continue their debate, but Javier seemed uneasy. Left out of the conversation, Lydia was downcast and Mirta pouted as if to say, "I told you so."

"I wish I were in New York," said Leticia. "It's lovely this time of year."

At this, Mirta rolled her eyes, and Lydia looked as though she were about to cry.

"Would you like another *empanada*?" Roberto asked dismally, and passed the tray.

Lydia shook her head but Mirta shrugged and popped one into her mouth.

Gloomily, Roberto resigned himself to finishing his beer, which had grown warm.

That afternoon, Hemingway worked on the galleys of *Death in the Afternoon* in his room at the Ambos Mundos. His pencil was worn down to a stub from scratching out entire sentences and rewriting them in the margin. When his head pounded from staring at the rows of typescript, he took off his spectacles and gently rubbed his eyes. The waning light cast a faint shadow across the tiled floor and he leaned out the window. A tanker on its way out to sea loomed improbably large against the ramparts of La Cabaña, belching dark smoke.

The day before, Joe had informed him that he needed to go back to Key West for a couple of days. When Hemingway asked why, Joe merely scratched his head and said he needed to take care of some business. It had to be Hoover gold, thought Hemingway. He would sample the cargo himself in Key West.

Hemingway's black mood evaporated as he showered and put on his freshly pressed *guayabera*. He walked up Obispo to the Floridita and found Constante polishing the marble counter to a fine sheen.

"¿Lo de siempre?" asked the *cantinero*.

"Por supuesto," said Hemingway.

The bar was nearly empty except for a few stragglers from the dining room, having finished a late lunch. Outside was the usual bedlam of Havana traffic mixed in with the cries of the *billeteros* and shouts of the shoeshine boys. The *cantinero* placed the first daiquiri before him, and Hemingway solemnly took a sip. It was refreshing and tart and the crushed ice dissolved on his tongue. He took a long swallow and slid the empty glass back along the bar.

"Uno más, Constante."

With the second daiquiri, Constante passed him a small plate of boiled shrimp, and Hemingway nibbled at them through the third and fourth. A tourist wandered in, sweating profusely, and ordered a Coca-Cola. He looked at Hemingway with a look of vague recognition, pursing his lips in concentration, but soon gave up and left to brave the heat once more. A sailor came in and asked him for a light just as he brought number five to his lips. Constante winced, but nothing could shake Hemingway's buoyant mood and he even offered to buy the man a drink.

Soon, the late afternoon crowd began to arrive, and Hemingway played poker dice with a salesman from Indianapolis. It was his first visit to Cuba, and his eyes popped out in amazement as Hemingway described the Havana Sport. After number seven, he announced he was hungry, and Constante ordered a Cuban sandwich from the kitchen. Between bites, Hemingway bought a round of drinks for some secretaries from the American embassy, just a few blocks away on the Plaza de Armas. He then offered to arm wrestle anyone at the bar, although no one took him up on this generous offer.

When Javier entered the Floridita, he found the writer with the eighth daiquiri in one hand, and the second Cuban sandwich in the other. After taking another bite and draining his glass, Hemingway engulfed him in a sweaty bearhug.

"¡Mi amigo!" he shouted.

Javier freed himself with difficulty and joined him in a Papa Especial. It was then that Hemingway announced he would be returning to Key West at the end of the month.

"Havana will miss you, Ernesto," said Javier.

"I'll miss Havana," replied Hemingway. "Where's your partner in crime?"

"Freddy's trying to find a lottery ticket," he explained.

"It figures," said Hemingway, lifting his glass in a toast. "Here's to the winning number!"

Javier dutifully finished his drink and Hemingway insisted on buying him another.

"It's a wonderful night to get drunk."

"It's not even dark yet," pointed out Javier.

"Be patient."

At his elbow was an empty glass with a number of swizzle sticks. Hemingway soon added another, and Javier counted nine.

"You won't be able to find your way to the *Anita* in the morning," said Javier.

"Please don't make me angry," said Hemingway. "We've had this discussion once before."

"Do you remember when we met? It appears that I'm destined to make you angry."

"I only get angry at my friends," explained Hemingway, "since no one else really matters. Friendship is a chain that only grows strong when it is tested, and our friendship is stronger than the chain they stretched between La Punta and El Morro to stop Sir Francis Drake."

"I'm honored to be your friend, Ernesto."

"Here's to friendship," said Hemingway, number ten in hand. "But I still owe you a boxing lesson."

"Nothing is owed between friends," laughed Javier warily.

Hemingway put down his glass and playfully raised his fists.

"So you say, but there's still lesson number three."

"It will have to wait until you return to Havana," said Javier.

Disappointed, Hemingway took up his daiquiri once more.

"This is truly the moment of truth," he said, holding the frosty stem of the cocktail glass between his thumb and forefinger.

Hemingway took a tentative sip of his eleventh daiquiri and then vanquished it decisively, wiping his mustache with the sleeve of his *guayabera*. Triumphantly placing the last swizzle stick in the glass, he announced that it was time for dinner. The crowd around him slowly parted as he precariously made his way out into the street with Javier in tow. A fresh breeze rustled the banyan trees in the Parque Central as Hemingway shadowboxed toward the statue of José Martí.

"Greetings, General," he said, bowing elaborately.

Javier took him gently by the arm and led him in the direction of El Pacífico. Skirting the Capitolio, Hemingway realized that they were passing directly in front of Nely's apartment. Sure enough, parked on Dragones was Colonel Segura's long black Cadillac.

Hemingway abruptly disengaged himself and declared:

"I've had enough Chinese food to last me!"

Executing an about face, he retraced his steps back to the Parque Central. Javier continued up the Prado to catch the trolley to El Vedado, and he watched Hemingway hesitate at the entrance to the Floridita before finally returning to the Ambos Mundos.

Hemingway had forgotten to close the shutters, and in the morning, the sun was directly on his face. He was awake for an instant before the pounding in his head started, and he realized he was still in his clothes, the *guayabera* sticky with vomit. Surprisingly, his shoes were lined up neatly on the floor. He groaned and rolled over, but the room was filled with merciless light and he staggered to the bathroom to splash cold water on his face. Hemingway vaguely remembered being on the rooftop of the Ambos Mundos, and executing a *verónica* with a tablecloth as a waiter charged him. Somehow, he had wound up back in his room, but the awful taste in his mouth precluded further speculation.

A hot shower helped somewhat, and by the time the waiter brought up a steaming pot of coffee, he felt sufficiently lucid to look out the window. Across the harbor, the flag atop El Morro fluttered invitingly. It was a perfect day for fishing. The marlin would be shooting along the Gulf Stream like torpedoes, and he cursed Joe for abandoning him. Without giving the matter more thought, he rang up Jane.

Unfortunately, Grant picked up the telephone:

"You must spend the day here, sport," he said. "Would you like me to send the car to fetch you?"

The coffee scalded the roof of his mouth, but Hemingway nonetheless gulped it down. The day had started out badly, and wasn't getting any better.

At Jaimanitas, Grant greeted him in a tennis shirt and white flannel slacks:

"Janie's had a late night, I'm afraid, so you'll have to make do with me. Hungry?"

Hemingway queasily followed him into the spacious tiled kitchen. Grant explained that he always made breakfast on Saturday mornings, and planted his guest on a stool as he fried bacon and expertly cracked an egg on the skillet.

"Over easy, what?"

Hemingway settled for a glass of tomato juice. They sat in the shade of the mango tree, the ripe fruit hanging from its branches. Grant noisily consumed several fried eggs, sopping up the yolks with buttered toast. The smell nauseated Hemingway, drowning out the lush scent of the garden. Hanging from the branch of a flame tree was a cage with a brilliantly colored parrot, squawking pitilessly.

"All you can hope for in life is a day like today!" said Grant, pushing back his empty plate with satisfaction.

Jane made her appearance wearing an outfit almost identical to her husband's. She had been drinking the night before, but her skin was fresh and clear and her eyes sparkled with pleasure at the sight of the bedraggled writer.

"Stoneface, you didn't tell me Ernest was here," she remonstrated. "What a lovely surprise."

She kissed Hemingway on both cheeks and sat beside him.

"I apologize for neglecting you, darling, but I've been so busy with my party that I haven't had time to think. How is Pauline? She must have concluded I'm terribly rude, since I haven't had time to write her. Will she be able to make it?"

Hemingway shook his head.

"The poor dear must be so busy. Have you decided upon a costume to wear?"

"Costume?"

Jane turned to Grant and said:

"Didn't you tell poor Ernest that it was a costume party?

That would be droll, if everyone came dressed up except him."

"He could come as Ernest Hemingway."

"That won't do," Jane scowled prettily. "I'll have to give it some thought."

While Jane pondered the matter, Grant produced a racket and said:

"How about a game of tennis?"

"Bad knee," said Hemingway darkly.

Jane suggested they have lunch at the Havana Country Club. Hemingway's appetite had returned, and he had a steak sandwich on the terrace overlooking the putting green. At the first hole, a foursome was teeing off.

"I didn't know Cubans played golf," said Hemingway.

"Not many do," admitted Grant, "and a good thing, too. Care to give it a try?"

"I've never played."

"You must, darling," said Jane. "It's ever so easy."

"Janie's quite a golfer herself," said Grant.

Resigned to the worst, Hemingway shrugged and followed Grant to the clubhouse, where he was outfitted with clubs and spiked golfing shoes. At the driving range, Grant selected a five iron and showed Hemingway how to wrap his hands around the grip.

"Nothing to it, sport," said Grant, lining up behind his own club. He swung in a graceful arc, and Hemingway watched the golf ball hang in the cloudless sky before it fell a few yards away from a little boy in a baseball cap, gathering the balls in an empty bucket.

"You missed him," said Hemingway.

Now it was his turn, and the ball sat serenely on the crisp Bermuda grass. Hemingway brought back the club as he had seen Grant do, and hit it with a satisfying *thwock!* To his surprise, it shot forward and rolled nearly as far as Grant's.

"Not bad, sport!"

Grant showed him how to shift his weight from his right foot to his left as he swung through. The club had a pleasing heft, and Hemingway soon began to hit the ball consistently. Perhaps golf was not such a bad game, after all. They walked to the tee box and Hemingway was delighted to see Freddy Huggins leaning nonchalantly on a golf club. Freddy introduced him to his father, who was resplendent in plus fours. Having spotted Grant in the clubhouse, Walter had invited him to join them.

"Huggins is the president of the Havana Trust on O'Reilly Street," said Grant.

"I was there once," said Hemingway.

Walter had been eager to meet the writer since Freddy had mentioned him at the American Club, and was delighted to golf with the president of Pan American Airways in Havana. There was no reason why he couldn't bring his business to the Havana Trust.

As they prepared to tee off, Jane appeared on the terrace and waved gaily.

"You're a very lucky young man, Mason," said Walter.

Grant blew his wife a kiss and invited Hemingway to go first.

"Here goes nothing," Hemingway said as he strode to the tee box.

Squaring his shoulders, he bent his knees as Grant had showed him, and brought back the club so that it was parallel to his shoulders. Then he uncoiled his long arms and connected solidly with the ball, sending it bouncing far down the long fairway lined by palm trees.

"You learn fast, sport," said Grant.

Walter was next, and he swung with a painful-looking jerk. As the ball sliced into the rough, one of the caddies scrambled after it, but Walter was unperturbed. He teed up another ball, and this time hit it right down the middle.

"So you hit it again whenever you miss?" whispered Hemingway.

"Not exactly," replied Freddy.

Freddy barely glanced at the ball before he hit it, and turned away as it landed just beyond his father's. Grant was last, and took a fierce practice swing before smashing the ball nearly all the way to the green. Walter let out a low, appreciative whistle.

Hemingway was easily on the green in two more strokes, and would have parred the hole if he hadn't missed the first putt. The sun was almost directly overhead, and he hadn't worn a hat, but there was a pleasant breeze which carried the smell of freshly cut grass. The second hole was a short par three beside a pond and Hemingway popped up the ball just a few feet from the flag.

"Beginner's luck!" he beamed.

The third hole was a different story altogether. Hemingway teed off first and swung the club with all his strength, but it merely nicked the ball, which dribbled a few feet away. As he was about to replace it, Grant said:

"Sorry, sport, that's just the first hole. Club rules."

"I think we can make an exception here, Mason," said Walter.

Grant shrugged and Hemingway hit a respectable drive.

But on the fourth hole, Hemingway's game collapsed completely. His arm grazed his hip as he swung, twisting the club head so that the ball bounced off the trunk of a palm tree, nearly hitting Freddy. From there, he topped it, and the ball burrowed into the grass before rolling a scant few yards. The next hole was even worse. Hemingway missed the ball altogether, nearly falling as the club whooshed through the air. There was a pained silence as he tried once more, but with the same result. His mouth set tightly, he bent over to put the ball in his pocket, and stomped down the fairway trailed by his caddy.

On the ninth hole, Grant gave him a few tips.

"Keep your eye on the golf ball," he said.

Hemingway drove cleanly down the middle, but landed in a sand trap. The caddy handed him a sand wedge, and he brought it back slowly, as he had seen Freddy do. There was an explosion of sand, and Hemingway expected to see the ball rolling towards the flag, but it was still at his feet. He tried again, but the ball only rolled a few inches in the sand. By then, the rest of the foursome had joined him and they stood solemnly around the sand trap. Hemingway's palms were wet with sweat and the club slipped out of his hands.

"Don't drop your shoulder," advised Grant.

Hemingway swung once more but only managed to bury the ball. Before Grant could offer more advice, Hemingway kicked the sand and yelled:

"I hate golf!"

Walter looked up to see the club spinning slowly in the air, its head glinting in the sunlight, as Hemingway stormed off the golf course.

"Temper, temper," said Grant.

They finished the hole and a waiter brought out a tray of daiquiris.

"Courtesy of Señora Mason," he explained.

The thought of relaxing at the bar with the lovely Mrs. Mason seemed like a good idea to Walter, but Grant was eager to play the back nine. Despite the heat, he had yet to break a sweat. Freddy looked bored, and toyed with his putter.

"Shall we carry on?" said Grant.

Walter reluctantly agreed. Having meticulously kept score, he saw that Freddy was one stroke behind Grant. They teed off and Freddy birdied the tenth hole, which evened the score.

"Splendid shot!" said Grant, peering at the scorecard. "I say, you wouldn't care to make a wager, would you?"

"I'm broke," announced Freddy.

"Come, come, now," said Grant slyly. "I'm sure your father will make you a loan."

To Walter's horror, Freddy accepted the wager. He proceeded to bogie the next hole, which Grant won handily.

Wiping the sweat from his forehead, Walter trudged behind them. Grant continued to hit powerful drives, but somehow Freddy remained only a few strokes behind. On the 13th hole he blundered, hitting the ball into the water, and Grant smirked until Freddy made up for it with another birdie.

As they approached the 16th hole, Walter tallied up the score and saw that Freddy was down by two strokes, but he gained ground by sinking an impossibly long putt.

Despite this, Grant seemed confident as they teed off on the second to last hole. He went out of bounds and lost a stroke, while Freddy managed a par. The score was now even.

"You're not trying to hustle me, are you?" chuckled Grant.

"Just lucky, I guess," drawled Freddy.

"I think your luck is about to change, sport," said Grant, taking out another fifty dollar bill.

Walter gulped as his son considered the offer.

"I couldn't possibly," said Freddy.

Walter breathed a sigh of relief but Grant said:

"I'll give you two-to-one odds."

"Are you trying to hustle me, Mr. Mason?"

Grant grinned and before Walter could object the stakes were raised.

The eighteenth hole was a dogleg par four with sandtraps on either side. Grant drove first and landed neatly in the elbow, with a clear shot at the flag. Walter held his breath as Freddy placed his ball just behind Grant's. From there, Grant hit a powerful five iron to the green.

"Why don't we forget about the bet?" said Grant magnanimously. "It's all in fun, anyway."

Freddy merely shrugged and took his usual careless swing. The ball appeared headed for the flag in a neat parabola but a sudden gust of wind brought it down in the rough. If he pitched onto the green, thought Walter, he could still par. But Grant was only a few feet away from the hole.

"I don't want to take your money," protested Grant.

But Freddy had already brought his club back. It scooped up the ball and lofted it just beyond the pin. Bouncing softly on the grass, it appeared to stop, but then dribbled back into the hole as the caddies hooted. Walter's jaw dropped as he realized that Grant could no longer win, but only tie if he sank the putt.

Grant squinted as he considered rising the slope of the green and carefully measured out the distance.

"Shhh!" hissed Walter to the caddies, who were already shaking Freddy's hand.

Grant lightly tapped the ball, and tilted his head as it rolled uphill with slow precision. It appeared headed towards the hole, but stopped several inches short.

"Bad luck, sport," said Freddy.

Each week, Javier continued to drop off the latest issue of *Bohemia* at the Havana Trust. The guard knew him by now, and nodded drowsily as he entered the lobby. Inside, Javier found Freddy at his desk, doodling on a piece of paper.

"Keeping busy?" he asked.

"I've got an idea," said Freddy.

"That's what I was afraid of."

"How about lunch?"

Over a bowl of won ton soup, Freddy described his latest brainchild:

"It has to do with radio. CMX broadcasts from the Tokio Cabaret on San Lázaro every day. It's called *Baila Conmigo*. Have you heard it?"

It was a popular show which aired in the afternoon and featured dance songs. Javier had often heard it blaring from the *bodegas* in the street.

"What if the bank were to sponsor a radio show?" continued Freddy. "We could call it the Havana Trust Hour, and have our own *conjunto*."

"Have you told your father about this brilliant idea?"

"Not in so many words," admitted Freddy.

Javier ate the last of his won tons and started back towards Trocadero Street.

It was purely by chance that he saw Jane's big yellow Chevrolet, which he remembered from the morning he met her at the San Francisco Dock. It was parked at an angle over the sidewalk, nearly blocking the narrow street. Around the corner, on Tejadillo, was her art gallery. It had once been the carriage house of the nearby convent, and it was just a few steps from the cathedral. Javier peered inside and saw a pudgy young man in a seersucker suit and bowtie standing behind the counter.

"Is Mrs. Mason here?" he asked.

"Who wants to know?"

Javier was startled by his querulous, high-pitched voice.

"Not just everyone can see Jane—um, Mrs. Mason," the young man corrected himself. "Do you have an appointment?"

"Don't be silly, Basil," said Jane as she breezed out of the tiny office at the back of the gallery. She was radiant in a madras sundress and greeted him with a Guerlain-scented kiss on the cheek.

"Now I've got egg on my face," said Basil.

"Never mind, dear, it looks wonderful," smiled Jane. Turning back to Javier, she swept a bare arm around the gallery and said: "What can I get for you, señor?"

Javier bent over to examine a crudely carved figure of an *orisha* wearing a red crown and holding a double-edged axe.

"Who's that?"

"That's Changó, the god of thunder," said Jane.

Surrounding Changó were his women: his wife, plain

Obba; his lover, the beautiful Oshún; and his favorite Oyá, the goddess of storms, wife of his enemy Ogún.

Javier's attention was drawn to the drab, unadorned figure of Obba.

"She only has one ear, you know," explained Basil. "Would you like to know why?"

"Don't disappoint him," said Jane. "He just loves to tell this story."

"The tourists love it!" said Basil. "Well, here goes: Obba is married to Changó, don't ask me why, and Oyá was very jealous. But Changó is in love with Oshún, so Obba asks Oyá how she can get him back. Follow me so far? Oyá said that Changó's favorite food was *quimbombó* [okra], and that Obba could cast a spell on him by cutting off her ear and adding it to the soup. Obba would do anything to keep Changó, so she cuts off her ear and wears a scarf to hide the scar. Anyhoo... Changó comes back around dinner time and sees this ear floating in the *quimbombó*. He was furious, let me tell you, and swore never to sleep with Obba again. What do you think of that?"

"It hardly seems fair," said Javier.

"That's a recipe I'll never try," laughed Jane.

Basil seemed eager to continue the conversation but Jane cut him off:

"Be a dear, Basil, and scamper off. Isn't it time for lunch, or something?"

Basil waddled off grumbling, and Jane drew the bamboo shade down over the window to close the gallery.

"Don't mind Basil," said Jane. "He can be trying, but he so loves making new friends."

"So do I."

"I'm so glad you came by," said Jane.

Javier followed her around the corner to where a policeman eyed the Chevrolet with a frown. His expression changed abruptly when he saw Jane and he greeted her with an adoring smile:

"At your service, Señora Mason."

Once the policeman continued on his way, a barefoot boy with dirty blond hair who had been hiding in a doorway darted out, and Jane tossed him a *centavo*.

"Isn't he adorable?" said Jane. "Pablito guards my car. I don't think anyone would steal it though, do you?"

Javier stood tongue-tied as she got behind the wheel, wondering how he could ever hope to see her again. Unexpectedly, Jane touched his arm and said:

"Would you like to come with me to Regla? Afterwards, I can drop you wherever you like."

Javier was expected back at *Bohemia,* but he could easily make up some excuse. He climbed into the passenger seat and they rumbled up Habana Street. The harbor was busy that afternoon, with a rusty old tanker making its way to Casablanca, and the bumboats crossing the channel. Jane drove south past the railway station, and then continued around the bay toward Regla.

"What takes you there?" asked Javier.

Regla was a poor fishing village known for smuggling and *santería*, hardly the place for a respectable American lady.

"Shopping," said Jane mysteriously.

The unpaved road narrowed but Jane speeded up, oblivious to the oncoming traffic. Javier clutched the dashboard as an enormous truck hurtled past.

"Cuban drivers!" bemoaned Jane.

A crowd of ragged children ran after the car as they approached Regla. Jane parked nonchalantly and took Javier's arm as they entered the maze of crooked streets lined with market stalls and cooking pots that bubbled volcanically. Huge green flies buzzed overhead and a fisherman waved them away from the glistening mackerels spread out on a newspaper.

"I love this place, don't you?" said Jane. "We could be in Mombasa."

"I've never been to Africa," said Javier.

"Don't bother to go. It's a terrible bore unless you want to shoot something."

She led him to where a gnarled old *bruja* squatted beneath a flimsy canopy. Javier wondered if he had ever seen anyone as old. Her mottled skin was stretched tight over skull-like features, and a few white hairs peeked out from under her kerchief. Looking up at Jane with interest, she pulled out several necklaces of small tortoise shells, and rattled them with a toothless grin.

"What are they?" asked Javier.

"They're called *ekeles*," explained Jane. "The *babalaos* use them to tell fortunes. Don't they look nice?"

She coquettishly draped one around her neck, but another old woman, equally wizened, hobbled up and tried to take it from her. Javier grabbed her fragile-looking wrist but she continued to pull on the *ekele* and curse in Lucumí, the language of the slave ships.

"What are they saying?" said Jane frantically.

"I can't understand a word of it," said Javier.

The necklace broke and the tortoise shells scattered on the cobblestones. A crowd gathered as the two old women snarled at each other, frantically gesturing with claw-like hands, seemingly ready to come to blows.

"Perhaps we'd better go," said Jane, backing away.

At this, the *bruja* forgot her assailant and turned her fury on Jane, clutching her hand and pointing at the other necklaces. As the crowd pressed around them, the air grew hot and fetid, and the stench was overpowering. Jane grew frightened and pulled away from the old woman, following Javier outside. To his surprise, he noticed she was shaking, tears glistening in her eyes.

"Are you all right?"

"I'm fine," said Jane, fumbling in her purse for a tissue. But she couldn't find one and the ringing in her head began.

"Tell me why you're upset," said Javier, pulling out his handkerchief.

"Did you see that old woman? It was as though she knew something about me, though I've never seen her before. She, she—," Jane broke into sobs on Javier's shoulder.

"She's gone, now," said Javier, gingerly putting his arms around her shoulder.

"Is she?" said Jane, dabbing at her cheeks with Javier's handkerchief.

Back in the car, Jane sat with her hands on the steering wheel, taking deep breaths. As always, the ringing in her head began softly, like a distant bell, and grew louder and louder. Her head soon throbbed with pain, and she gently massaged her temples.

"What's wrong?" said Javier.

"It's nothing," she said, waiting for the noise to stop, as it always did.

Jane regained her composure as they left Regla.

"Where can I drop you?" she asked, managing a weak smile.

"Anywhere you like."

"In that case, let's get a drink."

The road back to Havana led them past the Club Cazadores del Cerro, so Jane parked in front of the gun club. The bar was empty at that hour, but Jane ordered a shot of gin, which she downed with a pretty wince. The ringing in her ears had faded, and she managed a weak smile.

"Does that help?" asked Javier.

"No, but it doesn't hurt, either."

She left Javier and returned a few minutes later, freshly made up, with face powder and dark red lipstick.

"It's harder for men to do that, isn't it?" she said, as they stepped outside.

"Do what?"

"Put a new face on," said Jane. "A little paint, some perfume, and everything is fine. How do I look?"

"You're very beautiful."

"That's very sweet of you. If only I weren't such a coward."

"I think you're very brave," said Javier. "Very beautiful and brave."

"I'm not," insisted Jane. "I'm selfish and spoiled and I drink too much and part of me is all twisted up and dead. You might as well know all my bad qualities from the start."

"Is that all?"

"Heavens, no," said Jane, "I have very expensive tastes and I'm a terrible wife and mother and a number of prominent psychiatrists have given up on me. And there's more, much more to tell. You really don't want to have anything to do with me."

"Let me be the judge of that."

He leaned over to kiss her but she placed a finger on his lips.

"Promise me one thing."

"Anything," said Javier.

"Promise me that you won't fall in love with me. It would be such a bother if you did. For one thing, now is not a good time. For another, you're a sweet boy and I like you very much. Really, I do. So it would ruin everything."

As she dropped him off, he tried to kiss her once again.

"You promised!" laughed Jane, turning away. "By the way, I'm having a party next week. Won't you come?"

FOUR

Jane had been planning her 23rd birthday party for weeks, but when the day came, she was oddly blasé. Even as the guests began to arrive, she remained on the balcony of her bedroom and smoked a *margarita*. From the garden, their voices floated up to her, mingled with the sound of the servants scurrying back and forth. A moist breeze swept in from the beach, and she could hear the soft murmur of the waves.

"Would you help me, darling?" called Grant.

He stood before the full-length mirror and fretfully adjusted his turban. His robe was secured around his waist by one of Jane's silk scarves, from which dangled a fierce-looking scimitar.

"You look adorable," said Jane, kissing him lightly on the lips.

She wrapped the diaphanous blue veil around her face so that only her eyes showed, and pouted before the mirror.

"They're here," said Grant.

"It's my party," Jane reminded him tartly. "It can't start without me."

Grant went to greet their guests in the garden. The flame trees had been decorated with paper lanterns, each with a flickering candle inside, suspended from the branches like glowing fruit. Poinciana blossoms floated lazily in the pool, and on the terrace a bandstand had been erected beneath a thatched hut, with a parquet dance floor beside it. After an hour, Grant began to worry that out of some malignant whim, Jane had decided not to come down at all. But the sudden hush in the babble of voices told him that she was making her grand entrance. Jane perched regally atop a sort of palanquin, carried in by four of the waiters in blackface, while Armando the Filipino houseboy tossed rose petals in the air. They set her down by the fountain, and Jane lightly stepped off to much applause.

Her appearance was the signal for the music to begin, and the band began to play. It was the Conjunto Casablanca, who had played on the *Ile-de-France*. They wore snappy pink *guayaberas* and soon filled the garden with the beat of their maracas and *timbales*.

After the waiters deposited Jane, they darted back and forth among the guests, carrying trays of cocktails and flutes of champagne. Jane stopped to chat with Marie Antoinette and Don Juan before going on to greet Genghis Khan and his wife, Little Bo Peep. Grant trailed behind her with a sheepish grin, occasionally stopping to readjust his turban, which tended to slide down over his forehead, and shook hands with King Arthur and Cleopatra.

When Walter Huggins and his wife Beryl arrived, the party was in full swing. Grant had invited him after the golf game, and all week the banker had agonized over his costume. Beryl was quite content to go as Little Red Riding Hood, and Walter even found a wolf costume at a shop on Obispo. But at the last minute, he pulled out of the closet his old Stetson hat and cowboy boots, and decided upon Tom Mix, who had visited Havana the year before. Around his neck was a red bandanna, and he had even found a gun belt with two realistic-looking six shooters. This suited Beryl, who wore a rather revealing blouse embroidered with teepees and lariats.

"After all, we *are* Texans," she said.

Beryl was thirsty and took a daiquiri from one of the waiters. Walter rarely drank anything stronger than iced tea, and eyed his cautiously. It couldn't be very strong, he decided, and drained his glass. When he turned, he noticed that Beryl was gone. Had she gone in search of Freddy? He thought he saw her on the terrace, chatting with a man dressed like Robin Hood, in green tights and a feathered cap, and made his way towards her. Ali Baba was talking to the Big Bad Wolf by the pool, and he realized that his nemesis Tom Beales, the president of the Bank of New York, had rented the same costume he had seen on Obispo. Walter used the opportunity to greet his host.

"How's business?" said Grant.

"It's been better, but it's been worse," said Walter.

"I'm sure he wouldn't mind some of your business," said Beales. "By the way, Huggins, I thought you might want to know that Ernest Hemingway opened an account at the Bank of New York."

"You don't say?" said Walter cheerily, and resumed his search for his wife.

On the terrace, Robin Hood was nowhere in sight, and neither was Beryl. Had she found Freddy? His son had said he would be here, but Walter realized he didn't know what costume he was in. He thought he saw Freddy wearing bandoliers and a huge sombrero, but it was another young man he didn't recognize. Walter tried to imagine what he would wear, but drew a blank. Looking around him, he recognized Harry Guggenheim, the American ambassador, dressed as a clown with a bright red nose and floppy shoes. Guggenheim lived in Jaimanitas, not far from the Masons, and Walter often golfed with him.

"Howdy, partner," said the ambassador.

"I didn't know the circus was in town," replied Walter.

Guggenheim introduced him to a tall man dressed as a French courtier, with a powdered wig and an ebony cigarette holder. It was Dr. Fernando Alvarez Leal, who bowed circumspectly. Walter had read in the *Havana Post* about the law professor, who had been arrested on suspicion of being a member of the ABC, although nothing could be proved.

"It is a pleasure, Señor Huggins," said Dr. Alvarez Leal in excellent English. "Perhaps you can resolve my dilemma. Your illustrious ambassador assures me that President Hoover will be re-elected this year. Do you agree?"

"Without a doubt," said Walter.

While they chatted, Beryl continued her conversation with Basil Johnson, who led her back to the pool for another drink. Holding his martini in one hand and his longbow in the other, Basil invited her to stop by the art gallery if she were ever near Tejadillo Street:

"I have a wonderful statue of Changó for you."

"Where would I put it?"

"Wherever you like," said Basil. "If you buy Changó, I'll throw in his wife Obba for free. They're a matched set, you know."

"You don't say?" said Beryl.

Basil thought her quite beautiful in a faded sort of way, with cornflower blue eyes and blond hair untouched by grey. To Basil, it seemed that American women grew brittle and hard as they aged, but not her.

"Really, you must stop by the gallery," he urged her.

Beryl watched the plump, amiable Robin Hood disappear into the crowd. Walter was nowhere in sight so she strolled through the garden hoping to say hello to Jane Mason. Shortly after Jane's arrival in Havana, newly married to Grant, Beryl had invited her to the monthly luncheon of the Woman's Club of Havana. The luncheons were held at the Sevilla-Biltmore Hotel, and generally featured a speaker of note, generally someone visiting from the United States. Jane had accepted and absolutely charmed everyone, but then found excuses not to come again. The members often saw Jane out on the town, sparking wild rumors.

Beryl was surprised to note that her cocktail glass was empty. She could not remember the last time she had a daiquiri, but she decided to have another one if she could just find a waiter. She wandered through the garden, admiring the paper lanterns dangling from the branches of the flame tree, and soon found herself in the menagerie. A parrot squawked unhappily, and peacocks scrambled behind the bushes. As she retraced her steps back to the garden, Beryl heard an odd screeching noise. Out of the corner of her eye, she saw a flicker of movement in one of the cages and approached it hesitantly. Clutching the bars and frenetically waving its tail was a strange little monkey, as surprised as she was.

Meanwhile, Freddy helped himself to another martini. The question of his costume had been settled by Zoila Martínez, who found him red silk pajamas and a skullcap with a plaited ponytail, like a waiter at El Pacífico. She had also suggested that Javier go as the *gallego* at the Alhambra, but he took umbrage at this and refused to consider it. They racked their brains over *croquetas* at the Bar Campana, until Freddy found a Tarzan costume which had been used to promote the bank's baseball team. Together with a spear, it turned Javier into a formidable Ape Man. One of the waiters in blackface was quite taken with him and returned often with his tray full of drinks.

Basil apologized for being so snippy at the art gallery.

"No offense taken," said Javier.

"Jane was furious at me!" exclaimed Basil. "You have no idea the sort of people who just walk in there."

"I can imagine," put in Freddy.

"Where's your pal Hemingway?" asked Basil.

"I don't know," said Javier. "But whatever you do, don't interrupt him while he's drinking."

Their conversation was interrupted by a drumroll from the terrace, and Grant waved his scimitar at the huge birthday cake brought in the by the waiters. As the Conjunto Casablanca broke into *Feliz Cumpleaños*, there was a sound like a gunshot and a puff of smoke. A number of guests thought the house was under attack, and one even pulled out a revolver. But the top of the cake burst open and 23 doves fluttered out, procured from the Club Cazadores del Cerro. Delighted to be spared, they hovered over the pool before streaking off into the balmy night.

Captain Segura knew the sound of gunfire very well, and was not fooled. In the driveway, there was a tangle of cars as guests continued to arrive despite the lateness of the hour. For a moment, he thought his eyes were playing tricks on him. One woman was dressed in an elaborate hooped skirt, and her husband wore a blue waistcoat and a powdered wig. With a jolt of embarrassment, Captain Segura realized that he had forgotten to get a costume. Luckily, he was still in uniform, and that would have to do.

As his driver opened the door of the Cadillac, Captain Segura noticed Emilio Aragon's bulletproof limousine, which he had reportedly bought from a Chicago gangster. The sugar planter's bodyguards lounged sullenly by the curb, and Captain Segura recognized one of them, a hulking *guajiro* from Santa Clara. Seeing his old commanding officer, his hand jerked in an involuntary salute, but he caught himself in time.

Captain Segura ignored him and made his way into the house, where the guests were still talking excitedly about the flight of doves from the birthday cake. Accepting a glass of champagne from a waiter in blackface, he looked for Señora Mason. Before the outing on Hemingway's boat, they had met once before, at a reception at the U.S. embassy. But when the writer introduced them at the pier, she pretended not to know him.

By the fountain, Captain Segura saw Aragon dressed in a Roman toga, white with a purple stripe. Quite appropriate, he thought. Aragon was talking to a paunchy, pink-faced American in a huge cowboy hat. Captain Segura wondered if the man knew the risk he was taking. As someone close to Machado, Aragon was a logical choice for the assassins of the ABC. Their attacks were often in broad daylight, and planned with deadly precision. Last week, a car crammed with explosives had been parked outside the Presidential

Palace, and was discovered only by chance. They were apparently organized in cells which operated independently, so that even Chief of Police Ainciart's *apapipios* [informers] had been unable to penetrate them. Strangest of all was their flag, bright green with a Star of David and the words: *El ABC es la esperanza de Cuba.* [The ABC is the hope of Cuba.] What did it mean?

"How charming, Captain Segura," said Jane, suddenly before him. "You came as yourself!"

"Will you forgive my impertinence?" he said, bending over to kiss her proffered hand. "An unforeseen engagement prevented me from arriving earlier."

"What sort of engagement?" asked Jane. "Not another woman, I hope."

"Hardly one as lovely as you," he replied, lifting his champagne glass. "Duty, I'm afraid."

Captain Segura felt the blood rush to his face as she offered him a fleeting, fragile smile and turned to greet another guest. She was maddening, this *americana*. Her grinning dolt of a husband had come to see him once regarding security arrangements at the Arsenal Dock, where the seaplanes landed. Regardless of Hemingway, there would be other opportunities for them to meet. Where beautiful women were concerned, he was a patient man.

As Captain Segura sipped champagne, Walter found himself in conversation with Emilio Aragon. He had been searching for Beryl when he heard the sonorous voice with a surprisingly good American accent:

"Walter, my friend, it's been too long."

It occurred to Walter that they were not exactly friends, although they saw each other occasionally at the Havana Country Club. But Aragon was friends with everyone, it appeared. Walter had also seen him in Matanzas, since La Margarita was not far from the *central* of the Cuban Sugar Cane Company. Walter shook his meaty, moist hand and noticed the diamond ring on his little finger with distaste.

As often happened in Aragon's presence, he became faintly uneasy, without knowing why.

"We have much to discuss, you and I," said Aragon. "Perhaps we can play golf this Saturday."

By reputation, Aragon was a terrible golfer, and a sore loser.

"I'm afraid not," said Walter.

"Another time then, my friend," said the Cuban amiably.

When a tall army officer came to greet him, Walter quickly excused himself. By the bar, he recognized Freddy, dressed like a chinaman, talking to Tarzan.

"Pop!" cried Freddy. "Remember that idea I had about the radio show? Javier and I have it all figured out."

"What radio show?"

"You remember, the radio show sponsored by the bank. We've even got a name for it: *El Mono Sabio*. What do you think?"

"Can this wait until Monday?"

"Sure thing," said a downcast Freddy.

"Have you seen your mother?"

Freddy shook his head and Walter plunged back into the crowd.

"What did I say wrong?" said Freddy, but soon cheered up and went off in search of a waiter.

Left alone, Javier regretted bringing the awkward spear from the Alhambra. Like many of Freddy's ideas, it just wasn't practical. He thought of leaving it under the hedge when he spotted Jane. Champagne glass in hand, she was giving instructions to the leader of the Conjunto Casablanca at the bandstand. When they began to play she stepped down, dodging the dancing couples as the veils floated behind her.

They hadn't met since the drive to Regla, although he had stopped by the art gallery several times hoping to see her. Now, he wondered what to say to her. What exactly had passed between them? She was, after all, a married woman.

But something *had* passed between them. Was it as unexpected for her as it was for him?

Because of the brilliant blue silk of her costume, he was able to follow her progress across the dance floor. She whispered something to Armando, who scurried off to bring her another glass of champagne. Then she laughed with the stout man in the toga who had spoken to Mr. Huggins, and Javier felt a surprising surge of anger at the sight of his hand resting comfortably on her waist. But Grant was there, the turban tilting to one side, and didn't seem to mind. Jane coyly disengaged herself and disappeared into the throng of guests.

Where did she go? Javier anxiously scanned the crowd but soon gave up and regretted coming. The earlier breeze had died, leaving the air fetid and damp, and his Tarzan costume itched. He had lost sight of Jane and thought of going inside to look for her when he was struck by the absurdity of his position. She had made him promise not to fall in love with her. Was it a warning, or an invitation? Javier leaned the spear against a tree and moved away from the other guests. After a while, he found himself on a path along the walls of the estate, and wondered if it led to the beach. The band had momentarily stopped playing, and the noise of the party seemed oddly distant. Javier came to a gate and saw that it was open.

"Hello you," said Jane.

She stood just beyond the wall, looking out at the waves. It was a hazy night, and he couldn't make out her expression. Suddenly, Javier was embarrassed.

"I don't want you to think I was following you," he stammered.

"Silly boy, what if you were?"

"But I wasn't," he insisted.

Jane turned away and Javier felt his heart sink. He had dreamed of this very moment, yet all he felt was anger.

"I'm sorry," he said.

"Don't be."

"Your guests will wonder where you've gone. You should go back."

"Everyone seems to forget it's *my* birthday," said Jane. "I can do whatever I please."

Javier leaned towards her and found her lips surprisingly soft and yielding. Placing his palms against the rough stucco of the wall, he kissed her again. Jane tasted like champagne and tobacco, with a faint taste of lipstick.

"Remember your promise," she said.

Suddenly, there were footsteps on the other side of the gate, and Jane put her finger on his mouth until they receded. Hemingway had seen Jane on the dance floor, and followed her to the garden. He remembered the path to the beach, but got lost and found himself by the dog run, where a magnificent Doberman snarled threateningly. Startled, Hemingway headed back towards the other guests. The absurd costume that Jane had cobbled together irritated him, and he took off the eye patch.

"Why, if it isn't Captain Hook," said Basil.

"Where's Mrs. Mason?"

"Where indeed? Everyone seems to be looking for her. I was hoping you could tell me."

"What do you mean by that?"

"Nothing at all," said Basil, lightly touching his forearm.

Hemingway's arm jerked away as though he had received an electric shock, spilling what was left of his martini on his striped jersey, and Basil backed away in alarm.

"Don't touch me," said Hemingway in a low voice.

Basil took a deep breath to regain his composure. At that moment, Beryl arrived with her face flushed from the rum, and he thankfully introduced her to the writer.

"Freddy's told me so much about you!" gushed Beryl.

Hemingway squinted grimly at the blond woman in the cowboy hat and mumbled an excuse, but she continued to chatter excitedly away in a thick Texas accent. She wanted something from him, he was sure of it, and it had to do with lunch.

"What did you say?" he asked desperately.

"Why, the Woman's Club meets next week," said Beryl. "You'll be our guest of honor!"

"I'm leaving the day after tomorrow," said Hemingway.

Outside the gate, Jane ducked beneath Javier's outstretched arms and ran down to the beach, leaving behind her slippers. The wispy clouds had drifted away from the moon, and a milky light illuminated the water. Above them, the Conjunto Casablanca had started to play once more but the melody was lost in the hiss of the surf. Javier started uncertainly down the path and saw that the last of her veils had fallen off.

"Jane!" he whispered, afraid to raise his voice.

On the sand was an overturned skiff, and Jane disappeared behind it only to emerge at the water's edge. The slender curve of her back gleamed in the moonlight, and Javier watched her dive neatly into the ocean. No longer afraid, he followed her in, the cool foamy water lapping at his ankles. A wave crashed into him and he lost sight of her, but soon her blond head popped out of the water, and they both gasped for air, laughing.

Joe sat in the cockpit of the *Anita* and smoked another Lucky Strike. After two months in Havana, Hemingway had reluctantly agreed to return home, and this was to be their last day on the water. Not a bad run for a party boat, thought Joe. His quick trip to Key West had made it even more profitable.

Now, it was just like Hemingway to be late. But as Carlos loaded the hold with ice, Joe recognized the writer's familiar, rolling gait on the wharf. He appeared bleary-eyed from the night before, in no mood for small talk. In fact, when he got back from Jane's party and took off his pirate costume in the hotel room, the sun was already rising above the lighthouse of El Morro. Hemingway muttered what passed for a greeting and made his way into the cabin, where he lay face down on the bunk.

"Vamoose," said Joe, but Carlos was already untying the bowline.

The *Anita* followed a majestic Spanish battleship out of the harbor, rolling in its wake. Before them, a pair of frigate birds danced among the whitecaps, fluttering in the wind only to swoop down with a shriek. To the west, fleecy clouds scudded along the horizon. As Hemingway snored, Joe rounded the firing range on the rocky approach to El Morro and steered for Cojimar, running ahead of the current.

Hemingway awoke to the sound of waves sloshing against the hull and climbed out on deck for the first Hatuey of the day. Taking his usual place aft, he yawned as the sun tickled the back of his neck. Carlos had already taken the teasers out, and Hemingway watched them skip crazily in the wash of the propeller. Were the marlin out today? Carlos had told him that they were often drawn to the surface by choppy seas.

Across from Boca Ciega, Hemingway hooked a sailfish that became entangled in the line before throwing off the hook, and saw that they were being followed by a pair of flat-nosed *dentusos*. Taking out Joe's shotgun, he gleefully pumped a round of buckshot into the water, but the sharks sheered out to sea. They continued east and had lunch in Bacuranao, anchored off the mangroves where a fisherman sold them a bushel of crabs. The three men contentedly picked the meat out of the claws, doused in lime juice. With the sun overhead, Joe doubled back towards Havana, tacking against the current. By then, they had run out of baitfish and Carlos used strips of *chicharrón*, spearing the pork rind with the barbed hook. Hemingway caught a *peto*, which he threw back into the water, and then a small tuna.

"You promised me a marlin today, Carlos," said Hemingway.

"*Ojalá,* Don Ernesto."

Squatting on the deck, Carlos baited the Hardy rod with the tuna. Hemingway cast the line and the jig appeared to dive beneath the royal blue water, only to bob up at the end of the line. It appeared they would return home empty-handed, but then Carlos saw a black marlin slanting in from shore at a distance of 100 yards. Still hung over, Hemingway cast the big bamboo pole and watched the marlin slice through the bubbling curve of the wake, almost directly astern. It lifted its blunt head out of the water as though to crash the bait, but then plunged underwater. Hemingway reeled in the line as the marlin broke through the waves and hung in the air for an impossibly long moment, twisting as it fell. Once more, he cast the rod but the marlin seemed indifferent, swimming parallel to the boat with lazy strokes of its tail, occasionally gaining ground and then dropping back. Joe edged the *Anita* into a narrow turn so as to cut it off, but the marlin sounded. After a few minutes, it shot up again, its sword flashing in the sunlight.

The chase continued and they soon lost sight of land. The wind picked up and the clouds overhead were mottled with grey, a sure sign of rain. If a storm was coming they would need to start back, but Hemingway still clung to the gunwale, hoping to spot the marlin. The color of the water had changed from dark blue to a murky grey, and the air grew charged with electricity. Finally, he saw it leap in a shallow arc against the horizon, holding its sword aloft before diving beneath the waves for the last time. Behind it was a darkening wall of rain, blotting out the fading light. As Joe turned the *Anita* back towards Havana, the squall washed over them, and fierce raindrops peppered the deck.

Hemingway dried himself off in the cabin, but couldn't shake the chill. He shivered in the customs house until the rain let up, and then made a dash for the Ambos Mundos. But it was stuffy inside his room and when he opened the window a puddle formed on the tile floor. That night, he went to see Nely Chen. Luckily, Captain Segura was in Cienfuegos and they had dinner in their usual *reservado* in the Café de la Isla.

"Perhaps I will come visit you in Cayo Hueso," said Nely.

"You would not like it there, daughter," replied Hemingway.

"Will you miss me? No doubt you will amuse yourself with a beautiful blond lady."

Hemingway managed a weak smile, but only picked at his food. How did she know about Jane? Perhaps Captain Segura told her.

Later, when the fever began, Nely made him tea scented with honey and anisette and wiped his forehead with a cool cloth. Captain Segura said the *americano* was famous in his own country, though she didn't know why. When he learned that Hemingway came to see her (as she knew he would) he was amused by it. This infuriated Nely, who had hoped to make him jealous. When Captain Segura learned about Javier, there was a terrible row which ended with a tender reconcilation and a new apartment on Dragones Street. But Hemingway was different, somehow. Softly, she sang a song that her mother had taught her in Santiago de Cuba, a prayer to Oshún. The *orisha* was the goddess of rivers and might help him find his way across the water.

Hemingway couldn't understand the words but the strange rhythm of her voice lulled him to sleep. In the morning, the storm had passed but the breeze was stale with the stench of rotting fish. Low clouds hung over the tiled rooftops, and the streets were slick with stagnant puddles. Promising to see her when he returned to Havana, Hemingway wearily dressed and started back for the *Anita*, where Joe was ready to cast off.

During the crossing, Hemingway tossed fitfully in the narrow bunk and tried to fall asleep. He gave up an hour later, his head throbbing, the sheets damp with sweat. The sloping walls of the hull seemed to close in around him and he scrambled outside to see Joe at his usual place behind the wheel, sipping coffee from the thermos.

"Still awake, Mahatma?"

"I must have caught a cold," Hemingway muttered.

They would not see the lights of the La Concha Hotel for several hours, but a pale moon illuminated the wispy clouds. He could not bear to go back inside the cramped cabin and took a deep breath of the damp salty air. Trying to remember Nely's strange lullaby, he helped himself to Joe's coffee and peered over the gunwale at the shimmering purple waves that stretched to the horizon.

Back in Key West, Hemingway lay in bed for several days, still running a fever. Pauline had gone ahead with the boys to her parents' house in Piggot, Arkansas and the house on Whitehead Street was quiet except for the squawk of the flamingoes Jane had given them. His sister Carol had agreed to make the drive north with him, but his throat hurt and the cough had gotten worse. Joe sent over a bottle of amber-colored Cuban rum, and in the evening Charles came over to help him polish it off. Hemingway's pursuit of the black marlin grew more vivid with each retelling, and had now achieved Homeric proportions.

"Whatever you say," chuckled Charles.

When he was well enough to work, Hemingway took out the galleys of his bullfighting book, which he had been unable to finish in Cuba. Rubbing his tired eyes, he saw something he hadn't noticed before. Across the top of each page in purple ink was the heading:

HEMINGWAY'S DEATH

Was it a joke? In disbelief, he riffled through the pages and saw that they were all slugged with the same caption, shorthand for the title. Hemingway threw on a thick cotton sweater and stumbled to the Western Union office to angrily wire his editor. The next day, he shot off a letter demanding that the typesetter who was responsible be fired.

"Really, Ernest," said Carol. "I'm sure it was just a mistake."

"Stay out of this, Beefy," said her brother. "You don't know publishers. They're all bastards."

The doctor finally pronounced him fit to travel, and they set out in the new roadster that Pauline had bought while he was in Havana. Once on the highway, the power of the V-8 engine delighted him, and they roared through the Florida panhandle.

"Can't we stop?" whined Carol, as they shot past a diner. "I'm hungry."

"Not on your life," he said. "Someone might recognize me."

"That's ridiculous! We're miles from nowhere."

"We'll be there before you know it."

Hemingway was still weak from the fever, but he kept on driving. His sister managed to get a fried egg sandwich at a gas station, but it was dark before they pulled into a motor court in Georgia for a few hours sleep.

They reached Piggot the following day, and Carol happily took a train to Chicago. Once more Hemingway took to bed, and it was several days before he set out with Pauline for Wyoming. As they approached the high country, he took deep breaths of the brisk air redolent with pine needles. They slept in a log cabin, and awoke each morning to the smell of woodsmoke and freshly brewed coffee. Hemingway's strength returned, and after a few days he finished the galleys of *Death in the Afternoon,* sending them to New York. The book no longer meant anything to him, but at least it was out of his hands, and he celebrated that night with a bottle of moonshine whiskey. But he could not shake the nameless fear that had followed him from Cuba.

Javier wrapped a towel around himself and splashed cold water on his face. Only after banishing Jane from his mind was he able to get dressed and go to work. While waiting for the streetcar to take him to Trocadero Street, he realized that he had finally stopped thinking of her. But he was soon reminded of Jane's unsettling habit of tilting her head to one side, and began to count the hours until he would see her again.

Bohemia was on the verge of bankruptcy, and the office grew increasingly threadbare. This was of little consequence to Javier, who loved the near-chaos of squabbling editors and harried reporters, which built to a crescendo each week as the deadline approached. Somehow, the magazine emerged from the printing press as pristine as a newly laid egg, still warm and smelling of ink. It was then rushed to newsstands throughout the island, where it sold for 10 cents a copy. The publisher, Miguel Angel Quevedo, could hardly afford to pay what employees he had. But to appease Don Ramón, who had known his father, he had offered Javier a job as assistant to Pepe Dominguez, the advertising director.

At the beginning of the day, Pepe's suit was immaculately pressed, with a neatly folded handkerchief in his breast pocket. As he lit his first cigar, the rosy pate beneath his thinning hair gleamed with optimism. By late afternoon, Pepe's cigar would be an unrecognizable stump, and his handkerchief a wrinkled flag of desperation. When Pepe rallied his troops, Javier sat behind him, pretending to take notes as the advertising director interrogated his salesmen. First up was Raimundo Piqueras, a lean Catalan who pursed his lips doubtfully. Next came Waldo Romero, who rambled on in a slow melodious voice until Pepe lost patience and demanded he get to the point. The list was rounded off by Dick MacMechan, a bluff New Yorker who had been brought in to handle the American accounts. MacMechan, who understood little Spanish, could be found each afternoon at Sloppy Joe's. Pepe pleaded, cajoled, and finally banged his fist on the table, threatening them with imminent dismissal if the ads were not secured by Friday.

As the salesmen filed out of Pepe's office, Javier presented the idea of a radio show to be called *El Mono Sabio*. Pepe's ears perked up at the mention of the Havana Trust, and Javier explained how it would be broadcast on station CMX from the Tokio Cabaret on San Lázaro. The Conjunto Casablanca would play and then the audience would try to confound an eminent authority billed as "the smartest man in Havana." If he couldn't answer the question, a prize would be awarded.

"What do you think?" asked Javier eagerly.

Halfway through Javier's presentation, Pepe had begun to scan the correspondence on his desk, and now he looked up and said:

"Just who is 'the smartest man in Havana'?"

"I haven't figured that out yet," admitted Javier.

"Sure, *chico*," said Pepe offhandedly, "let me know when you find him."

Javier left dejectedly and returned to the desk that had been found for him outside the storeroom. Once again, he tried not to think of Jane. The difficulty was that this made him think of her of even more, as though in an attempt to erase her image, her features became clearer still: her delicate chin, her small, deceptively prim mouth, and her greyish eyes set perhaps a trifle too far apart.

This reverie occupied the balance of the morning, since he had relatively little to do other than run errands for Pepe. At lunchtime, he was able to leave the office without attracting undue attention, and he strolled down Galiano to have a Cuban sandwich at Woolworth's with Professor Filiberto Vargas.

Professor Vargas was well known to the readers of *Bohemia*, since he wrote a weekly chess column. As a young man, he had studied in Paris, and taught philosophy at the University of Havana until it was shut down by Machado's soldiers. In his column, Professor Vargas avidly followed the career of José Raúl Capablanca, world champion until his defeat by the Russian grandmaster Alexander Alekhine. But his passion was for chess problems, intricate puzzles in which a single move launched an inexorable combination leading to checkmate. The column proved too esoteric and it was soon replaced by a crossword puzzle. But after a flood of angry letters from chess players throughout Cuba, Professor Vargas was triumphantly reinstated. Despite the heat, the professor habitually wore a dark wool suit. He was almost completely bald, with a pointed goatee, and thick spectacles. A confirmed bachelor, he lived in a book-lined apartment with his mother on Concordia Street. Realizing that Professor Vargas was perfect for *El Mono Sabio*, Javier introduced him to Freddy.

"He'll do," said his friend. "A little dry, but that's okay. He's supposed to be 'the smartest man in Havana,' not a tap dancer."

After Javier had lunch with Professor Vargas, the thought of Jane finally overwhelmed him. Instead of returning to the office, Javier headed in the opposite direction toward the art gallery. Basil had warmed up to him and genuinely looked forward to his visits.

"I sold Changó to your pal's mom," he announced.

Javier raised an eyebrow and Basil explained that after the costume party, Mrs. Huggins had dropped by after one of her shopping expeditions on the Prado. She had taken Changó on the condition that Basil throw in not just plain Obba but lovely Oshún as well.

"It only seemed fair," Basil admitted. "I can't imagine where she put them, though."

Left behind, proud Oyá stood uneasily beside gloomy Ogún, her husband.

Javier heard the squeal of brakes as Jane's yellow Chevrolet pulled into Tejadillo, and smelled her perfume as she breezed in.

"My, but you two are getting friendly," she said.

"Who would have thunk it?" said Basil

"I'd better be going," said Javier with a look at Jane.

He was soon at Freddy's apartment on Neptuno. It would be several minutes until Jane arrived, and to calm himself Javier lit a cigar. But that didn't help, and he frantically changed the sheets on the bed and kicked Freddy's dirty clothes into the closet. From the balcony, Javier saw her car skid to a stop across the street. By the door was a shoeshine boy sitting on the box containing his brushes, talking to another boy who sold Chiclets. Yet again, they bemoaned the unfairness of Kid Chocolate's loss on points against Jack Berg in New York, when Jane passed by. Her appearance provoked not the usual compliments, but a stunned silence and sudden intake of breath, itself a subtle *piropo*. As the click of her high heels receded, the boys shook their heads sadly and returned to Kid Chocolate.

When Jane came in, Javier was forced to revise the image of her that had haunted him all day. In the sharp afternoon light, her eyes were not so much grey as gun-metal blue, and they were a perfect distance from the delicate bridge of her nose. She wore a breezy silk blouse and her strawberry blond hair was parted down the middle and pinned back in a demure chignon beneath her stylish feathered hat.

"I'm afraid Basil knows," she said, taking off her pearls and draping them over the ashtray.

"I know," said Javier.

"Not only that, but he knows that we know he knows."

"Does it matter?"

"Of course it does," said Jane crossly.

There was no time to argue, as Jane was soon expected back at Jaimanitas. After they hurriedly made love, a drowsy languor filled her and she dropped off to sleep. Javier lay on his side and noticed how her features softened in repose, her luxurious eyelashes nearly touching her cheek, the tiny lines on her forehead smoothed out, and her mouth no longer so tightly set. Asleep, she seemed oddly indifferent, not just to her lover but to the world. With his fingertip, Javier traced the tiny half moon beneath her lower lip, but Jane stirred and swatted his hand away. Her eyes fluttered open, and she briskly removed the hand resting on her thigh.

"You're a very naughty boy," said Jane.

"I'm as old as you are," said Javier.

"Just barely."

"It's a pity, since I know you like older men."

"Now, now," said Jane, sitting on his lap.

"What about Hemingway?"

"What about him?" said Jane irritably. "Pauline wrote and said they're off to Wyoming to shoot grizzly bears."

Jane stood up to dress, and the sheet draped over Javier slid to the floor.

"*¡Aguja!*" she laughed, darting away from him to pin on her hat.

Javier growled and lay on his stomach, watching the reflection of her face in the mirror as she applied lipstick and spritzed on some perfume. She was soon out the door, and he peered down from the balcony as she climbed back into the Chevrolet and drove off. His clothes were scattered about the room in a frantic path to the bed: his shoes by the door, his jacket on the floor, and his trousers on the bedpost. If he hurried, he had just enough time to put in an appearance at *Bohemia* before meeting Freddy at the Floridita.

When Jane told him that she would be away for several days in Miami, Javier plunged into a gloomy funk. His mother was astounded when he lost his normally ferocious appetite, and even Pepe noticed him sulking at his desk and patted him on the back. Freddy tried to cheer him up, and after a few daiquiris they went to the Zombie Club, where the justly celebrated *Mulatas de Oro* were performing. But Javier yawned throughout the show, and they left early.

The day Jane was to return, he impulsively rang up Jaimanitas. When Armando answered, he asked to speak with Mrs. Mason. Somehow, Grant picked up the phone.

"Who is this?" he demanded.

Javier didn't know what to say, and hung up.

The next afternoon at Freddy's apartment, Jane told him never to call her at home.

"Why not?" asked Javier.

"If you don't know, I won't bother to explain it to you."

"Does your husband know?"

"No, he doesn't."

"What would you do if he found out?"

"I told you he doesn't know!" said Jane fiercely.

As though to punish him, she didn't come to the art gallery for several days, and Basil shook his head bleakly whenever Javier stopped by. When he finally saw her, there was no trace of Jane's anger, and he prudently decided not to bring the matter up. Quite casually, Jane mentioned that Grant would be gone for several days in Peru.

Freddy recommended a small hotel in Varadero, and for one glorious night Javier had her all to himself. She picked him up on Neptuno and they left the city in the late afternoon, taking the new Carretera Central towards Matanzas, and the lovely beaches to the east. The Hotel de la Playa was set in a grove of *guayacan* trees dotted with pale blue flowers. It consisted of several tidy white cottages with gingerbread trim, each with a small porch facing the water.

Dinner was less than satisfactory, since the only other guests were a family of American missionaries who glared at them disapprovingly.

"Do they think I'm a fallen woman?" said Jane, trying to keep from giggling.

"They think I've seduced you."

"Isn't that the case?"

"If only they knew."

They took their plates of *arroz con camarones* back to their cottage, and listened to the croak of the tree frogs as the night fell like a soft blanket over the gentle waves.

"I wish you didn't have to go back tomorrow," said Javier.

"You know I don't have a choice."

"There's always a choice."

"You've got so much to learn."

In the morning, Javier woke up to find Jane already in

her bathing suit, and he had just enough time to put on his swimming trunks before she dashed outside. The sand was as fine as talcum powder, and it stuck to the soles of their feet as they dove into the shallow turquoise water. Jane swam out to sea with clean, strong strokes, and he was nearly out of breath when he caught up with her. They could see their shadows on the smooth, sandy bottom, just a few feet below. Later, they lay on their beach towels, warmed by the early morning sun, and Javier said:

"I wish this moment would never end."

"That would get rather boring, darling."

"Not for me."

"You're a silly little boy."

"Don't call me that."

"Please, Javier, don't spoil it."

But the moment had passed and Jane went back to the cottage. Javier followed her back, and her skin was salty from the seawater and the tiny grains of sand. Afterwards, she saw the sadness in his eyes and said:

"It's really better this way, don't you think?"

The following week, Jane announced that she would spend the rest of the month with Grant in Argentina.

"It's winter there," she explained.

"Send me a postcard," said Javier sourly.

Jane blew him a kiss and said that Basil would keep him company. But in the absence of a breeze, the sun beating down on the cobblestones of the Plaza de la Catedral drove away what few tourists there were, and Basil gratefully closed the art gallery for two weeks. Rather than stay in Havana, he went to the Isle of Pines, where a friend's aunt owned a small farm. Javier continued to pass by, hoping that Jane had somehow returned early from Buenos Aires.

As they did every summer, his parents had embarked for Spain, taking Lydia with them, and even Miguel had fled to his father-in-law's *finca* in the tobacco country of Pinar del Río. As always, Javier's grandfather refused to go to Spain and the two of them remained alone in the house During his lunch hour, Javier often went to visit him at the *almacén*. Carrying a loaf of bread and a link of *chorizo*, Javier would pass beneath the forgotten coat of arms into the courtyard once teeming with delivery trucks but now littered with empty jute sacks. His grandfather, who rarely stepped outside without his black beret, turned slowly from the open window and squinted with fading blue eyes, as though trying to recognize him. Then he took out his clasp knife, a steel blade in an olive wood handle which he always ate with. With practiced skill, the old Spaniard carved thin wheels of the peppery sausage, and they ate together in silence.

The summer doldrums even penetrated the offices of *Bohemia*. Business was slow, and only by means of a *siesta* did Pepe Dominguez manage to survive the steamy afternoons. The latest issue of the magazine had mentioned the mysterious disappearance of Raúl and Vivian Esnard. There was a rumor that they had been taken to Atarés, but Chief of Police Ainciart denied they had been even been arrested. Their apartment showed no sign of a struggle, and offered no clue as to their whereabouts. It was as though they had walked out for a stroll, and never returned. None of their neighbors had seen anything, or at least anything they were willing to talk about. Some of their friends even hoped they had gone to Key West, as the police claimed, and would soon return, wondering what all the fuss was about. But after a few days, this seemed unlikely. Javier remembered the afternoon he spent with them at the beer garden, and wondered what they had done to get in trouble with the *expertos*. Was Raúl a member of the ABC as Machado's newspaper, the *Heraldo de Cuba,* now claimed? If so, then Roberto was sure to be involved. Perhaps Lydia would forget about him in Spain.

The only one indifferent to the weather was Professor Vargas. One steamy afternoon, Javier found him at the Acera del Louvre, holding his ponderous head in his hands, bent over a devilish chess puzzle by Comins Mansfield. Being an indifferent player, Javier could make no sense of the pieces on the green and white squares. The black king was in the center of the board, protected by a rook and a phalanx of pawns, yet also threatened by both white knights and a bishop. The white king was in the corner of the board, yet not out of danger either. If the black rook moved, it opened the diagonal and pinned the white queen, threatening checkmate. The white rook protected the king's flank, but it was also vulnerable to attack. What was the solution?

"White to move and mate in two," challenged Professor Vargas.

Javier concentrated on the baffling position on the chess board, hoping it would help him drive Jane from his thoughts. But he soon realized that the key to the problem was the white queen, and this made him think of her even more.

It was Frank who told Roberto what really happened to Raúl and Vivian Esnard.

The Directorio planned a *tángana*, or demonstration, and at first light they met at the university. A row of *expertos* in khaki uniforms looked down impassively from the statue of the Alma Mater as the students gathered below. Grainy photographs of the young couple had been pasted to placards, which the students held up above their heads. Just when it appeared the crowd would surge up toward the soldiers, they proceeded up San Lázaro Street. At the statue of Antonio Maceo, another group waited, and together they marched down the Malecón chanting:

"*¿Dónde está Raúl? ¿Dónde está Vivian?*" [Where are Raúl and Vivian?]

As the students swarmed across the boulevard, blocking traffic in both directions, the waves crashed against the seawall, sending a cloud of cold, salty spray over their heads. Keeping in step, Roberto joined in the shouts. He was jostled from behind and quickened his pace, careful not to lose sight of Frank, whose plaid jacket bobbed in the crowd ahead of him.

The soldiers were lined up just before the fortress of La Punta, their carbines unslung, blocking the entrance to the Presidential Palace, and the students veered to the right, heading down the Prado. Mounted police cantered along either side of the street, and Roberto was thankful for the shade of the laurel trees. A crowd of onlookers had gathered to watch the *tángana* and many of them joined in the shouting, while others were afraid of Machado's thugs, the *porristas*, and silently went their way.

As they neared the Acera del Louvre, Roberto remembered the last time he saw Dr. Alvarez Leal. It had been many months since the *tertulia* had met, it being unsafe to discuss politics in public places. The law professor had been arrested more than once, though nothing could be proved and he was quickly released when the American ambassador protested. But he had left Cuba after two men tried to shoot him outside his house, and was reportedly in New York. As for Alberto Zayas Bazán, he had fled his parents' house in Miramar minutes before the police arrived, and was in hiding. There was a price on his head, 10,000 *pesos* dead or alive, in connection with a failed attempt on Machado's life. Alberto had laughed and said he would collect it himself someday.

Several military trucks with machine guns mounted in the back were parked in front of the Capitolio, and it was here that the students began to disperse. The shouting died down as many of them disappeared into the sidestreets, while others blended in with the passers-by. It was as though having come all this way, they had forgotten what they had set out to accomplish. The placards bearing the picture of Raúl and Vivian Esnard soon littered the Parque Central, but they were picked up by the policemen. There was nothing for Roberto to do except go home.

"Tonight," said Frank as they parted, and whispered the address in his ear.

The excitement of the march, and the feeling of being swept along in a giddy current, left him feeling hollow. Once it grew dark, Roberto nervously approached the apartment where they were to meet. It was on a nondescript street in the Vedado, just a few blocks from the cemetery of Colón. Were they being watched? It was deserted save for two old women savoring the cool of the evening on their front porch. Once he passed through the door, he realized, nothing would be the same again. He remembered the countless arguments he had participated in, a sea of words sloshing around in his head. What difference did it make? It was time for action, not words.

But the young men inside hardly looked like conspirators. There was Frank, who gravely nodded as he puffed his pipe, the sweetish smoke filling the room. Beside him sat Enrique Espuelas, a member of the Directorio, and Bobby Diaz, a gangly law student with acne scars on his gaunt cheeks. Carlos Medina had been a classmate of his at La Salle together with Luis Sifuentes, who cooly smoked a cigarette. There were others he didn't know, nine in all, and a tenth man who didn't introduce himself. He was older, with thinning dark hair, and smoked American cigarettes. Speaking with the precision of a lawyer, he asked each of them in a calm voice what they were willing to do to overthrow Machado.

That was how Roberto became an *abecedario*. They met once a week, always at a different location they learned of the same day. Roberto never learned the name of the tenth man, who was their only link to the other cells. If any of them were caught, they could only betray themselves, but not the others. They swore themselves to secrecy, but it was hardly necessary, since they all knew the punishment for a *lenguilargo*.

There was no one he could talk with about it, anyway. Certainly not Lydia, who was in Spain with her parents. A few days before her departure, he had sat with her in the parlor of her parents' house while Aunt Clara embroidered and pretended not to listen. As Lydia talked excitedly of the trip,

Roberto wondered how she would react if she knew. Would she think him heroic, or foolhardy? Would she admire him, or be afraid for his life?

"Roberto!" Lydia pouted. "You're not listening!"

"*Sí, sí, mi amor,*" he whispered, pressing her small soft hands with a sidelong glance at Aunt Clara.

Roberto had stood with Javier as the majestic ocean liner left the harbor, bound for La Coruña. He thought he saw her high on deck, a slight, girlish figure waving a white handkerchief.

"How about a drink?" offered Javier.

Roberto was in no mood to waste time with her brother, whom he regarded as a fop who spent all day carousing with his *yanqui* friends.

"*No, gracias,*" he said abruptly, and left Javier on the pier.

One Saturday morning, they left Havana in Frank's car and headed south toward Batabano, as though they were taking the ferry to the Isle of Pines. Before they reached the shore, they turned into a dirt road and continued through the desolate countryside. Soon they came to a small farmhouse on the edge of a swamp. A cloud of mosquitos hung over the brackish water, and the air was dank and sulphurous. Hidden beneath the floorboards were cartridges of cheddite, and a grizzled Spaniard showed them how to attach the fuses to detonate the explosives.

Roberto then practiced shooting the .38 caliber Smith & Wesson he had been given, placing a row of bottles on a fallen tree trunk. He held the long-barrelled, surprisingly heavy pistol in both hands, and slowly squeezed the trigger. It kicked back sharply, nearly flying out of his grasp, and the bullet shot well over the bottles. Roberto was ashamed, but the Spaniard seemed unconcerned, and showed him how to keep his arms bent as he fired.

"*Una vez más,*" he said in his thick accent, pronouncing the *s* as *th*. [One more time.]

When they returned to Havana, the tenth man ordered Roberto to report on the movements of a certain Senator who was a member of the Havana Yacht Club, and regularly went for a sail in the morning. Roberto sat by the pool and watched him leave the marina, preceded by his bodyguards. The Senator was a small, dapper man, dressed in white linen slacks and a red silk ascot. Carlos waited outside and saw him enter his car, a long black Lincoln, and speed off down First Avenue.

"When will it happen?" Roberto wanted to ask, but the tenth man would hardly have answered, even if he had known.

When they met the following week, Roberto was told to be ready the next day, and that night he carefully hid the pistol in the satchel which had once held his law books. On his desk was the last letter that Lydia had sent him. It was scented with lilac, and written on violet paper in her round, child-like handwriting. After a few lines, he could not bear to finish it.

In the morning, they met at the university, where Carlos waited in his car, a dark green Cadillac. There was nothing to say, so they sat in silence, occasionally glancing at their watches. Carlos drummed his fingers on the steering wheel, while Frank puffed on his pipe. In the back seat, Roberto sat beside Enrique, who methodically chewed his fingernails. He held the pistol, gleaming with gun oil, beneath his coat, and it was cool against his clammy fingers. At last Luis walked by, and whispered the address to Carlos before disappearing around the corner. That was the signal, and they drove down 23rd Street.

Carlos parked in front of a white bungalow in the shade of a grapefruit tree, and once more they waited. After a few minutes, the door opened and Alberto emerged carrying a large canvas bag. Roberto had not seen him for several months, but he remembered his unreadable expression from the *tertulia*. He entered the back seat without greeting them, and said:

"He just arrived at the Havana Yacht Club."

They crossed the Almendares River into Miramar, and Roberto noticed that a car was following them, a Packard with several people inside. But Alberto was unconcerned, and Roberto realized that the other *abecedarios* would cover their escape, or else finish the job if they failed. As they neared the Havana Yacht Club, Roberto felt nauseous, and opened the car window to take a deep breath. He could see Carlos' freshly barbered neck as he drove, and Frank's plump hand around the stem of his pipe. Beside him, Enrique squirmed nervously.

He knew it would be some time before their quarry left the Havana Yacht Club. They drove past it and headed towards Jaimanitas, and then doubled back to park several blocks away from the entrance. From their vantage point, they could see the entrance of the clubhouse where he would emerge. Suddenly, the black Lincoln pulled up to the driveway.

"Now," said Alberto in a gravelly whisper. Pulling the Thompson gun out of the canvas bag, he checked the pan and slid the safety all the way over.

The Senator stepped out into the light, once more wearing the absurd ascot, and spoke with his bodyguards before disappearing into the Lincoln. As it left the Havana Yacht Club, Carlos slowly followed in the Cadillac, with the Packard several car lengths behind.

Luckily, there were no other cars on First Avenue, and Carlos gunned the engine to pull up beside the Lincoln. Roberto briefly glimpsed the pale faces within as Alberto swung the Thompson out the window and opened fire. The deafening *bop-bop-bop* of the submachine gun and the sound of shattering glass drowned out the screams as Alberto raked the car from a few feet away. Then Carlos speeded up, and Roberto craned his neck to see the Lincoln swerve and nearly hit a banyan tree before coming to rest just before the colonnade of an elegant mansion.

"*Bien muerto, como perro,*" said Alberto, and carefully replaced the smoking Thompson in the canvas bag. [A good death, like a dog.]

The smell of cordite from the spent shells filled the car as they drove east towards Marianao. Roberto noticed that Enrique was shaking, and Frank's hand trembled as he lit his pipe. The Packard had sped off in another direction, and only after driving for an hour did Carlos stop the car, turning into an unpaved street of wooden houses. Robert stepped out and threw up behind the car, his vomit splashing on the tires.

"It will be your turn next," said Alberto.

The next day, the assassination was on the front page of the *Diario de la Marina*. Roberto didn't know that it was only part of the plan, nor did anyone else in his cell, except perhaps the tenth man. The rest was to come out later. That afternoon, he drank steadily from the bottle of rum they passed around, hoping to pass out, but once again he threw up amid general derision. The taste of rum had always made him wince, but after awhile he grew used to it.

Lydia returned from Spain a few weeks later. He told himself that it would put her in danger to be seen with him, but that wasn't it at all. He declined an invitation to dinner at her parents' house in the Vedado, and avoided the Havana Yacht Club in case she was there. That's what Alberto would have done.

The 1932 World Series between the New York Yankees and the Chicago Cubs was soon under way, and each afternoon, Roberto followed the game on a scoreboard in the Parque Central. In less than a week, it was all over, as the Yankees swept the Cubs in four games straight. In the third game, Babe Ruth pointed boastfully to the centerfield bleachers, and blasted Charley Root's fastball out of the stadium.

Roberto left the Parque Central and walked up the Prado to catch the streetcar, and there he saw Lydia. She was with her friend Mirta Rivero, waiting outside the Teatro Fausto to buy tickets for the latest Carlos Gardel movie. Hoping she hadn't seen him, he pulled his boater down over his forehead and kept walking.

Walter was roused by the dismal whirr of the ceiling fan. Beryl slept contentedly, but the damp sheets clung to his belly, where Olga's greasy fried chicken reposed. If the Havana heat didn't kill him, thought Walter, the food would.

Reluctantly, he padded downstairs, careful where he stepped. Once, in the twins' room, he discovered a scorpion the size of his forefinger, which the little girls gleefully stalked and set on fire. Now, it was eerily quiet, and he noticed the odd little dolls that Beryl had brought home the other day. They were lined up on the bookshelf, as though standing guard. What did she say their names were? Walter leaned over to get a closer look at the little man holding a double-headed axe. His eyes glittered like shards of glass, and his mouth was twisted in a malicious sneer. Beside him was a melancholy figure with a scarf over her head, and another woman, with gaily painted eyes and a necklace of yellow beads. As he studied their rough-hewn faces, an involuntary shiver ran through him.

Walter helped himself to the bottle of milk in the frigid-aire. It was nearly light out, and he realized he wouldn't be getting back to sleep. The thought depressed him because he would be listless and cranky all day. Perhaps he would go home early. There were fewer tourists during the inter-minably long summer, and the bank lobby seemed like a morgue.

The milk failed to settle his stomach. Returning to the bedroom, Walter filled the bathtub with cool water and soaked until his wife began to stir. His only consolation was that he would soon be dispatching Beryl to Texas. Each summer, she visited her family in Austin, and the girls attended Camp Waldemar in the Hill Country. For Walter this meant long, drowsy afternoons on the fairways of the Havana Country Club with his friends Ogden Crews and the Reverend Graham. It was several years since Walter had been home. His brother-in-law was now president of the bank, and his pince-nez spectacles and thinning hair parted down the middle gave him the appearance of a preacher. Even now, he looked down upon Walter, who was only too happy to remain in Havana.

Despite this, he remained irritable, and the weeks passed slowly. Olga visited her son in Bayamo, and Walter breakfasted at the American Club. Taking advantage of the early morning cool, he walked briskly down O'Reilly and was the first to arrive at the bank, even before Hopgood. Elmer nodded smartly, and Walter realized it was several weeks since he'd smelled liquor on his breath. Freddy and the other employees were careful to look busy when he passed by their desks, and even Hugo Pedraza did his best to remain awake throughout the long afternoons.

Pedraza was the first Cuban employee of the Havana Trust, who had begun as a bank teller and worked his way up to general manager. Nearly a quarter century later, his expression was as serious as ever, but there was the unmistakeable glint of irony, as though from a private joke. That was often the case with Cubans, though. One evening over a game of poker at the American Club, Walter mentioned it to Ogden, whose wife was also away for the summer.

"I know exactly what you mean," said Ogden. "Back home, you always know where you stand. Here, you can never be sure."

"What do they think of us?" mused Walter.

"Some of the young whippersnappers hate us, that's for sure," chuckled Ogden. "They think we want to take their country away from them. If we wanted Cuba, we would have kept it after the war. Hell, they can have it."

"That's for sure," said Walter, though he remembered the fierce, battle-hardened *mambises* who fought the Spaniards.

Many of the Cuban soldiers were barefoot, armed only with machetes and rusty rifles.

"Mark my words," said Ogden. "We're going to wind up back here whether we like it or not."

The next morning, Walter called Pedraza into his office, and asked him what he thought of the political crisis. The Cuban seemed surprised by the question, and took a moment to consider.

"It is a pity," he said in his courtly, heavily accented English. "Machado is a good president, but he is greedy."

"Aren't all the *políticos* the same?" asked Walter.

Pedraza pursed his lips and slowly opened both palms toward Walter:

"No, Señor Huggins. They are greedy for money. Machado is greedy for power."

Walter resolved to invite him and his wife to dinner as soon as Beryl returned to Havana.

There were less Americans in Havana that year, and receipts were down, so the New York office was demanding that Walter attract more Cuban customers. If the economic situation continued to deteriorate, Cubans would feel safer putting their hard-earned *pesos* in an American bank. But how to get them through the door? Once more, Freddy described his idea for *El Mono Sabio*.

"What's this about a monkey?" asked Walter.

"It's Cuban for a really smart guy, Pop," said Freddy, and described Professor Vargas. Listeners of the radio show would submit questions about Cuban history by sending them to the magazine.

"What if this *mono sabio* fellow doesn't know the answer?"

"That's the point, Pop! If they stump him, they get a prize."

"What kind of prize?"

"Maybe a free drink at the Floridita. Whatever! You know how Cubans are, they'll be dying to make this guy fall on his face. Everyone will want to listen to the show."

"Will *Bohemia* go along with this?"

"If we keep buying ads, the publisher will turn cartwheels in the Parque Central if I tell him to."

Freddy did not mention that Pepe Dominguez had been decidedly lukewarm about the idea, but he figured that an opportunity would arise to change his mind.

Beryl returned to Havana on the P&O ferry from Key West. Betty and Barbara were tanned and plump, and the servants looked on in amazement as the girls put a chair under the avocado tree and practiced lassoing it. But their homecoming was overshadowed by the spectacular murder of Clemente Vazquez Bello, the president of the Cuban Senate, and a close friend of Machado's. The newspapers reported that he had been gunned down while leaving the Havana Yacht Club. Like Chicago gangsters, the *abecedarios* had sped off in a getaway car. The police promptly rounded up all student leaders for questioning. But why Vazquez Bello?

A few days later, a gardener at the cemetery of Colón discovered a black wire running under the ground and called the *expertos*. A huge bomb was found buried beside the mausoleum of the Vazquez family, containing hundreds of pounds of cheddite, connected to a detonator. It was estimated that the explosion would have left a crater with a diameter of 500 yards. That was the real motive for the shooting. The *bomba sorbetera*, as it was dubbed, would have been set off during the funeral, which the president and his entire cabinet were expected to attend. They were saved only by the fact that Vazquez Bello's widow decided to bury him in Santa Clara rather than Havana.

But once the shock of the diabolical plan wore off, it was fodder for the wags at the American Club:

"It would have been one hell of a eulogy," said Ogden. "What a way to go!"

In response, the police arrested hundreds of students suspected of being members of the ABC. The jail cells at the

Jefatura were full and the prisoners were dumped into the rat-infested dungeons of El Morro. A cordon of soldiers surrounded the presidential palace, and all suspicious vehicles were stopped and searched. Machado's thugs beat up protesters on the street with their *vergajos*, truncheons made of twisted hide, and there were more disappearances like that of the Esnards. The ABC retaliated with several bombings, and a policeman was gunned down in broad daylight on the Malecón. The violence frightened off what few tourists there were, and business slowed down to a trickle at the Havana Trust.

To top it all off, Hugo Pedraza dropped dead one afternoon. Hopgood found him face down in a stack of loan documents and called a doctor, but it was already too late.

As his employer, Walter was asked to say a few words at the funeral. The coffin was drawn by four pairs of black horses, their coats curried to a glossy sheen. At the iron gates of the Colón cemetery, a bell rang and the priest fell in with the procession. In contrast to some of the gaudy mausoleums, in polished onyx and Tiffany glass, Pedraza's tomb was a discrete granite headstone, as befitted a banker. A long, flowery eulogy was delivered by his brother from Matanzas.

"We should have invited them to dinner," whispered Walter. "Then I'd know what to say."

"Hush!" said Beryl.

Finally, it was Walter's turn. Facing Señora Pedraza and her grown children and numerous grandchildren, Walter cleared his throat. He was often called upon to speak at the luncheons of the Havana Rotary Club, but now the words stuck in his throat.

"I knew Hugo Pedraza for many years," he began haltingly, and surveyed the small army of relatives surrounding the grave. The fierce morning sun beat down upon him, and he stopped to take out a handkerchief and wipe the thin film of sweat from his forehead. "I knew Hugo Pedraza for many years," he repeated, and it struck him that there was literally nothing else he could say about the man felled by a stroke in the line of duty.

One of Pedraza's grown sons coughed nervously, and a child began to cry. As Walter wondered what to do, there was a commotion in the crowd and a striking young woman dressed in black, her face pale behind a veil, threw herself on the coffin with anguished sobs. An angry murmur came from the family circle and the son stepped forward to lead her away. But another man intervened, and they began to argue. At the podium, forgotten for the moment, Walter strained to hear what they were saying, but the words were lost in the scuffle.

As it turned out, the beautiful young woman was not Pedraza's mistress, as many had assumed, but his daughter. A brief investigation revealed that Pedraza had another family altogether in Matanzas, with not just one but two daughters, and a son. Until the funeral, this fact had not been known by his family in Havana, or by anyone else outside of Matanzas. Pedraza had somehow managed to amass a considerable fortune, and his second family wanted their just share.

At the Havana Trust, Freddy gleefully thumbed through that week's issue of *Bohemia,* which Javier had dropped off.

"I never thought old Hugo had it in him," he said. "Listen to this, Pop. It says here that he had a *chinita* in Pinar del Río. No more kids, though."

Walter's stomach rumbled as he remembered Pedraza's frequent visits to the bank's branches throughout the island.

"She's a knockout, isn't she?" continued Freddy, showing his father the picture of the woman draped dramatically over the coffin. "Look, they even mention us."

"We don't need that sort of publicity."

That evening at the Floridita, Freddy commiserated with Javier:

"Pop really blew his stack. How did they find out about it, anyway?"

"Just bad luck," admitted Javier. "They sent a reporter to

photograph the tomb where the bomb was buried, and when the fight broke out, he came running."

"Right in the middle of Pop's speech, too. If only the police hadn't shown up."

"They sent the same reporter yesterday to talk to the woman in Pinar del Río," said Javier. "Who knows what he'll turn up?"

"Wait," said Freddy. "I've got an idea."

Later that week, they had lunch with Pepe Dominguez. He was suitably apologetic and promised that the Havana Trust would not be mentioned in any future coverage of the Pedraza affair.

"I'm afraid the damage has already been done," said Freddy darkly.

It was early afternoon and the advertising director of *Bohemia* was in an advanced state of dishevelment. The lapels of his jacket curled up around his sunken chest and a few strands of hair stuck to his damp forehead.

"What can I d-d-do?" he stammered.

So it was that *El Mono Sabio* premiered on station CMX from the Tokio Cabaret, co-sponsored by *Bohemia* and the Havana Trust. The small audience in the makeshift studio sat in folding chairs on the dance floor, while Professor Vargas sat at a small desk on the bandstand. The Conjunto Casablanca's first number was greeted with a round of applause, and then a beauty contest winner named Kiki Herrera asked the first question, from Ileana Diaz, a housewife in La Vibora:

"*Maestro*, when was the city of Havana founded?"

"Why that's an easy question, señorita," said Professor Vargas suavely. "But do you mean the founding of the city in its present site? That was established on November 25, 1519, and it was called Puerto de Carenas. But the first settlement was built on the southern coast, near Batabano, on St. Christopher's Day, four years earlier."

Listening to the radio that Freddy had placed in his office, Walter smiled at the sound of applause. But Professor Vargas continued:

"Between the founding of the two settlements, yet another Havana was built, at the mouth of the Almendares River. Is that the one you mean, my dear?"

El Mono Sabio quickly became a hit with listeners in Havana, and the magazine was deluged with letters containing obscure questions to befuddle Professor Vargas. Ironically, among the fans of *El Mono Sabio* was Emilio Aragon. One Saturday morning at the Havana Country Club, he admitted to Walter that on Fridays he took his lunch one hour later so as not to miss it. Across the fairway was Aragon's impressive new house, still under construction. It was an Italianate villa with a huge marble swimming pool and extensive gardens. The sienna walls were now finished, but stacks of red tiles lined the flagstones at the entrance.

"By the way, there's something I've been meaning to talk to you about," said Aragon.

He described to Walter a new real estate development on the beach just west of Jaimanitas. Plans had been drawn up to build a marina, a golf course, and even a hotel with a casino. It was to be called Altomar. Prosperity was just around the corner, and American tourists would soon return to the island. Aragon boasted that his resort would rival anything in Cuba, even the Hotel Nacional. In fact, President Machado himself was thinking of building a beach house there. Most of the financing had already been secured, but there might be room for an American bank like the Havana Trust.

"Are you interested, Huggins?" said Aragon, grasping Walter's elbow with a plump, sweaty palm. "Perhaps you should take a look at it."

"Perhaps I should," Walter replied.

Did the New York office want results? It was going to get them.

FIVE

Election Day came and went, although Hemingway cared little for either Roosevelt or Hoover.

Having finally put his bullfighting book behind him, he turned to several short stories that lay gathering dust in his steamer trunk. One was about his father, and he had started it in Europe but put it aside when the words wouldn't come. His father had been a doctor and Hemingway remembered his enigmatic, hawk-like eyes, keen yet somehow empty. Those eyes were expert at spotting quail, instinctively finding their usual cover and knowing when they would shoot up in a blur of feathers. But when he tried to describe his father's eyes, Hemingway stopped mid-sentence.

His oldest son Bumby visited, and they celebrated Thanksgiving with Pauline's family. In the fields outside of Piggot, the cotton had already been picked, and the rows of corn stalks were streaked with red sorghum. Driving with Bumby, he remembered how his father taught him to shoot. It was important not to stand between the quail and their usual cover, he warned, or else they would pop out of the thicket and the only shot would be over the shoulder. But that was many years ago, long before the poison seeped into his brain, when his father was strong and vigorous. Even then, was his death written on the lines of his face, if only he had been able to read it? The story lay inside him, Hemingway knew. All he had to do was wait for it to emerge, just as his father had waited for the quail.

Back in Key West, there was still much to do in the house. The carpenters were building a catwalk that stretched over the yard from Hemingway's bedroom to his writing studio, and Pauline insisted on having the plumbing redone. The workmen tramping in and out irritated him and he caught a train to New York, where he spent a couple of weeks at the Brevoort Hotel. At the taxidermist's, Hemingway picked up a bearskin that was shipped from Wyoming. He had shot it one snowy night in the mountains and it measured eight feet long from paw to paw.

As the Masons had suggested in Havana, he called their friend Dick Cooper, who offered to meet him at a speakeasy on 49th Street. Hemingway walked from the hotel, rubbing his hands in the chill night air, and asked a policeman where the Pigiron Club was.

"If you don't know, then you won't be welcome, pal."

Hemingway shrugged and asked several passers-by, none of whom knew. Finally, he slipped a few coins to a panhandler, who directed him towards an unprepossessing alley. Cooper had told him to ask for Studsy, and Hemingway was led down into a crowded, smoky basement.

"I was afraid you wouldn't make it, old man," said Cooper, trying to make himself heard over the wail of the saxophone. "Did you have trouble finding it?"

"These guys don't exactly advertise," said Hemingway.

Lighting a Turkish cigarette, the Englishman mentioned that he hoped to visit Grant and Jane in Havana:

"It's quite a town, what?"

"Depends who you know," replied Hemingway.

Squinting at his cocktail glass, Cooper said to the bartender:

"I don't precisely know what this is, but it's bloody marvelous. I'll have another."

"Make it two."

"Jane tells me you enjoy hauling big fish out of the water," said Cooper. "Frankly, I can't see the sport in it."

"It takes all kinds, I suppose. You hunt, do you?"

Soon, they were talking about Africa, and Hemingway recounted his plans to go on safari to Tanganyika in the fall. Cooper invited him to stay at his farm, and recommended he engage Bror Blixen as a white hunter.

"Absolutely the best!" he said cheerily. "But you must go elephant hunting, old man. Absolutely nothing like it. Once you hunt elephant, you won't want to hunt anything else. Once, I saw Blix drop a bull as he charged head on, tusks down, ears spread, trumpeting to open the gates of heaven, barely ten yards away. Do you know what the blighter said to me? 'I couldn't let him come forever.' That's nerve, what?"

"I've never hunted elephant," growled Hemingway.

"I won't hold it against you," laughed Cooper. "But I understand that you actually climbed into the bullring last summer in Madrid."

"What on earth are you talking about?"

"Don't be bashful, Hemingway. You've got *cojones*, I'll grant you that."

"I was in Cuba last summer."

"I say, Studsy. Be a good chap and get me another one of these. Where were we? Oh, yes, the bullfight. I was told it left quite a nasty scar. Do you mind terribly if I see it?"

"I'm not a bullfighter," said Hemingway irritably. "I haven't been in Madrid for over a year. You must be mistaken."

"If you say so, old man," said Cooper affably.

Hemingway warily sniffed his drink.

"Who told you that I was in Madrid last summer?" he asked.

"I forget his name. Some chap I met in Paris."

"Did he have a mustache?"

"I don't recall. Why don't we drop it?"

"You brought it up," said Hemingway. "I'm going to tell you a secret, Cooper. For the last few years, some bastard has been going around claiming to be Ernest Hemingway."

"But that's you, old man."

"I know that," snapped Hemingway. "He's an imposter! I've come close to catching him a couple of times and wringing his neck but he always slips through my fingers. It's a lousy business."

"Remarkable," mused Cooper. "But there's quite a bit you could get away with, if you catch my drift. Whatever happens, you simply blame it on the other bloody Hemingway."

"Let's drop it."

The next day, Hemingway caught the *Havana Special* back home. No sooner had he unpacked than he resumed work on his short stories, which he hoped to publish later that year. On most days, he awoke before dark and quickly dressed, careful not to wake Pauline. The catwalk to his writing studio had been completed, and he crept across it to begin work. The room above the carriage house had been replastered and painted sea-green, and on the polished wood floor was the bearskin, its glassy eyes staring at him vindictively. An old gateleg table had been hauled up to serve as his desk, and he sat upon a wooden cigar maker's chair.

Before long, the morning sun flooded the studio with light and a delivery truck sputtered down Whitehead Street. Pauline sent up his morning coffee, but had strict orders not to disturb him otherwise. The boys were playing in the yard and their voices floated up to him but he shut out the noise, concentrating on the empty page before him. When the going was good, the words flowed out of him effortlessly. Only later would he go back and revise what he had written in his rounded, almost girlish handwriting, changing a word, crossing out entire sentences, even ripping apart a page to start all over. Later, when it was typed, he would take a fresh look, often reading the words out loud to judge their cadence, and repeat the process, discarding the excess verbiage with the stroke of a pencil.

By lunchtime, Hemingway was nearly spent. He knew it was better to quit now, and start fresh the next day. That way, he could pick up easily where he left off, the well having replenished itself overnight. For the rest of the day he fished, usually with Charles on his powerboat, or with his sons from the pier. He offered the boys prizes for each catch, 25 cents for a tuna under 15 pounds, and $2.00 for a tuna over 30 pounds. For a sailfish, he promised them $5.00.

The Masons visited Key West together with Charlotte Eastlake, a slender girl with marcelled dark hair and pale green eyes. Charlotte was Jane's best friend and had just arrived from Paris after a row with her fiancé, Jack Halsey. Jane seemed refreshed and laughingly recounted that her picture had been taken by Cecil Beaton, and would be used in an ad for Pond's face cream to appear in *Ladies Home Journal*. There was a healthy glow in her cheeks, and no trace of the moodiness that Pauline remembered from the year before.

"Doesn't she look stunning?" said Pauline to her husband.

"If you say so," said Hemingway nonchalantly.

"I've never seen her look so lovely."

"Maybe she met someone new."

"Ernest, that's terrible!" she protested, though not without a smile.

Jane had taken up sculpture, and insisted on having Hemingway pose for her. She sat him atop a barstool and began shaping his head with gobs of modeling clay.

"I don't intend to sit here all day," he groused.

"Ernest, we've only just begun!"

"Call me Papa."

Jane had borrowed an old smock of Pauline's and her face was soon smudged with the dark green clay.

"Dick Cooper sends his regards," she said. "He told me you two got on swimmingly."

"You might say that. He threatened to visit you in Havana."

"I certainly hope not!" she joked. "I'm all yours this summer."

Hemingway grew weary of sitting still, and the modeling clay was put aside for the moment. That night, their guests joined them for a dinner of green turtle steak with black beans and yellow rice, and they drank several bottles of Tavel. Afterwards, in the garden, they finished another bottle of amber rum from Joe's seemingly never-ending stash.

"How are things in Cuba?" ventured Hemingway.

"Not too good, sport," said Grant. "Shooting in the street nearly every day, now."

"I've picked a fine time to visit," complained Charlotte.

"Ernest!" gasped Pauline. "Is it safe?"

"I've been shot at before," snorted Hemingway. "Besides, what would they want with me?"

"You never know," teased Jane.

"Really, Ernest. Why not go when all this passes?"

"How long can Machado hold out?" asked Hemingway, ignoring his wife.

"As long as he wants," replied Grant. "The army is behind him, and he's not afraid to break some heads. Those lunatics from the ABC have tried to blow him up once or twice, so he never leaves the palace except under armed guard. He's stopped paying the teachers, and every other day somebody goes on strike. One of these days, the whole thing will blow up. Roosevelt doesn't want him out until he repays the loans. He's picked a fellow named Sumner Welles to be the next ambassador. Don't know much about him, I'm afraid. Now, it's his problem."

"Some problem," said Hemingway. "Let the Cubans worry about it."

"Nonsense!" said Grant. "If Machado falls, then the whole house of cards comes tumbling down. At least he's somebody we can talk to. If the damned students take over, we'll have to go in with the marines. Now, to top it all off, the communists want to muck up the sugar harvest. It's terrible for business."

"Don't be banal, Stoneface," said Jane. "Is that all you can think of?"

"Politicians are all phonies," Hemingway concluded.

After the Masons returned to Havana with Charlotte in tow, the house was quiet once again. Hemingway's collection of short stories was complete save the one about his father. When he tried to write about Dr. Hemingway's death, he found it hard to remain at his chair. Behind the wire-rimmed spectacles he wore while writing, his eyes ached, and the muscles on his back grew sore from crouching over the desk. The rush of words had died down to a trickle, and he put the manuscript away. But the memory of his father's eyes wouldn't leave him. Even after fishing all afternoon with Charles in the Gulf of Mexico, he went home to Pauline only after several drinks. At night, he couldn't fall asleep, and often got out of bed before dawn to prowl through the half-paved streets. Soon, he knew, the marlin would be running within sight of El Morro.

Over a drink at the speakeasy, Hemingway agreed to charter the *Anita* once more. During the winter, Joe had added a fresh coat of green paint to the wheel house, and repaired the gashes in the hull made by swordfish. Charles was recruited, of course, and even Uncle Gus and Pauline's brother Karl agreed to come to Havana for a few days. In anticipation, Hemingway climbed into the cockpit and lovingly ran his hand along the gunwale, smelling the varnish. Out on the Gulf Stream, the *brisa* would clear his head and he would be able finish the story. Then he would go to Africa.

Over the holidays, O'Reilly Street was gaily decorated with colored lights, and many customers stared curiously at the frosted pine tree in the lobby of the Havana Trust. Freddy objected to the décor:

"It never snows here, Pop. Why don't we use a palm tree instead?"

"What kind of Christmas tree is that?" scoffed Walter.

As his son slinked away, Walter regretted his sarcasm. Freddy's radio show was a hit, and *El Mono Sabio* continued to be broadcast once a week from the Tokio Cabaret. Professor Vargas was indeed the smartest man in Havana, Walter had to admit, and many listeners who dropped questions off at the bank opened checking accounts.

Despite the untimely death of Hugo Pedraza and its scandalous aftermath, the year had begun well at the Havana Trust. The New York office had approved the financing of Altomar, although the groundbreaking ceremony had been put off until the current wave of shootings died down. Aragon had proudly shown Walter where the clubhouse would be, and pointed out the grove of scraggly palms where golfers would tee off.

"I'll reserve a berth for your yacht, Huggins," Aragon chuckled.

Walter's contentment was marred by a cable which arrived one afternoon at the Havana Trust from the redoubtable Commodore Halsey, the chairman of the board. The Commodore's military service had been limited to the presidency of the Oyster Bay Yacht Club, but his clipped, patrician tones never failed to intimidate Walter. He generally met with the Commodore at the annual board meeting in New York, but these were formal luncheons at the Harvard Club, beneath the stuffed kudu heads shot by Theodore Roosevelt on safari. Now, Commodore Halsey informed him that his son Jack would be passing through Havana on his way home from Paris. Walter had met Jack Halsey and his fiancée Charlotte Eastlake the year before in Paris, but all the young man had talked about was bullfighting. Why was he coming to Cuba? Had he been sent by his father to check up on him?

"You spent some time with Jack," said Walter, taking Freddy aside. "What's he doing here?"

"It's hard to say, Pop."

"I don't want any shenanigans while he's in Havana."

"What could go wrong?" said Freddy nonchalantly.

The afternoon Jack was due to arrive, Freddy waited as the ocean liner slowly nosed into its berth, and soon recognized him coming down the gangplank. Having shaved his mustache, Jack looked boyish, with a lock of dark hair hanging over his forehead.

"Welcome to Havana!" Freddy called out.

"Is that where I am?" quipped Jack.

Jack's luggage was loaded into the car, and they were soon on their way to the Hotel Nacional. But Jack insisted on getting a drink first, and they stopped at the Floridita.

"So what does a fellow do around here for fun?" he asked.

"Just about anything he wants," replied Freddy. "You're going to love this place."

"I already do," said Jack, sipping the daiquiri that Constante had placed before him.

"That's Ernest Hemingway's favorite drink," said Freddy.

"Hemingway?" said Jack, raising one eyebrow.

"The writer," explained Freddy. "His pals call him Papa."

"Of course they do," said Jack. "I knew him in Paris, in a manner of speaking. A frightful bore, really. All he wanted to talk about was bicycle racing. I was the one who suggested he go to Pamplona."

"No fooling?"

"A number of people have told me that I resemble him. Physically, I mean. On certain occasions, I've even been mistaken for him. Isn't that droll?"

Freddy couldn't imagine how anyone would think he was Hemingway.

"Never mind," said Jack. "I don't think I look like him, either."

Freddy explained that he was invited to dinner that night at his parents' house. After a few more drinks, he dropped Jack off at the Hotel Nacional.

"How is he?" asked Walter anxiously when Freddy returned to the bank.

"Same old Jack. I left him at the hotel to freshen up."

"Is he sober?"

"He was when I left."

Later that evening, Freddy collected him at the Hotel Nacional, and they soon arrived in Miramar.

"If it isn't the beautiful Mrs. H.," said Jack, giving Beryl a kiss on the hand.

Beryl blushed scarlet as he bowed with a flourish before the twins, saying:

"And how are the little missies?"

Mystified, Betty and Barbara exchanged giggles.

The evening proceeded smoothly as Jack recounted his adventures in the bullring.

"It sounds very dangerous," said Beryl, as the girls looked on wide-eyed.

"Well, it is," said Jack, pointing at his side, "and I've got the scar to prove it. Would you like to see it? A little deeper, and I wouldn't be here enjoying this wonderful tuna noodle casserole. They don't have bullfighting here, do they?"

Walter shook his head.

"C'est dommage," shrugged Jack, and deftly poured a shot from his hip flask into his glass of iced tea.

"How do you fight the bull?" asked one of the twins.

"There's nothing to it," he cried, and directed Betty to charge him, a forefinger on either side of her pig-tailed head. Jack took off his jacket and executed a graceful *verónica* as she passed, and solemnly intoned: "Now comes the moment of truth."

"Girls!" broke in Beryl. "It's well past your bedtime."

Jack grew more subdued after the twins left and stifled a yawn. After another iced tea, he sagged back on the couch.

"Jack?" said Walter.

Freddy rushed over and patted his cheek.

"Out like a light."

"Should we call a doctor?" asked Beryl.

"Let him sleep it off," advised Freddy.

Walter suggested they move him into the guest room, but Freddy said:

"Believe me, Pop. He'll be better off at the hotel."

Walter and Freddy each took a limp arm and dragged him to the car.

The next afternoon, Jack presented himself at the Havana Trust with a pink carnation in this lapel.

"I'm glad to see you're all right," said Walter guardedly.

"Why is that?" said Jack with a puzzled expression.

Walter and his son glanced at each other as Jack admired the model of the *HMS Victory* in Walter's office, running his forefinger along the hull, and counting the cannons.

"Ka-boom!" he said.

Walter warmed to the subject, explaining its role in the Battle of Trafalgar and pointing out the mother-of-pearl inlay where Lord Nelson fell. Jack nodded distractedly and moved on to the old engraving behind Walter's desk of La Margarita, the sugar mill owned by the bank.

"I've heard about this place."

"If you're staying a few days, I'd love to take you. The *zafra* has just started."

"That's swell, Mr. H.," said Jack, taking a swig from his hip flask.

He strolled about the office with a wink at Walter's secretary and then looked at his wristwatch:

"About that time, isn't it?"

His visit to the Havana Trust concluded, Jack repaired to the Floridita with Freddy.

"How about two of those *Papas Especiales*, my good man," he said to Constante.

Several rounds later, Javier came in and found them at the bar.

"Freddy tells me that you've gone fishing with Heming— Papa, that is," said Jack.

Javier nodded warily.

"What did he do in Havana besides fish?"

"Drank mostly," said Javier, "right where you're sitting. He also spent quite a bit of time with the Masons."

Seeing Jack's expression change, Freddy said: "Do you know the Masons?"

"Do I ever," said Jack, snapping his fingers for another daiquiri. "Jane is best friends with my ex-fiancée Charlotte. She and that booby Grant are the last people I want to see. You won't tell them I'm here, will you?"

"Not on your life," said Freddy.

"Another round, *mon ami.* This time, add some sugar."

It was then that Jack turned his attention to Leopoldina la Honesta:

"Now what do we have here?"

It was not until late the following morning that Freddy presented himself at the Havana Trust.

"Well, well," chuckled his father. "Look what the cat dragged in."

Walter's secretary brought him a cup of coffee and Freddy sipped it gratefully.

"Did Jack have a good time?"

"I don't know, Pop. I suppose he did."

"What do you mean, son?"

"Well, Pop—"

"Get on with it!" snapped Walter.

"I lost him."

"You what?" cried Walter, and felt a queasy rumble in his stomach.

"Like I said, Pop, I lost him."

"You'd better explain yourself, young man."

"It's a long story," began Freddy. "We left the bank to go to the Floridita since he kept asking about Papa—Hemingway, that is—and that's his favorite place. Anyway, we have a few drinks and Javier joins us, and then we have a few more drinks."

"Hmm," growled Walter.

"At the bar, we meet up with a friend of ours and—"

"Who?" demanded Walter.

"Just a friend, Pop. She has a couple of friends with her and we buy them drinks. You know how it is. Well, maybe you don't. That Jack's really something. Do you know that he dropped out of prep school and rode the rails? A hobo tried to— Anyway, by then we're getting hungry, so we go to El Pacífico, all six of us. Jack had heard about the opium den and—"

"Hell's bells!" cried Walter. "What opium den?"

"It's just for the tourists. The real opium den is on Zanja and—"

"Never mind!"

"Well, you wanted to know."

"Just get on with the story!"

"Let me tell it my way, Pop, or I'll get confused. So there we are at El Pacífico. Jack loves Chinese food, you know. During dinner he starts doing his bullfight routine with a tablecloth and a skewer. Do you know that he's a real bullfighter? He said that Hemingway stole the plot of his novel from him. Anyway, he nearly gores a waiter, so we have to leave in a hurry. We get in my car and—"

"All six of you?"

"Right. We drive to the Rumba Palace in Marianao to hear El Chori and—"

"Who's that?"

"El Chori's a *timbalero* who does a number with a frying pan and a Coca-Cola bottle you wouldn't believe. So there we are at the Rumba Palace, and Jack starts telling war stories. Do you know that he fought with the Arditi in World War I? That was after he drove an ambulance. He got wounded on the— Anyway, he tries to show his scar to a lady at the next table, and her husband takes a swing at him, and we have to leave before the police show up."

"Go on," said Walter grimly.

"Then we go to Chateau Madrid and Jack jumps on the dance floor with Leopol—our friend—and starts to rumba.

173

Then he tries this trick where he dances with a glass of water on his head. Have you ever seen that? Anyway, he spills it on this soldier and his fiancée, so we have to leave there, too."

"Is that where you lost him?"

"I'm getting to that! Everyone's hungry, since we never finished dinner at El Pacífico. Javier knows this place in Jaimanitas that's open all night, but Jack doesn't want to go because he might run into the Masons."

"What do they have to do with it?"

"That's a long story, too. Anyway, we head back to Havana, and try to get into the bar at the Sevilla-Biltmore. The manager takes one look at Jack and doesn't let us in, so we go to the Café Diana. They were just about to close, but Jack offers to pay the band to keep playing and orders champagne and starts arm wrestling with these sailors at the bar. By then, Javier had left, and I had to go to the bathroom. When I come back, they're gone!"

"Jack and the young ladies?"

"Jack and the sailors! The girls are still there, and they're hopping mad. The band wants to get paid, so they're mad, too. Then the waiter brings the bill for all the champagne, and—"

"And what?"

"Never mind. Anyway, I figured he'd gone back to the Hotel Nacional, so I went there this morning, but his room hadn't been slept in."

"Where is he?" cried Walter.

"I don't know."

Walter sagged back in his chair, and felt a trickle of sweat on the back of his neck.

"Don't worry, Pop," Freddy reassured him. "He's bound to turn up. After all, where could he go?"

The day Jane was to return from Key West, Javier anxiously passed by Tejadillo Street.

"Sorry," said Basil. "She wired that she wouldn't arrive till tomorrow."

Javier dejectedly started to walk out but Basil said:

"Hey, not so fast! You can take me out to lunch, can't you?"

Basil suggested the Lafayette Hotel, where they sat at the bar. Basil slurped down a glass of tiny oysters from Sagua la Grande, while Javier settled for a Cuban sandwich.

"You should try these," said Basil, ordering more oysters, which he doused with lemon juice and Tabasco. "They might do you some good."

"I don't think they'd help."

"I've got a question for Professor Vargas," said Basil. "When did they build the *buzón*?"

"The *buzón*?"

"You know, the big stone mailbox in the Plaza de la Catedral. It's the Roman god Janus, and you drop the letter in his mouth. What happens if he doesn't get the right answer?"

"You win dinner for two at the Floridita," said Javier gloomily, putting his sandwich aside after only a few bites.

"You've got it bad, don't you?"

"Does it show?"

"Only when you try to hide it," said Basil, spearing the last slippery oyster at the bottom of his glass with a fork.

Javier stopped by again at the end of the week, and his heart raced when he saw Jane behind the counter. Beside her was Charlotte Eastlake, peering at the statue of Oyá.

Jane introduced her friend and put in, "I was hoping you'd come by."

"Haven't we all," said Basil.

Jane stuck her tongue out at him and announced that they were terribly late. As she left, she whispered to Javier:

"Four o'clock."

That afternoon, Javier waited for her in Freddy's apartment. There was no need to look out the window, since when she arrived, he would hear the roar of the engine as the Chevrolet turned into Neptuno Street, and the click of her high heels against the pavement. Nonetheless, every time a car passed he jumped to the balcony. After a few minutes, he told himself she wasn't coming. Only when there was a knock on the door did he change his mind.

"Hello you," said Jane.

Javier flung the door open and lifted her over the threshold, like a bride. They stumbled to the bed and made love with their clothes still on, her skirt hitched up around her hips, his trousers fallen to his ankles.

"You don't waste time, do you?" Jane laughed breathlessly. "I'm glad I knocked on the right door."

It was only then they undressed, and Javier lay beside her until he felt himself stiffen and they made love again. Afterwards, he lay back against the pillows and watched her comb her hair before the mirror. As Jane dusted her cheeks with powder, he caught a glimpse of her face in the mirror. Her expression was shrewd and calculating, as though sizing up her own imperfections.

"I couldn't wait to see you again," he said.

"Key West was delightful," said Jane. "Ernest sends his regards."

"Did you think of me?"

"Of course I did, darling," said Jane briskly.

"Do you mean it?"

After a last stab of dark red lipstick, Jane turned away from the mirror and sat on the edge of the bed.

"Silly boy," she said, placing a finger on his lips. "Not another word out of you. You'll ruin everything. Ernest is coming back to Havana, you know."

"I don't want to talk about him."

"Don't be tiresome, darling," said Jane, putting on her gloves. "By the way, we're expecting you for cocktails. I've told Charlotte all about you."

"Does she know Jack Halsey was here?"

"No," said Jane, her eyes wide with surprise, "and neither did I. How on earth did you meet him?"

Javier recounted Jack's adventures in Havana, including his mysterious disappearance. Despite Walter's desperate efforts to find him, Jack didn't turn up until several days later, fresh as a daisy after a good night's sleep.

"Where did he go?"

"We never found out. I don't think he remembered."

"That's Jack for you. Is he back in New York?"

"I suppose."

"Let's not tell Charlie just yet, shall we? She'd take it rather hard. The poor dear has had a terrible time and I'm counting on you to be nice to her. She's perfect for you, by the way."

That night, Javier drove to Jaimanitas. Armando led him out to the verandah, where Grant awaited him in white tie and tails. The heat had wilted the mango blossoms, and they lay withered on the lawn, but the garden was fragrant with night-blooming jasmine.

"What will you have, sport?"

"Whatever you're having."

Soon, Armando returned with a pitcher of martinis, and Grant raised his glass in a toast:

"Here's to Cuba!"

"Then we'd better make it a double."

"Do you know that every time I leave I miss it terribly?" laughed Grant. "I sometimes think I'm becoming Cuban myself. I heard a great expression the other day at the American Club. When you go native here, you're *aplatanado*. Imagine that!"

"Many Cubans would like nothing better than to leave," said Javier.

At that point, the ladies made their appearance, Jane in a silvery gown by Poiret, and Charlotte in a black Chanel *robe du soir*.

"We're drinking to Cuba," announced Grant as Armando poured a round of martinis.

"Is there bullfighting here?" asked Charlotte.

"Don't be silly, dear," said Jane.

"I hope I never see another matador again."

"Why not?" asked Javier.

"That's a long story," said Jane, changing the subject.

"Things are topsy-turvy here, aren't they?" said Charlotte. "In Cuba, I mean."

"Plus ça change, plus c'est le même," said Jane.

"That's very true, darling," said Grant. "Someone said that if there were no Cubans, you would have to invent them. No offense, sport."

"None taken," said Javier.

"I've warned Charlie about Cuban men, but I don't know if she'll take my advice."

"I'm not a very good Cuban, anyway," said Javier.

"Why not?" asked Charlotte, as Armando refilled her glass.

"We Cubans are supposed to be happy. Isn't that what the tourist brochures say? I'm miserable most of the time."

"But that's just it!" exclaimed Jane. "The smile is just a mask. Cubans are really rather melancholy. Isn't that right, darling?"

They were soon on their way to the Sans Souci, a nightclub on the Calzada de Marianao. The tables were arranged around the bandstand in the garden, and the waiters moved between them with precision. Grant ordered champagne with dinner, and when the orchestra began to play, they danced beneath the illuminated royal palms. Charlotte was a good dancer and rested her cheek against Javier's chin. Her perfume was sweet and cloying, unlike Jane's, which was tart and lemony. Then they switched partners.

"This is torture," Javier whispered.

"Don't be banal, darling," said Jane.

The waiter began to prepare dessert, an elaborate Crêpes Suzette. He sprinkled rum in the pan, and there was a flash of blue flame.

"Another bottle of champagne," said Grant.

Jane pointed out a table of Cuban army officers at the other end of the dance floor and said to Grant:

"Look, Stoneface, there's Captain Segura! I don't think that's his wife, either."

Beside him was a stunning young woman in a yellow satin gown, her hair falling to her bare shoulders.

"Honestly, darling," said Grant. "What do you expect? I've heard she used to dance at the Alhambra."

"Who's Captain Segura?" asked Charlotte.

"Just another of Jane's boyfriends," said Grant. "Quite an amusing fellow, really. We had a bit of a problem at the airport and he took care of it."

"I'm sure he did," said Javier.

"What do you mean by that?" said Jane crossly. "I happen to know he's very well regarded at the embassy. I believe you're jealous."

"I'm afraid she's got you there, sport," laughed Grant.

"Be quiet," hissed Jane, pushing back her chair. "I'm going to ask him to dance."

"Have you gone mad?" said Grant incredulously. "This isn't New York, you know. That just isn't done here. What will people think?"

"Who cares what they think?" said Jane, studying her face in her compact as the waiter looked on. "Why shouldn't I ask him to dance? Are you going to stop me?"

"Don't," said Grant, laying a hand on her arm.

Jane pulled it back as though stung, and Grant looked around himself in embarassment.

"Janie, you said you weren't going to play these games any more. Say something, Charlotte!"

The impasse was broken when Captain Segura stood up and made his way towards them.

"My compliments, Señora Mason, you are lovely as ever," he said, nodding to Grant and gallantly kissing Jane's hand. Captain Segura then bowed to Charlotte and pointedly ignored Javier. "In your honor, I've asked the orchestra to play a *milonga*. I dared hope you would join me. With your permission, of course, Señor Mason."

"Of course, Segura. Why not?" huffed Grant.

The orchestra began to play, and they tangoed across the parquet floor with long, languorous paces. The other dancers made room until they had it to themselves.

"The nerve of that fellow," said Grant, storming off.

"They're quite a couple, aren't they?" asked Charlotte.

Javier shrugged and picked at the forgotten Crêpes Suzette.

"I'm hardly one to talk," Charlotte continued. "You don't need to keep your secret any longer. Jane told me that Jack was in Havana."

"Was he ever."

"We're quite a couple as well," Charlotte sighed.

"Why don't you drop him?"

"I did, you know, but I suspect we'll get back together."

"Why?"

"I suppose I was brought up to marry someone like Jack. It's all Jane and I know how to do, really. Do you understand?"

"No."

"I didn't expect you to."

On the last day of his life, Captain Segura rose early, as was his habit, and rode his favorite chestnut mare.

By mid-morning, the sun would cast sharp shadows on the hills, and the palm trees would shimmer in the heat.

But now the air was still cool, with the tang of freshly mowed grass. The bridle path led past the golf course of the Havana Country Club, and he could see the splendid new mansion of Emilio Aragon. It was nearly completed, and the gardeners were planting a row of orange trees by the long gravel driveway. Aragon was a close friend of General Ibañez, but the two men couldn't present a greater contrast. While Aragon was ebullient, with a great booming laugh, the general rarely smiled. In the war, General Ibañez had led a daredevil charge against the Spaniards near Bayamo, but now was pear-shaped and balding, with a bushy white mustache.

It was General Ibañez who had introduced him to the millionaire, and he remembered the night well. They were celebrating at the Jockey Club, and Aragon's fleshy hand was draped over the delectable thigh of Fina Lugones. She was a petite brunette with intoxicating dark eyes, and she had changed much since Captain Segura had seen her last, on the stage of the Teatro Payret. Now, she played the part of a rich man's mistress to perfection, wearing a mink stole despite the balmy heat. Pretending not to know him, she turned away with a bored expression.

Since then, he had seen Aragon quite often, and had been able to help him on several delicate matters. Aragon had returned these favors, and it was he who owned Nely's apartment on Dragones Street. He also invited him to his *encerrones*, scandalous parties where the guest were literally shut up in one of his many houses, with enough food, drink, and women to last for several days. There, he had renewed his acquaintance with Fina Lugones, if somewhat discreetly.

Captain Segura soon patted the mare's glossy flanks and turned back towards Camp Columbia, where he joined his wife and young daughter for breakfast. The early morning calm was fleeting and at exactly nine o'clock he crossed the parade ground to the office of General Ibañez. During the night, the general informed him, a crude bomb had exploded in the Vedado, killing a young man. This had become a common occurrence, but in this case, it was apparently an accident.

"No doubt the *expertos* have been there already," said General Ibañez drily. "But perhaps you will find something they missed."

Captain Segura remained at attention, waiting for the old man to continue. The general's contempt for Chief of Police Ainciart was well-known, and he had often mocked his effeminate manner as well as his warnings of a conspiracy to topple the government. But since the murder of Clemente Vazquez Bello, the army had begun to take the ABC seriously, and there had been attempts on the lives of several officers as well.

As General Ibañez returned to the papers on his desk, Captain Segura clicked his heels and saluted crisply. Soon, he was soon leaving Camp Columbia in the black Cadillac driven by his chauffeur. In the Vedado, the police had already erected a barricade around the house where the explosion took place, and held back an eager crowd of onlookers.

Captain Segura immediately recognized Sergeant Crespo—the one they called El Zurdo—guarding the door. Were the stories they told about him in the barracks true? He was called El Zurdo not because of the scar on the left side of his face but because his right testicle was shriveled and small as a raisin. The scar came from a knife fight with a Mexican pimp over a woman on Pila Street. It was rumored that El Zurdo had been the one who killed the young couple after Ainciart was finished with them. Esnard was guilty of nothing more than publishing a harmless broadsheet, and nothing could be proved against the girl, but the Chief of Police had decided to set an example. That had been a mistake, since it had given the opposition two valuable martyrs. No doubt El Zurdo had been following orders, but Captain Segura wondered if he enjoyed his work. The *experto* scowled impassively at him, his hand resting on the holster at his hip, and the two men locked eyes until he finally stepped aside with a grudging salute.

Inside, there was little to be seen. The bomb had exploded in the kitchen and blasted a hole in the wall, revealing the twisted pipes in the blackened plaster. The mangled corpse had two charred stumps where his arms had been, and his features were unrecognizable. There had apparently been no one else in the house at the time of the explosion. Captain Segura turned over the body with the tip of his boot and spat on the floor. He could expect little help from the *expertos*, and he was certain they would immediately report his presence to Ainciart himself. So much the better.

The Chief of Police was nothing if not meticulous, and no doubt his men would comb Havana for the remaining members of the cell. The dead boy's parents would be questioned, and their house would be searched. His friends would be watched and taken to the dungeons of Atarés if they were suspected of being *abecedarios*. His neighbors would be interrogated in case they had seen something. Anyone who had been seen with him in recent days would be arrested.

Captain Segura's report that afternoon to the general was succinct. The dead boy had been identified from the papers in his wallet as a law student named Bobby Diaz, who lived with his parents in Miramar. There was nothing to link him to the ABC, and he could very easily have belonged to any number of student groups, including the Directorio. The boy was an amateur, and that had been his undoing. But the *abecedarios* were fanatics, not professionals, and that was their greatest strength. Captain Segura was certain that his confederates had fled or gone into hiding. They had been planning something, of that he was sure. But for whom was the bomb intended? There was no way to know.

General Ibañez appeared to consider this, and carefully stroked his chin.

"Perhaps Ainciart was right, after all," he said. "These people are dangerous and unpredictable. You will continue to keep me informed on the progress of the investigation."

Captain Segura was about to take his leave when the general looked up unexpectedly and said:

"Be careful, Captain. The hunter can easily become the hunted."

It was not until later that evening that he was able to stop by Dragones Street. Having dismissed his chauffeur, he drove his own car, and parked it across the street from the Hotel New York.

When Captain Segura first saw Nely Chen at the Alhambra, he was astounded by her beauty. She was slender, with the supple body of a dancer, but had fulsome breasts for a *chinita*. Because of her olive skin, straight dark hair, and pale green eyes, she could pass for white, but her lips were astonishingly full with a mocking pout. Captain Segura was a connoisseur of beautiful women, and congratulated himself upon having discovered her before someone like Aragon. Nely had just arrived from Santiago de Cuba, and was kept by Adolfo Ibarra, who played *negrito* in blackface at the Alhambra. But when the actor made one too many jokes about Machado onstage, he was arrested by none other than El Zurdo. Nely pleaded for his life, and Captain Segura secured his release from Atarés on condition that he leave Cuba immediately. However, it was impractical to arrest all her other lovers, including the son of an American bank president and a wealthy young Spaniard. Although he was not a jealous man, he solved this problem by ending her theatrical career, and moved her from the seedy *solar* to Aragon's apartment on Dragones Street.

Nely was herself rather jealous of his other mistresses. There was a spectacular scene when she somehow learned that he had slept with Fina Lugones. Nely had thrown a bottle of rum at his head and left a vicious scratch on his cheek. Feeling the blood trickle down his face, he made a fist and knocked her down, almost as he would a man. Such encounters typically ended with a bout of passionate lovemaking, but this time Nely cried all night, holding a chunk of ice to her swollen jaw. In the morning, he found her muttering in Lucumí before the altar in her bedroom. It contained a figure of Oshún draped in yellow beads and peacock feathers. Was she casting a hex on Fina Lugones?

That was several months ago. Surprisingly, Nely had yet to learn of his latest find, a young *guajira* only recently arrived in Havana. Barely sixteen, she was a fair-skinned brunette from Guantánamo who worked as a seamstress in the Hotel Inglaterra. Captain Segura had seen her strolling in the Prado beneath an old fashioned parasol, probably discarded by a guest at the hotel. It was only a matter of time before Nely found out, however, and he was already planning ways of placating her.

Still more surprisingly, Nely did not make a fuss when he asked Señora Mason to dance at the Sans Souci, and appeared to have reconciled herself to his friendship with the beautiful *americana*. More than once, he had accompanied her to the Club Cazadores del Cerro, and he had to admit she was a crack shot, for a woman. Captain Segura found American women cold, and in this regard, Señora Mason was no different. Therefore, he was amused to learn that she was cuckolding her husband, although he had yet to learn the name of her lover. This piece of information could be useful some day, he thought. Despite her frigid demeanor, she had a wild, impulsive streak that intrigued him.

But that night, his thoughts were far from Señora Mason or the *guajira* from Guantánamo. When he arrived with his usual bouquet of yellow frangipanis, Nely took him to task over the time:

"Do you suppose that I'll always wait for you?"

"*Sí, mi chinita,*" said Captain Segura.

"You're quite mistaken."

"Am I, *mi chinita?*"

"You're very lucky that I'm still here. I could well have been out."

"Then I would have found you, *mi chinita.*"

185

She pushed him away and only after much coaxing did he persuade her to sit on his lap. But Nely was still petulant and said:

"Perhaps you're so busy that you don't have time for me."

"I have thought of you all day, *mi chinita.*"

"Did you think of Señora Mason as well?"

"No, mi chinita."

This failed to satisfy her and she scampered off his knees with feline grace.

"Really, you must learn to lie better than that," she taunted him.

"Why would I lie, *mi chinita?* You can read my thoughts."

It was a game he never tired of, a sly burlesque worthy of the Alhambra itself. By the time she permitted herself to be cajoled into bed, he had a painful erection and a telltale spot of moisture had appeared on his mustard-yellow uniform.

"I think you'd rather be with Señora Mason tonight," Nely continued even as she undressed. "Do you think of her as you make love to me? Or is there someone else who's caught your eye?"

"Do not torment me, *mi chinita.*"

Much later that night, weary from his exertions, Captain Segura glanced at his wristwatch. He had told his wife not to expect him home until the early hours of the morning, if at all. Outside the apartment, the street was deserted, and even the doorman of the Hotel New York was napping in the lobby. Captain Segura took a deep, satisfying breath. Playfully swishing his riding crop through the air, he contemplated the marble dome of the Capitolio, which gleamed in the violet sky. It had been built atop a garbage dump, and had no doubt lined the pockets of Machado's cronies. Greed would topple it one day, as it would Machado. With a bit of luck, he would be there to pick up the pieces.

Lost in this pleasant reverie, Captain Segura failed to hear the squeal of tires until it was too late. By then, he was on the run, pulling out his Luger. He realized he would not reach the safety of his car in time, and heard the *bop-bop-bop* of the Thompson as the shots ripped through his chest. The force of the bullets flung him to the ground, and as he fell he tried to fire in the direction of the speeding car, but the heavy revolver slipped from his grasp. He tried to lift himself up and crawl towards his gun, but his hands were slick with his own blood and he collapsed once more on the pavement.

Havana 1933

"Did you see the [revolution] in Cuba?"
"From the start."
"How was it?"
"Beautiful. Then lousy. You couldn't believe how lousy."

Ernest Hemingway, *Green Hills of Africa*

SIX

In 1933, Fred Astaire was all the rage in Havana.

Having tired of Carlos Gardel and newly disdainful of the tango, Mirta Rivero dreamed of tap dancing on the wings of an airplane high above Copacabana. Her best friend Lydia López Angulo dutifully accompanied her on Saturday afternoons to the Teatro Fausto, where *Flying Down to Rio* was playing. But no sooner had the lights dimmed than a tear ran down her cheek and she sobbed all through the movie.

"Shhh!" said Mirta, who was beginning to lose patience.

"I can't help it," sniffled Lydia.

"You're too good for Roberto."

"I don't care. I still love him!"

After Lydia returned from Spain, Roberto had been cold and distant. The last time she saw him, he had been walking in the Prado and rushed past without saying hello. Mirta told her to forget him, just as she had Carlos Gardel and before him, Maurice Chevalier. But at the thought of Roberto, Lydia burst into tears. This turmoil soon reached the López Angulo household in the Vedado. Doña Inés was alarmed at her daughter's fits of weeping and complained to her husband.

"I'll speak to the boy's father!" cried Don Ramón.

"You'll make yourself look ridiculous," said his wife, clearly alarmed at the prospect. "Are you going to challenge him to a duel or something?"

The thought of an affront to his dignity silenced Don Ramón, who agreed the matter was best left to her. Doña Inés had lunch with Lourdes Perez at the Havana Yacht Club, and found her equally distraught.

"Inés, I'm afraid to show my face in your house," she admitted.

Not only had Roberto insulted the family of such a lovely girl as Lydia, he had been seen with Alberto Zayas Bazán, who was hiding from the police. What's more, he was rumored to be an *abecedario!* Lourdes and her husband were worried sick that he would be killed like poor Raúl Esnard. Her sister lived in Caracas, and they had tried to get him out of the country, but he refused, saying Cuba needed him.

"Can you imagine that?" cried Lourdes, nearly in tears. "Now, he thinks he's José Martí!"

"*Cada loco con su tema,*" said Doña Inés, shaking her head sadly. [To each his own.]

Doña Inés came home from the Havana Yacht Club resigned to the worst. She took Lydia to visit her family in Trinidad. The Angulos had lived for generations in the house off the Plaza Mayor which still bore their coat of arms, a fierce-looking bat. Doña Inés hoped that a change of scenery and the cool air of the Escambray mountains would make her forget Roberto, but the sadness in the girl's eyes only deepened. What's more, Lydia returned to Havana with a surprising resolution. She had decided to study in the United States, like her brother, and applied to Smith College. This prospect alarmed Doña Inés even more than Lydia's crying spells, and she dreaded the day her husband found out. Once again, she prevailed upon Javier, who was even gloomier than usual.

"What about Freddy Huggins?" she asked, having been impressed with his manners.

"What?" cried Javier.

But his mother would not be put off and Javier knew it was best to humor her.

Needless to say, the evening ended like the *Fiesta de Guatao*. Lydia looked lovely, if a bit severe, wearing a black lace shawl from Madrid. Javier had to admit that Mirta was charming, wearing her hair like Ginger Rogers, and Freddy had turned out in a freshly starched *dril cien* suit and a bowtie. They forsook the Floridita for the more sedate Zaragozana, and the girls ordered champagne cocktails before dinner. Out of the corner of his eye, Javier watched Mirta's plump, perfumed hand creep closer to his on the tablecloth.

Afterwards, they had a pleasant stroll up the Prado to the Malecón. In the winter, the northers sent the waves crashing over the seawall and often closed off the boulevard to traffic. That night, the wind had picked up and they stepped back as the spray threatened to drench them. Freddy suggested they take in the show at the Tokio Cabaret.

"You're on your best behavior tonight!" said Javier sternly, out of his sister's hearing.

"Trust me," said Freddy.

Mirta was delighted, since the Tokio Cabaret was somewhat risqué, and even Lydia brightened at the prospect.

At the door, they were greeted warmly and given one of the best tables, just across from the stage. Everyone in the smoky nightclub seemed to know Freddy, from the waiter to the cigarette girl, and a bottle of champagne was sent to their table. As the evening progressed, Freddy sat back and lit a Rey del Mundo, obviously pleased with himself.

Things took a turn for the worse when Zoila Martínez mounted the stage clad in a green sequined dress, to wolf whistles and much applause.

"What's she doing here?" whispered Freddy.

"I thought she was still at the Alhambra," replied Javier.

As it turned out, Zoila had been called in unexpectedly when her friend Omara Fuentes came down with a cold. Halfway through her first number, she saw Freddy and sashayed down among the audience, ruffling his hair as he squirmed uncomfortably.

"Does she know him?" wondered Lydia.

"Maybe she thinks he's someone else," said her brother.

Zoila's second number was a melancholy *habanera* entitled *Amor Perdido,* and as she sang she draped her feather boa over their table.

"Freddy, who is she?" asked Mirta.

The third and (as it turned out) last song was sung from Freddy's lap. When Zoila finished, she emptied what remained of the champagne on his head, extinguishing his cigar, and screamed vile imprecations in which Javier distinctly heard the name of Kiki Herrera.

"*¡Sinvergüenza!*" she cried triumphantly, and stormed off to a standing ovation.

On the way home, Lydia burst into tears and Mirta glared poisonously out the window. After dropping the girls off, Freddy looked so forlorn that Javier agreed to have a drink with him at the Floridita.

"It was all a misunderstanding," he said, a puddle of stale champagne forming on the floor.

"I warned you, Freddy."

"Holy mackerel! How could I have known Zoila was going to be there? Besides, there's nothing between me and Kiki. It's strictly a professional relationship."

"I'm sure of that."

After another drink, Javier agreed that Zoila *se botó* an untranslatable expression meaning that she went over the top.

"But she does have her good points," admitted Freddy.

"I'm sure of that, too," yawned Javier.

Freddy reluctantly dropped him off in the Vedado. The breeze had died down and the streetlights flickered against the colonnades of the houses. Lighting the cigar his friend had given him, Javier savored the calm of the moonless night. At the gate of his parents' house, he saw a flicker of movement.

"Who's there?" he called out.

There was no answer but as he approached he saw Roberto Perez crouched in the shadows.

"What are you doing here?"

"Please be quiet," the boy whispered.

Javier wanted to laugh at the sight of him, cowering like a frightened animal, but the urgency in his eyes stopped him.

"I need to see Lydia."

"*¿Estás loco?*" cried Javier. "It's a bit late for a social call."

"I have a letter for her."

"Lydia doesn't want to hear from you."

"*Por favor*," pleaded Roberto. "The police are after me."

They heard another car and Roberto flattened himself against the wall.

"Don't be absurd," said Javier. "What are you afraid of? Go home and come back tomorrow."

"I can't," said Roberto. "The *expertos* have already been there."

"What will you do?"

"A boat is coming for me tomorrow night. Until then, I need to hide."

"*Coño*," said Javier, and fried an egg.

His Model A was in the garage, and with Roberto crouching on the floorboards they drove through the Vedado. There was no traffic on the Malecón, but as they passed the Hotel Nacional they heard a snatch of music from the orchestra in the garden. Muralla Street was deserted save for a weary prostitute who looked at them hopefully but then turned away and headed for the waterfront.

"You'll be safe here," said Javier, opening the gate of the *almacén*. "No one comes here except my grandfather."

There was a musty smell of rat droppings in the courtyard which once bustled with delivery trucks. Javier turned on the light, a naked bulb on the ceiling, and led him up the stairs to one of the empty storerooms. Roberto went to sleep almost immediately, and that was how Javier fond him the next morning. Curled up on the dusty floor, he seemed innocent as a child, but in his hand was a pistol. Javier leaned over and plucked it from his fingers. As the church bells pealed outside, Roberto sat up with a groan and rubbed the sleep from his eyes before drinking the *café con leche* Javier had brought him.

"I've got to leave," he said, wiping his lips with his sleeve.

"Don't forget this," smiled Javier, holding the Smith &Wesson by the trigger guard.

Roberto tucked it under his belt, as he had seen George Raft do in *Scarface*.

"Did Lydia get my letter?"

"She gave me this," said Javier, handing him the note Lydia had given him in return. "Where will you go?"

Roberto shrugged and dusted himself off.

"You're not very good at this, are you?" said Javier. "No one knows you're here, but if the *expertos* are out you'll never leave Habana Vieja. Let's wait until it gets dark."

"Why are you helping me?"

"I'm the only chance you've got."

After Javier left, Roberto laid the revolver on the floor. His friend Frank gave him the news that Bobby Diaz was dead, killed while assembling the bomb they planned to detonate beneath Captain Segura's car. They had watched him for weeks, observing from the lobby of the Hotel New York each time he visited his mistress. But when the bomb exploded, the police began to arrest all suspected *abecedarios* and he spent the night at an apartment on San Rafael Street they kept for just this purpose. Frank said he would meet him there, but he grew restless and stepped outside. This was what saved him, since when he returned a police car was parked in front and several *expertos* stood guard. Had they arrested Frank? There was a number to call in case of an emergency, and an unknown voice told him that a boat would pick him up at a cove in Barlovento used by bootleggers and take him across the Florida Straits.

Roberto took out the letter Lydia had written on her violet stationery. It smelled faintly of lilac and he read it over and over again, as though the words could summon her voice. She promised to wait for him no matter what happened, as he hoped she would. Lydia wanted to study at Smith College, and perhaps he could take a train from Key West and meet her there. When it was all over, they would be able to return to Cuba.

A few hours later, Roberto heard footsteps on the stairs and undid the safety catch of the revolver. He squatted in the corner, his back to the wall, and pointed the gun at the door, but it was Lydia's brother. This time he brought dinner, a plate of fried rice and spare ribs from a nearby *fonda*. Roberto was ravenous and scarfed it down with greasy fingers.

"Captain Segura is dead," said Javier.

Roberto looked up from the remains of his plate.

"You don't seem very surprised," said Javier, and showed him that morning's edition of the *Diario de la Marina,* which showed his body lying in a pool of blood.

"Bien muerto, como perro," spat Roberto.

Alberto had finished the mission in his own way, he realized.

"He had a wife and a little girl. Did you know that?"

"I don't know anything about him except that he served Machado."

"That's all you need to know, isn't it? You and Alberto already know the answers, so you don't need to ask any more questions. What will you do when the killing stops?"

"Our goal is not just to eliminate Machado but also what brought him into existence. We Cubans must control our own destiny. When we're in power, we'll fight for social justice and political equality. We'll help the *guajiros* and nationalize the monopolies. We'll—"

"Is it worth dying for?" broke in Javier.

"It's worth killing for."

"We'd better go," said Javier tersely.

It was already dark and they drove south to avoid the police on the Malecón. The Via Blanca took them around El Cerro towards Marianao and the beaches to the west of the city. The road led past Jaimanitas and Javier caught sight of Jane's house. Was she there?

"Drop me off here," said Roberto when they reached Barlovento.

A path led down to a few shacks at the mouth of a mangrove-choked stream, and the bootlegger's cove lay just beyond the rise. Roberto climbed out of the Model A but stopped before starting down.

"Why don't you join us? We seek all Cubans with clean hands."

"Your hands are soaked in blood. You're no different from them."

"Before long you'll have to choose between us."

Javier watched him make his way down to the water, and soon Roberto was lost in the shadows. A car sped past, heading toward Jaimanitas, and he smelled the gasoline fumes mixed together with the briny sea air. Across the bay, he could see the lighthouse of El Morro, its beacon sweeping over the dark waves.

The night before he left Key West, Hemingway dreamed of the great blue river. It was there, he knew, just beyond the horizon, the royal blue water dotted with strands of gulfweed, whipped into eddies by the strength of the current. A few fathoms below, the marlin sped along the edge of the stream like silvery boxcars, flashing in and out of sight beneath the waves.

Hemingway had already packed, including the manuscript of his unfinished story, so there was little to do that morning except say goodbye. Pauline reminded him once more to book rooms at the hotel for Uncle Gus and Karl, who would be arriving next week, and to give her love to the Masons. His son Patrick was sullen because he wanted to come along on the *Anita,* and baby Gregory inexplicably broke into a wail and had to be taken upstairs by Ada, the nanny. As Pauline drove him to the Navy Yard, she reminded him of a few more things he had to do in Havana.

"What did you say?" said Hemingway, turning towards her absently.

Pauline realized he was caught up in the thrill of departure (as he was before every trip) and would forget everything she told him.

"Nothing at all, dear."

Hemingway stepped over the transom and saw that Charles was already aboard. Joe's son tossed them the bowline, and the *Anita* backed away from the rotting pier built for battleships but now used by shrimp boats. They soon passed the lighthouse at Sand Key, where two pelicans perched on the pilings. A fresh breeze propelled the clouds, like puffs of white smoke, across the brilliant sky and a plume of spray swept over the bow. Landfall was fifteen hours away, and Joe was at the wheel drinking coffee from his thermos, while Hemingway scribbled in his log and Charles sat in the shade of the wheelhouse.

"I hear there was another shooting in Havana last week," said Charles, running his long fingers through his hair.

"I hope they got the right guy," chuckled Hemingway, looking up from his writing.

"That's not funny."

"I didn't mean it like that," said Hemingway, to mollify his friend. "I don't think they'll be after us, do you?"

"I suppose not."

As night fell, the water turned a dark, shimmering purple. Hemingway saw a green sea turtle, far from home, scudding just beneath the surface, and the irridescent bubble of a

Portuguese man-of-war. They were making good time, nearly ten knots an hour, and by 1:30, they spotted the lighthouse of El Morro. Since it was a clear night, Joe decided to enter the harbor rather than wait until morning. To their left loomed La Cabaña, and they heard the familiar noises of the city floating over the water: the squeal of brakes, tinny music from a radio, and distant voices. At the edge of the pier, an old black man in a tattered straw hat lay upon a crate and looked at them indifferently before nodding off to sleep. Hemingway wanted to get a drink, but the gates of the customs house were closed and they couldn't get cleared until morning. Some water had splashed in through the porthole, and he reluctantly settled into his damp bunk.

When he opened his eyes, he realized the other bunks were empty, and heard Joe's gravelly voice on deck. Scrambling upstairs, he saw Charles on the wicker fishing chair, sipping coffee. It was a dazzling morning, and the sunlight sparkled on the greenish water of the harbor. Since last night, a black-hulled freighter had entered the channel and moored opposite Casablanca. Just off the pier, a fisherman standing on a skiff began pulling up his net, and it emerged from the water full of silvery *machuelos* which fell like coins at his feet. The *brisa* was already blowing to the east, and the seagulls floated lazily overhead.

While Joe dealt with the customs official in broken Spanish, Hemingway and Charles wandered into the Plaza de San Francisco. It was already noon, and the belltower of the church cast a narrow shadow. The clerks hurried out of the Lonja del Comercio on their way to lunch, and an old chinaman sold tamales from a gasoline can balanced on a pole, crying: "*¡Pican! ¡No pican!*" A horse-drawn carriage carried an American tourist over the cobblestones, with a ragtag group of little boys trailing behind. But there were fewer market stalls, and a bum sat disconsolately at the base of the fountain, holding out a bony, outstretched hand. Hemingway also saw more police than he remembered, in their familiar blue uniforms with black braid.

They walked to the Plaza de Armas, where soldiers with Springfield rifles stood guard in front of the American embassy. Obispo Street was as busy as ever, with a man in a Model T honking his horn as he attempted to maneuver around a *gallego* selling brooms from a pushcart. Making his way perilously between them, Hemingway checked into his old room on the fifth floor of the Ambos Mundos. At the desk, he found a cable from Pauline wishing him *bon voyage*, and a note from Jane inviting him to Jaimanitas on Sunday.

Charles and Joe decided to have a early dinner at the Perla, where for 10 cents they had a steak covered with onions and parsley, and a mound of *moros y cristianos* [rice and black beans] while Hemingway strolled up Obispo. The shoeshine boys on the corner of Compostela Street saw him coming and ran ahead yelling, *"¡El Hemingway! ¡El Hemingway!"* When he reached the Floridita, Constante already had a *Papa Especial* waiting for him. Javier and Freddy were at their usual spot, tossing a cup of poker dice for the next round.

"We've missed you, Ernesto," said Javier, disengaging himself from his bearhug.

"Call me Papa," Hemingway reminded him with a grin.

"Maybe you can help me," said Freddy, recounting his strange dream of the night before, when he found himself crossing Fifth Avenue, not in Miramar but Manhattan, and three riderless horses passed by. He ran after them, but they rounded the corner and vanished.

"Not a good sign," remarked Hemingway.

On Saturday, the winning lottery number would be picked by the orphans at the Beneficiencia, so Freddy had spent the morning scouring the *billeterías* on O'Reilly for lottery tickets containing either 53 or 35. Then it occurred to him that in the *Chino de la Charada*, the number corresponding to a horse was one. It followed that his lucky number was either 51 or 15.

"What do you think, Papa?"

"It's hard to say."

"Fifty-one plus fifteen is 66," calculated Freddy. "On the other hand, 53 plus 35 is—" he paused briefly "—88. Eighty-eight minus 66 is 22, and if you multiply 22 times three you get 66, right? Maybe that's it."

"If you say so, Tex," agreed Hemingway, hoisting his third daiquiri.

He asked the Trío Matancero to play *El Manisero*, and told them all that had happened since he left Cuba: the feverish crossing, the drive to Wyoming, fly fishing for cutthroat trout, his trip to New York, and the final, impatient days in Key West.

"Much has changed here," said Javier.

"For the worse?"

Javier looked over his shoulder uneasily.

"It's dangerous to discuss politics here," he said. "There are *apapipios* everywhere."

"Good!" boomed Hemingway, wiping the crushed ice from his mustache with the back of his hand. "There are many other things I'd rather talk about. How's your novel coming along?"

"I haven't written much lately."

"Neither have I. What's *your* excuse?"

"I'm afraid I don't have one. I don't know if I'll ever write a novel."

"Maybe you're better off, Harvard. It's the toughest racket there is. You need the dedication of a monk and the confidence of a trapeze artist. When I was your age, no one would even look at my stuff. Even now, a lot of what I write is crap."

"Then why did you become a writer?"

"I didn't have a choice. It hurts like hell to write, but the only thing that hurts more is not to write. There are many things I'd rather do, like fishing for marlin and drinking with my pals. But if I couldn't write, I couldn't bear the pain. I'd kill myself."

"Don't talk that way, Ernesto."

Hemingway shrugged and philosophically puckered his lips as the tart daiquiri slid down his throat.

"I know who you are," came a loud, whining voice from across the bar.

A fleshy man in a wrinkled seersucker suit staggered towards them. In one hand, he held a highball glass, and in the other a handkerchief with which he wiped his flushed forehead.

"You're the writer who's out to catch a giant marlin," he said. "Zane Grey, right?"

Hemingway stared straight ahead, finishing his daiquiri, but Javier noticed that the back of his neck had reddened. Freddy's eyes darted nervously from the tourist to the writer and back to the tourist, whose highball sloshed over his shirt as he wedged himself against the bar. Dabbing at his belly with his handkerchief, he said:

"What do you say I buy you a drink?"

"No, thank you," said Hemingway.

"I know we've met before," he said, leaning closer to the writer, his plump lips nearly touching his ear.

"What did you say?" asked Hemingway, putting down his empty glass, the muscles in his jaw twitching.

Javier had interposed himself between the two Americans, and took the tourist by the collar.

"Nerts to you!" the man squealed as he was propelled out of the Floridita, to the cheers of the shoeshine boys.

Javier returned to the bar straightening his tie, but Hemingway stared stonily ahead.

"I fight my own battles," he frowned. "When I want your help, I'll ask for it."

Javier's face fell and they drank in silence. Leaving the Floridita, they saw the tourist unceremoniously propped up against the marble statue of Francisco de Albear. A policeman stood above him, his arms akimbo. For dinner, Freddy suggested the rooftop of the Hotel Plaza, opposite the new Bacardi Building.

The breeze had died down, and it was a dank, humid night. From the restaurant, they looked across the Parque Central to the wedding-cake towers of the Centro Gallego. Javier and Freddy ate ravenously, but Hemingway had lost his appetite and mechanically chewed his steak. Finally, he pushed aside his plate and turned to Javier.

"Sorry," he grunted. "I don't know why I said that back there, but I did."

"He was just a drunk," said Javier.

"If we see that sap again, just step out of the way while I cool him."

Suddenly, there was a murmur of voices in the restaurant and Freddy put down his fork and cocked his ear. From the street below came a faint popping noise. Then there was silence, followed by the wail of a police siren.

"What's that?" asked Hemingway.

"It's the ABC," said Javier.

They leaned over the railing and saw the flashing lights of a police car in front of the Hotel Inglaterra. They heard another explosion, louder than the first, from the direction of the Malecón, and the sound of breaking glass. There were confused shouts and several people came running down the Prado, darting frantically in front of the cars. Several policemen stood on the corner, as confused as the people fleeing across the busy street. A truck pulled up and several soldiers jumped out with rifles. But from behind them, in the Parque Central, came a third explosion, followed by more screams. The normally frenetic traffic around the park had ground to a halt amid the blaring of klaxons and the shouts of angry drivers.

"The *expertos* will be busy tonight," said Freddy.

"It's a damn shame," muttered Hemingway.

"I told you things have changed," said Javier.

Hemingway continued to study the confusion below with a frown, but soon changed the subject: "Say, I brought my boxing gloves. If you haven't gotten too soft over the winter, we could go a few rounds tomorrow."

"*No, gracias.*"

"Too bad," said Hemingway, trying to hide his disappointment. "I still owe you another boxing lesson."

"I'll remember," said Javier.

The traffic had resumed by the time they left, although policeman were posted on the street corners and soldiers patrolled the Parque Central. Leaving Javier and Freddy, Hemingway walked in silence along Monserrate. But instead of turning toward the Ambos Mundos, he continued until he came to Dragones Street. More soldiers surrounded the Capitolio, and the policemen posted in front of the Hotel New York eyed him suspiciously. Would Nely be there? Her apartment was on the fourth floor, and he rapped lightly on the door. After a few minutes, the door opened a crack, and an unshaven man in an undershirt peered out. It occurred to Hemingway that she might be home, after all, but then another woman crowded behind him, her eyes wide with fear.

"Is Nely Chen here?" he asked.

The couple looked at each other questioningly and shook their heads no. Perhaps she had gone back to Santiago de Cuba when Captain Segura was shot. Hemingway muttered an apology and started back down the stairs, wondering if the Floridita was still open.

The next morning, he awoke to the *clickity-clack* of a horse's hooves on the street below and the mournful cry of a cock. His black mood of the night before vanished as he saw from his balcony that the sky was clear. Hemingway splashed cold water on his face and dressed in moccasins, khaki shorts held up by a rope, and his favorite striped fisherman's jersey. At the hotel desk, he bought a newspaper and read that during the night bombs had exploded not just in the Prado, but throughout the city. As he walked to the waterfront, the sun was beginning to rise over Casablanca, leaving a pinkish streak on the clouds at the end of the bay. First one, then two seagulls swooped low over the glassy water and glided down the middle of the channel before banking to the right towards La Cabaña.

"How do you like it now, gentlemen?" said Hemingway on the pier.

As Charles responded with a yawn, Hemingway heard footsteps and turned to see Carlos Gutiérrez. He gave him a strong *abrazo,* and the old fisherman showed him the bait he had brought wrapped in a crumpled newspaper: half a dozen gleaming *cero* mackerels, their eyes still clear.

"Today will be a good day, Don Ernesto," said Carlos, his melancholy eyes lightening.

The engine rumbled to life and the *Anita* was soon under-way. The channel was empty except for the fishermen jigging for kingfish and a bumboat making the early run to La Cabaña. Barely a quarter mile from the shore, Hemingway saw what Carlos called the *hilero*, the edge of the Gulf Stream: a line of dark blue water, like the border of another country. Squatting on the deck, Carlos gravely took a fish from the icebox and passed the hook through its mouth and out the gill, tying the mackerel's mouth shut with the leader. Then he tossed it overboard and handed the rod to Hemingway.

But no sooner was the bait in the water than the wind picked up and a wave crashed against the hull of the *Anita.* A pack of smoky grey clouds appeared on the horizon, and the seagulls overhead keened ominously. Another wave swept over the bow, drenching them with spray, and Hemingway steadied himself against the gunwale. Joe reluctantly turned the *Anita* around and they made their way back to the harbor. Hemingway dried himself with a towel as they docked, barely an hour after they left, and glared at Carlos.

"Mañana," said the old fisherman apologetically. *"Mañana seguro."*

By that afternoon the skies were clear, but it was too late to go out gain. They had drinks at Sloppy Joe's and feasted on lobster at the Miami Restaurant on Neptuno Street. As they stepped out into the Prado, Hemingway saw that soldiers in broad-brimmed hats were patrolling beneath the double row of laurel trees, and a machine gun had been set up at the entrance to the Parque Central. The explosions of the night before had not closed down the Alhambra, and Joe pointed out a poster announcing that night's performance. It was called *La Isla del Encanto*, and featured a dancer billed as La Chinita.

"I won't understand a word," protested Charles.

"You won't need to," said Joe, rubbing his hands in anticipation.

Hemingway and Charles reluctantly followed him down Virtudes Street to the old theater, which reeked of cigar smoke and stale cologne, and an usher took them to their seats. The show had just started and the audience was laughing uproariously at the warm-up act, a magician who kept dropping his magic wand, forcing his buxom assistant to retrieve it. They were both swept away by a line of scantily dressed rumba dancers, and the stage was cleared.

La Isla del Encanto began with the sea voyage of the *gallego*, a portly, mustachioed Spaniard wearing a red sash and a black beret, and his sidekick *negrito*. Through various odd circumstances, they boarded an ocean liner whose crew consisted entirely of chorus girls in revealing sailor suits. A fierce storm flung them overboard, and they found themselves on a deserted island. The *gallego* plucked a coconut from a convenient palm tree, and *negrito* convinced him that the only way to open it was by breaking it over his head. The *gallego* knocked himself out in the process, but when *negrito* took the coconut, he revived and indignantly chased him around the palm tree. Meanwhile, La Chinita appeared stage left, clad only in palm fronds and peacock feathers. Both the *gallego* and *negrito* stopped to ogle her.

"Where the hell is that island, Mahatma?" said Joe, nudging Hemingway in the ribs.

Hemingway had been yawning throughout the show, but now rubbed his eyes as La Chinita bent over to pick up the coconut, exposing her round, caramel-colored behind. The performance was soon halted when a fight broke out in the back of the theater. A student stood up and yelled, *"¡Abajo Machado!"* and was set upon by two tough-looking men in the row behind him. The other students joined in the brawl, and order was restored only when La Chinita returned to the stage, and an American battleship disgorged the chorus girls.

After the curtain fell on the final *comparsa*, Joe wanted to get another drink at Sloppy Joe's. But once outside, Hemingway said:

"You two go on. I'm going to walk down the Malecón and get some fresh air."

"Just stay out of trouble," said Charles.

Hemingway watched as his friends headed back across the Prado. He bought a bouquet of sunflowers from a *mulata* on the corner and re-entered the Alhambra. The lobby had emptied except for the usher, but Hemingway brushed past him.

"How do I find La Chinita?" he asked a stage hand removing the fake palm tree.

With a smirk, the man cocked his thumb backstage. Hemingway parted the faded red velvet and froze in his tracks when he saw one of the rumba dancers taking off her sailor suit. He stared at her dumbly, but she merely smiled and pointed to the end of the corridor with a wink. Hemingway knocked on the door of the dressing room, and the voice within thrilled him. He entered and found La Chinita sitting before the mirror, her silk dressing gown threatening to slide off her slender shoulders. Seeing his reflection, she said:

"Welcome to Havana, Señor Hemingway."

Nely Chen had returned to the Alhambra after the death of Captain Segura. On that terrible night, she heard a faint *bop-bop-bop* shortly after he left her apartment, but thought nothing of it until the *expertos* came to her door. That was the first time she saw Sergeant Jesús Crespo. He was a squat, ugly man with mournful dark eyes and a purplish scar across his left cheek. Behind him were two guards with carbines slung over their shoulders. They didn't allow her to get dressed, but merely wrapped a blanket around her and hustled her into the waiting car. Nely knew immediately what had happened. Dragones Street should have been empty at that hour, but the police had cordoned off the sidewalk from the crowd and she could see the incandescent flashes of the newsmen's cameras as they jostled to get a picture of the bullet-riddled body.

As the car headed south towards the train station, Nely realized with dread that they were taking her to the fortress of Atarés. They climbed the hill past the sentries at the gate, and Nely was taken down a flight of stone steps to the women's prison. Chief of Police Ainciart himself interrogated her. He was a slight, sallow man with thin lips and sly, hooded eyes. His narrow face was dominated by round, horn-rimmed spectacles that gave him the appearance of a malignant owl, and he wore a cloying perfume which made Nely sneeze. As Sergeant Crespo stood behind her, Ainciart questioned her in his odd, high-pitched voice about Captain Segura and the *abecedarios*. The interrogation lasted all morning, but the dreaded chief of police apparently decided she knew nothing about the killers. After Ainciart had left, the leering guards whispered to themselves and Nely was afraid of what they would do to her. A look from Sergeant Crespo silenced them, and they let her go.

For several days, she could not get him out of her mind. She was afraid to leave the apartment, terrified that Sergeant Crespo would arrest her again and take her back to Atarés. One afternoon, she peeked out from behind the drawn curtain and saw him talking to the doorman of the Hotel New York. She could not forget his eyes, black and impenetrable, threatening to suck her down into the darkness. Zoila had told him that the knife fight which had left the scar on his face was over a woman. Who could love such a man? Nely could tell much from a man's face, but his morose expression puzzled her. Even after he left, she sensed that he was out there, watching her.

When Nely learned that her old room in the *solar* was empty, she packed her things. Zoila's brother Elpidio wasn't afraid of anyone, not even El Zurdo, and stopped by to pick them up. But how to make her escape? There were two soldiers posted on the corner where Captain Segura had been shot, and late at night, she could hear their weary voices drifting across the street. The problem was solved when Zoila walked by to distract them, and Nely dashed out dressed in a man's raincoat, with a fedora pulled over her head. Nely was delighted to return to Zulueta Street and offered a prayer of thanks to Oshún, as the *babalao* had taught her.

It was her mother who had taken Nely to meet the *babalao* when she was a little girl. He lived in the hills above Santiago de Cuba and was a wizened, copper-colored old man whose yellowish eyes gleamed like coals. Dressed entirely in white, he squatted on a reed mat, surrounded by shrines to the many *orishas*. Some were elaborate, such as Changó's throne, carved from *acana* wood and draped with red and white beads, while others were more modest, like Oshún's peacock fan. Nely watched silently as he took the *ekele* and touched it to her forehead. Then he let the *ekele* fall from his hands to the floor.

"You are a daughter of Oshún," he whispered, stroking her cheek. "She is a powerful *orisha*. Follow her and she will never mislead you."

In his low, raspy voice the *babalao* told her a story about Oshún. When the *orishas* lived on earth, she was a lovely young girl who loved to wander through the hills. One day Ogún, the god of iron, saw Oshún and wanted her for himself. But she was in love with Changó, the god of thunder, and ran away. Ogún pursued her and as he was about to seize her, she leaped into the river and was swept away by the current. Yemayá, the mother of all *orishas*, took pity on her, and placed Oshún under her protection. That is how she came to be the goddess of rivers.

Remembering the *babalao's* words, Nely prayed to Oshún in her bedroom and filled a yellow bowl of water with five flat, smooth stones that she gathered on the bank of the Almendares River. But she was still afraid of what Sergeant Crespo would do if he found her. There were many soldiers about and policemen regularly patrolled the Prado, since it was a popular place to plant bombs. Nely often thought of joining Adolfo Ibarra in Mexico. The actor had plucked her from a cabaret in Santiago de Cuba and brought her to Havana, but Zoila heard that he had taken up with a Mexican cigarette girl. Instead, Nely decided to return to Santiago, where the *babalao* would hide her and she would be safe from the *expertos*. Each morning a train left the station for the long ride along the spine of the island to Oriente, but when the time came to go, she couldn't bear to leave Havana.

Then Fina Lugones told her that it was the *abecedarios* who had killed Captain Segura, and that she was free to come and go as she pleased. If Sergeant Crespo arrested her, she would speak to Emilio Aragon and that would be the end of that. Relieved, Nely decided to return to the stage of the Alhambra. Captain Segura had expressly forbidden it, but he could hardly object now.

One morning she put on her favorite yellow satin dress with a long slit running down her thighs, and ventured out on the Prado. A policeman stopped to tip his hat, but she merely smiled and walked past. A plump young man in a white linen suit followed her part of the way, and despite a last, desperate *piropo* from an older man in a *guayabera* on the corner of Virtudes Street, she continued towards the theater. In the lobby, Nely inquired if Señor Espuelas could be found, and was quickly shown to his office. An old friend of Adolfo

Ibarra's, the impresario was a slightly dilapidated man with nervous eyes and a single lock of hair plastered over his bald head. He eyed Nely appreciatively and said that *sí*, something could be done, *por supuesto*.

Many of the other girls in the chorus line remembered Nely and tried to make her life miserable. But she had always been a particular favorite of Señor Espuelas, and soon had her old dressing room back. About this time, *La Isla del Encanto*, in which *negrito* and the *gallego* were marooned on a mysterious island like Cuba in many respects, was nearing the end of its long run. Its star, the Venezuelan actress Coco Fuentes, had been a great beauty in her day, and claimed to have slept with every president of Cuba, from prim Tomás Estrada Palma to Machado himself. One night when Coco was too drunk to appear on stage, Señor Espuelas gave Nely her big break. Appearing as La Chinita, she was met with raucous applause, and one man even leaped onstage and had to be pulled off by the usher. The next night, tickets to the Alhambra were sold out, but when Coco appeared in her peacock feathers, the audience booed and a tomato was thrown. Needless to say, Coco was put on the next boat to Caracas, and Nely replaced her in *La Isla del Encanto*, breathing new life into this tired chestnut.

Nely no longer thought of El Zurdo but she was haunted by a strange dream. More than once she woke up just before dawn, bathed in a cold sweat. In her dream, she was walking through a forest on a dank, moonless night. Thick branches blocked her way, and she noticed to her horror that they were pale limbs sprouting from the ground. They pulled at her as she tried to run, dragging her deeper into the fetid darkness. Only after saying a prayer to Oshún was she able to go back to sleep.

As always, Nely had many admirers and *La Isla del Encanto* became the talk of Havana. It was the week of *carnaval*, and the *comparsas* gathered on the Malecón and began their riotous procession down San Lázaro to the Prado, where bleachers were erected, and finished in the Parque Central beneath the stern features of José Martí. The police were afraid that the ABC would use this opportunity to set off a huge bomb, and Ainciart threatened to cancel this year's *carnaval*. But in their clandestine radio broadcasts and their newspaper *Denuncia*, the *abecedarios* declared a temporary truce during the festivities.

From their seats above the Prado, Nely and Zoila watched the *comparsas* wind down the avenue like a gaudy, glittering serpent. The Havana Yacht Club was the best of all, with the young men in blackface, wearing outlandish African costumes, pounding on kettle drums and skillets. First came the flag bearer, holding up the banner with the purple, intertwined initials HYC, followed by the *faroles*, giant paper lanterns that cast an eerie glow.

Next came the float sponsored by the Havana Trust. Behind the undulating rows of rumba dancers was a truck decorated with longhorns and cactus, replete with cowgirls, and Nely recognized Freddy in a oversized Stetson sitting atop a papier-mâché horse, drinking a daiquiri.

"¡Hijo de puta!" cried Zoila, frantically looking around her for something to throw.

But her shrill voice was lost amid the screams of the crowd and the squeal of the *cornetas*. Freddy waved gaily as the cowgirls threw chocolate coins, and the *comparsa* continued down the Prado. Despite this, it was a somber *carnaval* compared to previous years, and nothing like the orgiastic celebrations that Nely remembered from Santiago, which lasted all night and into the next day. Despite the truce, a phalanx of mounted police cautiously trotted beside the rumba dancers, and a row of soldiers greeted the revelers at the entrance to the Capitolio, their carbines unslung.

The night Hemingway came to her dressing room was no different from any other night. It was a particularly bawdy crowd and a fight broke out in the back of the theater. During the final rumba, after *negrito* and the *gallego* are freed from the

213

cooking pot of the savages upon the intervention of La Chinita, a student leaped up and cried,

"¡Abajo el asno con garras!"

His friends cheered wildly but they were shouted down and two burly men started beating him with blackjacks. The other students joined the fray and order was restored only after Señor Espuelas and several stage hands threw them out without refunding their tickets. The rumba was allowed to continue amid whistles and catcalls, and as usual, there was a standing ovation for La Chinita.

Back in her dressing room, Nely was peeling off the heavy makeup she used to whiten her skin when there was a forceful knock on the door. She had heard from Zoila's brother that *El Hemingway*, as he was known on the waterfront, was back in Havana, so she was not surprised to see him. But Nely had forgotten how big the *americano* was: He literally filled the doorway, dressed in a *guayabera* which barely covered his broad shoulders, holding a bouquet of sunflowers.

When she greeted him he nodded bashfully, but with a hungry look in his eyes. Hemingway followed her back to the *solar*, and as they ascended the dilapidated marble staircase, he peered skeptically into the courtyard criss-crossed with clotheslines. But her room was tidy and bright with pots of yellow frangipani blossoms. There were the same yellow candles he remembered, together with a picture of the Virgen de la Caridad del Cobre. Leaning out of her balcony, he could see the statue of Máximo Gómez on horseback and the moonlit ocean. Nely lightly ran her fingers from the knot of muscle between his shoulder blades to the small of his back.

"What did you catch today?" she asked.

"Nada."

"Then perhaps your luck is about to change, Señor Hemingway."

"Call me Papa."

Javier had not spoken to Jane since the assassination of Captain Segura, but she rang him at *Bohemia* and insisted he meet some friends who were honeymooning in Havana. When he arrived at Jaimanitas on Sunday afternoon, Armando led him to the terrace.

"So good of you to come, darling," said Jane, a scarlet poinciana blossom behind her ear.

Grant was close behind and pumped his hand.

"Meet Harry Dobbs," he commanded, introducing Javier to a lanky young man in a tennis sweater. His wife Francine was a pale girl in a red polka-dotted beach hat.

"*Encantado,*" said Javier.

"Do you know that you're the first Cuban I've met?" said Harry. "I mean, apart from the bellboys and waiters at the hotel."

"I'm honored," said Javier, and excused himself with a slight bow.

"What's wrong with him?" whispered Francine in alarm.

"Jane said he went to Harvard," explained Harry.

Javier walked to the other end of the terrace and looked out over the flame trees to the blue green water. There were several people he didn't know, friends of the Masons from the Havana Country Club and the American embassy.

Grant cleared his throat to get their attention and offered a toast to the newlyweds:

"I must say I received a shock when Francine agreed to marry you, sport. Of course, I've never been able to figure out why Janie married me. All I can say is you're very lucky that your bride made the same mistake that mine did. May you both be every bit as happy as we are."

"I need another drink," said Jane.

Javier brought her a glass of champagne and they watched a sleek cruise ship steaming toward the harbor.

"I suppose we should toast Charlie as well," said Jane. "She's engaged to Jack Halsey, you know."

"Again?" said Javier with raised eyebrows.

"I'm afraid they've set a date this time. Poor sweet thing. You were her last chance."

"Where's the honeymoon?"

"Tahiti, I think."

"I didn't know they had bullfights in Tahiti."

"Jack is through with all that. She wouldn't marry him unless he promised to give it up."

Grant soon joined them, a bottle of champagne in hand, and refilled their glasses.

"Sorry about Charlotte, sport," he said.

"Don't be silly, darling. He couldn't care less."

"You're not conspiring to run off with *my* bride, are you?" said Grant with a wink.

"If only he would," said Jane.

There was an uncomfortable silence until Harry took Javier by the elbow and led him away.

"I say, I hope I didn't say the wrong thing," he said contritely.

"Hardly," said Javier.

"It's just that I hadn't expected to find so many Americans here. We're quite taken with Havana."

"It's the bee's knees," put in Francine.

"Now I know why they call it the Paris of the Caribbean," continued Harry. "But Paris has got nothing on this place. It's so close to the United States, but it really is quite a different country, isn't it?"

Their conversation was interrupted by Jane's shrill laughter as she recounted the story of Grant's encounter with the Cuban soldiers. A few days before, several *expertos* had demanded to search the house.

"What did they want?" asked Javier.

"God only knows," said Jane. "Perhaps to borrow a cup of sugar. But Stoneface here brings out his thirty-ought-six and points the business end out the front door. 'Stand clear,' he yells, 'or I'll shoot!' Can you imagine that? They must have thought he was a lunatic."

"It wasn't quite as dramatic as that," said Grant, reddening.

"Oh, yes it was. John Dillinger couldn't have done it better himself."

"You make it sound like a lark," said Grant. "You know what these fellows are like. We could have been in danger."

"You were in danger of shooting your foot off. What would you have done if they fired back?"

"I'm glad you found it so amusing, dear. Why don't we talk about something else?"

"I want to hear this," piped Francine. "What happened next?"

"Why don't you tell her, darling?" said Jane.

"If you insist," said Grant, joining in the spirit of the joke. "Jane had the good sense to call a friend of ours who is well connected to Machado himself. I still remember the look on that soldier's face when Jane said, 'It's for you!' and handed him the telephone."

Emilio Aragon had threatened to speak to General Ibañez and get the *expertos* assigned to guard duty at the Isle of Pines if they did not leave the house immediately.

"Good show!" laughed Harry.

At this point, all heads turned as Hemingway made an appearance, with Charles a few steps behind. As always, Javier was amazed how the writer instantly became the center of attention wherever he was. He seemed to expand somehow, appearing even bigger, or perhaps it was the space around him that seemed to shrink. Harry and his wife gravitated towards him, and Grant snapped his fingers for more champagne. It was some time before Hemingway disengaged himself and found Javier.

Hemingway had returned to the Ambos Mundos just before dawn, yet he appeared well-rested, his skin ruddy from the sun. He had atoned for his sins of the night before by attending mass at Espíritu Santo, Father Saralegui's parish church, and invited the Basque priest to join him on the

Anita. Joe preferred to nurse his hangover at the Perla, but Charles had joined him and they caught a cab to Jaimanitas.

"Fancy meeting you here," he grinned.

"I'm afraid I can't stay long," said Javier.

"Let me know when you go," whispered Hemingway. "I don't know how much more of these ballroom bananas I can take, either."

Hemingway wandered down into the garden looking for Charles, and Jane crept up behind him, laying her hand lightly on his forearm.

"*Enfins seuls,*" she said.

"I'd rather be out on the stream," admitted Hemingway. "I'm sure the marlin are biting today. I can feel it."

"You can't fish all day, can you?"

"Yes, I can, daughter."

"I'm so glad you came," she said. "It's been so depressing lately."

"So I've heard."

"Would you mind terribly if I joined you in Africa? I won't be a bother, I promise. Say that I can come."

"We'd love to have you, I'm sure."

"Pauline and I get on so well. Please say that I can come, Papa."

"Why not?"

"Let's drink to it, then," she said, and they clinked glasses.

Down by the fountain, Armando was passing out canapés. Jane had put on her bathing cap, and joined Francine and some of the other guests in the pool, floating contentedly in the water.

Hemingway found Charles frowning at his half-empty glass of champagne.

"Am I the only sober one here?" he said.

"Not for long," replied Hemingway.

Javier had wandered down by the beach but soon climbed back up to the house. As he passed by the pool, Jane playfully splashed water on him.

218

"Why the sour face?" she said.

Javier absently hunched his shoulders.

"Be a dear and get me a towel, will you?"

As Jane stepped lightly out of the pool, the water dripping from her bare arms, Javier draped a towel over her shoulders.

"This is unbearable," he whispered.

"Don't be obvious, Javier."

Armando rang a tiny gong to announce that luncheon was served. In Hemingway's honor, the centerpiece of the buffet table on the terrace was a glistening ice sculpture of a marlin, its bill already starting to melt. Around it were piles of plump langostinos and Morro crab claws.

"I thought you'd rather like this," Grant told Hemingway. "It was Janie's idea."

The writer heaped his plate full and joined Javier by the pool.

"Let's eat and clear out of here," he said.

"Just say the word."

But there were more toasts, and more guests arrived, and then the trouble began. Jane was showing Hemingway a painting she had bought from an artist named Antonio Gattorno, who was a friend of Freddy's. It was a colorful oil painting depicting a group of Siboney maidens dancing in a grove of banana trees.

"Doesn't it remind you of Gauguin?" she said.

Hemingway was intrigued by the coolly stylized features of the naked dancers, almost oriental in appearance, swaying voluptuously to a long-lost rhythm.

"I hate to spoil the fun, darling," said Grant, "but I wish you'd take down that awful thing."

"Easy there, Mason," said Harry. "I rather like it."

"It certainly goes with the furniture," said Francine.

"This is a free country," said Grant, then stopped himself: "It is, isn't it? Anyway, I'm entitled to an opinion, seeing as I live here, and I have to say I just don't like it."

"Why not?" asked Hemingway.

"I'm no expert," replied Grant. "So if I told you, it probably wouldn't make any sense. But I know what I like, and I just don't like it."

"No," said Jane, "that's not good enough. I'm sure our guests want to hear *why* you don't like it."

"All right, darling," said Grant, undaunted. "For starters, none of it is real. The natives weren't like that, they were savages. Headhunters, and what not. Small wonder the Spaniards wiped them out. Second, what in Sam Hill are they doing? The rumba? That hadn't been invented yet. I don't even think they had music. And what's Hatuey over there smoking, an H. Upmann? They didn't have cigars then. Or did they? Anyway, I think this fellow Gattorno is just making it all up."

There was a moment of silence and Jane said:

"Grant, that's the most idiotic thing I've ever heard you say."

"That's a bit harsh, isn't it?" said Francine. "She didn't mean it, Grant."

"You stay out of this, Frankie," snarled Jane, and turned back to her startled husband. "I meant what I said. That's one of the most stupid comments I've ever heard. How can you be so ignorant? It's a work of art. Of course Gattorno made it up. That's what artists do—they make things up."

"You've made your point," said Grant.

"Is there any more of this?" said Hemingway, finishing the last of his champagne.

"I should say so," said Grant. "Armando! Where is that goddam gu-gu when you need him?"

"I haven't finished yet," said Jane. "You don't have to be an expert to appreciate art. You don't even have to understand it. But why make fun of it? Does it make you feel better? Does it help if you can stuff it in a little box and put in in the closet with your socks?"

"You're hysterical, darling."

"Why do you always say that when you disagree with me? Doesn't anybody understand what I'm saying? What do you think, Ernest?" cried Jane.

"I'm not getting involved," said Hemingway prudently.

"I'm sure our friends don't need to hear any more of this," said Grant.

"No, but you do."

"I've heard plenty," said Grant, advancing towards her.

"It's hopeless," said Jane, backing away from him. "You don't know how I've tried to make you see. But you won't see, and you never will."

"Let's change the subject, shall we?"

"Do you think that will make the problem go away?" said Jane, suppressing a sob. "Do you think that will change anything?"

"Please, Janie."

"This is a swell party, isn't it?" Jane laughed, wiping the tears from her eyes. "Let's get a drink somewhere."

"You've had enough," said Grant.

"Javier will take me if you won't."

As all eyes turned toward him, Javier shifted uncomfortably.

"Cat got your tongue?" said Jane to Javier. "I thought that was what you wanted."

"This has gone far enough," said Grant.

Jane heard a sound like a distant church bell in her head. She knew that if she shut her eyes, and put her hands over her ears, she could make it go away, but—.

"What's wrong, Jane?" said Hemingway.

"Do you know what bothers me the most?" she said, taking a gulp of warm champagne. "It's the thought that you might be right, Grant. Come to think of it, I don't like this painting, either."

Jane hurled her glass of champagne at the painting and left the room sobbing.

"Exit stage right," said Grant.

Armando, who had been cowering by the door, gathered courage and said:

"Champagne, anyone?"

SEVEN

The next afternoon, Pauline's Uncle Gus and her brother Karl arrived on the *Oriente,* which regularly plied the New York-Havana run. Hemingway dutifully waited at the Ward Line Dock as it nosed into the harbor, dwarfing the fishing boats. As soon as the passengers started down the gangplank, a *conjunto* began to play and several brown-skinned young boys on the pier waved frantically.

"*¡Guan cen! ¡Guan cen!*" they yelled.

Uncle Gus was a sprightly old bachelor who carried a raincoat draped over his arm despite the heat. He tossed a few pennies at them and was startled to see the boys dive into the oily water and emerge with the coins in their teeth. Karl Pfeiffer craned his neck hoping to spot his brother-in-law, who towered over the swarm of porters on the pier. Their bags were soon loaded into a cab and they headed for the Ambos Mundos. Hemingway had hoped to go fishing, but as soon as they left the hotel, they felt the first tentative raindrops.

"Don't worry," said Hemingway. "It'll pass."

Uncle Gus regretted having left his raincoat in his room at Hemingway's insistence, but they continued down Obispo. After a few minutes the sun peeked out briefly and then it began to rain once more, this time in earnest. It was a dense, tropical shower which darkened the sky and instantly soaked them. They ran for cover in a café off the Plaza de Armas, and watched the warm torrents of water thrash the palm fronds and splatter on the wooden bricks in front of the Ayuntamiento. The square was soon flooded, and where it was unpaved a reddish mud oozed out of the water.

When it showed no sign of letting up, they dashed back to the Ambos Mundos. Once in dry clothes, Uncle Gus and Karl were content to write postcards, but Hemingway paced bitterly in the lobby, feeling like a caged animal, and listened to the drumbeat of the rain on the cobblestones. After dinner, Karl announced that he would go to bed early, but Uncle Gus caught a second wind and challenged Hemingway to a game of gin rummy. He produced a pencil and pad to keep score, though after the second game, Hemingway yawned elaborately and said that they would be up at first light tomorrow.

"That's fine with me, Ernest," said Uncle Gus as they headed to the elevator.

Hemingway decided it was too late and too risky to see Nely. He had barely turned off the light in his room when there was a knock on the door.

"Rise and shine!" said Uncle Gus cheerfully.

Hemingway groaned, but his black mood passed when he saw that the sun was out. The rain had cooled the air and swept the filth on the streets out to sea, and it was a lovely morning as they headed for the Plaza de San Francisco. A *pregonero* maneuvered his handcart over the sparkling cobblestones, loaded with tomatoes, avocados, and chayotes, spread out on palm leaves. and a beggar leaned over to drink from the fountain. They found Carlos already on the *Anita,* wiping the dew from the roof of the wheel house while Charles hung his damp clothes out to dry on the bow. They had passed a fitful night on board, huddled in their bunks as the raindrops pummeled the cabin.

Hemingway was eager to shove off. In the shadow of El Morro, a boy in a dinghy cast a line for mutton fish, while a pair of terns passed overhead. Carlos put out a feather jig and soon added a tarpon and a pearl-grey jack to the mackerels in the baitbox. The old fisherman looked up at the sky and frowned but nonetheless began to bait the hooks. As for Uncle Gus, he was happy just to be on the water.

"You're the guest of honor," announced Hemingway, offering him the rod.

"I wouldn't dream of it!" Uncle Gus protested, squinting in the sunlight.

But he nonetheless took it as the bait skipped just shy of the teasers. Joe headed out to sea, following the terns, and Uncle Gus soon turned the rod over to Karl. Hemingway opened a bottle of Hatuey and saw that they were well within the Gulf Stream. The water was a vivid purple, and he imagined the marlin cruising several fathoms beneath the surface, like cars along a submarine highway, oblivious to them.

"What will the weather be like in Africa?" asked Uncle Gus, who would finance the safari.

"We'll be there in December," Hemingway replied. "That's summertime and it'll be hotter than hell."

"I hope we can find some shade," said Charles.

"I sure do envy you," Uncle Gus laughed fondly.

Though Carlos sniffed the air pessimistically, the tip of the Hardy rod began to twich. Karl had never fished before but managed to raised a slender striped marlin which skipped in a shallow arc across the wake. After a few leaps, it was so close to the stern that they could make out the faint purple hoops along its back.

Then the sharks closed in. They were ugly, shovel-nosed *galanos*, eagerly circling the marlin, their tails slashing through the waves. Hemingway went into the cabin for Joe's shotgun, but they had already sunk their teeth into the marlin's flank. The water grew cloudy with blood, and it thrashed helplessly as the mako sharks gorged themselves on its flesh. Soon, they were gone, but others would come, lured by the blood. When they pulled up the leader, more than half of the marlin was gone, its backbone nearly picked clean. They cut the line and the carcass slid back into the reddish water.

"Apple-cored it!" Hemingway told his dejected brother-in-law. "That's what happens when they get tired—they can't escape the sharks."

After lunch, they doubled back towards Havana. Determined to catch a fish, Hemingway let the bait drift far beyond the teasers. Off the Tarara Club they saw a fishing skiff with its tattered sail raised. Carlos asked the fisherman if he had caught anything. The old man leaned back against the stern, one hand on the tiller, and shook his head sadly.

"No luck today, Mahatma," said Joe.

"Luck has nothing to do with it, Josie."

At the entrance to the harbor, a huge oil tanker timidly followed a pilot boat into the channel. Joe pulled away from shore before cutting off the engine, and the *Anita* drifted with the current. It was eerily quiet, except for the gurgle of the waves against the bow and the creak of the hull. Carlos weighted the line and secured the bait at varying depths, an old trick of the marlin fishermen, but after an hour he pulled it in with a dour shrug. Hemingway tossed his bottle of Hatuey overboard, and he and Charles took turns firing at it with the .22. Tiring of target practice, they resigned themselves to the afternoon somnolence. As a last resort, Carlos baited a sash-cord handline with the tarpon and let it drop to 100 fathoms, hoping that the marlin might be feeding deep. To Hemingway's amusement, he fell asleep, the line wrapped around his big toe, his mouth hanging open.

"I hope we have better luck tomorrow," grumbled Hemingway.

"I thought you said luck had nothing to do with it," said Uncle Gus, a twinkle in his eye.

After they docked, Carlos started to say something, but Hemingway cut him off:

"Whatever you do, just don't say *mañana seguro*!"

As the crestfallen Cuban turned away, Hemingway led his guests to the Floridita.

"The day can yet redeem itself, gentlemen," he said, as Constante presented them with a row of frosty daiquiris.

"No thank you," said Uncle Gus, and ordered his usual seltzer water.

Having already downed his, Hemingway shrugged and drank Uncle Gus's daiquiri as well. He soon spotted Javier and Freddy entering the bar, accompanied by Antonio Gattorno. Hemingway took to him immediately, and they were soon talking about Paris, where Gattorno had spent several years. Since he spoke little English, the diminutive painter nodded happily to Uncle Gus, who nodded in return, equally cheerful. The talk of Paris depressed Javier, who went home early, and Freddy said he needed to be at the Havana Trust in the morning. Gattorno had no such compunction and gladly joined them for another round.

Hemingway commandeered a barstool in his favorite corner, his back against the wall, and from this command post he supervised the production of daiquiris. With each new drink, he tossed the swizzle stick in an empty glass, which resounded in a satisfying *ping*. As the lemony crushed iced slid down his parched throat, he waited for the alcohol to take its effect, but he could not forget their dismal day on the water.

"That damn Carlos!" he fumed.

"He seems like a nice enough fellow," said Uncle Gus.

"It's never today *seguro*," said Hemingway.

Unable to follow the conversation in English, Gattorno nodded blithely and sipped from the daiquiries which appeared before him. Finally, he gathered up courage and blurted out:

"Would you like to buy a painting, Señor Gus?"

"I'd have to see it, I suppose."

"I show it to you, yes?" said Gattorno eagerly.

"I've seen one of your paintings," said Hemingway, "at the home of Jane Mason."

"*Ay*, Señora Mason," sighed Gattorno, and the words failed him momentarily.

Though he had lost count of the swizzle sticks in the glass, Hemingway ordered another round. Uncle Gus soon excused himself, and Joe complained that he was hungry and wandered back to the Perla with Karl stumbling after him. Charles remained stoically at the bar until he patted his stomach with a resounding burp and left as well. Hemingway blinked and realized that only Gattorno remained. The painter was not only matching him drink for drink but appeared reasonably sober.

"Let us drink to the marlin that got away," said Gattorno, switching back to Spanish.

"He was a bastard," recalled Hemingway.

"Maybe he thought the same of you."

"If so, then we can respect one another. If I were a fish, I would want to be a marlin."

"It would be amusing to see you hanging from a hook at the dock," said Gattorno. "Let me see, how many *arrobas*? You would fetch a great price at the market. How much for a pound of *americano*?"

"That depends on whether it's white meat or dark," chortled Hemingway.

Constante had replaced the tray of banana chips on the bar and Gattorno eagerly helped himself as Hemingway continued to drink. When he thought he saw two Gattornos eating banana chips, he steadied himself on the barstool.

"Ernesto," said the painter, plucking at his sleeve, "there is someone who wants to speak to you."

Hemingway took a gulp from his latest daiquiri and said: "Make him go away, Gattorno."

A stocky, olive-skinned man with a hooked nose stood a few feet away.

"He claims to know you."

"I can assure you that he's mistaken."

"He is very insistent, Ernesto."

Hemingway loudly smacked his lips and drained his glass. Placing it down on the bar, he said:

"No one has the right to interrupt a man while he's drinking, Gattorno."

He climbed precariously down from the barstool and let his arms hang down by his side, shifting his weight to the balls of his feet.

"You don't remember me, do you?" said the olive-skinned man.

"Tell me why I should, *cabrón*," said Hemingway.

In response, he grabbed Hemingway's jersey and butted his head against his chin. The writer was slammed back against the wall, and felt a trickle of blood at the corner of his mouth. Gattorno gallantly cocked back his fist but the man put the palm of his hand against his chest and almost gently pushed him out into the street. Hemingway's head cleared as he rubbed his jaw and he said with a grin:

"Is that the best you can do?"

The following afternoon at the Floridita, Freddy heard several versions of what happened next. As Constante described it, Hemingway's assailant charged forward only to be met by a vicious right hook that felled him on the spot. Miguel, the *tres* player of the Trío Matancero, recalled that it was the *americano* who hit the ground. Leopoldina la Honesta was more ambivalent, saying that the two men grappled on the floor until the police came. All agreed that Gattorno got the worst of it. The man with the hooked nose managed to slip away in the confusion, and for lack of anyone to arrest, the police took Gattorno to the Jefatura. If not for Uncle Gus, who got the American consul out of bed, he would have spent a night in the hoosegow.

Hemingway's luck returned on Saturday morning, when the sky was blessedly clear. The fishing smacks had raised their white sails to take advantage of the *brisa*, and a flock of terns circled over the bobbing masts. Even Carlos was cheerful, his lined, leathery face split with a smile as he showed Hemingway the *machuelos* in the baitbox.

"*Ahora sí*, Don Ernesto," he said.

They were trolling off Bacuranao when Hemingway raised a marlin that skimmed over the waves in a series of greyhound leaps. He methodically hauled it in and Carlos gaffed it just beneath the dorsal fin. It was the first strike of the season, a fine striped marlin weighing close to 150 pounds, gun-metal blue with pinkish lines that soon faded in the sun.

After Uncle Gus returned to New York, and Charles went back to the hardware store, Hemingway used the opportunity to work. Pulling out the unfinished manuscript he had brought on the *Anita*, he locked himself in his hotel room with several sharpened pencils. Hemingway remembered he was on a train to Key West with Bumby when he got the telegram from Carol about his father. He got off in Philadelphia to take the overnight train to Chicago, and it was not until he reached Oak Park that he learned Clarence Hemingway had shot himself. But he didn't want to think of his father as he saw him the last time, lying in his coffin, the gaping wound behind his ear carefully sewed up.

His father was an expert hunter, and he remembered hunting red squirrels with him in Michigan. That was his father's country: pine forests, swampy creek bottoms, and grassy fields. His father had given him a single barrel twenty gauge shotgun, and told him to wait until the squirrel jerked his tail and fire at the first sign of movement in the leaves. He had been nearly Bumby's age then, and he recalled his father's quick, sure footsteps on the pine needles. How could the boy have known that the man would put an old Civil War pistol to his head and pull the trigger?

But music from a café on Obispo distracted him, and the sound of his father's footsteps faded. The story somehow eluded him, just beyond his reach. After filling a page with uncertain handwriting, Hemingway put down his pencil and hurried to catch the last show at the Alhambra. His wife was due to arrive the next morning.

Bumby now lived with his mother in Chicago, but he spent his summers in Key West, and Pauline brought him to Havana. They spent long, languid days on the Gulf Stream. Javier didn't want to go fishing, and Freddy was avoiding the waterfront for fear of Zoila's brother, but Jane often joined them. There was no mention of the disastrous luncheon at Jaimanitas, nor of Gattorno's painting. One afternoon, while Grant was at work, Jane suggested they go shooting at the Club Cazadores del Cerro. Leaving Bumby to help Joe oil the reels aboard the *Anita,* they took the road to Regla which passed by the gun club.

In the clubhouse, Hemingway gleefully selected a handsome 12 gauge shotgun of Grant's, and he and Pauline followed Jane out to the shooting pavilion.

"It caused quite a stir when I first started coming out here," said Jane. "Some of the old boys objected rather strongly."

"I should think so," chuckled Hemingway.

Jane walked out on the deck and put the gun to her shoulder, her left hand far forward on the stock, and her weight resting lightly on her left foot. She moved the muzzle first to one side, then the other.

"Pull," she said in a low voice.

The grey pigeon shot out of the sunken trap and flew low above the grass toward the white fence. The first shot missed narrowly, but the second blew its head off and the bird collapsed mid-flight in a bloody heap of feathers. There was a hushed murmur of approval from the other shooters but Jane cursed under her breath as she walked back towards the pavilion.

"No excuse for that," she hissed.

Jane broke the shotgun and briskly reloaded both barrels. Her cheek against the comb, she leaned forward to anticipate the pigeon's flight, and Hemingway imagined her stalking a leopard in the Serengeti.

"*¿Lista?*" called the trapper.

"*Lista.*"

There was a deadly pause until Jane called out: "Pull!"

The pigeon flew out of the trench with a flutter and Jane dropped it with the first barrel. When the second charge slammed into it, it was already falling.

Hemingway let out a low whistle and Pauline shifted uncomfortably. Now it was her husband's turn, and she knew that if he missed he would be in a terrible mood the rest of the day. Putting on the wire-rimmed glasses he wore while he wrote, he stepped briskly onto the deck. Grant's shotgun had a pleasant heft in his hands, and the long barrel gleamed with gun oil. Hemingway brought the gun up and lifted his right heel, his heart pounding. Since his eyes were bad, he decided to shoot at the sound of the trap.

"Pull," he said hoarsely.

Pauline saw the flutter of wings against the pale sky and breathed a sigh of relief as the pigeon virtually disintegrated in an explosion of feathers. Hemingway rejoined them with a broad grin.

Now it was her turn. The shotgun she had taken was far too heavy and she selected another. The sun beat down on her and she stopped to put on a pair of eyeshades. Pauline remembered an ugly, greenish bruise she had gotten while shooting last year and was careful to place the butt against her shoulder. Then she glanced back and saw her husband lighting Jane's *margarita* and laughing at something she said.

"Pull," said Pauline.

The pigeon swooped out of the trap and flew high. Her two shots whizzed harmlessly by and the bird was soon out of sight.

"Bad luck," commiserated Jane.

"Poor old Mama," said Hemingway.

Pauline declined to shoot again, and they had a drink at the bar. One of the boys brought out a folding canvas chair for her, and she fanned herself while Jane and her husband shot skeet. Jane laughingly joked that she might join them on safari, with or without Grant, and this set in motion an unpleasant train of thought. When Pauline met Hemingway, he was married to Hadley. She had joined them on vacation in the south of France, and that was how it began, as a harmless little game. Pauline tried to dispassionately analyze her own feelings, which were complicated, and wondered if there would come a time when Jane's feelings might have to be considered.

And what of his feelings?

Shortly after he arrived in Havana, Sumner Welles spoke at the American Club.

Walter sat with Ogden Crews and Freddy, sipping his iced tea as the Reverend Graham offered a benediction. Then the new ambassador approached the podium. He was a tall, fastidious-looking man, nearly bald but with prominent eyebrows and a small mustache. Despite the wilting heat, he wore a dark three piece suit, and his gleaming white collar appeared newly starched. Surprisingly soft spoken, he began his speech by thanking the American colony for its warm welcome.

"Hell, Machado had half the army on the Malecón to greet him," said Ogden *sotto voce*.

Among his priorities, Welles noted, was to establish a reciprocal trade treaty, with closer commercial cooperation between the two countries.

"At least until Machado pays back the Chase Manhattan Bank," whispered Ogden, and Walter looked at him askance.

Welles added that this proposed treaty would stabilize the sugar crop by letting Cuba allot a certain tonnage for export to the United States, at a fair price. He assured them that President Roosevelt would offer Cuba a fair deal, while not overlooking the domestic interests of the United States.

"I've heard that before," said Ogden.

Welles paused to take a sip of water, and then concluded his remarks:

"In short, gentlemen, we intend to be good neighbors."

"He's a smooth one, all right," said Ogden.

His friend's sarcastic tone irritated him, and Walter turned toward Freddy, who had nodded off and seemed about to fall from his chair. Walter elbowed him in the ribs, and Freddy awoke with a start.

"Did I miss anything?" he said.

"Not much," said Ogden in amusement.

Walter gave Freddy a stern look as the room erupted in applause.

"Sorry, Pop," said Freddy. "Late night."

"As usual," said Walter.

"Let's see who lasts longer," said Ogden as they rose from the table, "Welles or Machado."

Walter left the American Club blinking in the harsh sunlight, and started down the Prado toward the Havana Trust.

"I'll be along in a minute, Pop," said Freddy as they crossed the Parque Central.

Walter shook his head sadly as his son went in search of a lottery ticket, and encountered an altercation at the entrance to O'Reilly. An old chinaman's fruit cart had been overturned, and anemic pineapples littered the cobblestoned street. He argued fiercely with the driver of the horse-drawn carriage that had knocked it over, while the tourist inside looked on bewildered. A crowd had gathered, blocking traffic, and the stalled cars honked their horns as a weary policeman mopped his forehead with a handkerchief. The cacophany of screams in rapid-fire Spanish and Chinese combined with the heat to give Walter a dull headache.

He stepped carefully over the pineapples and soon reached the Havana Trust. Passing between the Corinthian columns, he walked briskly past Elmer, who straightened up and stifled a yawn. Walter went upstairs and Miss Garcia informed him that Emilio Aragon was waiting outside his office.

Lately, the Cuban seemed to be away quite often, either in New York or his vast *central* in Matanzas. But when he was in Havana he dropped by unexpectedly, often for no other reason than to chat or have a cup of coffee. Since the financing of Altomar, they saw each other frequently. Aragon regularly invited Walter and Beryl to extravagant parties at their newly completed house overlooking the ninth hole at the Havana Country Club. These were elegant affairs attended by cabinet ministers, high ranking officers, and other intimates of the president, as well as their bodyguards. A row of limousines snaked out into the street, and soldiers patrolled the fairway beyond the high wall, armed not with golf clubs but rifles. Aragon dressed his servants in powdered wigs and livery, and they announced each guest's arrival with much fanfare. Resplendent in tails with a silk shirt and diamond studs, he greeted them beneath the marble loggia, engulfing their hands with his moist palms.

Walter had also attended smaller, more intimate gatherings, without Beryl or Señora Aragon at a *chalet* in the Vedado owned by Fina Lugones, Aragon's mistress. She was an exotic-looking beauty who once sang at the Zombie Club. Aragon cheerfully admitted that he often took her to New York and installed her in a suite at the Plaza, naturally on a different floor than his wife. Several other charming young women attended these parties, and one lovely *mulata* sat on Walter's lap and planted a kiss on his shiny pate. Aragon later intimated that he would be happy to arrange a rendezvous with her, but the mere thought of it made Walter break out in a sweat.

Aragon had also become part of Walter's regular foursome at the Havana Country Club. His imitations of prominent *políticos* left Ogden Crews in stitches, and his cigars won over even the staid Reverend Graham. Although he showed up at the clubhouse in a natty tam o'shanter bubbling with enthusiasm, he often cheated. Walter discovered this one Saturday morning morning when he was paired with the Cuban. On the 11th hole, Aragon searched for his ball beneath the cane breaks at the edge of the fairway and found it lodged neatly between the leafy stalks. Ascertaining that their opponents were out of sight, he winked at Walter and deftly kicked the ball into a clearing. Before Walter could protest, Emilio swung his club back, but the ball ricocheted against a palm tree and landed in the water.

That afternoon at the Havana Trust, Aragon greeted him with a damp *abrazo*. Wiping the sheen of sweat from his forehead with a billowy white handkerchief, he winked at Miss Garcia.

"Why is it that at our age, women seem more beautiful than ever? Can you answer that, my friend?"

Walter bristled at the thought of Aragon seducing his hard-working young secretary, but the jovial Cuban somehow forced a smile out of him. He had an annoying habit of pacing about Walter's office, and now he stooped before the HMS *Victory*, running a glistening forefinger along the topsail.

"Perhaps your ambassador should have come in this," he said slily.

"It's a warship," parried Walter. "Is that what you expected?"

"We have high hopes for Mr. Welles," said Aragon, ignoring the question. "No doubt he explained his position at the American Club today. Were you there?"

Walter nodded.

"Then you probably heard the same pleasantries he offered upon his arrival. What does he really intend to do?"

"Why not take him at his word?"

"Because he is a diplomat. Diplomats rarely say what they mean, and even then, only for a very good reason."

At last, Aragon eased himself onto the chair opposite Walter's desk, and accepted a tiny cup of coffee from the blushing Miss Garcia. He dispatched it with a noisy slurp, and described his recent visit to Matanzas. Despite the efforts of the communists to organize a strike, the *zafra* was nearly over, and the smokestacks belched dark plumes over the endless rows of sugar cane. Aragon's cutters and their families lived in filthy huts, and it was little wonder they joined the strike. But he had replaced the striking cutters with Haitians eager to work for lower wages.

"Someday you will sell me La Margarita," smiled Aragon, glancing at the picture of the sugar mill on the wall.

"It's not for sale," said Walter, as always.

"Everything is for sale in Cuba. Have you not learned that yet, my friend?"

Walter knew of the Cuban's passion for cigars and offered him a Rey del Mundo from the cedar-lined box on the table. Aragon vastly preferred his own Partagas *robustos*, favored by Machado himself, but to be polite he lit it and blew a cloud of smoke towards the ceiling.

"But I did not come to discuss La Margarita," said Aragon, "at least not today. You are aware of the interest that President Machado has in Altomar, are you not? Despite the cares of state, he somehow finds the time to inquire about my lowly efforts. He has often expressed an interest in seeing Altomar, and would surely have done so if not for the cowardly attempts on his life."

Not long after the murder of Vazquez Bello, the *expertos* had found a small fishing boat in Havana Harbor literally crammed with sticks of dynamite. Presumably, this had been part of a failed attempt to blow up Machado's yacht. Aragon himself had been shot at one afternoon as he strolled along the Malecón, and Walter suspected that several burly bodyguards waited in the bank lobby.

"I have spoken of you more than once, Walter, and *El Presidente* has long wanted to make your acquaintance. He personally sent me to invite you and your lovely wife to a reception in honor of your illustrious ambassador."

No sooner had Aragon taken his leave than Walter telephoned Beryl with the unexpected news.

"Tonight?" she cried. "Why, there's no time to get ready!"

But when Walter came home to change into evening dress, she was already trying on a white satin gown with a ruffled *décolletage*.

"How do I look, dear?" she said, twirling before him.

"Dandy," muttered Walter, struggling to wrap his cummerbund around his formidable waist.

As Felix drove them along the Malecón towards the Presidential Palace, Walter noticed the armored trucks full of soldiers surrounding the statue of Máximo Gómez. Before the white marble palace with high stained glass windows, a fragment of the old city wall remained, and now served as a checkpoint for the police, who thoroughly searched each passing car. Sharpshooters were posted around the gold-rimmed cupola, and *expertos* frisked the guests as they entered the vast foyer.

"I'm so thirsty!" bubbled Beryl as a waiter approached with glasses of champagne.

"I need to keep my wits about me," said her husband.

Nonetheless, Walter tasted his champagne and scanned the crowd for Aragon. He recognized several people who had been at the luncheon at the American Club, including Tom Beales, who was chatting with Grant Mason. Ambassador Welles was surrounded by dignitaries, but the Cuban had yet to arrive.

Meanwhile, Beryl found the white-gloved waiter and whisked another glass from his tray. She had enjoyed the daiquiries at Jane's party, and now discovered that champagne tickled her nose. The week before, Beryl had made an appointment at Casa Inez, a fancy new beauty salon on the Prado. After a facial and a manicure, she left with a confident pat of her French twist. It was a lovely day, and Beryl felt an exquisite thrill as a darkly handsome man in a white linen suit followed her progress across the street. She towered over the delicate, small-boned Cuban women, and had often felt ungainly. But that afternoon on the Prado, Beryl took pleasure in the fact that many of them grew fat as they approached middle age, if not before. It was no wonder that Cuban men looked elsewhere, and practiced their *piropos* so assiduously. Beryl let the last of the champagne roll down her tongue, and with a giddy hiccup she imagined what she would wear for her next stroll down the Prado.

At that instant, Walter took her by the elbow and whispered urgently in her ear:

"It's time, dear."

"Whatever for?" she protested as he led her through the crowd.

"For President Machado," said Walter.

Beryl saw that Aragon was frantically motioning them to a spot in the receiving line where the Cuban president was greeting his guests. He was tall for a Cuban, with bushy white hair and a broad, squarish face. He wore round horn-rimmed spectacles which made him appear more youthful, but his forehead was lined with wrinkles and the skin around his jowls sagged disconcertingly. Was this the man that the newspapers lauded as *el egregio*, and that the students called *la bestia*? Beryl wondered how such a tired old man had come to merit such extravagant praise and unremitting scorn. Aragon introduced her, and President Machado bent over to kiss her fingertips. His right hand was plump and fragrant with *eau de cologne*, and he kept his left hand behind his back.

Beryl felt Aragon's palm on her bare back, and she moved on to let Walter greet the president. The two men were soon in an animated discussion about Altomar, as Aragon beamed happily. President Machado spoke in surprisingly good English, his voice a deep rumble. After a few minutes Emilio nudged Walter as well, and President Machado gave him a warm *abrazo*, placing both hands on his shoulders.

As Beryl turned to leave, she noticed with a shudder that one of the fingers on Machado's left hand had been lopped off, ending in a stump at the first joint.

One morning, Joe mentioned that he would be going back to Key West for a couple of days.

"What for?" asked Hemingway.

"I've got to take care of some business," said Joe, taking off his cap and scratching his head.

"Suits me fine!" said Hemingway unexpectedly. "I've got work to do, anyway."

But Bumby watched intently as his father pointed a menacing finger at Joe:

"Just don't stay away too long, Josie—we might not be here when you get back, you know."

"Sure thing, Mahatma."

Joe had decided to build up his inventory before the repeal of Prohibition, when he intended to open a new saloon named after Sloppy Joe's in Havana. The next afternoon, he entered the Perla and sat at his usual table beneath the listless ceiling fan. Joe ordered a steak with yellow rice and crispy *tostones* which came to fifteen cents. For another dime, he got a bottle of Hatuey. He had cleaned his plate and was elaborately picking his teeth when his old partner Domingo entered the bar.

Domingo was a stooped, sad-eyed Catalan who owned a *bodega* on Lamparilla Street. Joe had met Domingo when he first started coming to Havana, and his expression hadn't changed much since then.

"How's business?" asked Joe.

"*La calle está dura*, Señor Russell," said Domingo, opening his lined palms in a gesture of resignation. [Times are tough.]

"It's no picnic for us, either," commiserated Joe.

Domingo nodded sourly, and ordered a glass of brandy. As in previous years, their transaction was a simple one. Domingo would meet Joe in a secluded cove in Barlovento with the merchandise.

"This will be the last time," said Joe, sliding a wad of money across the table.

"Who knows?" said Domingo, breaking into a weary smile as they clinked glasses.

As Joe sipped his beer, he noticed two well-dressed young men at the bar. They were students, by the look of them, with brilliantined hair and white linen suits, seemingly out of place on the waterfront. They finished their drinks without talking, as though waiting for someone. But Domingo paid them no heed as he reminisced:

"Do you recall when we met? Those were the days of the *vacas gordas*. Now, we have only *vacas flacas*." [Fat cows and thin cows.]

"What's going to happen?"

Domingo looked over his shoulder and put a finger to his thin lips.

"It is not good for one's health to ask questions like that, or to answer them. Do you understand, Señor Russell?"

Joe nodded and finished his beer. The students had left the bar and now stood idly in front of the café. The lunettes atop the church cast wavy shadows across the square, and the red-tiled customs house seemed empty. A beggar had doggedly kept his place by the fountain, waiting for the office workers to leave the Lonja del Comercio.

"What do you think of our new ambassador?" asked Joe.

"Does it matter what any of us think? I have heard it said that he is a *maricón*."

Out of the corner of his eye, Joe saw one of the students light a cigarette. Who were they waiting for? Something about them made him uncomfortable. He emptied the bottle of

241

beer into his glass and watched it foam up against the rim. Havana, it occurred to him, was becoming a very dangerous place.

Joe had already gotten his clearance papers from the broker, and had filled the tanks at the Standard Oil dock, where the gas was 28 cents a gallon, so there was nothing to do but shove off. At dusk, the streetlights blinked on in the Plaza de Armas, illuminating the American flag above the embassy. He headed west along the Malecón toward Barlovento, and the abandoned pier where Domingo would be waiting for him, but it was still too early. The coast was dark except for the flickering light from a fisherman's hut behind the mangroves. Joe guessed that he was about a mile offshore, too far for a Cuban patrol boat, and he cut the engine.

Breathing in the salty air, Joe tried not to think about the two boys in front of the Perla. Most likely they were members of the ABC or one of the other student groups. Or perhaps they were *lenguilargos*. Either way, it was not his problem.

The *Anita* soon drifted back towards Jaimanitas, and Joe checked the time in the glow of the binnacle light. It was a cloudy night, and the lights of Havana cast a murky glow. He scanned the shore until he saw the signal, and then flashed the running lights. Domingo was waiting on the edge of the pier holding a hurricane lamp. Behind him, his nephew Diego stood guard with a shotgun. Joe moored and followed them to where an old truck was parked. In the back, under a sheet of burlap, were the sacks of liquor. From out of the shadows came two enormous black men, their eyes shining in the darkness, to load the hold of the *Anita*.

Joe took a deep breath to calm his nerves. In the cabin was a Winchester pump gun in a sheep's wool case soaked in gun oil, and the Colt pistol that he kept for sharks. But he had never had to use them for anything else. When the contraband was loaded, he drank a valedictory toast with Domingo.

"Here's to better times."

"*Ojalá*," said the old Catalan.

Joe stoppered the bottle and tossed it to one of the men, who flashed his teeth in a wide grin. Casting off, he heard the rumble of the truck's engine as it started up the road, and watched the pier melt into the darkness. Joe steered north, relieved to be returning home, and in a few hours Havana dipped below the horizon. Joe opened the thermos of coffee and took a desultory bite from his sandwich, but he had lost his appetite. He had the same uneasy feeling as when he saw the two students at the bar, like a tingle at the back of his neck. It was late morning when he passed the stakes at the Western Dry Rocks. Big Al Skinner, who weighed 300 pounds and tended bar at the speakeasy, was waiting for him at Woman Key.

"Some Cuban fellows have been asking about you," said Al in his deep-throated rumble, a 40 pound sack of rum under each arm.

"What for?"

"They wouldn't say, boss."

Joe spit over the side and pulled up anchor. This was the last run, all right, and the thought cheered him as he docked. He had dinner at home with his wife and children, and listened to Gracie Allen on the radio. In the morning, he walked over to the speakeasy, and Al cocked his thumb at the café across the street. Seated at the table were two young Cubans. It was only a matter of time before they came looking for him, so he decided to go to them.

"You *muchachos* looking for me?" he said.

The Cubans had seen him cross the street and looked up without surprise. One was tall with hard, expressionless eyes, while the other appeared younger, with a wispy mustache.

"We have heard that you will be returning to Havana soon, Señor Russell," said the tall one.

"Where did you hear that?" said Joe.

"What we know is of no importance. We have a business proposition for you."

"I'm not interested "

"Please hear us out, Señor Russell," said the younger one.

"Hear you out? I saw a boat at the Navy Yard with bullet holes in the stern. You boys wouldn't have anything to do with that, would you?"

"You will be well paid, half now and half in Havana."

"I'm sure I will," said Joe, "and if somebody talks I wind up as shark feed. What good will your money do me then?"

"We're wasting our time," said the other Cuban, preparing to leave.

But his friend looked up at Joe and said:

"We need your help, Señor Russell."

Joe sat down wearily and once more felt the tingle at the back of his neck.

"I assume you boys want a one-way ticket to Havana," he said.

Joe planned to leave early the next morning, so as to be in Havana that night. He had assumed that they wanted to smuggle guns into Cuba, and was relieved when they denied it. Still, something was not right. When he arrived at the pier, the Cubans were already there, together with a third man.

"Wait a minute," said Joe. "You didn't say anything about him."

"Let me explain," said the younger one, who had introduced himself as Roberto. "He won't be on the manifest."

"There's nothing to explain. If the crew manifest says two passengers, that's how many are getting off in Havana."

"No one will be getting off in Havana," said the older one, whose name was Alberto Zayas Bazán.

"You fellows lost me somewhere," said Joe.

"You must trust us," said the third man. He appeared to be in his forties, with a touch of grey in his thinning hair, and smoked a cigarette in an ebony holder. "Fernando Alvarez Leal, at your service."

It occurred to Joe that these characters were more dangerous than a shipment of Thompsons, but it was too late to turn back now.

"Let's go then," he said finally.

Joe realized that there would be discrepancies in the paperwork, but a few dollars to the harbormaster would take care of that. As they passed Sand Key, Dr. Alvarez Leal went down into the cabin while Alberto lit a cigarette and leaned against the gunwale. He was in his early twenties, Joe guessed, but had the eyes of a killer. The younger boy sat in the fishing chair and appeared friendly. Joe remembered the two students at the Perla and imagined them sprawled on the cobblestones in a pool of blood, their expensive suits riddled with bullet holes. They were just boys, all of them.

"We will remember this, Señor Russell," said Roberto.

"I'd like it if you paid up and then forgot all about me," said Joe.

"You do not understand. After the revolution we will remember both our friends and our enemies."

"You and your pals have long memories, I'm sure. But how do you know it will be different after the revolution?"

Roberto seemed not to understand the question.

"The revolution will bring many changes," he continued.

"Don't be so sure."

"Machado is a bloodthirsty tyrant," said Roberto passionately. "When he is gone, Cuba will at last be free."

"He's not the first," said Joe, "and he won't be the last. I don't mean to piss on your parade, son, but getting rid of him won't solve the problem. It's never that easy."

"You misunderstand me, Señor Russell. Machado is just the symptom, not the disease. There is much work to be done before Cuba can achieve political and economic independence. But the leaders of the so-called opposition think that talk can change the world. The time for talk is long past."

"Sure, but is it worth getting a bullet in your gut?"

Roberto was about to reply when Alberto turned towards him.

"Shut up!" he hissed.

Roberto reacted as though he had been slapped.

"No harm in a little friendly conversation, *amigo*," said Joe.

At that point, Dr. Alvarez Leal climbed out on deck. Roberto quickly entered the cabin, red with shame, while Alberto lit another cigarette, his back to the others. It was a hazy day, and the water had a greyish, metallic sheen. The air was hot and Joe wondered if it would freshen by tomorrow morning.

"Are you interested in politics, Captain?" asked Dr. Alvarez Leal.

"Not if I can help it," said Joe. "Even less if it's none of my business."

"You must forgive my students. They tend to be very passionate about the revolution. But are you truly as cynical as you would have me believe? Scratch a cynic and you find the worst sort of idealist."

"I'm getting paid to take you to Havana. What you do when you get there is your problem. If you want to blow yourselves up, be my guests."

"Do you play chess? The greatest chess player of all time is a Cuban named Capablanca. Several years ago he beat the Russian grandmaster Nimzowitsch in a rather famous game. The Russian found himself in the unenviable position of being forced to move, and weakening his defenses. In chess, that's called *zugzwang*, and that's the position the Cuban government finds itself in. It's only a matter of time, now."

"You and this Capablanca fellow can play all you want. I heard about that boy that got gunned down in the street by the *expertos*, trying to escape, they said. Was he a chess piece?"

"Not at all. He died for what he believed in."

"I don't know what that poor boy believed. But you and me, we're old enough to know better."

"Perhaps that's our misfortune."

The *Anita* skimmed over the darkening waves and in a few hours they saw the lights of Havana, a crescent-shaped glow just over the horizon. Alberto had said that a boat would be waiting for them off Cojimar, so Joe veered to port and made for the fishing village.

"Now what?" he said.

"Now we wait," said Alberto.

The sea was calm and an eerie mist hung over the water. There were no lights on the beach and no sign of movement. An hour passed and Alberto said:

"Take us in."

"This is as far as I go," said Joe.

At this, the Cubans looked at each other and spoke rapidly in Spanish. Alberto was surely armed, Joe realized, and there was little he could do if they forced him to approach the shore. But Dr. Alvarez Leal did not seem like a violent man. Or was he?

Joe had cut the engine while the Cubans argued. It was growing late, and he wondered if he should simply drop them off in one of the deserted coves along the shore. But what if the *expertos* were waiting? After another hour, they heard the low rumble of an engine. Was it a patrol boat? Alberto pulled out his revolver and crouched behind the gunwale.

"Wait," said Dr. Alvarez Leal.

They peered through the haze and saw a single flashing light that appeared to drift over the water. That was the signal, and Joe turned on the running lights. As they boarded the other boat, Alberto scowled impassively, and Dr. Alvarez Leal seemed preoccupied and shook Joe's hand with a curt nod. But Roberto stood on deck and said:

"I will not forget you, Señor Russell."

"And I'll remember you, son," Joe shouted across the water. "Just take care of yourself."

As he feared, it was too late to get cleared that night. Joe anchored in front of La Cabaña and leaned back in the fishing chair. Lighting a Lucky Strike, he watched the sleeping city across the harbor.

During a performance of *La Isla del Encanto*, Nely thought she saw El Zurdo in the audience. What could he be doing at the Alhambra? When she went offstage, she peered out from behind the tattered velvet curtain, and scanned the faces of the crowd through the miasma of stale cigar smoke. The audience was full of students and many of them could be *abecedarios*. In fact, Chief of Police Ainciart had often threatened to shut down the Alhambra. Were they the ones El Zurdo was after? If he was there, she didn't recognize him.

It was the *abecedarios* who had killed Captain Segura, and Nely was even more afraid of them than the police. A few days ago, a dockhand found the body of a young man in an alley off Jesús María Street. His throat was slit from end to end in a ghastly rictus, and on his chest was a sign that said:

El ABC dará esta muerte a todos los lenguilargos.

Nely shuddered at the thought of it. She had not seen Sergeant Crespo since she left the apartment on Dragones, but she often had the distinct feeling she was being followed. Yet she felt safe with Hemingway. The *expertos* would not bother her so long as she was with the famous writer, who had many influential friends.

In many ways, he reminded Nely of Captain Segura. They were both sons of Changó, with the same wolfish smile, at once welcoming and fearsome. But unlike Captain Segura, he was a hurried, impatient lover. The *americano* was afraid to be seen with her in public, since he was becoming well-known in Havana, and a pesky reporter from the *Havana Post* was following him around, hoping for an interview. Moreover, he explained, an imposter claiming to be Hemingway had been in Havana several months before, leaving unpaid bills and even picking up sailors. There had already been one unpleasant incident in the Floridita. Hemingway and Nely usually had dinner at their usual *reservado* at the Café de la Isla, although he insisted that she slip out a few minutes before he did, so that no one would see them leaving together. Surprisingly, Zoila took a dislike to him, which Nely ascribed to her best friend's generally negative attitude towards men. Zoila was now singing several nights a week at the Zombie Club, where she met many wealthy *políticos,* including one who offered to take her on his yacht, but Nely knew that she was still in love with Freddy.

When Hemingway's wife came to visit, he left word at the Alhambra that he would not be able to see her for several days. But Nely prayed to the *orishas,* and bought five sweet pastries to place before the altar, since Oshún had a sweet tooth. Apparently this was efficacious, since no sooner was his wife on the ferry back to Key West than Nely heard the same knock on her dressing room door. Often his back was sore from hauling in the huge marlins, and Nely drew a hot bath scented with anisette blossoms and rubbed almond oil into his aching shoulders. But he always left the *solar* before daylight, to join his fishing companions at the Ambos Mundos.

There were nights when she waited for him in vain, and Zoila said that she saw him dancing with a blond *americana* at the Zombie Club. He is a man, thought Nely. Let him enjoy himself while he can. But why should I suffer? It was not difficult to encourage the attentions of Antonio Ramirez, a young pianist at the Alhambra. He was very poor, having recently arrived from Camagüey, but very handsome, with green eyes and long, elegant fingers. One night when Hemingway came to her dressing room, she told him that she was otherwise occupied. But the writer merely responded with that same self-satisfied expression that Captain Segura had. This irritated Nely to no end. She waited for him one morning in the Plaza de San Francisco, hiding behind the market stalls, and saw Señora Mason. The *americana* drove her big yellow car to the entrance of the customs house, and emerged smoking a cigar, like a man. Nely remembered her from the night she danced with Captain Segura at Sans Souci. He had explained that she was the wife of a business associate, and Nely had chosen to believe this ridiculous explanation, but now she knew they had been lovers.

That afternoon, Nely told Señor Espuelas that her mother was gravely ill and she needed to be at her side. Once more packing her cardboard suitcase, Nely took the train to Santiago de Cuba, riding not in the crowded third class car full of *guajiros* with chickens but in a tidy Pullman berth with an elderly lady visiting her grandchildren.

There was much that Nely wanted to ask the *babalao*, who seemed ageless. He hardly ever left his room, sitting on a goatskin stool, surrounded by his *orishas*. Remembering the traditional greeting of a daughter of Oshún, she lay down and touched first one elbow to the ground, and then the other. Then she kneeled down on the straw mat beside him as he touched the *ekele* to her forehead, and let it fall at his feet. He repeated the process several times, picking up the chain of tortoise shells only to drop them once more.

Expectantly, Nely leaned forward to hear his faint voice. His yellowish eyes glowing in the half-darkness, the *babalao* spoke to her once more of Changó. One day, the god of thunder grew restless and decided to experience life as a man. But he grew so unhappy on earth that he hung himself from the branch of a *siguaraya* tree. Having taken his own life, he wandered disconsolately for seven days in the kingdom of the dead. When his father Obatalá found out what happened, he rescued him and returned him to the world of the living. Somehow, the experience frightened Changó and forever changed him. He never spoke of it again, and no one ever found out what happened to Changó in the underworld.

Nely left the presence of the *babalao* bewildered. He had answered none of her questions, and she had been too afraid to reveal the real purpose of her visit. The next day, she gathered up the courage to ask him. But the old man was horrified by her request and grew very angry:

"The power of the *orishas* is not a weapon, my child. It is a gift, and gifts must be accepted with an open heart. Drive these thoughts from your mind and trust in Oshún. You are her daughter and she will lead you out of the darkness."

Nely sulked all the way back to Havana. What good were the *orishas* if they couldn't prevent someone from taking her man? Somehow, the *americana* had bewitched not only Captain Segura but also Hemingway. Could it be that she was a *santera* as well? Whatever the reason, it was clear she had potent magic of her own.

A cousin of Zoila's knew of a *bruja* who lived in Regla, a fearsome old woman who had been born in Africa and could cast fearsome spells. One morning, Nely took the ferry across the bay, and prayed to Nuestra Señora de Regla to forgive her for what she was about to do. Crossing herself, she entered a square crowded with market stalls, and immediately recognized the *bruja*, squatting on a blanket beside several chains of tortoise shells which she sold to tourists. She was a gaunt crone with malignant eyes and filthy white hair. Nely explained what she wanted and the *bruja* clucked her tongue malevolently. Steadying herself against the stall, she got to her feet and grasped Nely's wrist in her gnarled hand. The old woman lived in a wooden shack at the end of dusty street, where the cobblestones gave way to packed earth and rats burrowed into the refuse. Inside, it was dank and foul-smelling, and for an instant Nely wanted to wrench her arm free and return to Havana. But it was too late to turn back.

She described Señora Mason, and the *bruja* appeared to know who she was. But for the spell to take effect, she would need something of hers, something that the *americana* had touched. Nely nodded grimly and placed the coins in the old woman's outstretched claw.

It was easy to find the art gallery where Señora Mason sometimes went, near the cathedral. Nely waited around the corner for her to drive off and went inside, where a plump *maricón* wearing a bowtie was reading the *Havana Post*. Nely's eyes darted nervously about the room, and she was astounded to see the figures of proud Oyá, the goddess of storms, and her husband Ogún, flanked by the leprous Babalú Ayé. Was Señora Mason a *santera* after all, as she feared? Upon closer inspection, she saw that they were not images of the *orishas* at all, but dolls made for the *americanos*. Relieved, she curtsied to the young man, who put down his newspaper and looked at her strangely. Surely there must be something of hers, Nely thought desperately, and pretended to be a customer. Soon, she found what she was looking for, a half-smoked cigar that Señora Mason had left in the ashtray. When the young man looked the other way, she snatched up the stub and popped it in her purse.

Back in Regla, the *bruja* was delighted when Nely unwrapped her hankerchief and showed her the slender cigar. Her eyes gleamed in the half-light as she carefully pulled away the outer layer of tobacco with a scraggly fingernail. Nely gasped when she saw that the *bruja* had fashioned a small doll from the dried husks of banana leaves, covered with gaudy bits of cloth. She rubbed the doll against the charred end of the cigar and muttered an incantation in Lucumí. Then she grinned tooth-lessly and pressed it into Nely's hand.

That night, when Hemingway came to see her, Nely was terrified that he would find the image of Señora Mason, since it was hidden in a shoebox beneath her bed. But he was too tired to make love, and simply rolled over and went to sleep.

Charlotte Eastlake was married in grand style at her family's estate in Oyster Bay. It was a beautiful spring day and the wedding took place on the lawn facing Long Island Sound. Jane, the matron of honor, retouched her friend's mascara before she walked down the aisle.

"I feel like I'm trussed up and ready for supper," said the reluctant bride, wiping her tears.

"You'll get used to it, Charlie," replied Jane.

During the reception, Grant chatted with the groom, Jack Halsey. For their honeymoon, the newlyweds planned to take the train to San Francisco, where they would board a yacht bound for the South Seas. There, Jack planned to indulge his new passion for sportfishing.

"A bit safer than bullfighting, sport," said Grant.

"For the marlin as well," admitted Jack. "But I like to live dangerously."

"The fishing is marvelous in Havana."

"Perhaps, but I don't think I'll be going back anytime soon."

Jane had to admit that Charlotte never looked lovelier. The orchestra began to play a rumba, of all things, and she and Jack twirled around the dance floor to great applause. Jane herself danced with Commodore Halsey, the father of the groom.

"How's the trouble in Cuba?" asked the silver-haired banker.

"People are always asking me that," said Jane, "but it's not as bad as it seems."

The next day, Jane and Grant took the overnight train to Miami, and then the *Caribbean Clipper* to Havana. By early afternoon, the seaplane was circling the harbor and soon hove up to the Arsenal Dock. After the crisp afternoons of Long Island, Jane found the heat annoying, but it grew cooler as they neared Jaimanitas.

That night, Jane couldn't sleep, and she smoked a *margarita* on the balcony. Her bedroom overlooked the garden, and she could smell the night-blooming jasmine. It was a murky night, but the spotlghts were on and she saw a shadow flickering across the lawn. Jane leaned over the balcony and strained to hear footsteps, but it was absolutely still except for the gentle rush of the surf. Was it just her imagination?

"Grant!" she cried. "Wake up!"

Rubbing his eyes, her husband reluctantly sat up in bed. "There's someone out there," said Jane.

"Go back to sleep," he yawned.

"I tell you there's someone out there," she insisted.

Grant knew from experience that it was best to humor her, and wearily put on his bathrobe. Armando was roused out of bed, as was the chauffeur, and together they scouted the grounds, but found no sign of an intruder.

"Don't you see, darling, it's just your imagination," he assured her.

"Perhaps I'm going crazy after all," she said.

"Let's not joke about that."

Jane managed to fall asleep but awoke tired and restless. Her son Tony howled pitilessly all morning, and Jane told the nanny to take him out into the garden. The inchoate fear of the night before continued to haunt her. If no one had been out there, then what was she afraid of? As she sipped a cup of tea, Armando brought the post that had arrived during her trip. There were the usual letters she never answered, like the monthly invitation to the Woman's Club bridge tea at the Sevilla-Biltmore. Suddenly, everything seemed unspeakably dreary.

Jane decided to stop by the art gallery, and as she drove along the Malecón, she thought of Javier. Even after the dreadful scene that Sunday, she half-expected him to be waiting for her. But it was better this way, she thought. Turning into Tejadillo, she saw to her surprise that it was shuttered. Where was Basil?

"Anybody home?" she said, unlocking the door.

There was no answer. The art gallery appeared to have been closed for several days, but she noted with pleasure that Gattorno's painting, which she had brought from the house, was still there.

"Basil?" she called up the stairs to the room where Basil lived.

In reply, there was a low moan. Jane found Basil lying in bed wearing lime green pajamas. There was a rank, sour smell in the room and the floor was littered with dirty clothes and newspapers. On the nightstand was a half-empty bowl of won-ton soup, and beside it, the scarred statue of Babalú Ayé.

"You poor ghastly child," said Jane.

With great effort, Basil propped himself up on plump elbows. Jane saw that red blisters covered most of his face, like burn marks. A few days ago, the rash had appeared on his forehead and quickly spread all over his body. Was it something that he ate? Basil had sent for a doctor, who was baffled but nonetheless prescribed a salve. This only made it worse, and the blisters itched even more. All else having failed, he had brought Babalú Ayú upstairs in the hope the *orisha* would cure him.

"I'll take whatever help I can get," Basil explained.

Opening the window to let the air in, Jane tidied up by kicking the dirty clothes under the bed, and saw an ashtray with one of her *margaritas*.

"I didn't know you smoked," she said.

"Maybe that's what it was."

"This won't do at all," said Jane.

As Basil protested weakly, she piled what clean clothes she could find into his worn leather suitcase, and helped him into his paisley bathrobe. His slippers were beneath a fetid pile of socks and he managed to waddle down the stairs to her car. Back at Jaimanitas, she installed him in one of the guest cottages behind the pool house. It was a cool, pleasant room with wicker furniture, quiet save for the screech of the monkey from the menagerie. Basil's appetite picked up when Armando brought cucumber sandwiches, delicately holding his nose, and he and Jane played hearts and drank manhattans.

Jane had agreed to meet Hemingway at the Ambos Mundos, and bring Bumby and Patrick back to Jaimanitas, where they would stay for several days. As she was about to set out, Tony began crying once more and she decided to take him along. Once more she made the drive back to Habana Vieja, and saw Hemingway in the hotel lobby. They had fished that morning, and Bumby proudly told her how he had landed a tarpon. Five-year-old Patrick, who had arrived from Key West on the ferry the night before, stood shyly behind his father.

"He's still getting his sealegs," explained Hemingway.

Jane agreed to join him on the *Anita* the next morning, and soon set off, leaving Hemingway to work before dinner. Bumby sat in front and the two younger boys in the back as she drove down Obispo to the Plaza de Armas. To avoid the late afternoon traffic, Jane decided to head south past Atarés and then take the Calzada del Cerro to Jaimanitas.

"Can I go fishing, too?" asked Tony.

"We'll see, little man," asked Jane. "You wouldn't want a big swordfish to eat you up, would you?"

This possibility gave Tony pause, but Bumby put in:

"Don't worry, Mrs. Mason. He'll be all right."

Patrick enthusiastically agreed.

"You're both very brave," said Jane, "just like your Papa."

The boys beamed and Jane squinted in the glare as they sped through El Cerro in the hills of Marianao. Here, just below the manicured fairways of the Havana Country Club, the building boom had ground to a halt, and many houses were left unfinished.

"Are we home, yet?" asked Tony.

"We'll be there soon," said Jane.

As the big Chevrolet climbed up the hill, the road narrowed, and it was then Jane saw the bus heading towards them. She turned sharply to avoid it, but the wheels spun in the gravel and they slid over the shoulder of the road. At first the boys laughed, thinking it was part of a game, but then the car tipped over and tumbled down the hill with agonizing slowness. Jane gripped the steering wheel as the boys desperately clutched at her arms, wide-eyed with surprise, too scared to cry out. The roof buckled as it scraped against the ground and it seemed an eternity until it finally came to a stop. The door was jammed, but they were able to scramble out the window. The wheels of the upended car continued to spin languidly, and Jane saw that they had come to rest in a baseball diamond at the bottom of the embankment. The bus was nowhere in sight, but several cars had stopped and a man shouted down if anyone was hurt. The boys had a few bruises but they were otherwise delighted with the adventure.

"I can't wait to tell Papa!" said Patrick excitedly.

When Grant heard about the accident, he rushed home to find Jane sitting in the garden, placidly stirring a pitcher of manhattans. Basil sat on a lawn chair, reading a Philo Vance mystery, and the boys splashed noisily in the pool.

"We're absolutely fine!" laughed Jane.

"But darling," protested her husband, "you could have been killed."

"You should be so lucky," she replied. "It was marvelous fun, wasn't it, boys?"

From the pool came a shriek of laughter.

"If you want to feel sorry for someone," continued Jane, "poor Basil is in an awful state. Just look at him!"

"That's the last time I try one of your cigars," said Basil.

With a frown, Grant noticed that Basil was wearing his favorite silk pajamas.

"It hardly sounds like fun," he said, turning back to Jane. "Does Ernest know?"

"Poor Ernest! They found him at the Floridita and dragged him to the telephone. I suspect he's still there."

"I wonder if you shouldn't see a doctor. You haven't been yourself lately, darling."

"Thank heaven for that," replied Jane. "Basil and I were going to have another drink before dinner. Won't you join us?"

The next morning, Jane awoke with an uncharacteristically fierce hangover. Even her usual remedy of tomato juice with a raw egg and Worcestershire sauce did nothing to help. Grant was alarmed when he heard she was going fishing:

"Janie, a day in bed would do you wonders."

"I promised Ernest I would bring the boys. Besides, Tony is dying to go. I told him that a giant marlin would gobble him up but he refused to listen."

"Nonsense! I'd feel better if you stayed at home, and certainly if Tony did. We've all had rather too much excitement lately."

"If you say *nonsense* one more time I don't know what I shall do," said Jane. "Tony can stay home, but I'll not be the one to tell him. As for me, it's a beautiful day and I'd much rather spend it on the water with Ernest than playing cards with Basil."

"How long is he staying?"

"Until that horrible rash clears up. The poor boy is terrified it will ruin his looks. By the way, I want you to be nice to him."

They cast off from the San Francisco Dock at 9:30 and the *brisa* quickly revived her. While still in the harbor, Carlos put out a feather for bait and Bumby explained yet again to his father how he climbed out of the car, with Patrick filling in the gaps.

"Looks like I missed all the excitement," said Hemingway. "How are you feeling, daughter?"

"Not you, too!" said Jane. "I'd have wrecked the car earlier if I'd known it would get me so much attention. Poor Stoneface was turning somersaults this morning."

The first strike came just after 11:00. A striped marlin smashed Hemingway's bait and jumped twice before spitting out the hook, and Bumby reeled in a *dorado*. They were heading back from Boca de Jaruco when Carlos cried out:

"¡Aguja!"

Patrick pointed excitedly as the marlin broke through the swell and followed behind the frothy wake. Jane's bait, a tarpon, was already in the water, and the marlin appeared to nibble at his tail, his slender bill riding above the water.

"Give him some slack, daughter," Hemngway advised.

Carlos began to pull up the teasers as the boys scrambled behind the fishing chair, anxious see the marlin jump.

"Now! Hit him!"

Jane snapped back the rod to set the hook and squealed with pleasure as the fish sailed gracefully out of the water. It was royal blue with lavender stripes on its dorsal fin, a small, feisty marlin that weighed forty pounds and and leaped nine more times before Carlos gaffed it.

"Look, Papa!" said Patrick. "Mrs. Mason caught the biggest fish ever!"

"I can see that," said Hemingway.

Incredibly, only a few minutes after they hauled the marlin over the transom, Jane had another strike, perhaps its mate. It jumped eight times before Carlos pulled in the leader and Hemingway grabbed it by the bill.

"Hurray for Mrs. Mason!" yelled Bumby.

Exhilarated, Jane breathed deeply and leaned back in the fishing chair. She felt a shiver of pain in her back, but the tension soon drained from her muscles. They weighed the two marlins at the dock, and she posed for pictures with the boys. Hemingway wanted to celebrate at the Floridita but she was afraid to see Javier there and they went instead to the rooftop bar at the Ambos Mundos. They ordered *mojitos* and watched the afternoon light cast an amber glow on the towers of the cathedral. When she returned to Jaimanitas, she found Grant playing cards with Basil.

"Gin!" cried Basil, triumphantly throwing down his hand, and Grant sighed wearily.

"I hope you two have been getting along," said Jane.

"Don't worry, Mr. M., your luck's bound to change."

He wore one of Grant's polo shirts, and his spirits had improved, although the blisters still covered his forehead.

"By the way," Basil added, "Armando makes a great manhattan. Do you suppose I could have another?"

Jane went fishing the next day, and the day after that,

hoping to put out of her mind the fear that had been shadowing her. Her affliction began as it always did, a faint ringing in her ears, oddly familiar like a melody she couldn't quite recognize. She knew that she could make it stop any time she wanted, but she let it grow louder and louder. Yet as the *Anita* reached the open sea, the sound lost itself in the rush of the waves and the squawks of the seagulls, and Jane sat in the shade of the wheel house, smoking a *margarita.*

They anchored in Boca Ciega, and the *Anita* drifted lazily in the shallow inlet. From the icebox, Hemingway produced a bottle of Tavel that Pauline had brought from Key West on her last visit. Opening it with a flourish, he filled their glasses as Joe whittled away at a wheel of Manchego cheese and a link of *chorizo.* Carlos had bought some avocados in the market and he sprinkled the wedges with pepper and lime juice before passing them around. No sooner had Jane finished than she changed in the cabin and went for a swim, her legs straight as she executed a neat dive from the bow.

"Come on in, Ernest," she called, splashing in the turquoise water.

He shook his head, but nonetheless followed Jane's lissome figure as she swam towards the shore. She emerged on the small, rocky beach and lay on her back, where a fisherman drying his net in the sun unabashedly gawked. The blonde *americana* would be his story at the *bodega* tonight, thought Hemingway, and for many nights to come. Jane's slender arm was draped over her eyes and she appeared to be sleeping. With a delicious yawn she waded back into the water, and swam to the *Anita* with slow, deliberate strokes.

Hemingway was anxious to be underway. As the engine rumbled to life, he dabbed coconut oil on the bridge of his nose, and put on his green-tinted Crooks lenses. But Jane stared sullenly at the sea grape trees on the shore.

"What ails you?" he asked.

"It's nothing," said Jane sharply.

"If you say so, daughter," said Hemingway. "But I'm quite a good listener, you know."

"I'm not your daughter!" said Jane, and went below, where Carlos was cleaning up the remains of lunch.

She began sobbing and Carlos emerged from the cabin with an incredulous shrug.

"Well, what do you know?" said Joe.

"You said it, Josie," smiled Hemingway with a wink, and finished the last of the wine.

There was no more fishing that afternoon. The sky grew overcast, although a shaft of light occasionally burst through the clouds like a spotlight on the darkening water. Jane remained below as the *Anita* entered the harbor behind a rickety old schooner. The skiffs of the marlin fishermen had returned empty handed, and their sails drooped forlornly as they rowed to Casablanca. Carlos shook his head mournfully at the dockhands waiting on the pier. As soon as the stern line was tied, Jane stepped off without a word.

"Jane," said Hemingway, running after her. "I can't let you go off like this."

"How do you propose to stop me?"

"That's not what I meant," he said quickly. "But I know that something is wrong. Why won't you tell me what it is?"

"Why do you think something is wrong? Look, Ernest, I really don't want to talk about it. Everybody wants to talk about what's wrong with Jane except Jane. But there's nothing wrong with Jane, nothing that you can fix, anyway. Don't worry, it has nothing to do with you."

Hemingway started to speak but Jane cut him off.

"That's it, isn't it? You think this is all about you. Would it make you feel better if it was? Then you could write about it, I suppose. But this isn't your book, it's mine."

"I'm sorry," Hemingway mumbled.

"Don't be sorry, Ernest. There's no need to apologize unless it's your fault. But you want it to be your fault, don't you? Then you could have something to apologize for."

Jane was crying again, and he tried to take her in his arms, but she slapped him hard across the face.

"There, that felt better, didn't it? Now you have something to write about!"

Jane left him on the dock, rubbing his cheek, and she ran out to where the chauffeur was waiting. It had grown louder, now, and she shut her eyes tightly all the way back to Jaimanitas. Grant was not yet home, but Basil was in the library, playing solitaire.

"I'm cured!" he said triumphantly as she entered. Indeed, the blisters on his face appeared to be fading.

"I need a drink," said Jane.

Armando soon brought a pitcher of manhattans, and Jane quickly drained her glass before having another.

"Slow down!" protested Basil. "I'll never keep up at this rate."

As the liquor had its intended effect, she felt the pain deadening in her head.

"Rough seas?" asked Basil.

"Just a squall or two," said Jane.

When Grant made his appearance, they were chattering gaily over a second pitcher of manhattans.

"I spoke with Ernest," he said dolefully. "He was very concerned."

"Was he really, darling?" said Jane, and this set Basil giggling.

"I don't think this is very funny," said Grant.

Basil bit his thumb, trying to keep from laughing, and Grant faced him and said:

"I trust you're feeling better, sport."

Basil nodded sheepishly.

"Will you excuse us?"

After Basil tiptoed out, Grant said:

"You've been seeing too much of him."

"Don't take it out on poor Basil."

"I meant Ernest. What happened on the boat today?"

"Here we go again!" laughed Jane bitterly. "What did he say?"

"He didn't say anything."

"That's because nothing happened. Jane went fishing, Jane cried, and Jane left. Are you quite satisfied?"

"It's starting again, isn't it?" said her husband.

"You don't give up, do you? You're no different from him, really. If something *happened*, as you put it, that would be different. At least you'd know what to say, instead of staring at me with those puppy dog eyes. I'm sorry to disappoint you, darling."

"Please, Janie," he said.

But it was too late, and she started crying again, though this time she couldn't stop. Jane locked herself in the bathroom and Grant banged on the door with the palm of his hand and threatened to break it down. She was better by then, and ate a cold supper that Armando brought up on a tray. Afterwards, she drank a few more manhattans, and by bedtime, she thought she would make it.

Relieved, Jane stood on the balcony and breathed in the damp air scented with night-blooming jasmine. Smoky grey clouds veiled the moon and the water was a dark purple. It was late, and the lights of the fishing village had started to flicker out.

It began once again and this time she knew that it would soon overwhelm her, like a giant wave. Jane tried to concentrate on the sound of the water lapping up against the beach and the hum of the cicadas in the flame trees, but they were blotted out by the eerie, mournful ringing growing louder and louder, like the peal of a churchbell. She knew that she should go inside but the breeze was cool against her cheek and she balled up her fists and put them to her ears.

"Darling!" she cried, but she was already falling.

Jane remembered the awful, endless moment when the car slid over the embankment and tumbled end over end, turning the boys' laughter to terrified silence, and it so terrified her that it was a relief when she finally hit the ground.

EIGHT

Javier heard that Jane had tried to kill herself from a reporter at *Bohemia* who covered the more lurid goings-on of the American colony. He immediately rushed to the hospital, where the nurse informed him that Señora Mason was not receiving visitors. The Anglo-American Hospital was located in the Vedado, and he sat in his car as though waiting for her to step outside. But he knew that she wouldn't, so he drove to Tejadillo Street and parked in front of the art gallery, as though she were there. It was closed and shuttered, and he thought of driving to Jaimanitas, but of course she wasn't there, either. If he wrote her a letter, the doctors would simply turn it over to Grant. Even if he knew she would read it, what could he say?

Javier returned to *Bohemia* and made his way to his desk. The office of the magazine had the look of a city under siege. It had been closed several times by the police, and the publisher had spent a night at the Jefatura before some *político* friends secured his release. Many of the employees had not been payed for several weeks, and more than a few desks were empty. The ceiling fan spun impotently in the stifling air, and the advertising director, Pepe Dominguez, holed himself up in his office and rarely emerged. Even Professor Vargas no longer came to the office, despite the success of his radio show, and delivered his weekly chess columns by messenger. Javier realized that once more his absence had gone unnoticed and he decided to quit at the end of the summer and leave for Paris.

During the next few days, the heat gave way to rainstorms. Javier was surprised when Grant telephoned, but nonetheless agreed to meet him for a drink at Sloppy Joe's. The rain had stopped, so Javier walked from Trocadero Street, only to sprint across the Prado when the sky opened up once more. By the time he entered the bar he was dripping wet, and found Grant nursing a shot of rye.

"Jane asked me to see you," he announced matter-of-factly. "She knew you'd worry."

Javier ordered a beer, but it was flat. He pushed it away and stared straight ahead.

"Damned lucky to be alive," continued Grant, lighting a Chesterfield. "It wasn't a big fall but she landed on her back. The doctor thinks it may be broken but they don't know, yet."

"How did it happen?"

"One of the newspapers printed some garbage that she was shot. Nothing so dramatic as that, I'm afraid. She fell off the balcony. She was a bit tight, I think. That's all there is to it."

"Is it?"

"You're not making this any easier, López. I don't blame you for anything that took place. If it hadn't been for the accident, none of this would have happened. The doctor thinks she might have strained her back then. Terrible scare with the boys, what? Poor Ernest was beside himself. And Jane shouldn't have gone fishing the next day. But I don't blame Ernest, either. It's nobody's fault."

"May I see her?"

"That's not such a good idea, sport."

"Why not?"

"Doctor's orders," explained Grant. "She was in quite a state, you know. It's best that she doesn't see anyone for a while. As soon as she can travel, I'm sending her to New York."

"Will she be all right?"

"You know how Jane is," said Grant. "It will take more than this to keep her down."

As Javier waitied for him to finish, Grant drained his rye and replaced it on the bar. Several tourists charged inside amid shouts and laughter, their clothes dripping wet.

"Is there anything I can do?" asked Javier.

But Grant appeared not to have heard, and stared into his empty glass. There was no point in continuing the conversation, and Javier walked out into the rain.

Freddy found him slumped over the bar at the Floridita and tried to cheer him up by inviting Kiki Herrera and a friend of hers to join them. They had dinner at El Pacífico, and then drove to a *frita* in Marianao, but Javier drank steadily and refused to dance. Freddy reluctantly dropped the girls off and they walked down the Prado towards the Malecón. It was silent except for the distant music of the female orchestras, and the footsteps of a policeman who looked them over suspiciously. The laurel trees seemed to genuflect over their heads in the ghostly moonlight, and they came to the statue of Juan Clemente Zenéa, the poet executed by the Spaniards in La Cabaña, who sat on his marble pedestal and gazed wistfully out to sea, his muse reclining at his feet.

"I don't see why you want to leave," said Freddy. "This is the most beautiful city in the world."

"I suppose in Paris I'll miss Havana," admitted Javier.

The following afternoon, they found Hemingway in the Floridita. He had dropped Pauline off at the P&O ferry and spent the day in his hotel room, unsuccessfully trying to write.

"What have we here?" he boomed as he entered the bar, clapping Javier on the back. His drink spilled, but Constante soon had three more daiquiris lined up. "What do you say, Harvard?"

Javier shrugged and dried his shirtfront with a handkerchief.

"How's the fishing?" asked Freddy.

"The big one's still hiding, but Papa's going to find him."

Hemingway quickly dispatched a daiquiri and described his latest exploits on the water.

"Why don't you boys join me tomorrow?"

"I've made enough of a mess on your boat," said Freddy.

"Hell, Tex, a swordfish rammed us so hard it nearly split the hull. Josie's had to patch her up so many times that you can puke all you want. How about your *amigo* here?"

Javier shook his head sullenly.

"Had enough fishing?" said Hemingway, gulping down another *Papa Especial* and snapping his fingers for one more.

"Javier's going to Paris," explained Freddy.

"I'll be there in November. What are you going to do?"

"I'm going to write my novel."

"No better place to do it. I've done my best to talk you out of it, but let's hope you have better luck than me. I can't write a goddam word anymore. Maybe I'll give it up and become a white hunter. What do you say?"

"Bag a lion for me," said Freddy.

"Hell, shoot one yourself. You two can be native bearers. None of my pals wanted to come, except for Charles. That's what friends are good for, stabbing you in the back. All my friends are either sons of bitches or bastards. The only trouble is trying to figure out which is which. What do you think?"

"I've got to go," said Javier.

"Not so fast," said Hemingway, grabbing his arm. "I still owe you a boxing lesson, remember?"

"How about another drink?" asked Freddy.

Hemingway ignored the question and began to shadow-box against the wall, holding his daiquiri in his right hand, close to his chest, and jabbing with his left.

"I guess they don't teach boxing at college. I never got around to going, you know, I was too busy getting shot at by the Austrians. Just what did you learn at Harvard?"

"Not much," Javier admitted.

"Then welcome to Professor Hemingstein's boxing academy for young Cuban gentlemen," he said, putting down his empty glass.

"It's getting late, Ernesto," protested Javier.

"Call me Papa," said Hemingway, his smile frozen. "I've got the gloves back at the hotel. Tex can time the rounds."

Javier turned to leave but Hemingway playfully shoved him against the bar and once more assumed a boxing stance.

"I don't think this is such a good idea," said Freddy.

But Javier had turned to face Hemingway and their eyes met. They finished the last round of drinks and walked down Obispo to the Ambos Mundos, Javier a few steps ahead. Hemingway threw punches in the air, trailed by several cheering shoeshine boys. Scattered on the floor of his room were crumpled sheets of paper and empty bottles of Vichy water. The boxing gloves were in the closet, and Hemingway tossed a pair to Javier before taking off his shirt.

"Why don't we go have a few more drinks?" suggested Freddy.

"Shut up," said Hemingway.

He moved the furniture into the corner and kicked the bottles under the bed. As Javier loosened his tie, Hemingway strapped on the gloves and took several deep breaths before jumping up and down to loosen up.

"What about the people downstairs?" asked Freddy.

"They're used to it," Hemingway replied.

Freddy waited till the second hand of his watch passed twelve and reluctantly signalled for them to begin.

"Let's see what you got, Harvard," said Hemingway, leaning forward, his head bobbing behind raised fists.

Javier hesitantly circled him, but Hemingway charged and landed a jab to his forehead. His eyes smarting with the pain, Javier lashed out wildly, but Hemingway danced out of the way.

"You forgot lesson number one: *Never get mad.*"

Javier stayed out of reach of Hemingway's long arms. When he swung again, Javier ducked and stepped forward, throwing a right hook. Hemingway easily parried it and scored with a blow to his side.

Freddy announced that the two-minute round was over, and Hemingway went to the sink and splashed water on his face.

"I'm getting thirsty," said Freddy. "Why don't we go upstairs to the bar and forget all this? Hell, we could call room service."

"We're just getting started, Tex," said Hemingway, once more raising his guard.

Javier was still dizzy from the shot to his head and his ribs ached from the sucker punch, but he managed to ward off the jabs with his forearms and wait for an opening. Hemingway's muscles were toughened from weeks of hauling billfish out of the sea, but he was slow. Javier remembered that he was nearly blind in his left eye, and if he could get inside his swing, he could land a punch. He waited for Hemingway's right hook, and crouched low so that the glove went over his head. Feinting with his right, he threw an uppercut. But Hemingway's head jerked back at the last instant, and he connected with a left to Javier's chin.

Immediately, Freddy called time.

"You forgot lesson number two," said Hemingway triumphantly. *"Never let the other guy see your cards."*

Drenched in sweat, he dried himself off with a towel, and spat on the floor.

"Had enough?"

Javier rubbed his jaw but shook his head. Once more, they began to circle each other.

"You know what your problem is?" said Hemingway, between raspy breaths. "You think too much. That's not good for a boxer, or a writer."

He bared his teeth and lunged forward, but Javier spun away. Hemingway turned and swung with his right, and would have caught him squarely on the mouth if Javier hadn't ducked and counterpunched. Hemingway raised his glove at the last second, but their momentum carried them against each other, and Hemingway roughly pushed him away.

"You're learning, Harvard."

Javier saw that despite his strength, the older man was becoming tired, gasping for air, and his reflexes were slowing. Hemingway began to favor his bad knee, and had to steady himself against the bedpost. But his eyes had grown small and piggish, and Javier realized he was moving in for the kill.

Hemingway usually feinted before taking a half step forward to land his Sunday punch. Javier had tried to get inside, only to receive a sharp left to the jaw, so this time he sidestepped to the right. Hemingway shoved him against the wall, and brought down the glove to chop him on the side of the head, but grunted with irritation when he saw that the younger man was still moving forward. Hemingway whirled around, expecting a flurry of punches, but Javier had stepped back and eyed him defiantly.

"Time's up!" announced Freddy.

"No, it's not over yet," said Hemingway, catching his breath and wiping the sweat from his forehead with the back of his glove.

Hemingway stood with his back to the wall, and shifted his weight to his toes. Suddenly he was laughing again. Javier noticed that his face was split by the same fierce, wolfish smile he remembered from the day they met at the Floridita. Then Hemingway said:

"It's time for lesson number three. You may not like it, but Papa's going to make you like it."

"What's lesson number three?" asked Freddy.

Hemingway stepped forward and forced Javier towards the center of the room, waiting for him to lower his guard. He jabbed with his right, waited a split second, feinted once more, and when Javier raised his glove he took a half step back and swung hard with his left. Hemingway had purposely led with his right in each round, saving his left cross for the end. To his immense surprise, it failed to connect and he felt a sharp pain in his bad knee. Javier had stepped just beyond the murderous reach of the swing. When he saw Hemingway lose his balance, he put his weight into a punch that caught him just above the left eye.

Hemingway didn't see it coming and stumbled back against the wall. His knee gave way and he fell with a crash.

"*Now* it's over," said Javier, taking off his gloves.

Lying on the floor, amid his dirty clothes and manuscripts, Hemingway touched his glove to his rapidly swelling eyebrow.

"You've earned your diploma," he looked up with a grin, but Javier had snatched up his jacket and was already out the door.

"Was that lesson number three?" asked Freddy.

Hemingway told Nely that two men had set upon him with *vergajos* as he left the Floridita. She sent Zoila to the butcher for a steak to place over his black eye, and drew a hot bath.

"Was it the *porra?*" she asked.

"It must have been," said Hemingway. "I took a crack at one guy and they ran off, so I didn't get a good look at them."

While Hemingway soaked in the tub, Nely took out the shoebox beneath the bed, and looked at the doll the *bruja* had given her. It was dirty and shriveled, and the seams had come undone, spilling the flakes of tobacco stuffed inside. Nely ripped the foul thing apart and threw it away.

That night, Hemingway stirred restlessly in bed, peeling off the damp sheets from his skin and staring at the ceiling. Nely listened to his breathing and realized that he was awake and thinking of the blond *americana*, whose magic had proved much more powerful than hers. When he got up and put on his clothes, she pretended to be asleep, and heard the door close softly behind him.

It was still dark when Hemingway arrived on the waterfront. A drunk sang softly to himself, clutching a bottle of rum, and there was the clatter of high heels on the cobblestones and a woman's laughter, a whore with her last customer of the night. As dawn broke, a fisherman rowed his dinghy to the middle of the harbor to cast his net for *machuelos*. The water was smooth as a pane of glass, and ripples fanned out from his oars.

Hemingway had breakfast at the Perla, where two students had been gunned down by a passing car the day Joe left for Key West. The shattered glass had been replaced and a fresh coat of paint covered the blood stains, but there were still bullet holes in the wall. Finishing his coffee, he caught up with Carlos making his way across the square. The old Cuban carried several pink snappers wrapped in a newspaper under his arm, and they stopped to buy mangoes at a stall. Joe was yawning in the cockpit, having slept onboard, and the three men silently prepared to set out. The swelling had gone down but there was still an ugly bruise above his eye. Carlos looked questioningly at Joe, who hunched his shoulders and put a finger to his lips.

A pair of skiffs bobbed off La Punta, their lines dangling over the coral bottom, and Joe wheeled around them. The sun was at Hemingway's back, and he let the bait trail behind the teasers while a cormorant soared overhead. They raised a marlin later that morning, but he ignored the bait. For lunch, they anchored in Boca de Jaruco and ate the mangos, but Hemingway refused to go swimming despite the heat. Joe had seen his black moods before and was content to sit at the wheel while Carlos tried to stay out of the way.

That afternoon, Hemingway half-heartedly landed a dolphin which he threw back in the water, to Carlos' dismay. The spray made the cut over his eye sting but he knew it would act as a disinfectant, and he leaned back and studied the turquoise wash of the *Anita's* propeller. More than once, he had almost thrown the unfinished story about his father away. But something had happened, as though the hook had been set, and now it was nearly within his grasp. He could feel it deep inside him, like a giant marlin several fathoms beneath the surface, pulling at the line with tremendous force.

Carlos turned his dark brown face to the sky as if in prayer. There was a chill in the air as clouds advanced from the west, and they entered the harbor just ahead of a blow, with towers of dark rain on the horizon.

"Mañana seguro," said the old fisherman, but Hemingway had already started down the pier.

That night, he couldn't sleep, and he leaned out the balcony and looked over the rooftops to the Plaza de Armas. The spreading branches of the ceiba tree in front of the Templete were illuminated by spotlights, and raindrops still clung to the leaves. His throat was scratchy and he pulled the blanket over himself, managing to doze off in an armchair. When he woke up it was still dark, and he thought he was still dreaming. He heard the murmur of voices, a young boy asking where his grandfather was buried.

Suddenly, his mind was clear. Hemingway pulled out the sheaf of papers from his drawer. With his penknife, he whittled the pencil to a fine point and began to write. He remembered driving over the red brick streets of Piggot with Bumby during Thanksgiving, and passing by the rows of corn. Once again, the boy asked where his grandfather was buried. But that was not how it began, he realized, that was how it ended.

Hemingway tore up the first page and began again. Once more, the man was driving through the main street of the town with his son, past flashing traffic lights, to the newly picked fields lined with bales of cotton. The boy was asleep, and the man thought of hunting quail with his father. It was his father who had taught him to shoot quail, to pick out their hiding places and figure out which way they would fly.

Hemingway sat in bed with the paper on his knees, scribbling furiously, and rapidly filled a page before replacing it with another. The words were rushing out of him unchecked, but he stopped and read what he had written. Only when he was satisfied did he begin again, this time writing slowly and deliberately. The sun had risen and was streaming in through the window, and he heard the musical call of a *pregonero* and the snap of a metal shutter being opened on Obispo. These were sounds that he loved, but it made no difference. The story was taking shape and he knew that if he did not write it down now, it would be lost forever. The lead of his pencil broke and he searched frantically for another. Finding one in his dresser, he continued to write, and remembering how his father could look across the lake and see whether a flag had been raised on the dock, or count sheep in a far-off hillside.

By then, Hemingway had worked for several hours and filled eight pages. The words were still rising to the surface like a bubbling spring, and to choke them off he went down to the Plaza de San Francisco and found Joe having lunch at the Perla.

"You picked a fine day to disappear, Mahatma," said Joe, who had sent Carlos home after waiting all morning.

Hemingway shrugged and realized he hadn't eaten all day. Suddenly ravenous, he wolfed down a plate of *picadillo* and white rice, washing it down with a bottle of Hatuey. More than anything else, he wanted to go back and write, but he knew he would have to wait. Even though it was too late to go fishing, he made Joe take him out into the Gulf Stream so he could clear his head. The *brisa* had picked up and the sea was choppy, but they headed east for a mile until they passed the old stone house on the point that marked the bay of Cojimar. It was then they saw the porpoises. Carlos pointed excitedly out to sea, where hundreds of them swam against the current like a herd of ponies, leaping in low, graceful arcs. Joe smiled as Hemingway chattered away, and marveled how quickly his black mood of the day before had passed, like a summer storm. Only much later that night, after several drinks at the Cunard Bar, did Hemingway stumble back to the hotel.

In the morning, he heard the voices again, as in his dream of the night before. Hemingway snatched his spectacles from the nightstand and began to write sitting up in bed. There was a knock on the door and when there was no answer, a maid with fresh towels poked her head in. The eccentric *americano* didn't bother to look up, and the only sound in the room was the scratch of his pencil.

In another time and place, a boy was lying in a clearing against the trunk of a hemlock tree, with a girl and her brother, the pine needles tickling his bare feet. To get there, he had followed the trail from the cottage, through the woods down the fallen log over the creek bed, to the field of sheep sorrel by the Indian camp, where the hemlock bark was stacked for the tanneries. The boy was hunting squirrels and he waited carefully for the squirrel to bark so as not to waste a shot, because his father had only given him three cartridges to hunt with. The girl was plump and brown with laughing dark eyes, and she had lain with him on the bed of pine needles.

When Hemingway put down the pencil, he had written nine more pages, and he knew that he was close to the end of the story. If he continued writing, he could finish it today, but his vision was blurry. It was not yet noon, and Joe and Carlos might still be waiting at the dock. By the time he arrived, storm clouds were moving in and the fishing skiffs were already returning to the harbor, so there was nothing to be done. They waited out the rain at the Perla, drinking Hatueys and playing dominoes with Kaiser Guillermo.

That night, Hemingway tried to write but his temples throbbed with pain. He knew that the voices were fading and if he did not complete the story soon it would never be finished. Unable to sleep, he feverishly paced from one end of the room to another, listening to the distant thunder, but after a few slugs from the bottle of rum on his dresser he fell in bed exhausted.

The sound of traffic in the street below awoke him the following day. Leaning back against the headboard, Hemingway took up the sheaf of paper and once again propped it on his knees. He could finish it now, he knew, and remembered how his father's beard had frost in the winter, giving him the appearance of an old man.

Once more, he was driving with Bumby in the late afternoon through the Arkansas countryside. The boy stirred and asked his father about the Indians, his voice drowsy with sleep, and his father told him how they used to hunt squirrels in the branches of the hemlock trees. But that was not all the boy wanted to know, and he asked about his grandfather.

On the train, when he learned of his father's death, Hemingway had told Bumby that his father was dead and he would have to continue on to Key West by himself, like a brave little fellow. He could not say that his father had shot himself, because he did not yet know from his sister's telegraph, and he could not tell him that his father was a coward, although he already knew that.

Now, as they drove home in the fading light, the boy wanted to know where his grandfather was buried, and the man promised to take him, though he knew he never would. He had loved his father, but he had never understood what he was afraid of, or what made him put the old Civil War pistol behind his ear and pull the trigger. Was it really cowardice, or a special kind of bravery he could not yet begin to understand?

Even though he had slept for several hours the night before, Hemingway was exhausted, and the pounding in his head had started again, but the man and the boy continued to talk as fathers and sons often do, not saying anything in particular, but reassured by the sound of their own voices. His back was sore from sitting up in bed, and his fingers were cramped from clutching the pencil. That morning, he wrote seven more pages, and he knew that he was done.

Lately, the New York office had been asking Walter a number of troublesome questions, and the latest cable demanded a progress report on Altomar. But during the past few days, he had been unable to reach Aragon, who was in Matanzas. Given the sugar cane strike, which threatened to cut short the *zafra*, it was understandable that the Cuban had not returned his calls. But what was happening at Altomar?

Returning home one evening, Walter had instructed his driver Felix to continue down Fifth Avenue, past Jaimanitas, until they reached the construction site. Walter stepped out of the car and peered through the chain link fence at the pilings erected on the rocky beach, where the marina would be built. The sea grape trees near the water had been cleared, and a hole had been dug for the foundation of the sleek Art Deco club house, but little else had been done. Commodore Halsey would not like this, thought Walter.

The next morning, he closeted himself in his office and contemplated the *HMS Victory*, as he liked to do at the beginning of each day. It was a fleet of ships such as this that battered the walls of El Morro when the British took the island in 1762. Perhaps Welles should have entered Havana in a warship, as Aragon had suggested.

Walter buzzed Miss Garcia and dictated a curt letter to him, demanding an explanation for the construction delays, and threatening to call in the loan. Hopgood, the bank's vice president, had opposed the financing of Altomar, saying it was too risky. If the construction remained behind schedule, he could imagine Hopgood's pinched features breaking into a triumphant smile. For once, Aragon made an appointment, and came by to see Walter a few days later.

"We have something to discuss, my friend," he said.

"You can say that again! You're running out of time."

"Walter, Walter, Walter!" moaned Aragon in mock despair.

He ruefully recounted his recent troubles in Matanzas. The Communist-led strike had nearly ruined the *zafra* of the Cuban Sugar Cane Company, and only when troops were brought in could they finish the harvest. As if that weren't enough, the train carrying the sugar cane to the mill had been attacked by rebels, and several hundred hectares of land had been set on fire.

"They are little more than hoodlums, with no regard for property," continued Aragon bitterly. He seemed tired, with fleshy bags beneath his eyes. But then he brightened, regaining his usual optimism: "Fortunately, I also have good news. Our troubles will soon be over."

"That's what you told me last month," said Walter.

Aragon leaned closer and said in a low voice:

"What I am about to tell you is strictly confidential. There are negotiations underway now that will resolve the present crisis. While your Mr.Welles sees fit to meet with student agitators and terrorists, Ambassador Cintas has been meeting with President Roosevelt in Washington, D.C. More I can not say. Do you know what this means, my friend?"

Walter's eyes narrowed suspiciously.

"It means that we will soon be able to resume construction at Altomar!"

That week, a bomb went off in the American Club, of all places. Long after the fall of Machado, the incident remained part of the club's lore, recounted over poker games in the members' lounge. The bomb had been placed in the mailbox, and exploded precisely at noon, sending jagged shards of metal and glass flying into the dining room. Cesar, the head waiter, thought the American Club was under attack by revolutionaries and dived beneath the buffet table. One resolute member had been contemplating taking another bite of his club sandwich, but instead walked to the bar.

"I think I'll have a martini," he said, as the bartender's head slowly peeked over the counter.

The bomb was still the topic of discussion several days later, when Ambassador Welles spoke at lunch. An aide whispered the anecdote to Welles as he ascended the podium.

"I understand there's been a bit of excitement around here lately," quipped the ambassador to nervous laughter, "and that you make one hell of a strong martini."

"Hear, hear!" cried several members, and Ogden nudged Walter in the ribs.

"There have been times in the past few weeks," continued Welles, "when I've wanted one myself."

"Hear, hear!"

"But I felt it was important to give you gentlemen a progress report on my work to date. As you know, we've been burning the midnight oil at the embassy since our offer of mediation was accepted by President Machado. By the way, Mrs. Welles and I regret we've not been able to accept your many kind invitations. But I'm glad to say it's been worth the hard work!"

"He's talking through his nose again," said Ogden.

"If at times our progress has seemed incremental, or even minimal, it is because of the sheer complexity of the situation. Those of you who have lived and worked in Cuba for many years know that the relationship between our countries has never been better. It has also never been more complex, involving a host of political and economic variables, all with important ramifications. It is in the context of this complicated relationship that President Roosevelt's Good Neighbor Policy must be seen. If the United States is to be a good neighbor of the Republic of Cuba, then we must work toward a fair and equitable way to resolve the situation we presently find ourselves in..."

Walter had barely slept the night before. Above his head, the ceiling fan stirred the sluggish air as the ambassador's reedy voice droned on, and he nearly nodded off.

"Pop!" whispered Freddy.

Walter's head jerked up as Welles concluded his remarks. Grant Mason took the floor and said:

"Ambassador Welles, let me ask a question that is on all of our minds. When are we going to quit dilly-dallying and put an end to this nonsense?"

One member laughed out loud but several others began to talk excitedly and Welles raised both hands for silence.

"That's a good question, Mason, but hardly one that I can answer given the delicacy of the negotiations. While the United States is prepared to intervene, as is our right—and I might add, duty—under the Cuban constitution to guarantee public safety, that hardly seems necessary at the present juncture."

"That's fine for the politicians," said Tom Beales, "but we're all businessmen here. Many of us here agree with Mason that the only way to resolve the crisis is through military intervention. It's the only thing that's worked in the past, and it's the only thing the Cubans understand. Whether Machado stays or goes, it's going to come to that, and the sooner we admit it to ourselves, the better."

"Hear, hear!" cried the members excitedly.

Welles coughed nervously and drank from the glass of water on the podium.

"Please, gentlemen!" cried the president of the club, trying to make himself heard over the hubbub. "Ambassador Welles may just order the marines to come here if we don't show him some common courtesy."

This quieted the audience down somewhat, but Welles had lost his equanimity and his eyes flickered nervously from one face to another. Like a pack of wolves moving in for the kill, the members demanded to know what would happen next. Much to everyone's amazement, Walter stood up and tapped his glass of iced tea with his fork until there was silence.

"It seems to me," he said, "that I've heard all this before. Too much blood has been spilled already. If the marines do land, what makes you fellows think it will solve anything? When they go home, what then?"

Welles stared first in relief, and then in mounting terror as Walter concluded:

"Cuba's a pressure cooker and if we make a mistake it's liable to blow up in our faces. The Cubans have to solve their own problems, once and for all, whether we like it or not."

Walter was so accustomed to keeping his own counsel that when he impulsively voiced his opinion, he was just as surprised as anyone else. There was a hushed silence, but the members soon shouted him down and began arguing furiously among themselves. Welles drained his glass of water, and wiped his shiny forehead with a handkerchief. With a weak nod to the president of the club, he darted out the side door, his aide scurrying behind.

"I didn't know you had it in you," said Ogden.

That night, Walter tossed and turned so much that Beryl banished him to the guest room. He awoke tired and irritable, and rather than brave Olga's pancakes, he went so far as to skip breakfast. Perhaps Aragon was right, and the crisis would soon end. But Welles hardly seemed optimistic. What would Commodore Halsey do if Altomar went bust? Would he inject more capital to keep the bank open as he had when Mr. Gordon absconded? With the situation as uncertain as it was, Walter decided to send Beryl and the twins to Texas a few weeks early, accompanied by Freddy.

"But I'll miss all the excitement!" he protested.

"That's what I'm hoping," said Walter.

Freddy had been downcast since the demise of his radio program. Astonishingly, despite the deepening political crisis, the number of phone calls to CMX and letters to *Bohemia* grew, and listeners even stopped by the Havana Trust hoping to submit a question that would stump "the smartest man in Havana." What turned out to be the final program began well enough one afternoon at the Tokio Cabaret. Professor Vargas sat at his usual place, his hand appearing to prop up his huge head, when Kiki Herrera read the question submitted by one of their most faithful listeners, Marta Portuondo from

Luyano. It concerned the Giraldilla, the famous bronze statue atop the moated castle of the Real Fuerza off the Plaza de Armas. The statue was said to portray the wife of Hernando de Soto, scanning the horizon in vain for her husband, who had left Havana to explore Florida and later died on the Mississipi River.

"*Maestro*, what does she hold in her hands?" asked Kiki Herrera breathlessly.

The professor's mind worked at a dizzying speed and his tendency was to instantly blurt out the correct answer. But in order to build suspense, Freddy had instructed him to wait several minutes before answering, and clear his throat as though nervously stalling for time. In the meantime, the Conjunto Casablanca played a quick *bolero* followed by a drumroll.

"In her left hand, she carries the Cross of Calatrava," began Professor Vargas triumphantly, and added with a flourish: "This was the order of Juan Beltran de Villamonte, the governor of Havana in 1634, who commissioned the statue."

"But what about the right hand?" asked Kiki Herrera on cue, as Freddy beamed.

Professor Vargas hesitated, as though racking his encyclopedic brain for the correct answer, but before he could open his mouth, there was a racket as a door was forced open at the back of the studio. Kiki Herrera screamed as an angry young man burst in and began chasing Freddy around the dance floor.

"*¡Por favor, Angel!*" screamed Kiki Herrera, chasing him in turn.

Angel, her *novio*, lunged at Freddy across the table, knocking down Professor Vargas, who tumbled into the Conjunto Casablanca. Freddy ran around the tangle of musical instruments with his pursuer a few steps behind, and jumped onto the bandstand. Angel would surely have caught him if not for the conga player, who was a porter at the railway station between musical engagements. He seized Angel by the scruff of the neck and lifted him up as he flailed his fists, while Freddy cowered behind Professor Vargas. This might have ended the struggle if Kiki Herrera had not come unexpectedly to her fiancé's help by hitting the conga player on the head with the heel of her shoe, and it took the rest of the band to subdue them both. The struggle took place under a live microphone, which provided much excitement for listeners. Unfortunately, Walter happened to be listening to the program in his office at the Havana Trust, and promptly called the radio station to cancel the show once and for all.

Beryl was oddly absent-minded the day of their departure, and checked yet again to see if she had forgotten anything. The girls were looking forward to returning to Austin, and tossed their lassoes in the garden. As for Freddy, he moped by the door while Felix loaded the suitcases into the Buick.

After dropping his family off at the P&O terminal, Walter went directly to the bank. Hopgood was in Indianapolis visiting his mother, and the work had piled up. Loan documents lay in irregular heaps on his desk, and there was another cable from New York demanding to know when work on Altomar would resume. Walter loosened his tie and and rolled up his sleeves. A mosquito hovered malignantly over his desk, and after much effort he was able to squash it with a damp forearm. His spectacles were cloudy, and Walter squinted as he dried the lens with a handkerchief. For once, he regretted not going to Texas, and imagined himself sitting in the cool shade beneath a live oak tree on the Guadalupe River.

His secretary looked up when Walter stepped out of his office, but he waved her off. As Elmer held the door open, Walter couldn't resist sniffing the air, but could detect no liquor on his breath. O'Reilly was empty save for a woman huddled miserably on the sidewalk with a small child. Walter stepped around them and walked disconsolately to the Plaza de Armas, hoping for a sea breeze. As he fanned himself with a sweaty palm, he noticed an old man pushing a cart filled with wilted flowers. A tattered shirt hung from his shoulders, and the remains of a straw hat clung to his head. Walter watched his painful progress around the square, and realized he was heading towards him, perhaps mistaking him for a tourist. He appeared to be saying something, and pointed at the flowers with a gnarled finger.

Walter fled back to the Havana Trust. Altomar continued to trouble him, and he decided to spend a few days at La Margarita, which never failed to calm his nerves. Perhaps away from Havana, he could clear his head and decide whether or not to call in the loan. He dispatched Felix to pick up his things at the house, but when he returned, Walter sent him home and impusively got behind the wheel of the Buick himself.

There was little traffic as he left Habana Vieja and rounded the bay. Approaching Matanzas, the road curved around the lush green hills topped with royal palms. Walter turned south to reach La Margarita, and remembered how the neatly paved road had once been a path of reddish clay rutted by oxcart wheels. Verdant fields of sugar cane filled the landscape, and he could see the white administrator's house, surrounded by a verandah. Walter drove with the windows open, and he could smell the hay and the discarded stalks of cane drying in the sun. As he passed through the gates he saw the schoolhouse which he had built so the children of the cutters could learn to read, and the baseball diamond hacked out of the sugar cane field. The bleachers had been erected on the site of the old *barracón,* the long wooden house where the slaves had been shut up every night. As always, La Margarita filled Walter with an odd sense of pride. It was little wonder that Aragon wanted to get his hands on it. He would send the troublesome *guajiros* away, cut the cane with gangs of Haitian laborers, and send it to be ground at the mechanized mill of the Cuban Sugar Cane Company.

Walter went to bed early, and slept well for the first time in many nights. The only sound was the hiss of the cicadas, and the occasional bark of a dog. At dawn, he made his way to the stable, where he had an old mare saddled. Walter had brought along his riding boots and Stetson hat, and as the first streaks of pink crossed the greyish sky, he trotted down the tidy paved street lined with white picket fences toward the baseball diamond. The sugar cane fields began at the outfield, and stretched over the hills to the horizon. It was quiet save for the distant barking of a dog, and the air was surprisingly cool. Gaining a rise, he saw La Margarita spread out before him, the streetlights glowing in the half-light, the steeple of the church glistening with dew. Walter continued to nudge the horse forward, and followed the royal palms that appeared to climb the slope like pilgrims. Beyond them, he knew, was the sea.

Back in Havana, his contentment vanished as Walter puttered through the empty house. Olga offered to make him dinner, but he sent her away and gnawed on a piece of cold chicken at the kitchen table. Something caught his attention as he made his way to the bedroom and he noticed the odd little statues that Beryl had bought last year, perched on the bookshelf. The obsidian eyes of the one holding the axe glinted in the light and he wondered what they were doing there. Walter specifically remembered asking the maid to get rid of them, but here they were. Annoyed, Walter picked up the fierce little man. What did Beryl say his name was? With a shrug, he put it back.

Arriving the next morning at the Havana Trust, Walter learned that the bus drivers had gone on strike, and several of the tellers were late for work. The stevedores had threatened to walk out as well, which would effectively close the port. Walter decided to keep the bank open no matter what.

"Elmer!" he snapped. "Look sharp!"

"Yes, sir!" said the guard, roused from his lethargy.

Pauline visited once more in June, and told Hemingway of the travel arrangements she had made. She had booked passage on the *Reina de la Pacífica*, which left Havana on August 7 for Santander. From there, they would go to Madrid for the *corridas*. Charles would meet them in Paris, and they would sail from Marseille in the *General Metzinger* on November 22, bound for Mombasa. Jane was still in the hospital but when Pauline suggested they visit, Hemingway demurred.

"Poor old Papa," said Pauline. "It ruins everything when you're sad."

"I shouldn't have let her come fishing after the accident. She was feeling punk."

"How could you have known what would happen?"

"It's a bloody shame."

"Yes, it is," agreed Pauline, who was relieved that the game had ended, for now. "But there's nothing you can do now, and it does no good to talk about it."

"It never does."

Once Pauline returned home to begin packing for Africa, Hemingway was alone. After the day's fishing, he spent his afternoons at the Floridita, although Javier no longer went and Freddy was in Texas. He sat at his usual corner to the left of the bar, with his back against the wall, sipping daiquiries and taking notes for an article that he had agreed to write for a new magazine called *Esquire*. Apart from an occasional *bombazo*, things were quiet in Havana, although a grim impatience hung over the city. Constante saved him a newspaper so that Hemingway could read *El Bobo*. It was Gattorno who introduced him to the satirical cartoons drawn by Eduardo Abela that appeared in the *Diario de la Marina*. *El Bobo* was a plump, unassuming fellow with four hairs sticking out of his bald head, and a seemingly complacent expression. One cartoon that month showed him in a baseball uniform, kneeling at home plate, praying for this to be the last inning.

As for the imposter, he appeared to have left. One night, Hemingway had dinner with the photographer Walker

Evans, who was in Havana taking pictures, but there were few Americans in Havana and he kept to himself. The blistering summer heat chased away what few customers had braved the explosions, and the Floridita was nearly empty. Leopoldina la Honesta bemoaned the lack of business and wiped the sweat from her forehead with a gardenia-scented handkerchief. Gazing at the *americano* with sad eyes, she wondered what he was writing about.

Most evenings, Hemingway waited for Nely outside the Alhambra, where *La Isla del Encanto* was still drawing crowds. They walked down Galiano Street and had a late supper at their usual *reservado* in the Café de la Isla, but when he felt the familiar black mood creeping over him he walked her back to the *solar* and chastely returned to the Ambos Mundos. One night, standing on Virtudes Street, he saw Nely leave the theater on the arm of a slender, dark-eyed young man in a *guayabera*. She looked back over her shoulder, but he ducked into a café. When he saw her later that week, Nely protested indignantly that she had waited for him in vain.

"It seems you found someone to wait with," he said.

"What if I did, Señor Hemingway?"

Hemingway glared at her and stormed off, but that night he couldn't sleep and the following night he took her to dinner at El Pacífico. Their quarrel was forgotten and Hemingway returned to the Ambos Mundos just before dawn.

Grant informed him that Jane would soon be leaving for New York on the *Morro Castle*, and they were having a small farewell party for her birthday. After several daiquiries for courage, Hemingway bought a dozen white roses from a *gallego* on Mercaderes Street and finally presented himself at the Anglo-American Hospital. A nurse led him to Jane's room, and he found Grant with Basil and Gattorno, as well as a few other people he didn't know.

Jane had been propped up in bed, encased in a plaster cast that came up to her chin. She was pale and drawn, but her hair was carefully parted in the middle and someone had applied lipstick and dabbed a spot of rouge on each cheek. Her guests wore party hats and the room was filled with huge bouquets of flowers. Adding his roses to the pile, Hemingway gingerly sat on the edge of the bed. Unable to turn her head, Jane smiled weakly to no one in particular, and he leaned over to kiss her cheek.

"How are you, daughter?"

"I never thought I'd fall for you," she whispered.

"Keep your chin up," he said, swallowing hard.

"I don't have much choice, do I?"

The doctor had prohibited champagne, but Armando came in with a chocolate cake and a single candle, which Grant held a few inches from her lips so she could blow it out. They sang *Feliz Cumpleaños,* and Basil cut the cake and handed a piece to Hemingway. He wasn't hungry and he left it on the dresser beside an odd little statue of a man whose face was covered with boils.

"That's Babalú Ayé," said Basil proudly. "He's watching over her."

"Do you really believe in that mumbo-jumbo?" scoffed Hemingway.

"It worked for me!"

There was much he wanted to tell her, but now wasn't the time. Grant carefully put a party hat on Jane, and they sang Happy Birthday again, this time in English. Gattorno unveiled a sketch he had made of her, and Basil passed out more cake. Grant took Hemingway aside and said:

"I certainly appreciate you coming, sport."

Hemingway nodded absently.

"It's been awfully hard on all of us," continued Grant. "Especially Janie, of course. I'm afraid she'll be in the hospital for a long time. Bad luck all around, what?"

"I suppose you could call it that."

"Drop us a line from Nairobi, will you? Jane would love to hear from you. And do give my regards to Philip Percival. Best white hunter in Tanganyika, for my money!"

Jane began blinking and the nurse whispered something to Grant. The party was soon over, and Hemingway stepped out into the humid, sultry air. Looking at his watch, he saw that he could still make the fights at Miramar Gardens. Kid Chocolate had sailed for Europe, but the other boxers were fast and good, their dark, sinewy bodies shiny with sweat under the floodlights. Hemingway shouted himself hoarse, and lost a dollar betting with Basil, who was delighted to accompany him.

Joe was eager to return to Key West, but Hemingway persuaded him to stay another week. As the time for their departure grew near, he insisted on going out every morning in the hopes of seeing the giant black marlin that had eluded him the year before. Even on days when a foul wind swept over the *Anita* and menacing clouds hung overhead, Hemingway leaned over the stern, desperately squinting at the dark blue water for any sign of him. His eyes soon ached and he gently pressed his eyelids with his fingertips.

But on the day before they were to leave Havana, the sun poured in through the mahogany shutters, and he looked out over Habana Vieja to the flag fluttering from El Morro. The trade wind was up, and he riffled through the pile of clothes on the floor for his striped jersey. Hemingway walked briskly to the Plaza de Armas, where a platoon of soldiers stood guard in front of the American embassy, and turned left into Officios Street. At the Perla, Kaiser Guillermo offered him a *café con leche* with his usual mustachioed frown. It was steaming hot, and Hemingway sipped it impatiently. Since the bus strike, Havana was full of bicycles, and an enterprising Canary Islander dropped off passengers in an ox-drawn cart at the Lonja del Comercio.

"¡Chur-ros!" cried a *pregonero* crossing the square. *"¡Chur-ros!"*

A few forlorn market stalls were set up against the church, but shiny green avocados were stacked in a pyramid on the cobblestones, and Hemingway bought an armful for 15 cents.

At the San Francisco Dock, he saw that the *Anita* was already loaded with ice. Carlos looked up from filling the baitbox, and Joe smoked a Lucky Strike in the cockpit.

"What took you so long, Mahatma?" he grinned.

"Today's the day, Josie!"

The *brisa* had swept away the briny smell and the air was cool and clean. The *Anita's* engine purred as Joe followed a cargo ship out the channel, and they passed the fishing smacks anchored in front of La Cabaña, with the live fish cars moored beside them. Carlos pulled up a *machuelo* dangling from the line, and sat cross-legged on the deck to bait the hook. Kissing the fish for good luck, he handed the rod to Hemingway, who cast it beyond the wake.

Still within sight of El Morro, Hemingway hooked a snapper that Carlos promised to grill for lunch. He spotted a pair of swordfish, shooting through the waves like torpedoes, but they ignored the bait and continued on their way. Carlos pointed to a sailfish, a hundred yards to port, leaping out of the water and appearing to dance atop its slender tail. Joe steered in its direction but Hemingway waved him off, saying,

"That's not what I came for."

Joe anchored in Cojimar opposite the watchtower, where a soldier wearily surveyed them from the battlements. Carlos served the snapper with the avocados, but Hemingway only nibbled at his lunch, impatient to set out again. The breeze had freshened, and the whitecaps peppered the bow with spray, but the sky remained clear and they continued east to Boca de Jaruco. For once, his eyes didn't hurt and his head was clear as he pointed the rod out the stern, his finger on the spool of line.

"*¡Aguja!*" cried Carlos.

The black marlin struck the bait without warning, blasting out of the water with a sound like a howitzer. The reel spun furiously and singed his fingertip, and Carlos helped him strap on the harness as the marlin sped away from the boat.

Joe had cut the engine and Hemingway increased the drag to prevent a backlash, but he was afraid the marlin would be spooked, and let it run out. When the time was right, he would know it. Placing the butt of the rod securely in the harness, Hemingway took a deep breath and readied himself for the fight.

"Sock him!" shouted Joe.

Screwing down the drag, Hemingway leaned back in the fishing chair, pressing his heels against the deck. He felt himself derricked up by the harness, and the rod was nearly torn from his hands. But he leaned forward and flung himself back once more, his knuckles white against the cork grip. Just when he thought the hook had been set, the rod snapped back and the line went slack.

"He's gone," Hemingway said hoarsely.

Joe turned the *Anita* to port so as not to tangle the line and Hemingway cursed under his breath, thinking it had thrown off the hook, but Carlos continued to peer over the gunwale.

"*¡El pan de mis hijos!*"

The black marlin crashed through the swell nearly four hundred yards away, still trailing the leader, its sword pointing straight up, and toppled backwards like a fallen tree. Joe gunned the motor to cut the distance between them, and Hemingway jumped to his feet and tried to take in line, but it was no use. The marlin sounded again, and the reel screeched to a halt. His first impulse was to let it take more line, but he held his ground. Still holding the rod, he was pulled towards the transom, skidding on the deck, but Carlos grabbed his waist.

"Cut the engine!" Hemingway yelled.

Hemingway realized that Joe had already put the engine in neutral, but the *Anita* was still moving: the marlin was towing them stern-first. Joe quickly backed up, and Hemingway was able to wind the reel. The marlin leaped once more, much closer now, and Hemingway caught a glimpse of its dull black eyes before it fell back in the water. It had a broad, serrated sword and an ugly, blunt head, with stubby fins and a half-moon tail. Its rounded back had a coarse, purplish hue, but its belly was a metallic lavender which gleamed in the early afternoon light just before the waves closed over it.

If he was to beat it, Hemingway realized, he would have to use everything he had learned about the great blue river. The black marlin was powerful but stupid, and lacked the stamina of the younger striped marlin. He could not hope to match its power, though perhaps he could trick it into squandering its strength.

Each time the marlin sounded, Hemingway waited for his chance. Joe put the engine in reverse, and when the marlin shot up to the surface, he was able to take in a few yards before the next dive. Soon the spool began to fill with line once more. It circled back as though to get a better look at them, and leaped once more, barely 50 yards from the stern. It was a long, clean jump, and the big fish soared above the crest of the wave and appeared to float in the air. Its pectoral fins were spread out like wings, and it turned slowly as it hit the water. A long plume of spray caught the light, and the drops glittered like coins as the sword sliced through the leader.

Hemingway fell back against Carlos as the black marlin leaped for the last time, the hook still in its mouth, and dove triumphantly beneath the dark water.

"He's well and truly gone," he said.

Carlos stared open mouthed at the tangled coils of line floating in the breeze, and Joe let out a low whistle.

"That was the one," Hemingway said softly, and sank back into the fishing chair.

He felt neither anger nor frustration, but a certain emptiness. The knot of muscles between his shoulderblades tingled and his hands were numb. With difficulty, he unstrapped the heavy leather harness and licked his cracked lips. The marlin had bested him.

They returned to the harbor in silence, with Carlos shaking his head and muttering to himself. Joe thought of the dinner his wife would cook for him in Key West, and merrily drummed his fingers on the steering wheel. As usual, the dockhands waited for the *Anita*, ready to raise a cheer, but Carlos bitterly spit over the side.

Joe agreed to fish the next morning, and Carlos appeared with several gleaming *guaguanchos* for bait, but Hemingway's back was sore. They had already secured their clearance papers and there was nothing to do but fill up the *Anita's* tanks. Hemingway wired Pauline that they would arrive the following afternoon, and he spent the afternoon packing.

That night, the staff of the Ambos Mundos gave them a farewell party on the rooftop. Joe was pleased that the sky was clear, and declared that it was a fine night to cross the Florida Straits. The manager brought up a cake in the shape of a marlin, and Hemingway saved the bill for himself, covered in chocolate frosting. Carlos had brought his wife, who was as plump and cheerful as he was thin and dour, and even Gattorno came by. He had been working late, and there were bright smudges of paint on his face and hands.

From the rooftop, Hemingway looked across the channel to the lighthouse of El Morro as the searchlight swept the black water, shimmering beneath the violet sky. It was almost time to go when there was a commotion at the door and Nely arrived with some rumba dancers from *La Isla del Encanto*. She had left the Alhambra as soon as the show was over, but had been delayed by a gun battle between students and the police on the Prado. Along the way, she had stopped at the Floridita and brought the Trío Matancero, who began serenading Hemingway with *El Manisero*. Even Carlos began to sway to the music, and Gattorno found himself dancing atop a table with a chorus girl.

By then, it was nearly midnight, and the revelers accompanied Hemingway and Joe down Obispo to the Plaza de San Francisco. Carlos untied the bowline for the last time, and a pilot boat escorted them through the ghostly, moonlit harbor.

Nely stood on the dock and watched the *Anita* pass beneath the walls of La Cabaña. Hemingway stood in the stern, trying to shake the sadness with a forced smile, and waving at the rumba dancers that had come to see him off. Even at a distance she saw him clearly, outlined against the glow of the binnacle, but soon the boat reached the open sea and was swallowed up by the darkness.

NINE

The night Hemingway left, Roberto Perez waited across the street from the Alhambra. In just a few minutes, the curtain would fall and the men would spill out into Consulado Street, smoking and laughing, and in anticipation the whores were lined up beneath the streetlight. Roberto had already been approached once, by a petite *mulata* in a tight red dress, but he had angrily moved away.

"*¿Qué te pasa, mi amor?*" she called out after him, "*¿Te da pena?*"

Roberto blushed, and to hide his embarassment, he turned up the collar of his jacket and stuck his hands in his pockets, feeling the cold steel of the Smith &Wesson. There was a bar around the corner, and he thought of getting another drink to steady his nerves, but a policeman stood at the entrance and he thought better of it. Since he had returned to Havana, Roberto had lived in a tiny room above a Chinese laundry on San Isidro Street, near the train station. At night, the only way he could deaden his nerves and fall asleep was by drinking himself senseless. He felt the familiar ache for the liquor and looked for another bar, but realized there was no time.

The doors of the Alhambra swung open and among the first to leave was Rafael. He had been seated in the back of the theater, and he put on his *jipijapa* hat and took it off, their pre-arranged signal, making his way down the street bare-headed. Roberto knew he would circle around the block and turn down Animas Street, where Tony and José María were waiting. Further up the street was Francisco, nicknamed the *Guajiro* because he came from a small town in Oriente, and his brother Fermin. Waiting in a car were Pablo and Manuel, ready to pick him up by the cast-iron lions in the Prado and speed up Zulueta to the Malecón, where they would make their escape. Roberto had not been told where Alberto would be, but he knew he was nearby, ready to finish the job if they failed.

What of the others? Roberto was the only survivor of the original cell. Bobby had been killed in the bomb blast, Enrique had been gunned down by *porristas* in front of a café, and Carlos had been shot while unloading the shipment of Thompsons at Bacuranao. As for the tenth man, he never found out what became of him. But it had been easy to replace them all. Tony and José María were students of Dr. Alvarez Leal, and Rafael was the son of a wealthy doctor. The brothers from Oriente had been recruited by Alberto while he was in hiding in Santiago de Cuba, and Pablo and Manuel had gone to Belén.

They usually met in a house in Marianao owned by Pablo. Alberto was a wanted man with a price on his head, and he had managed to elude the *expertos* for several months. They looked upon him with awe, but he said little and preferred to let the others talk, his small, cold eyes flickering from one to the other. José María was the loudest of all, and won most of the arguments simply by shouting them down. If the ABC were to support the mediation, he argued, wouldn't that amount to yet another betrayal by the *políticos*? Tony countered that if the *yanquis* were to rid them of Machado, then so much the better. Why shouldn't they accept their help? Some of Alberto's fatal glamour had rubbed off on Roberto for bringing Dr. Alvarez Leal back to Havana, and they looked to him to settle the argument. But it mattered little to Roberto who was right. He had asked himself these questions so many times that he no longer cared what the answers were.

Their voices blended into one another and their faces became indistinct. It was Bobby who had ungainly ears that protruded from his reddish hair. Had he betrayed them, or was that Luis? Bobby had pale, freckled hands, but they had been blown off by the bomb intended for Captain Segura. No, it was Luis who was the *lenguilargo*, and wound up with his throat slit from end to end. Frank had been arrested after Captain Segura was shot and taken to Atarés. Roberto remembered that he was never without his pipe. He wore an absurd plaid jacket that he had bought at Dartmouth, and liked to drink whiskey instead of rum, just like an *americano*. But he had been pushed out of a police car by the *expertos* and shot in the back while he ran.

Roberto's silence disconcerted them, but soon José María picked up the thread of the argument and blustered that to exchange one master for another was still slavery, while Tony charged that no price was too great to pay for freedom. Then the others joined in, raising their voices, until Alberto silenced them with a gesture. Even José María grew quiet and looked at him sheepishly.

In his low, raspy voice, Alberto explained what they were to do. Their various attempts against the life of Chief of Police Ainciart had failed. His house on the banks of the Almendares had been heavily fortified, and he was always accompanied by a platoon of bodyguards. But since the death of Frank, Alberto had become obsessed with killing El Zurdo. He was one of Machado's most vicious henchman, and was believed to have killed Raúl and Vivian Esnard, after the soldiers raped the girl in front of her husband, for Ainciart's amusement. He had no family, lived in the barracks, and rarely left the barracks in Atarés.

It was purely by chance that they discovered his one weakness. Without fail, each Tuesday night El Zurdo boarded a streetcar for the Parque Central. From there, he walked up the Prado to Virtudes Street, and continued to the Alhambra, where he attended a burlesque show entitled *La Isla del Encanto*.

Roberto greeted this discovery incredulously. The thought of El Zurdo watching rumba dancers in the dilapidated old theater would have been quite funny, if it did not present them with an opportunity to kill him. The week before, they had waited in their assigned places and watched him emerge alone from the lobby of the Alhambra dressed in a boxy suit and a striped hat crammed atop his head. Roberto had seen him from behind, and was surprised how squat he was, with short legs but powerful shoulders. Afterwards, Alberto announced that the date was set for next week, and that Roberto would be the one to pull the trigger.

Now, he stood on the street corner and watched El Zurdo leave the theater. He wore the same suit as the week before, and his dark face was hidden beneath the brim of his hat. Roberto waited for him to cross the street and fell in behind him. There was nothing to distinguish him from the other men who attended that night's performance of *La Isla del Encanto*. The ill-fitting suit and the straw boater gave him the appearance of a clerk on holiday, not an assassin. Roberto felt once more for his revolver, but it was not yet time.

Once again, he thought of Lydia, and remembered the last time he had seen her. Roberto had written her from Key West, but had no way of knowing if she had received his letter. When he returned to Havana, he waited in his car a few blocks away from her parents' mansion in the Vedado, and caught a glimpse of her returning home with her mother, the chauffeur holding open the door of their car. That night, as he drank himself to sleep, he tried to remember every moment they had spent together, from seeing her with her friends during the *paseo,* to his attempts to talk to her in the Havana Yacht Club and the Centro Gallego. There had been the bewildering luncheon at her house, surrounded by her scowling father and beautiful, melancholy mother, and the rest of her family; the glorious night they saw Carlos Gardel at the Teatro Fausto with her brother, when he managed to steal a kiss; and the disastrous afternoon at the Tropical beer garden, where Raúl and Frank got into a tiresome argument. There were other times, too, and he tried to remember every word she said, and the musical sound of her surprisingly deep voice, and the way her smile suddenly illuminated her sad features, like the sunlight shining through dark clouds. As he drank, these moments blurred together, like the faces of his friends.

Trying to see her again was out of the question. He thought of asking Javier to give her another letter, but that would only endanger them both. Not even his parents knew he was back in Havana, and to be seen in public would compromise the others in his cell. He had no doubt that it was Alberto who had cut Luis' throat, without animosity or regret. He also knew Alberto would kill him as well, if he needed to.

Roberto had fallen behind, and realized that he had lost sight of El Zurdo He ran forward, elbowing his way past two students, and breathed a sigh of relief when he saw that he had turned into the Prado. On each visit to the Alhambra, he had taken the same route back to the Parque Central, where he boarded the streetcar. Roberto knew by heart the streets that crossed the Prado: Ánimas, Virtudes, and then Neptuno. It was here that Alberto had told him to come from behind the *experto*, press the gun barrel between his shoulder blades, and press the trigger.

It was clear, and a full moon hung over Havana. On such a night, the Prado should have been full of people, but due to the strike it was getting difficult to get around the city. The only buses running were those driven by *porristas*. A couple passed Roberto, a man and his wife out for a stroll, and then a policeman. Roberto knew that he was a coward, and felt the fear welling up inside him, but the policeman was merely making his usual rounds, and didn't look twice in his direction.

El Zurdo crossed Ánimas, and Roberto narrowed the gap between them. He noticed for the first time that his suit was threadbare, and the collar of his shirt had a ragged edge. The squarish jacket hunched over his shoulders, and the sleeves were too short for his arms. He walked slowly and deliberately, apparently lost in thought. Why did he come to the Alhambra each week? Even *expertos*, he supposed, had a night off from killing.

Roberto managed a grim smile at the thought. It was not time yet, and he slowed his pace as his quarry continued toward Virtudes. He had to wait for a car to pass, and he had a sudden impulse to kill him then. But their movements had been carefully calibrated, like clockwork, and he would have to run a block to reach the cast-iron lions where the car would be. As El Zurdo crossed the street, Roberto was just a few feet behind him, and he smelled his rank odor of perspiration, and fought back the anger. Was he the one who shot Frank in the back? Clicking off the safety with his thumb, he knew it made no difference if he hated the man he was about to kill, nor would it make him feel better afterwards. Alberto had told him that anger could cloud his judgement, and slow his reflexes. It was not vengeance he was after, although this man certainly deserved to die. Why, then?

Roberto realized it made no difference why he had to die and as Sergeant Crespo neared the corner of Neptuno, he took out the Smith &Wesson and ran towards him. Suddenly, he remembered Frank's annoying habit of emptying his pipe on the heel of his shoe and he stopped a few feet away and screamed:

"¡Asesino!"

Sergeant Crespo turned to see the boy standing before him with the long-barrelled pistol aimed at his chest. Roberto felt his arm trembling as he grasped the weapon with both hands, and he saw his quarry's face for the first time. It was not the face of a killer, he noted with surprise. He was an ugly man, almost simian in appearance, with heavy brows and a slightly flattened nose, and a purplish scar running across his left cheek. But it was his eyes that caught Roberto's attention. He had expected them to be cunning and cruel, but instead they were unbearably sad. There was no trace of surprise, as though he accepted his death sentence, and welcomed it. It was the face of a condemned man.

Something made Roberto hesitate, and Sergeant Crespo pulled a revolver from the holster beneath his jacket and shot him in the throat. Roberto's gun misfired and it flew from his hands, and he found himself on the ground, gazing up at the laurel trees, which appeared to be reaching up to the full moon. There was an explosion and more shots, followed by screams, and he heard the sound of running footsteps, very far away. Roberto felt the warm blood spurting from his throat, and he tried to block it with his hand, but it seeped through his fingers and he began to choke.

Someone was shouting his name, and then it was eerily quiet and he was floating over the Prado, high above the laurel trees, swept by the cool breeze out to sea. Soon, his memory of the girl dissolved in the pale night.

Once she heard the news, Lydia refused to leave her room. Her mother sent her meals up, but she had only a few spoonfuls of soup. When Don Ramón knocked on her door there was no answer, only muffled sobs.

Just a week ago, Doña Inés had become hysterical after discovering a letter from Roberto in Lydia's drawer. After reading it, Don Ramón could not help but smile at the hopeless passion his daughter had inspired.

"She'll soon forget him," Don Ramón told his wife.

"Don't you see, you fool?" cried Doña Inés, incensed at his complacence. "He's back in Cuba!"

"But the police are after him," said Don Ramón.

The thought of her only daughter compromised by an revolutionary with a price on his head sent Doña Inés into a prolonged fit of weeping.

"My father wouldn't have tolerated this!" she sobbed.

"But what would you have me do, *mi amor*?" Don Ramón had said helplessly.

Now, there was nothing to be done for the poor boy shot dead on the Prado. They would soon be leaving for Spain, and Don Ramón hoped that the ocean crossing would help Lydia forget him, and cure her of the absurd idea of attending Smith College, which he assumed was near Harvard.

Another cause for worry was his father, who still insisted on being driven to the *almacén* on Muralla Street each morning. He spent all day in his old office, either dozing off or playing dominos with Father Saralegui, and when he returned home there was a far-away look in his dim blue eyes. Don Ramón had hired a young man named Pepin to keep an eye on him. One afternoon, Pepin discovered that the old man was missing, and frantically ran through Habana Vieja calling his name. He found him on the waterfront, watching an ocean liner leave the harbor.

Even his oldest son was short-tempered and irritable. The recent strikes had begun to take a toll on business, and Miguel feared the worst was yet to come. A friend of his from Belén had approached him, claiming to be an *abecedario*, and suggested that a financial contribution might be prudent. Don Ramón adamantly refused:

"Let them fight among themselves. Why should we take sides? Whoever wins will want to do business with us."

"It might be worse if they think we're *machadistas*," insisted Miguel, who rarely contradicted his father.

"Let them think what they will," said Don Ramón, abruptly ending the discussion.

As for Javier, he was rarely home and spent all of his time drinking at the Floridita. At first, this had not troubled his father, whose greatest fear had been that Javier would become a revolutionary like Alberto. But as the months passed, Don Ramón saw that his youngest son might never amount to anything.

This preyed upon his mind one afternoon at the Centro Gallego. Reclining upon his favorite leather armchair with one of his Por Larrañagas, Don Ramón was cheered by the sight of his old friend Dr. Eduardo Heydrich, who was visiting Havana. Immediately, he called for two glasses of brandy and the box of cigars. But Dr. Heydrich had his own worries. His oldest daughter Adelaida had refused to even consider marrying one of the most promising young surgeons in Matanzas. What's more, she refused to return to convent school, and even threatened to seek employment as a stenographer in Havana.

"Can you imagine such a thing?" cried Dr. Heydrich.

"Perhaps," said Don Ramón, lighting his friend's *perfecto*, "it is time to bring up a certain matter that we discussed last year..."

In the midst of these tribulations, the family's Sunday luncheons were uncharacteristically strained. As Don Ramón tipped his spoon into his *caldo gallego*, fragrant with hamhocks and sorrel, he noticed that his father had spilled his bowl onto Father Saralegui's ample lap. Doña Inés attempted to smile gamely, but Lydia's place remained empty. Miguel ate with singular ferocity, oblivious to all else, while his wife tried valiantly to feed the two little boys, who soon began to fight and were banished to the kitchen with their nanny. Aunt Clara was little help, complaining about the humidity and feebly fanning herself. But it was the sight of Javier, sitting with a distant look in his eyes, that emboldened Don Ramón to bring up the delicate subject of Adelaida Heydrich. After the dishes were cleared, Don Ramón summoned his son upstairs and offered him a Por Larrañaga. His book-lined study, which smelled of leather and cigar smoke, was singularly calm after the tension of the dining room.

"*Mi hijo...*" began Don Ramón, but paused to study the plume of brownish smoke curling up from his *perfecto*. He spoke of his own youth, of the bleak years before the war, when he sold salt cod from a pushcart in Habana Vieja, until his father had saved enough to lease the *almacén* on Muralla Street.

Javier listened patiently to this recital, having heard it many times before.

As he spoke, Don Ramón found himself growing nostalgic and remembered his father's pride in the crumbling old palace. The furnishings had been sold off to pay gambling debts, and all that remained of its former elegance were some painted beams of the *alfarje* ceiling. But his father, already well past middle age, surveyed it with the passion of a much younger man. He envisioned the courtyard full of wagons, with burly men unloading sacks of flour, crates of oranges, and barrels of olive oil, to be resold at a healthy profit. Don Ramón's eyes grew moist, until he remembered his objective and cleared his throat.

"But it was not until I met your mother—" he ventured, but Javier interrupted him.

"There is something we must discuss," he said.

Almost relieved, Don Ramón put down his Por Larrañaga.

"I've decided to go to Paris."

"And when did you reach this momentous decision?" said his father slowly.

"We've discussed it before," said Javier. "I've tried to fit in, but now I know there's nothing for me here. Since I returned to Havana, I've felt as though I don't belong. I felt the same way at Harvard, you see, but I thought that when I came home everything would be all right. Now it's only gotten worse. I feel like I'm walking a tightrope, neither here nor there."

When Don Ramón grew angry, his lips curled in a tight smile beneath his mustache, a quirk which disconcerted many who had sat across a bargaining table from him.

"And just what do you plan to do in Paris?"

"I want to write a novel," said Javier resolutely.

It was at this point that Don Ramón raised his voice. Waiting anxiously at the bottom of the stairs, Doña Inés winced when she heard the door slam as Javier stormed out of his father's study. She went upstairs to find Don Ramón still at his desk, slowly shaking his head.

"I take it he doesn't want to meet her," she said.

"Inés," he said wearily, "how soon can we leave for Spain?"

Despite the heat, something compelled Javier to remain in Havana. Even after the *fracaso* of the radio show, Javier continued to appear at *Bohemia*. The magazine had barely managed to remain open during the lean summer months, and the publisher had taken to carrying a revolver around Havana. But *Bohemia* continued to be published each week, and the newsroom buzzed with rumors. One reporter announced breathlessly that Welles had given Machado an ultimatum, and that his resignation was imminent. But then Machado declared in a fiery radio speech that he intended to serve out his full term, *ni un minuto más o menos* [not a minute more or less] until May 20, 1935. Another reporter declared that U.S. warships were on their way. But when pressed, Welles himself declared that he had no intention of invoking the Platt Amendment, and his goal was to mediate between Machado and the opposition, not bring about another American occupation of the island. Despite the new amnesty law, the shooting continued, and the strike which had begun in the sugar cane fields had spread to Havana.

One sweltering Friday afternoon, Javier decided to stop by the Floridita to see Hemingway, whom he hadn't seen since the ill-fated boxing lesson at the Ambos Mundos. Constante told him he'd already left for Key West, and Javier walked down Muralla. It had been several weeks since he had visited his grandfather at the *almacén*. Within the thick stone walls it was surprisingly cool. As Javier ascended the stairs he nodded to Pepin, who sat reading a newspaper. He found his grandfather in his office, gazing out the window at the harbor.

"Ramón," he snapped, turning towards him. "What are you doing here? I told you to wait for me at the dock. Will you never learn? *El ojo del amo engorda el caballo.*"

"It's Javier," his grandson reminded him.

This gave the old *gallego* pause, and he looked at him anew. As Javier took out their lunch of bread with *chorizo* and manchego cheese, his grandfather carefully opened his clasp knife.

"In the hills near Betanzos, there is a stream where my father used to take me fishing," he began. "Do you know it?"

Javier shook his head.

"It is a beautiful stream. The water is clean and cold, and we used to sit in the shade of a an old pine tree and fish for trout. Would you like to go?"

"No, *Abuelo*," said Javier impatiently, and regretted he had come.

His grandfather solemnly nodded, remembering a sunny afternoon before he joined the army and was sent to fight the rebels in Cuba, so many years ago. He did not know who the pleasant young man was before him, although he reminded him of his lazy, good-for-nothing son, and was kind enough to bring him lunch from time to time.

"What did you say your name was?" he asked.

By the time the ferry pulled into Havana Harbor, it was nearly dusk. Hemingway noticed that crates were stacked haphazardly on the wharf, with no stevedores in sight. A freighter was anchored opposite Casablanca, and laundry hung from the railings. The cab drivers had joined the strike, and there was no one to meet them as they left the terminal, not even the little boys who dove into the water for pennies.

"Nothing is going right, is it?" said Pauline.

Pauline's dislike of Cuba had only grown that summer. During her last visit to Havana, she had discovered a huge, hairy spider in her bathtub at the Ambos Mundos, and run out of the bathroom shrieking, much to her husband's amusement. The last few days in Key West passed in a blur, and she regretted spending the weekend in Havana before boarding the *Reina de la Pacífica*, due to sail Monday evening. Pauline was looking forward to the time they would spend in Paris, where she planned to do some shopping, but Africa filled her with foreboding. Secretly, she hoped her husband would change his mind and put off the dreaded safari one more year. But it was too late now, she feared.

Her sister Jinny was accompanying them to Europe. She was fine-boned and slender like Pauline, and smartly turned out in a plaid skirt and matching beret. This was her first time in Cuba and unlike her sister, she avidly drank in the sights and sounds of Havana, wanting to miss nothing.

The youngest boy, Gregory, had been left behind in Key West with his nanny, but Patrick (whom his father called Mex, short for the Mexican Mouse) and Bumby (who hated to be called John) would be coming as far as France. For them, just being with their father was a great adventure, and they were delighted when he hired a horse-drawn carriage to take them to the Ambos Mundos. It rambled precariously over the cobblestones, and as they entered the Plaza de Armas, they saw that a group of demonstrators had gathered before the American embassy. They were shouting slogans the boys could not understand, and one held a sign that said,

Abajo la guerra imperialista.

They were the stevedores who had refused to unload the freighter, burly men not intimidated by the row of soldiers who glared at them from the steps of the embassy.

"What are they doing, Papa?" asked Bumby.

"They're protesting."

"Why?" asked Patrick.

He was astounded that his older brother didn't know the answer, since he generally knew everything, and troubled by the doubt in his father's voice, since he always knew everything.

"When people don't like something," his mother explained patiently, "they protest."

"Can we protest, too?" asked Patrick.

"Don't be silly, sweet," said Pauline. "It's their revolution, not yours."

The family was soon settled into the hotel, and Hemingway was pleased to find his old room on the northeast corner of the fifth floor much as he left it. Pauline wanted to nap but Jinny was eager to explore the city. They walked up Obispo but the normally crowded street was deserted. Many of the stores had closed early, the *bodegas* were shuttered, and even the shoeshine boys were gone. But there was another demonstration in the Parque Central, with students marching around the statue of José Martí, singing in unison:

> *"¡Ya llegó el inning final,*
> *que se vaya el animal!"*
> [It's the final inning,
> the animal should go.]

The corner opposite the Hotel Inglaterra, where baseball scores would ordinarily be posted, was full of students carrying unfurled banners. Several of them carried a pole with what appeared to be the papier-mâché head of a donkey with incongruous talons. Jinny was intrigued by the students and wanted to get a closer look, but Hemingway warned that soon the *porristas* would come to disperse them. There were soldiers on the steps of the Capitolio with carbines, but the students were content to remain in the Parque Central. As the cars passed, they blinked their lights and honked their horns, shouting encouragement and shaking raised fists out the windows.

They had dinner at the Zaragozana, but the restaurant was nearly empty and the waiter kept looking outside, as though waiting for someone. The Morro crabs were in season, and Hemingway gleefully cracked the claws with a wooden mallet and sucked out the sweet white meat. He washed the crabs down with lemon-yellow Albariño and sat back contentedly in his chair.

"What's it all about?" asked Jinny.

"Do we have to talk politics?" asked Pauline.

"There's nothing to talk about," said Hemingway. "Machado either goes or he stays. Either way, all hell will break loose. It's as simple as that."

"It's never as simple as that," said Jinny.

The boys anxiously listened to the adults, turning from one to the other, following the conversation like a tennis match. Hemingway frowned and poured himself another glass of wine, holding the bottle by the neck, and Pauline threw her sister a dark look.

In the morning, when Hemingway went downstairs for a copy of the *Diario de la Marina*, the hotel manager ruefully informed him that there were no newspapers because the pressmen had joined the strike. Hemingway had hoped to see *El Bobo*, but settled for a *café con leche*. It was just two weeks since he had last fished for marlin, but he missed it keenly and wished that Joe and Carlos were waiting for him at the San Francisco Dock.

Hemingway had asked his publisher to send the galleys of his short story collection to Havana, so he could correct them during the crossing. That morning, the steel shutters of the *bodegas* remained shut and none of the *pregoneros* had ventured out into the fierce heat. Even the Farmacía Taquechel next to the Ambos Mundos was closed, although the white ceramic jars of powders and salves remained at the window. At the post office, the proofs had not arrived.

"That's swell," he muttered to the bewildered clerk.

Hemingway was beginning to worry, since everything was closed and it appeared that all of Havana was on strike. Would the *Reina de la Pacífica* be able to dock? Hemingway went to the shipping office for news, but it was boarded up. In the Plaza de San Francisco, there was a smell of sour milk, and a woman and two filthy children crouched beneath the empty market stalls with outstretched hands. Just stepping outside had made him thirsty, and Hemingway imagined how the first *Papa Especial* would feel sliding down his throat. To his dismay, he saw that the Floridita was closed, and a drunk lay sprawled against the door.

Hemingway walked up Zulueta until he came to the *solar*. There was no answer at Nely's door and he thought of leaving a note, but had neither pencil nor paper. Her neighbor was a plump *mulata* who habitually wore her hair in curlers beneath her scarf, but when Hemingway rang her bell she stuck her head out suspiciously.

"*¿Dónde está Nely?*" he asked.

"*No sé,*" she snapped, and slammed the door.

Hemingway continued down the street and saw that at least Sloppy Joe's was open. Two tourists were at the bar with their backs to him, and he was content to avoid them as he drank a bottle of Hatuey. Thus fortified, he crossed the Prado to the Alhambra and saw that the theater door was padlocked, and a policeman stood guard. Apparently, the *expertos* had at last shut down the Alhambra, a suspected meeting place of the *abecedarios*, and Nely had returned to Santiago de Cuba.

When Hemingway returned to the hotel, Bumby greeted him wide-eyed with excitement.

"Papa, we got shot at!" he cried gleefully.

"Papa, we got shot at!" echoed Patrick. "But they missed!"

Before Hemingway could react, Pauline said:

"You'll scare your father, boys. There was a shot, I think, but it certainly wasn't at us."

They had been walking along the Prado when they heard a faint report from the Malecón, like a car engine misfiring. It could well have been a shot, so they crouched behind the cast iron lion on the corner for a few minutes before scurrying back to the Ambos Mundos.

"What's a trip to Cuba without a little revolution?" said Jinny.

That night, Grant Mason joined them for drinks on the rooftop. He had remained alone at Jaimanitas when his wife and son went to New York, and he was glad of the company. Leaning over the railing, they looked out over the brooding city.

"The whole house of cards is about to collapse," said Grant.

"What do you mean?" asked Jinny.

"Welles was trying to bargain with Machado but he wasn't making progress as long as the army supported him. Now the unions have everyone by the throat. Welles is furious because they've thrown a monkey wrench in the works. The ABC is against the strike, but some of their members are against the mediation and have split off. Machado is against the strike, too, so now he's cut a deal with the communists to end it. Imagine that!"

"How will it end?"

"Welles thinks they'll all shake hands and go home at the end of the day, but there are too many guns out there. If you ask me, the only way this will end is if a destroyer sails right into the harbor and points its guns at the Presidential Palace. That will show Machado we mean business!"

"And that solves the problem?"

Grant took a sip from his martini and turned to face her. "I didn't say that."

"It sounds to me that there would be much more killing then," said Jinny, raising her voice.

Grant seemed surprised by her outburst, but answered patiently, as though speaking to a child:

"Is this your first time in Havana? I've been here six years. You assume that Cubans act rationally, but they don't. Just wait and see."

"You've got it all figured out, haven't you?"

"Jinny!" gasped Pauline.

Jinny's dislike of him was evident, but Grant was either unaware or ignored it.

"It's the moment of truth," he smiled, draining his martini and holding the olive lightly between his teeth before swallowing it. "Isn't that what you call it, Ernest?"

Hemingway remained uncharacteristically silent, looking out across the channel at the lighthouse of El Morro. Beside it, the Cuban flag hung limply in the stillborn air. During the afternoon, another ship had entered the harbor, and was lined up behind the freighter, anchored off Casablanca.

On Sunday, the manager informed them that the hotel employees had stayed home out of solidarity with the striking workers. His wife changed the sheets on their beds, and brought up a pot of watery coffee and a stale loaf of bread for breakfast. They could hear the church bells in the cathedral, and after mass they returned to the hotel, although Bumby was eager to go back to the Prado and get shot at again. As dusk fell, Hemingway wandered back to the wharf and saw to his delight that the *Reina de la Pacífica* had moored. Its gleaming white hull was illuminated by spotlights, and its smokestacks loomed over the docks like the towers of a citadel.

In the morning, Hemingway left the hotel early, determined to be at the post office when it opened. But the doors remained closed, and no one could tell him anything. Pauline was an expert at packing and unpacking, and their luggage was already in the lobby when he returned. Her husband informed her that the proofs had not arrived, but she wondered if that was why he was angry.

"Poor Grant," she said, to change the subject.

"Grant?"

"Jinny can be so trying. Honestly, I didn't know where to hide the other night. After all that's happened, too. It must be very difficult for him."

"I suppose so."

"He told me that Jane would have to stay in New York for several months after the operation."

It was no easy task to transport their luggage to the pier. There were no more horse-drawn carriages to be found, but by late morning two Spanish sailors presented themselves with a pushcart at the Ambos Mundos, and the manager helped them load the suitcases. After the deprivations of Havana, Pauline was delighted to settle into their comfortable stateroom. She savored the excitement of an ocean liner soon to leave port, with white-jacketed stewards rushing about, and porters straining to lift steamer trunks. From the deck, Havana seemed less malevolent, almost like a toy city, with miniature streets and churches and even castles. Jinny was still in a petulant mood and shut herself up in her cabin, while the boys played hide and seek among the lifeboats.

But Hemingway was restless and decided to stop by the post office one more time.

"You'll miss the boat, Ernest," said Pauline.

"We're not due to sail for another two hours," said Hemingway. "There's a chance the galleys may have gotten here."

"What if something should happen?"

"Don't be silly."

He walked briskly down the gangplank and crossed the waterfront. There was still a crowd in front of the American embassy, where Welles was meeting with representatives of Machado's government, but they appeared to be waiting rather than protesting. Obispo remained empty and the *bodegas* were still closed, and for the first time he noticed that the windows of several stores had been shattered. Had it happened today? When he got to the post office, he saw that it remained closed, and realized he wouldn't get the galleys until he reached Spain.

As Hemingway started back towards the ship, he was startled to see several students running frantically up the street. It occurred to him that they were being chased by the police, but others followed. They appeared to be heading to the Parque Central, and he looked at his watch and decided he had time to spare. Something had happened, he could feel it. There was confused shouting, but he couldn't understand what was being said. Hemingway nearly collided with a young man in a rumpled suit and grasped him by the shoulders.

"What is it?" he demanded.

"Haven't you heard?" cried the student, hoarse from excitement. "Machado has resigned!"

It was as though an electric current passed through him, and Hemingway felt the tension mount in his chest. He wanted to know more but the student ripped himself away and ran toward the Parque Central. Hemingway followed him, and heard a radio blaring from an open window. The announcer was saying something about Machado. Had he left Havana? Up ahead, a crowd was blocking traffic in front of the Centro Asturiano. Hemingway asked a man if Machado had resigned but couldn't hear what he said above the wail of the klaxons. But someone had apparently heard something because the crowd continued forward, waving banners and shouting:

"¡Viva la revolución!"

Hemingway moved cautiously into the mass of people flowing through the stalled cars in the street. He overheard a man saying that Machado had submitted his resignation to the Congress, which was now deliberating in the Capitolio. Another man said breathlessly that he had already left the island and was on his way to Miami.

"How can you be sure?" asked Hemingway.

"It's been on the radio all morning," someone said.

"But how do you know it's true?"

"Señor, it must be true!"

The crowd soon filled the Parque Central, trampling the shrubbery and surging around the royal palms like a vast, amorphous organism. At the edge of the park were the blue-uniformed police, standing behind a hastily erected barricade. Hemingway could not help but examine his own emotions even as he was swept ahead by the human current. Part of him watched cooly as he was jostled by the man behind him and almost stumbled. He noted with approval that he was not afraid, although it occurred to him that he should be, since there was death in the air.

Hemingway worried about missing his boat but was carried along by the press of bodies. Ahead of him, a student tripped and was nearly trampled, but managed to regain his balance as the crowd surged forward. By then, the first row of students had reached the barricade, and several tried to climb over it. The policemen pushed them back and began to swing their truncheons, but soon broke ranks and ran back toward the steps of the Capitolio, where there was a wall of sandbags. The wooden barricade gave way, and it seemed as though the policemen would be overrun.

But surprisingly, order was restored. The policemen scrambled up over the sandbags, where the soldiers waited with machine guns, and the pursuing students stopped short. They milled about in confusion until they linked arms to form an unbroken line. Stomping their feet, they began to chant:

"¡Abajo la bestia!"

Hemingway found himself joining in the shouting. Looking over his shoulder, he saw that the Parque Central was swarming with more protesters. Several had climbed atop the statue of José Martí and draped a Cuban flag over his outstretched hand, while others had hung banners from the streetlights. A solid mass of people stretched from the Prado and appeared ready to storm the Capitolio.

From behind him, Hemingway heard shouts of anger and saw that a fight had broken out. A white-suited black man was pummeling a student with his fists, creating a momentary gap

317

in the crowd. Others came behind him, swinging their deadly *vergajos* of twisted hide. At first the students watched in horrified silence, but then several joined in the fight and engulfed the *porristas*. As though healing itself, the organism reformed as the students linked arms once more and held their ground. Hemingway glanced at his watch and saw that only a few minutes had passed since he entered the Parque Central.

When the first shots were fired, he thought that someone had lit a string of firecrackers. Then he heard the rapid fire of the machine guns and saw the muzzles peeking over the sandbags, spouting flame. There were screams of pain, and a man fell to the right of him. He stooped down to grasp his arm but the crowd surged forward and he had to leave the wounded man behind. Several of the students were cut down as they rushed the Capitolio, appearing to stumble but then failing to get up. The policemen began to fire their revolvers as well, picking off the others before they reached the sandbags. The charge broken, the survivors retreated from the deadly line of fire and fled back toward the the Parque Central.

Hemingway turned away from the shooting and dove into the mass of sweating bodies. He had faced death only once before, that night during the war when he heard the terrible *chuh-chuh-chuh* of the mortar fired from across the river, and his breath was sucked out of him by the white-hot blast. There wasn't time to be afraid then, and he had always wondered how he would react if he confronted it again. Now, he felt the fear bubbling up inside him, flooding him with an odd exhilaration. No longer ashamed, he broke into a run, while the police continued to fire from the Capitolio.

As the protesters scattered in their flight across the Parque Central, Hemingway saw a *porrista* bludgeon a student and kick him as he fell. Now, the man was moving towards him with surprising speed, his *vergajo* raised to strike. There was no time to avoid him, and at his back were the staccato bursts of the machine guns. Letting his momentum carry him forward, Hemingway made a fist and brought it up to the man's face, which crunched satisfyingly. Jumping over his assailant, he made it across the street and crouched behind the colonnade. The mob had dissolved into terrified individuals running for cover, dodging the bullets, screaming above the klaxons, and hiding behind trees. The shooting soon stopped, but the policemen advanced from the wall of sandbags, their revolvers drawn. They moved slowly toward the Parque Central, stepping over the bodies, and started to erect the fallen barricade once more.

Hemingway looked at his right hand and saw that his knuckles were bleeding. Since the policemen were arresting anyone still standing, he ran back towards the wharf and soon boarded the *Reina de la Pacífica.* As it left Havana Harbor, he stood with Pauline by the railing. She had swabbed iodine on his swollen hand, and told him that she had heard from the captain that the rumors were false and Machado remained in the Presidential Palace, surrounded by his troops.

"Everything will be all right, now," Pauline reassured him.

The day began badly for Walter, and only got worse.

At breakfast, the coffee grew cold and he saw to his dismay that the pancakes were dense and flat, like tortillas. He summoned Olga and she emerged with a fresh pot of coffee, oblivious to the disaster.

"These are *not* pancakes," Walter growled, pushing the plate away.

Olga blanched and escaped to the kitchen.

Walter groaned, and wished he had his usual morning paper. Since the massacre of the students in front of the Capitolio, the strike had paralyzed the city and even the *Havana Post* had not been published for a week. But worst of all was the heat. Even before he reached the door, his starched collar was damp with perspiration. Outside, the leaves of the *barrigona* palms hung listlessly in the stillborn air. Putting on his fedora, Walter resolutely marched across the driveway, but it was no use. A malignant drop of sweat formed on his forehead and dribbled down his cheek, and he felt swampy half moons forming beneath his armpits. His pants stuck to his thighs, and by the time he reached the car, he was soaked.

Holding open the door of the Buick, Felix told him the news:

"Machado is gone, Señor Huggins."

"Where did you hear that?" snapped Walter.

"The radio, Señor Huggins."

"If I had a dollar for every time I've heard Machado has left the country, I'd be a wealthy man!"

With a shrug, Felix pulled the visor of his cap down over his forehead and sped past the sculpted banyan trees on Fifth Avenue. Walter opened the window as they crossed the river, hoping the breeze would cool his already flushed face, but there was a blast of hot air and gasoline fumes.

"Machado indeed!" he muttered.

There was little traffic on the way to the Malecón, but as they passed the monument to the *Maine*, a huge eagle cast from the wreckage of the sunken battleship. Walter saw the first groups of students holding up green banners. Several cars rushed by in the other direction, their horns blaring, and Felix slowed down beneath the Hotel Nacional. The students had marched from the university to the statue of Antonio Maceo, singing and shouting, and the crowd had overflowed onto the Malecón itself. As the car lumbered to a halt, Felix turned back to his employer with a triumphant expression.

"You were right all along, weren't you?" said Walter.

"*Por supuesto*, Señor Huggins," said Felix triumphantly.

The crowd swarmed around them, and only when Walter leaned out the window and waved his arm were they able to advance. The houses along the Malecón had green flags hanging from their balconies, and the people shouted encouragingly at the students. There were cries of *"¡Abajo la bestia!"* and Walter was more anxious than ever to get to the Havana Trust. If Machado had fallen, where was Emilio Aragon?

The road was clear until Galiano Street, where another group of students had gathered. The approach to La Punta was blocked by several trucks with military insignia, but the soldiers appeared to be joining in the celebration. A man stood on the seawall firing a pistol into the air, and tiny puffs of smoke drifted over the sea of green banners. Where were the *expertos*? Surely they would arrest him, thought Walter.

There was no getting through the jubilant crowd. Felix began the laborious process of turning the Buick around and heading back up the Malecón, but Walter realized he would make better time on foot.

"If you go back to Galiano, you might be able to circle back," said Walter. "I'll probably be there before you will."

"Be careful, Señor Huggins," Felix warned him.

Walter stepped out of the car and put on his jacket as Felix headed in the other direction. Rather than try and pass the roadblock at La Punta, he turned down the Prado. Walter could see the dome of the Capitolio at the end of the boulevard, and he was grateful for the shade of the laurel trees. Several students ran past him, yelling hoarsely, and Walter took off his fedora to wipe his forehead. Across the Prado, several of the students appeared to be running in and out of a mansion with a tiled facade. Walter heard the tinkle of broken glass, and saw that they had emerged on the balcony and were throwing furniture out on the street. Who lived there? Were they looting it? Where was the police?

Walter quickened his pace and was soon in front of the American Club. He thought of calling Aragon, but there was no time to waste and he cut across the Parque Central towards O'Reilly. Cars frantically circled the park, the drivers honking their horns and shouting. Walter noticed a cloud of black smoke rising from the office of the *Heraldo de Cuba*. Had the students set fire to Machado's newspaper? There were more soldiers in front of the Capitolio, but they appeared to ignore the mayhem. Mesmerized by the sight of the burning building, Walter continued along the park and saw that the sidewalk was littered with twisted machinery, the remains of the printing press.The looters had taken a roll of newsprint and were rolling it down the street like a giant roll of toilet paper.

His jacket was already soaked with sweat and he peeled it off and slung it over his shoulder. There were more looters in the Manzana de Gómez, methodically shattering the plate glass windows of the stores, but Walter saw that O'Reilly Street was empty. The sight of the Havana Trust at the corner of Aguacate immediately reassured him. Walter ran up the steps but found the doors locked.

"Open up!" he shouted.

Walter heard timorous footsteps, and the lock turned slowly. Finally, Elmer peered out the door.

"What's wrong with you?" demanded Walter.

Elmer stepped back to let him in and Walter saw he'd been drinking. His collar was undone, and there was stubble on his bulbous chin. The lobby was empty except for one of the tellers, who crouched behind the counter.

"Hell's bells!" cried Walter. "Where is everyone?"

Elmer swung the door shut and leaned back against it in relief.

"The whole place has gone nuts, Mr. Huggins," he said.

"But we haven't," said Walter firmly. "The Havana Trust is open for business today, like any other day. Do you hear me?"

Elmer nodded dimly and the teller quickly looked the other way as Walter stormed upstairs. Freddy was still in Texas and Hopgood would not be back from Indianapolis until Monday, so their desks were empty.

"Is anybody here?"

In response, his secretary darted to her desk, and Walter realized he'd been shouting like a madman.

"I beg your pardon, Miss Garcia. I didn't see you."

"Have you heard the news, Señor Huggins?" she asked.

"Who hasn't?"

"It's a miracle!" she said.

"I guess it is," said Walter curtly. "Get me Emilio Aragon. Call him at home, if you have to."

Walter shut the door of his office behind him and took a deep breath. Who knew what had happened? Perhaps it was another rumor, and order would soon be restored. But if Machado had resigned, his successor would surely be someone acceptable to Welles, who would end the general strike and get the Cubans back to work. Altomar would be built, after all.

His secretary knocked on the door.

"What is it?"

"There's no answer, Señor Huggins."

"How can that be? One of the servants must be home."

"The line went dead, Señor Huggins."

"Try again, and keep trying until you reach him!"

Alone once more, Walter sank back into his chair and wondered what to do. Perhaps Aragon had gone to Matanzas, and would return once the soldiers had taken back the streets. He had said that the Cuban ambassador was meeting with President Roosevelt to demand the recall of Welles. Had this last-minute effort succeeded? Probably not, since Welles was said to be an old friend of Roosevelt's. Was Machado really gone, then? What lever did Welles pull to force him from office? Did he threaten an invasion, like the hotheads in the American Club wanted?

Miss Garcia tremulously poked her head in and said:

"The telephone is not working, Señor Huggins."

Walter dismissed her with an angry wave of his hand.

Perhaps young Mason was right, he thought, and the only way to restore order was by landing the marines on the Malecón. Walter's eyes came to rest on the *HMS Victory*. His predecessor, Mr. Gordon, sat here on just such a morning, when the Marques de Valenzuela killed himself and nearly ruined the bank. Opposite his desk, Nelson's flagship plowed on through invisible waves.

"So it goes, old boy, so it goes," Mr. Gordon had said. Where was he now?

But Walter had not yet given up. If the phones were dead, there had to be some other way of finding out what happened. If anyone knew, that is.

"I'm going to the American embassy," he told his secretary. "It's time someone got to the bottom of this."

"There is shooting outside, Señor Huggins."

"It's all right. I'm just going to the Plaza de Armas."

Walter started past her but stopped when he saw her worried frown.

"Tell me something, Miss Garcia. Is it really a good thing that Machado is gone?"

"Of course, Señor Huggins," she said, her voice full of unexpected fervor.

It occurred to Walter that his secretary sympathized with the *abecedarios*.

"Will things be better now?" he asked.

"What could be worse?" she replied. "He is a *bestia*. What could possibly be worse?"

Walter descended into the lobby and saw that Elmer still cowered by the door.

"I thought I told you to keep it open!"

Elmer swallowed hard and pulled back the bolt. With one hand he took out his revolver, and with the other, he pried the heavy door open.

"Put that thing away before you kill yourself!"

Elmer reluctantly slid the gun back in its holster, and Walter stepped out into the blazing sun. There was still no sign of Felix. O'Reilly remained deserted, but he could hear shouts from the Plaza de Armas, where the crowd was waving palm fronds and a band was playing the Cuban national anthem. The embassy was only a few blocks away and Walter started down the street.

Just a few steps past the Havana Trust, Walter heard footsteps and turned to see a man charging towards him. He was a lean *mulato* in a white chauffeur's uniform, and he rapidly cut the distance between them. Walter tried to move out of the way but they collided, the man frantically taking hold of Walter's arms as they staggered back towards the wall.

"What do you want?" cried Walter, struggling to free himself.

The man appeared not to understand, but continued to force Walter back against the rough stone wall. His fingers pressed into Walter's fleshy shoulders, and for an instant they remained locked in this awkward position, like dancing partners. Walter shouted at him in alarm, trying to push him away, but he remained silent, his yellowish eyes wide with terror, the sweat running down his pockmarked face.

"Help me!" he finally whispered.

Before he could reply, there were more footsteps from around the corner and Walter was swung out into the street with surprising force. He spun around like an ungainly top and nearly toppled over the curb as his assailant broke into a run up O'Reilly. Several men raced after him, and one of them careened into Walter, sending him sprawling. It appeared as though the fugitive might get away, but they soon reached him, and he lashed out with his fists in an effort to defend himself.

"*¡Porrista!*" cried a woman, only a few steps behind.

Another man followed with a machete, and he leaped over Walter to join the mass of writhing bodies. The *mulato* somehow got up, but the woman had grabbed his ankle and the others pulled him back down. By then, he had regained the use of his voice, and screamed as they hacked him apart.

Walter felt a sharp pain in his ribs and found himself on his belly. Pressing against the dusty cobblestones, he slowly forced himself up and got to his knees. There was a foul taste in his mouth, a combination of blood and vomit, and his vision was blurred. Walter's glasses had been knocked off, and he ran his hands along the ground, hoping to find them. The screams continued, and the mob continued to slash at the man with the machete, ignoring Walter. A line of blood dribbled toward him, and he singlemindedly avoided it, edging away on his hands and knees, hoping to spot the glint of his spectacles. Then someone kicked him and he collapsed with a grunt.

Walter lay on his back, barely able to move, and heard their triumphant voices as they carried the dead man away. He was afraid to call for help lest they come back, but managed to roll over. Crawling back towards the sidewalk, his hand brushed against something metallic and he saw that his spectacles were miraculously in one piece. He delicately balanced them on his nose, but winced when he felt something warm and wet on his cheek. There was blood on his fingers, and he dried them on his already soiled shirtfront.

O'Reilly was empty once more, quiet save for the distant shouting from the Plaza de Armas, and Walter blinked in the harsh light. Still on his knees, he saw something a few feet away on the curb. A film of dirt and perspiration covered his spectacles, and he carefully wiped them with his tie. That's not right, he thought, it can't be. But as his blurred vision resolved itself, he saw that it was indeed a human hand, neatly chopped off at the wrist.

When word reached *Bohemia* that Machado was about to resign, Javier accompanied the reporter who was dispatched to the Presidential Palace, carrying the tripod for the camera and extra film cartridges. As they started down Trocadero they heard cheering, as though at a baseball game. The Prado was full of people waving palm fronds, from the Malecón to the Capitolio, and the laurel trees were draped with green banners. A makeshift band played the *Bayamesa*, the Cuban national anthem, and the squeal of a *corneta* could be heard above the roar.

"¡Abajo Machado!" cried a man, not angrily, but joyously, and a cheer went up as though someone had hit a home run.

Javier and the reporter soon came in sight of the gilded cupola of the palace, from which a Cuban flag still waved. It remained surrounded by guards, their jackboots gleaming in the harsh light, but the crowd had started to grow. Unlike at the Prado, it was strangely quiet. They jostled their way toward the door of the press room, but a guard waved them back with his carbine. Realizing they were unlikely to get inside, they turned left into Zulueta, heading towards the statue of Máximo Gómez.

A collective shudder ran through the crowd as several cars pulled out of the porte-cochere of the palace. Was it Machado? Someone was leaving and the sea of bodies parted as the motorcade headed for the Malecón. Once it had sped away, the guards withdrew, and the crowd once more surrounded the palace.

"¡Viva la revolución!" cried a man, and the crowd took up the chant.

Several military trucks with mounted machine guns were parked in front of La Punta, but the soldiers watched indifferently as more people approached the palace, carrying green flags and stomping their feet. At first, the people approached the entrance tentatively, unwilling to believe their eyes. Crossing the street in groups of two or three, they stepped gingerly across the lawn, as though waiting for the guards to return. The massive doors were unlocked, and they wandered into the sumptuous lobby. The first ones to enter crossed the polished marble floor reverently, but then others followed, their voices mounting with excitement. No longer awed by the splendor, they began to shatter the high windows and smash the gilt chairs against the wall. The offices were ransacked, with desks torn apart, and books hurled outside. The door to the pantry was discovered and they began to carry out the canned goods that were stacked on the shelves. A man emerged from the wine cellar with a bottle of champagne, its neck broken, the foamy wine flowing on his face. More bottles were taken out into the ballroom only to be shattered, and the dark red stain spread along the marble floor.

From his vantage point on Zulueta, Javier saw several people emerge from the palace carrying chairs and other pieces of furniture, and a car even managed to pull up to the entrance to be loaded. He expected the soldiers to come back any minute, but they remained by the trucks in front of La Punta. The door of the press room had been torn off its hinges, the phones had been ripped from the walls, and two men were in the process of taking a radio out through the open window. Then from the pantry came a high-pitched squeal as several men emerged with a crate containing a huge pig. Out on the lawn, they smashed the wooden slats and cut the pig's throat with a machete. Carving himself a bloody haunch, one of the men disappeared into the crowd. Still more people continued to rush into the Presidential Palace, though by then there was nothing left to take. Javier noticed that a large sign had been posted above the front doors, probably taken from one of the nearby houses, saying:

SE ALQUILA [To rent]

Javier spent the rest of the morning doggedly typing the reporters' notes with two index fingers, and running them to the typesetter in the basement for the next issue. One reporter claimed that Machado had already left Cuba on his yacht, but another heard that he had gone to his heavily fortified *finca* outside Havana with his bodyguards. Then Ambassador Welles read a statement announcing that Machado had resigned in favor of General Ibañez, who in turn appointed Carlos Manuel de Céspedes as provisional president. Camp

Columbia was in the hands of the young officers who had led the revolt, but it was unclear who controlled the garrisons at Atarés and El Príncipe.

Throughout the morning, until the telephones went dead, reports came in of looting in Havana and throughout the island. Following the sacking of the Presidential Palace, the mob set fire to the *Heraldo de Cuba* and destroyed the homes of prominent *machadistas*. The police were barricaded in the Jefatura, and armed gangs of *abecedarios* hunted down the *expertos*. José Antonio Martinez, the head of the *porra*, was gunned down in the Prado as he tried to flee. Chief of Police Ainciart was discovered trying to escape in woman's clothing, and was set upon by a mob. Like many others, his mangled body was tied to the hood of a car and displayed throughout the city to cheering crowds.

Then word came that Dr. Fernando Alvarez Leal was to speak at the university, and Javier drove the reporter in his car. As they sped down San Lázaro, the cheers grew louder. Dr. Alvarez Leal stood beneath the statue of the Alma Mater, surrounded by *abecedarios* holding Thompson guns. Ill at ease, he held up his hand and pleaded for silence, but the students only screamed louder. Dr. Alvarez Leal hated crowds and was more comfortable lecturing before polite, well-mannered law students. Now, he took out a carefully folded piece of paper from his vest pocket and tried to be heard above the shouting.

"My friends," he began haltingly, "this is a momentous occasion. The events of today will forever be remembered as a victory in the fight against tyranny. But let us remember that with victory comes reponsibility. Let us remember that—"

Javier strained to make out what he was saying but the students had begun chanting, "*¡El ABC es la esperanza de Cuba!*"

A few steps above Dr. Alvarez Leal, Javier recognized Alberto, who fired a pistol into the air. This was a signal for more shooting, and the *abecedarios* fired off quick bursts from the Thompsons as others broke into the *Bayamesa* yet again.

"I didn't hear a word he said," grumbled the reporter as they returned to *Bohemia*.

The office was abuzz with a rumor that two American destroyers, the *Taylor* and the *Claxton,* would enter Havana Harbor by nightfall. The wealthy *machadista* Emilio Aragon and his mistress had a narrow escape as they boarded a Pan American seaplane at the Arsenal Dock. An angry crowd had formed on the pier, and a carload of *abecedarios* soon arrived and attempted to board. The pilot pulled away from the dock without the luggage or any other passengers, and as the *abecedarios* opened fire, he managed to take off for Miami. But soon it was all over. Machado boarded a plane bound for Nassau at Rancho Boyeros Airport accompanied by members of his cabinet. Many other prominent *machadistas* were in hiding, having fled one step ahead of the *abecedarios*.

It was nearly dusk when Javier returned home. After his parents left for Spain with Lydia, he had remained with his grandfather, and now ran jubilantly up the stairs shouting,

"*Abuelo*, have you heard the news?"

His grandfather was not in his room, and when Javier returned downstairs, the maid told him that he had not yet returned.

"Where is he?"

The girl shook her head blankly and Javier frantically asked the other servants if they knew where he was. The chauffeur had set out with his grandfather that morning for the *almacén* but had not been seen since. Javier felt the fear in the pit of his stomach. Why hadn't he returned?

Javier immediately set out once more in his car. The Vedado was quiet, but he knew the students were still marching along the Malecón, so he drove down Paseo and turned left on Zapata, heading for Habana Vieja. Entering Chinatown, he began to see the ABC flags hanging from the balconies. The narrow streets were clogged with people joyously banging pots and pans, as though it were *carnaval*. At Dragones Street, a group was marching towards the Capitolio, shouting, "*¡Se cayó* *el tirano!"* [The tyrant fell!] Javier braked to let them cross, and drove slowly through the crowd until he came to the military trucks parked around the fountain of La India. As Javier tried to pass, one of the soldiers waved him over with the barrel of his carbine.

"Where are you going?"

"None of your business," said Javier. "Let me through!"

The soldier brusquely motioned for him to get out of the car.

"You're making a mistake," said Javier.

"I think it is you who have made a mistake, *come-mierda*," said the soldier.

He held the carbine by the stock and nudged the barrel against Javier's chest, pushing him back toward the other soldiers, who stood by the fountain smoking cigarettes and watching the students approach the Capitolio. But a car splashed with green paint pulled up and a young man in a straw boater emerged.

"Who is this man?" he demanded.

His voice carried a shrill authority and the soldier's smile was erased.

"Are you dumb, or merely stupid? I asked what this man has done."

The fear engulfed the soldier's face and he slowly pointed the weapon at the ground. The other soldiers remained by the fountain as several young men came out of the car carrying Thompsons.

"We meet again," said Alberto, who was the last to step out.

Javier took a deep breath as the soldier walked back to the truck.

"This is not a night for a *paseo*," said Alberto.

"You've got to help me," said Javier.

Alberto was thinner than he remembered, and his jacket hung loosely around his seemingly frail shoulders. There were weary lines on his forehead, and it had been several days since he'd slept, but there was an odd exhilaration in his voice. The other *abecedarios* deferred to his obvious authority, and fanned out around him, as though standing guard.

"We're looking for someone," said Alberto. "I'm afraid we can't have you in the way."

"Looking for someone? Is that what the revolution is about?"

The young man who had stepped out of the car first raised the Thompson at Javier, but Alberto waved him off with a slight gesture.

"Would you have the killers go free? The debt must be paid in blood."

"This is not a gangster movie, Alberto. We were friends once. Do you suppose the killing will stop when this debt of yours is paid? This is not what Roberto died for."

"Roberto was a coward."

"Then was his death meaningless? And that of all the others?"

"The man I'm looking for killed Roberto, if that will make you feel any better."

"There's no time to argue, Alberto. I've got to find my grandfather."

Alberto looked at his old classmate with flat, expressionless eyes before whispering something to his lieutenant.

"You'll need this if you're stopped by my people," said Alberto, and handed him a green card embossed with a Star of David. "But watch your back, *gallego.*"

It was what Alberto had called him at Belén.

"The same to you, *mi amigo*," said Javier, and offered him his hand.

The *abecedarios* sped away and the soldiers looked in the other direction as Javier got back in his car. He crossed Zulueta Street, but the way was blocked by the smoldering wreck of a black Cadillac, the kind favored by *machadistas*. There was no getting around it, so Javier left the Ford at the curb and continued on foot toward Muralla Street.

The old city walls had run along Monserrate Street, and on the other side was Habana Vieja. In contrast to the Capitolio, the old city was quiet, although he saw suspicious eyes through the closed shutters of the old houses and heard an occasional shout from the direction of the waterfront. Javier crossed the Plaza Vieja and soon reached the *almacén*. The gate was locked, and he tried the key but saw that it was barred from within.

"*¡Abuelo!*" he shouted, banging his fist on the old wooden door. The windows were shut behind thick iron bars, and he could detect no movement through the weathered *rejas* on the second floor.

"Pepin!" yelled Javier as he opened the gate, but no one was there.

Javier vaulted up the stairs to his grandather's office, but his chair was empty. He wished he could call home to see if his grandfather had returned, but a telephone had never been installed in the *almacén*, and the lines were probably still dead, anyway. Then he remembered the old man had taken to wandering down by the docks, and he set out for the waterfront. Muralla stretched from the Plaza Vieja to the Plaza de San Francisco, and he was soon in sight of the water. Soldiers guarded the customs house, so Javier continued along the wharf, past the La Máquina and Santa Clara docks. The stevedores had not yet broken the strike, and a number of ships remained in the harbor, unable to dock. Crates were piled up on the piers, and there was a rotten stench from the spoiled produce.

"*¡Abuelo!*" he called out.

One of the soldiers looked in his direction but Javier kept walking. Soon, he reached the Paula docks. Beyond Jesús María Street was the dock used by the United Fruit Company, and the Ward Line Dock. Javier could see across the bay to Casablanca, where the fishing fleet was anchored. Their masts wobbled in the stale breeze, and the fading light flickered on the oily water. Javier asked a watchman by one of the warehouses, but he'd been drinking and offered him a swig from his bottle of *aguardiente*. A fisherman sat on the dock, his pole dangling over the side, but he hadn't seen anyone. An old chinaman walked along the Alameda de Paula but scampered off when he saw Javier approach. The sun was setting when he finally spotted the old *gallego*, unmistakeable in his black beret, casting a fragile shadow at the water's edge.

His grandfather had left the *almacén* and strolled down to the wharf, as he was fond of doing in the cool of the evening. Somehow, he was not surprised to see the *muchacho* who reminded him of Ramón.

"It's time to go, *Abuelo*," he said, taking his arm.

Something about his voice triggered a distant memory of Spain. It was a sunny afternoon in the village where he was born, which he knew he would never see again.

"In the hills near Betanzos, there is a stream where my father used to take me trout fishing. Do you know it?"

"No, *Abuelo*," said the young man. "I've never been. Will you tell me about it?"

TEN

Javier had already booked passage on the *Orinoco* when a storm struck Havana and the port was closed. The delay gave Doña Inés the opportunity she needed, and she decided to take matters into her own hands. It was obvious that her husband's ham-fisted attempts to influence their younger son had come to naught. A lighter touch was needed, and when she learned that Sophia Heydrich and her two daughters were spending several days in Havana, she invited them to lunch on Sunday.

"This is unforgivable," protested Javier when he got wind of it. "It's clear what you have in mind and I don't want any part of it."

"You can think what you like," said Doña Inés indignantly. "It's all the same to me. Sophia is a very dear friend of mine and it would be very rude not to invite her and her lovely daughters simply because you're such a *guajiro*. Besides, you don't have to eat if you don't want to."

That morning, Javier contemplated having lunch at the Floridita when he smelled an *ajiaco* bubbling in the kitchen. When Panchita, the cook, stepped out into the garden to pluck a few sprigs of *yerba buena*, he lifted the lid of the huge cauldron and saw chunks of pork together with yucca, corn, plaintains, and much else simmering in a fragrant broth. As she had been ordered to do, Panchita soon returned and chased him out of the kitchen with a huge wooden spoon.

335

Javier duly appeared at the family table on Sunday afternoon. Don Ramón graciously welcomed his old friend's wife, and sat her to his right. Senora Heydrich was a lively, talkative woman with a musical laugh, and happily admitted that she had left Eduardo behind in Matanzas because he grew intolerably *pesado* when they went shopping. Her youngest daughter Teresita sat in Lydia's place, Javier's sister having enrolled at Smith College after her return from Spain. She was a dark-haired beauty of sixteen, and flirted so effectively with Miguel that his cheeks reddened and his wife jabbed him in the ribs with her fork.

Javier had positioned himself at his usual spot, beside his grandfather. Panchita ladled out huge portions of the sumptuous stew, and Javier's mouth watered even before Father Saralegui completed his benediction. The music of spoons against earthenware bowls momentarily suspended all conversation, except that of Señora Heydrich, who recounted the prodigious feats of her dressmaker on the Prado. Javier laid siege to the *ajiaco*, determined to take no prisoners, but try as he might he could keep his eyes from wandering toward Adelaida Heydrich, seated beside her mother.

Several years before, Javier had met Adelaida at the Heydrich's beach house in Varadero. He remembered her as a stocky, beetle-browed girl who insisted on pulling the ribbons from Lydia's hair and preferred to play chess rather than take a *siesta* with the other children. Was this the same girl? Some of the plumpness remained in her heart-shaped face, but she had a trim figure and dainty ankles. To her mother's despair, she had refused to pluck her eyebrows, as was fashionable, but Javier found that they deliciously set off her creamy complexion. Her dark hair was tightly pulled back but a curl had escaped and lingered just behind her right ear. Most surprisingly, while her mother chattered with Doña Inés and her sister teased Miguel, she devoted her attention to the *ajiaco*, and even asked Panchita for more. Javier had never seen a woman eat that much.

Miguel's young sons José and Ignacio were dressed in matching *guayaberas* and proudly sat between their mother and Father Saralegui. Now five and three, they had been deemed old enough to eat with the grown-ups, but picked indifferently at their food and soon began to torment each other. Having been sternly reprimanded by his father, Ignacio turned his attention to Adelaida, and began tossing tiny bits of bread into her bowl of *ajiaco*.

"*¡Niño!*" cried Aunt Clara, vainly swatting at him from across the table.

Ignacio thought this was great fun, and was about to launch more bread with a soup spoon when Adelaida reached out and pinched the last joint of his thumb until he yelped and scampered back into the kitchen, his brother a few steps behind.

Aunt Clara's jaw dropped in surprise, but she did not miss the tiny smile of complicity that passed between Javier and Adelaida.

Dessert was another favorite of Javier's, a luscious *flan*. Afterwards, Don Ramón and Miguel retired to the study for Por Larrañagas and brandy, but rather than join them, Javier lingered in the dining room. Through the window, he saw the ladies seated in the shade of the gazebo. Aunt Clara had felt faint and retired to bed, but Doña Inés chatted gaily with Señora Heydrich and her youngest daughter, while Adelaida stared moodily at the fig trees.

"I apologize for my nephew," said Javier, joining her in the garden. "He's terribly spoiled."

"I suspect all little boys are," said Adelaida. "I wouldn't know, since I don't have any brothers."

"That's a pity."

"Not at all! I suspect you're just as spoiled."

"Why do you say that?"

"It's rather obvious, isn't it?"

Javier bit his lip and noticed that his mother and the others had drifted back towards the house. He could hardly leave her sitting there alone.

"That's hardly an answer," he said.

"I thought that the eminent Harvard graduate had all the answers."

"You don't like me very much, do you?"

"Don't flatter yourself," said Adelaida, her honey-colored eyes flashing. "Listen to me, Javier López Angulo. I don't appreciate this any more than you do, so don't expect me to laugh at your jokes like all the silly girls at the Havana Yacht Club."

This note of discord wafted across the garden and Señora Heydrich soon came to Javier's rescue, clutching her beaded purse.

"It's terribly late," she cooed, adding: "Do join us for tea before we leave Havana. Wouldn't that be lovely, Adelaida?"

Javier grimly watched them take their leave, and expected the worst when his mother took him aside.

"What did you think of Teresita?" she asked slyly.

"Nice enough, I suppose," said Javier. "I'm afraid I spent all my time talking to that irritating Adelaida."

Doña Inés hardly seemed discouraged and said:

"She's very intelligent, you know. But Teresita is one of the prettiest girls in Matanzas."

Javier had already quit his job at *Bohemia*. As the time approached for his departure, he wandered ruefully around the city, playing dominoes with his grandfather and walking with him along the waterfront as the fishing fleet came in at the end of the day. But his conversation with Adelaida still rankled him.

Somehow, Señora Heydrich did not seem surprised when Javier presented himself at the Sevilla-Biltmore, where she and the girls were staying.

"How nice of you to stop by and see us!" she said. "Adelaida and Teresita have talked of nothing else all day."

There was an uncomfortable silence, but the girls soon descended in the elevator.

"It's too lovely a day to stay inside," declared their mother. "Why don't we go for a stroll?"

338

They left the hotel and were soon on the Prado, walking in the shade of the laurel trees. Señora Heydrich told Teresita about a new hairdesser at Casa Inez, and Javier soon noticed that the singsong of their voices seemed to recede. Indeed, they soon fell several steps back.

"I wanted to apologize," began Javier.

"Is that why you came?" said Adelaida. "I was wondering."

"I felt that I must have offended you."

"Really? It seems you're always apologizing. *C'est trés amusant.*"

"Do you speak French? I'm leaving for Paris next week."

"Paris is terribly dreary this time of year," scoffed Adelaida. "It does nothing but rain, all day long. What would the French do if not for the restaurants?"

"I'm hardly going for the food," said Javier, deflated. "I'm going to write a novel. But I didn't want to go thinking I'd insulted you somehow."

"I think that you're the most arrogant man I've ever met," said Adelaida sharply. "I was hoping you'd fallen in love with Teresita—they all do—since that would get me off the hook."

"I beg your pardon?"

"My parents are desperate to marry me off. I'm almost nineteen, you know, nearly an old maid. They've even threatened to send me back to the nuns if I don't get married. It doesn't matter to whom, really. I suppose they picked your name out of a hat."

"If Paris is so dreary, I suppose you'd rather spend the rest of your life in Matanzas."

"Now you *have* insulted me!" said Adelaida, leaving him behind.

Javier hurried to catch up, leaving Señora Heydrich and Teresita still further behind.

"Why don't you leave Matanzas?" he asked.

"Don't you think I want to? Sometimes I think I'll burst if I don't go!"

339

"I'll think of you in Paris."

"Then you must be sure to send me a postcard of the Eiffel Tower."

"You're not making this very easy, are you?"

"Para tumbar el coco hay que subir el árbol," said Adelaida. [To knock down a coconut you have to climb a tree.]

As Javier pondered this, they reached the Malecón. The brisk wind sent the spray crashing over the seawall, and he felt the cold drops against his cheek. He touched her arm to start back, but the girl was indifferent to the threatening whitecaps.

"Why, Javier!" said Señora Heydrich, out of breath as she caught up to them. "You're the most charming young man I've ever met. You must visit us in Matanzas."

"Por favor, Mamá," said Adelaida wearily, "he's sailing for France next week. Why on earth would he come to Matanzas?"

Teresita giggled but soon skittered away as the spray doused her new hat from El Encanto.

"¡Ave María Purísima!" cried Señora Heydrich. "You're as *pesada* as your father. It's that German blood of the Heydrichs. What will Javier think of us?"

Javier had already packed his clothes in a steamer trunk when he announced that he was putting off his departure for a few more days. The *Orinoco* sailed away, but the *Oriente* would leave next week for New York, and from there he could take *Berengaria* to Boulogne.

"What's gotten into that boy?" thundered Don Ramón. "First he wants to leave, then he wants to stay. Can't he make up his mind?"

"Be quiet, Ramón!" protested his wife. "You'll ruin everything!"

The *Oriente* sailed away as well. The following Sunday, Javier drove his yellow Ford through the Vedado and around the harbor. The road to Matanzas hugged the coast past Cojimar and Boca de Jaruco until it reached the lush green hills and palm-fringed valleys of Yumurí. From a rise, he saw the city of Matanzas, couched among the hills overlooking the bay.

Dr. Eduardo Heydrich lived in a white stucco mansion on the Malecón, its wide portico supported by delicate Ionic columns. Lunch was a somewhat less boisterous affair than at the López' in Havana, and the Heydrichs usually spent Sunday afternoons *en famille*. When Javier was announced, Dr. Heydrich emerged to greet him. He was nearly as tall as Javier, with an absent-minded look in his longish face, but a twinkle in his eyes.

"What took you so long, my dear boy?" he said, taking Javier's elbow and leading him inside. "You have no idea what's been going on here."

"What do you mean?"

Before the doctor could answer, Señora Heydrich fluttered toward Javier. Her husband seemed relieved to pass the bewildered young man off to her in the sitting room. Teresita was entertaining two well-dressed boys, brothers by the look of them, neither of whom got a word in edgewise. Dr. Heydrich happily resumed his chess game with Dr. Fuentes, a prematurely balding young man with a melancholy expression. Javier was cursorily introduced to cousin Finita, who smiled and returned to knitting her *mañanita*.

"I can't imagine what's keeping Adelaida," said Señora Heydrich to her younger daugher. "Would you ask her to join us, dear?"

Teresita frowned, but there was an edge to her mother's usually syrupy voice so she went upstairs, leaving her two suitors to catch their breath and prepare for the next round.

Adelaida came down in due course, and Javier noticed that Dr. Fuentes looked up from the chessboard to give her a longing gaze.

"I thought you were leaving Cuba," she said.

"So did I," admitted Javier.

Neither had anything more to say, and Javier sat awkwardly on the couch beside Finita. Much to her mother's

341

dismay, Adelaida wandered over to the chessboard, where her father was beating Dr. Fuentes yet again, and Teresita's lilting voice filled the room. Then Señora Heydrich suggested they take the air along the Malecón.

"It's cold," grumbled Dr. Heydrich, pondering the sacrifice of a pawn.

At a stern glance from his wife, he pushed the chessboard away and gently pulled Dr. Fuentes along with him. Teresita soon joined her mother outside, followed by her young men. Only Finita remained, for the sake of appearances, and the room was silent save for the click of knitting needles.

"Have you come to apologize again?" asked Adelaida.

"No," said Javier.

"Then why are you here? I take it you're not in love with my sister."

"No, I'm afraid not."

"Then why didn't you go to Paris?"

"I don't know," said Javier, but then corrected himself: "Actually, I do."

Finita listened intently but Adelaida hissed and pointed to the door. The old woman scurried out of the room trailing yarn.

"Well?" asked Adelaida.

"I suppose that I'll have to marry you," said Javier at last.

"Now I *know* that you're the most arrogant man I've ever met."

"Let me explain," said Javier. "It's all very clear to me now. As I was driving here this morning from Havana, I kept asking myself *why*. I just couldn't figure it out. Now I know there can't be any other explanation. Don't you see?"

"You seem to believe that I'm in love with you. I'm not, you know."

"I know that!" said Javier brightly. "But that doesn't matter, just yet. For now, you can send me away, or torment that poor doctor, or go back to the nuns, or do whatever you please. I'm very persistent, you see. Since I came back from Harvard, I feel as though I've been sleepwalking. It's terribly hard to look for something without knowing what it is. But now I know."

Rather satisfied with himself after his speech, Javier took a deep breath. Adelaida looked at him rather oddly, as though seeing him for the first time.

It was Finita, peering through a crack in the door, who rushed off to tell Señora Heydrich the good news.

Walter spent the tumultuous days after the *Machadato* in the Anglo-American Hospital. The gash in his cheek needed stitches, and his chest was swathed in bandages to heal his broken ribs. He had cabled his wife, telling her to stay in Austin, but she promptly boarded a train to Miami and flew to Havana on the *Caribbean Clipper*.

Beryl found the hospital room filled with flowers sent by the employees of the bank. Walter's face was swollen and numb, and every time he took a deep breath there was a searing pain in his side. His eyes blinked open and he saw her through the boozy fog of sedation.

"Beryl!" he said thickly. "There's fighting in the street!"

"Don't be silly," replied his wife, taking off her gloves and sitting on the edge of the bed.

Walter felt her cool fingers on his forehead, and then Beryl turned and said smartly to the nurse:

"I think we'll go, now."

Walter remained in bed for the rest of the week, supported by a mound of pillows while Beryl fed him tomato soup. The twins had remained in Austin, and Freddy would bring them to Havana at the end of the month. Reverend Graham and his wife came to visit, and they played a rubber of bridge in the bedroom.

When Walter returned to the Havana Trust, he found Hopgood in his office, huddled with several lawyers from New York over a stack of financial statements. It was only

343

after liquidating various assets such as La Margarita that the bank once again became solvent. Since Emilio Aragon's disappearance, the Altomar Realty Co. had gone bankrupt, and the land west of Jaimanitas became the subject of various lawsuits. Rather than foreclose on the property and face litigation in Cuban courts, the bank wrote off the loan and amortized the loss over several years. Together with a fresh dose of capital from Commodore Halsey, this allowed the Havana Trust to re-open its doors.

But no sooner had the lawyers boarded the *Oriente* for New York, there was another revolution, and the government fell after less than a month. It appeared as though the battleships would be returning to Havana Harbor, and Ambassador Welles advised American families to repair to the Hotel Nacional for safety. Walter was prepared to abandon the house in Miramar but Beryl stopped him in his tracks.

"That's the silliest thing I've ever heard," she declared.

This proved to be true, since the officers loyal to President Céspedes barricaded themselves in the hotel and were surrounded by their own troops, who blasted them with artillery until they surrendered.

By then, the new general manager of the bank arrived in Havana, none other than Harry Dobbs. While Walter was in the hospital, Commodore Halsey had asked Grant Mason for advice, and the latter recommended his old classmate from Yale. He and Francine had been quite taken with Havana on their honeymoon, and were delighted to go back. Since Jane was still in New York, Grant lived a bachelor life, and invited them to stay at Jaimanitas until they could find a place of their own.

Harry was a scratch golfer, and he and Grant faced off against Walter and Freddy one Saturday morning at the Havana Country Club. Walter's ribs were still sore and he could barely swing his club without wincing. Blessedly there were no wagers, and Harry noticed Emilio's abandoned house on a rise above the fairway. An angry mob had broken down the door and looted it from top to bottom, smashing windows and carting off furniture. The orange trees had withered and died, and the sienna walls were charred from the fire. Harry picked his way through the rubbish beneath the marble loggia and peered in through the boarded-up windows.

"It's safe to say that you can pick it up for a song," said Grant.

When Walter arrived at the Havana Trust each morning, Harry had already been there for an hour, happily installed in Hugo Pedraza's old office. Although he didn't speak a word of Spanish, he was an energetic and efficient manager, and soon the Havana Trust was sailing as sweetly as the *HMS Victory*. Walter invited him to lunch at the American Club, and introduced him to some of the old Cuba hands, but Harry generally preferred to have a sandwich at his desk and work right through lunch, or else meet Grant for a game of squash.

Soon, Walter found that he had time on his hands, since Harry reported directly to New York and rarely needed his help. He began to leave early, stopping for a martini at the American Club, and then pottered listlessly around the house until dinner. In the evening, he listened to *Amos and Andy* until he fell asleep. Walter slept late and was in no hurry to get to the office, and once told Felix to drive west on Fifth Avenue to Altomar. There was nothing left save a few pilings sticking forlornly out of the rocky beach. Even the chain link fence had been taken down and sold for scrap.

It was Beryl who suggested they leave Cuba.

"I have no interest in taking a vacation," said Walter.

"That's not what I meant," said Beryl. "It's time we went home."

"But *this* is our home!"

"No it's not, dear."

When Walter submitted his resignation in a letter to Commodore Halsey, he felt as though a great weight had been lifted from his shoulders. Beryl looked forward to returning to

345

Texas, and the girls once more began lassoing shrubbery in the garden. As for Freddy, he had never gotten along with Harry, and soon quit. Almost overnight, their house in Miramar was full of packing crates. Beryl complained that Walter was in the way, and he happily repaired to the bar of the American Club. Over drinks, he recounted his now legendary encounter with the *porrista*, and the scar on his cheek gave him a jaunty, piratical air. When they learned he was leaving, his friends regarded him with something akin to envy. Even Reverend Graham joined him in a daiquiri, and Ogden Crews clapped him on the back saying, "You're free at last!"

Walter had no regrets on his last day at the bank. When he cleaned out his desk, he realized that all he wanted to take was the engraving of La Margarita on the wall and the model of the *HMS Victory* that Mr. Gordon had left him. Then he thought better of it and took the ship into Harry's office. The new president of the Havana Trust distractedly looked up from a stack of loan documents when Walter entered.

"I wanted you to have this," said Walter. "I think you'll need it."

"That's swell of you, Walter," replied Harry, thinking that Grant's young son would enjoy playing with it in the swimming pool.

Miss Garcia burst into tears and even Hopgood grew misty-eyed as he wished him good luck, but Walter smiled mischievously as he descended into the lobby.

"It won't be the same without you, Mr. Huggins," said Elmer wistfully.

Walter shook the guard's hand and noticed with satisfaction that he'd been drinking. His car was outside, but he placed the picture of La Margarita in the back seat and told Felix to meet him at the American Club. With a spring in his step, Walter walked up O'Reilly Street for the last time, crossing Aguacate and Villegas streets toward the statue of Francisco de Albear by the Floridita. Facing the Hotel Inglaterra, he entered the Parque Central beneath the statue of José Martí, and passed between the cast-iron lions of the Prado towards the Malecón. A female orchestra was playing *El Manisero* in one of the cafés, and Walter hummed happily to himself.

It was only when he saw the lighthouse of El Morro, floating on the rim of turquoise water beyond the laurel trees of the Prado, that he realized how much he would miss it all.

When Hemingway returned to camp, it was already dark, and the others were sitting around the fire drinking gimlets. They had left the highlands of the Serengeti for the flat, brushy country south of Lake Manyara. Near Kijungu, they had pitched their tents in the gap between two wooded hills, just a few miles from a salt lick.

But it was already February, and the rains would soon make the roads impassable. Each morning, a damp mist hung over the hills, and the sky was grey with mottled clouds. Unfailingly, it rained before lunch, a weak drizzle followed by intermittent squalls that left the ground slick and foul-smelling. That evening it cleared, but Hemingway was already wet and the water dripped from his Stetson hat.

The throaty voice of Philip Percival, the white hunter, drifted over the camp, followed by Pauline's familiar trill and Charles' polite laughter. They had been doing just fine without him, thank you, and Hemingway mumbled a greeting and stomped to the circle of green tents. Handing the boy the Springfield rifle, he ordered him in Swahili to draw a bath, and soaked in the canvas tub until the warmth seeped back into his bones. Soon, attired in his flannel pajamas, dressing gown, and mosquito boots, he joined them and accepted a drink from Percival.

Hemingway had spent the day fruitlessly following kudu tracks. As always, Charles had shot the first one, a freak bull with 38-inch horns that twisted forward, which now hung in

347

the skinner's tent. Hemingway remembered that nearly two years ago, just off El Morro, it was Charles who caught the biggest marlin.

"Poor old Papa," said Pauline.

"Here's to *nada*," said Hemingway, saluting them with his gimlet.

"Whatever you say," put in Charles.

Hemingway frowned and sipped his drink. He didn't want to talk about hunting, although that is what they invariably talked about at night. They had been on safari for over two months, and he had killed lions, gazelles, leopards, rhinos, and countless hyenas who strayed too close to camp, but not a kudu.

Charles was embarrassed by his good fortune, and wished that Hemingway had shot the first kudu. Accustomed to his friend's childish moods, he regarded them as indifferently as the summer showers in Key West. But he had grown weary of Africa and missed his wife Lorine, who would later join them in Haifa.

As for Pauline, the thrill of being on safari had quickly worn off. The natives unnerved her with their heavy-lidded eyes and the way they worshipfully addressed her husband as B'wana. She had no interest in shooting kudu, or anything else, and spent the day listening to the drumbeat of the rain on the tent flaps. Pauline, too, wished her husband had shot the kudu instead of Charles. Each night, he stayed up drinking with Percival, and staggered back into the tent muttering to himself. Lying in the narrow cot beneath the mosquito net, she wondered why he was angry, since he had everything he ever wanted. Except for a pair of kudu horns, of course.

"Another spot of the giant killer?" said Percival.

Hemingway nodded as the white hunter moved behind the glow of the campfire to the canvas cooling bag where he kept his seemingly inexhaustible supply of gin. The ruddy Englishman was hardly what Hemingway expected. He had imagined white hunters to be roguish, implacable killers, with an ominous air of mystery. Instead, Percival was officious and mild-mannered, a shopkeeper rather than a paid assassin.

As Percival mixed the gin with the lime juice, he wondered how long it would take Hemingway to bag a bloody kudu. Despite himself, he had grown fond of the bluff, boastful American, who would be an excellent hunter if not for his poor eyesight and lack of patience. He made up for it with an almost touching eagerness to learn, constantly asking questions and jotting things down in a notepad he kept in one of the many pockets of his tailored bush jacket. The white hunter thought Charles was a good chap, but felt sorry for the Memsahib, who clearly wanted to be someplace else. He did not like being out in the field so late in the rainy season, and looked forward to seeing his wife at their farm in the Mua Hills. But he was, as the saying goes, drinking their whiskey.

Or gin, for that matter. Percival handed Hemingway his gimlet and settled his comfortable bulk in the canvas chair. Would it be another long night? He had nearly run out of stories about Teddy Roosevelt and the gossip from the Mathaiga Club that he usually regaled his clients with, and came with the price of the safari. To his dismay, a gloomy silence had fallen over the Americans, like a dark cloud.

"Spot of trouble in Cuba, what?" he ventured.

"You might say that," replied Hemingway.

"You were there for the revolution, weren't you?"

"Which one?"

On August 12, the Hemingways were at sea and heard on the ship's radio that Machado had resigned. The newspapers were full of it when they landed at Santander, recounting the subsequent slaughter. Shortly after they reached Madrid, they learned that a hurricane had slammed into Cuba, causing widespread damage. Then on September 4, a group of sergeants led by a *mulato* named Fulgencio Batista had revolted against their officers and seized Camp Columbia. The timorous Carlos Manuel de Céspedes speedily resigned. In less than a month, the provisional government established by Sumner Welles had collapsed. A doctor named Ramón Grau San Martín became president with the support of the Directorio.

After the bullfight season, Hemingway proceeded to Paris. There, still smarting from the lukewarm reviews of *Winner Take Nothing*, he read in *Le Figaro* that the ABC had attempted a *coup d'etat* on November 8 and occupied the fortress of Atarés. The *abecedarios* finally surrendered, but were machine-gunned by the soldiers as they emerged beneath a white flag, and the ABC seemed all but finished.

Then while Hemingway was in Nairobi, recovering from amoebic dysentery in the hospital, he learned that on January 15, Batista had double-crossed Grau San Martín and the students. With the support of the new American ambassador and the surviving *abecedarios*, he installed retired soldier Carlos Mendieta in the refurbished Presidential Palace. From Havana, Grant had sent the latest installment of *El Bobo*, in which a little boy in a cinema asks if a new movie is coming on. No, replies *El Bobo*, it's the same one.

"I think we saw our share of fireworks," recalled Pauline.

"Really?" said Percival. "It must have been quite extraordinary, if you can believe the newspapers. Life's a bit dull around here, I'm afraid."

Hemingway did not want to talk about Cuba, either, and debated whether or not to have another gimlet when the boy announced dinner. It was a surprisingly formal affair, even with their pajamas on, and Percival produced two bottles of claret. The candles were lit in the dining tent, and they were served roasted gazelle chops, mashed potatoes, and green corn. Hemingway ate with gusto, dousing his meat with chutney. Since his illness, he had lost weight, and Pauline was delighted to see his appetite return. But they ate silently, lost in their own thoughts. After coffee, Charles made his usual excuses and returned to his tent. Soon after, Pauline yawned and turned in, but Hemingway was not sleepy and finished a third bottle of wine.

It was bad form to let a client drink alone, so Percival accompanied him back to the campfire, which the boy had rejuvenated with another log. Hemingway had brought a bottle of port from Nairobi and filled Percival's glass.

"Tomorrow's the day," Hemingway announced. "I can feel it!"

"God save us," said Percival amiably.

"I think I'll be at the salt lick at first light," said Hemingway. "I could take some food and spend the night there."

"There's a village just west of Kijungu," shrugged Percival, filling his pipe. "You could bed down there, if you like. It's all the same to the kudu."

"Very funny," growled Hemingway.

He stared at the rising flames in silence, but soon brightened at the thought of sleeping in a Masai hut. Pouring the white hunter another glass, he studied him intently, noting for the first time that his hands were large and brown, but with meticulously trimmed fingernails, and that there was a white line across his forehead, from years of wearing a bush hat in the sun. Taking out his pad, he wrote it down.

Percival savored the sweet, tawny port and wondered at the change in the mercurial writer's mood. One minute he was torturing himself over a kudu and the next he was grinning from ear to ear like the damn Cheshire Cat and scribbling something or other. One could never tell with the bloody Americans. But as they spoke, he had an eerie feeling he could not put his finger on, and he felt a tingle at the back of his neck. Once, he had been on the Serengeti Plain, tracking a gazelle, when he realized that he himself was being stalked, by a cheetah. It was astounding how easily the predator could become the prey.

"I hear there's great fishing up the coast from Mombasa," said Hemingway. "Have you ever caught a marlin?"

"I don't believe I have, laddybuck," said Percival warily.

ELEVEN

My grandparents' wedding took place on a warm spring evening in the cathedral of Havana. Father Saralegui celebrated mass, and the bride and groom emerged beneath a white silk canopy onto the torchlit Plaza de la Catedral. The guests cheered as several horse-drawn carriages drew up to take the wedding party to the Centro Gallego, where the reception was held.

Although the American destroyer *Wyoming* remained in Havana Harbor, its ominous grey bulk dwarfing the fishing smacks, the bombing had resumed and constitutional guarantees were suspended yet again. Once more, policemen patrolled the Prado, and a cordon of soldiers surrounded the Presidential Palace. But that was of little consequence to Javier and Adelaida as their carriage traversed the cobblestoned streets toward the Parque Central. The towers of the Centro Gallego gleamed in the pale violet night as the wedding party approached. A top hat perched precariously on his head, Javier alighted from the carriage to take Adelaida's arm and they ascended the grand staircase of yellow marble to the ballroom.

It was with evident relief that Don Ramón led Dr. Heydrich to his favorite armchair by the window and offered him a Por Larrañaga. As the guests continued to fill the ballroom, the two old friends looked out at the illuminated statue of José Martí, partially hidden by the royal palms.

"Do you recall that afternoon we sat here, just you and I, with two excellent *perfectos* such as these?" said Dr. Heydrich.

"Indeed I do," said Don Ramón, as the delicious smoke curled up toward the gilded ceiling.

In principle, Dr. Heydrich was pleased to be rid of his willful, often truculent daughter. Or rather, he was delighted that the responsibility for her happiness had passed out of his hands. But in recent days, he had grown weary of the mindless gossip that passed for conversation between his wife and Teresita, and he already missed his older daughter's quiet, thoughtful voice, and their games of chess in the evening.

As for Don Ramón, he took the same satisfaction in the marriage as he did in the signing of any other contract. He was equally glad that his younger son's future was no longer his concern. In fact, he could write all the damn novels he pleased. *¿Por qué no?*

From within came the sound of the orchestra, and Don Ramón took Dr. Heydrich by the arm and led him to the ballroom. Javier and Adelaida moved slowly around the dance floor to a *habanera* by María Teresa Vera they would never forget called *Veinte Años*. Then Dr. Heydrich stepped forward to dance with his daughter, while his new son-in-law danced with Doña Inés, who was resplendent in a new silk gown from Madrid. The guests from Matanzas clapped at the sound of *Las Alturas de Simpson,* the *danzón* played at the Heydrichs' own wedding, and those from Trinidad were soon tapping their more aristocratic feet to the infectious rhythm.

It was only after the orchestra took a break and several toasts were offered to the young couple, that the Conjunto Casablanca mounted the bandstand amid much applause from the younger guests. Sporting the same natty *guayaberas* from Jane's birthday party, they launched into the bawdy *son* which had opened *El Mono Sabio.*

This immediately brought Freddy Huggins to the dance floor with Mirta Rivero. Following his departure from the Havana Trust, Freddy spent a dismal winter in New York, thinking up radio jingles for an advertising agency on Madison Avenue, and grew even more homesick for Havana. It was purely by chance that he encountered Lydia's best friend Mirta one damp, chilly afternoon before the Christmas windows on Fifth Avenue. Senator Rivero had fled to New York shortly after President Céspedes had resigned, and installed his family in a penthouse on Park Avenue. There was no love lost between Mirta and Freddy from that disastrous night at the Tokio Cabaret, but he looked so pathetic out on the street, shivering in his raincoat, that she invited him home for dinner. Luckily, Señora Rivero had left Cuba with her cook, and Freddy soon found himself before a plate of *lechón asado, moros y cristianos,* and *tostones.*

As Freddy later explained to Javier, one thing led to another, and he was soon a regular guest at the Riveros' penthouse, which had become a meeting place for exiled *políticos* such as Dr. Fernando Alvarez Leal, who had prudently left Cuba after the slaughter of the *abecedarios* at Atarés. But when his old friend Colonel Mendieta became president, Senator Rivero returned triumphantly to Havana. Freddy was more despondent than ever. He had no wish to go to Austin, where Beryl's brother had hired Walter to run the family bank, and it took just one scented letter from Mirta for Freddy to quit his job and board the *Havana Special.* Now, he was giving golf lessons at the Havana Country Club.

Mirta was an excellent dancer and they whirled between the other couples to the next number. Freddy was momentarily distracted by the sight of a stunning *mulata* with violet eyes, who took the stage in a green sequined gown. Zoila Martínez had just returned from a tour of Mexico, where she had gone with Nely Chen, and if she recognized Freddy among the dancers, she didn't show it as she sang.

Freddy was trying to catch her eye over Mirta's shoulder when he felt a sharp pain, and realized that Mirta had brought her stiletto heel down on his toe. Freddy yelped and hopped briefly on one foot, but Mirta smiled sweetly and said,

"Did you lose something, *mi amor?*"

Among the many dignitaries at the Centro Gallego was Dr. Alvarez Leal, who had returned to Cuba on Senator Rivero's yacht. Amazingly enough, he had survived the countless double-crosses of the past year to become Minister of Justice in the latest cabinet. There had been several threats against his life and his bodyguards were posted at the entrance to the ballroom, but he had lived with danger so long that it made little difference to him. To his wife's despair, he was a terrible dancer, and while she danced with a handsome officer, he stood by the wall with his old nemesis at chess, Professor Filiberto Vargas, who continued to submit his weekly columns to *Bohemia*.

"How I envy them!" said Professor Vargas, nodding his bespectacled, egg-shaped head at the young couple.

Javier and Adelaida were to leave Havana the next morning. They planned to visit Lydia, who was studying for her examinations at Smith College and had been unable to attend the wedding. Then, they were to embark from New York on the *Ile-de-France,* bound for Le Havre.

"They'll be in Paris just when the chestnut trees bloom. There's a lovely little café on the Rue de Medicis where I used to play chess. Do you know it?"

Dr. Alvarez Leal nodded distantly and brought his ebony cigarette holder to his thin lips. He tried to remember a tantalizing chess problem which the professor had shown him last year, in which a seemingly suicidal move by the white queen held the key. But he had not played chess for many months, and soon gave up. It seemed so long ago since the *tertulias* with their students in the Acera del Louvre. So many things had changed since then.

At the other end of the ballroom, he noticed Jefferson Caffrey, who became the American ambassador after Sumner Welles was declared *persona non grata.* It was rumored that Batista, who ruled the country from Camp Columbia, rarely made a move without consulting him. The thought of the uneducated sergeant, now the most powerful man in Cuba, brought an ironic smile to his face. Through indirect channels, Batista had let it be known that he wanted to attend the reception, since he was eager to do business with Don Ramón and many of his Spanish friends. But the Centro Gallego steadfastly refused to admit him, since he was a *mulato,* and the matter was quickly dropped to avoid further embarrassment. Clearly, not everything had changed in Cuba.

The orchestra began to play once more and Javier reclaimed his bride from the arms of Don Ramón, who acceded with a courtly bow. Adelaida was breathless from her new father-in-law's energetic *pasodoble,* and Javier bent over to lick a single, fragrant drop of sweat that ran down her cheek. Laughing, they hid from their guests in a small alcove beneath the statue of an angel that seemed ready to soar across the ballroom.

The newlyweds had barely exchanged a word since their wedding vows, but neither had anything to say now. Knowing that when they were discovered, his wife would be taken from him, at least for the next dance, Javier put his arms around her, his chin resting gently on her forehead.

Charlotte Halsey's honeymoon in Tahiti ended abruptly when her husband was severely beaten under somewhat mysterious circumstances. When he failed to return to the yacht by morning, Charlotte dispatched the crew to scour the waterfront. They found him lying face-down on the pier, nearly all of his teeth knocked out.

Jack remained in his cabin the entire trip back, the bamboo shades drawn over the portholes, writing in his diary and eating from tins of applesauce. Charlotte happily sunned herself on deck with no regrets for her erstwhile pallor, and was genuinely sorry to see the yacht pass beneath the unfinished arches of the Golden Gate Bridge. Jack spent the winter in

357

New York getting a new set of teeth. By then, Jane was back in Havana, and Charlotte gratefully accepted her invitation to visit.

That month, the flame trees were in bloom, and the branches were heavy with red poinciana blossoms. Charlotte found her best friend lovely as ever. She had grown her strawberry blonde hair down to her shoulders, and her skin had a healthy pink glow. Jane laughingly showed her the jagged scar along her back from the operation, and Charlotte shuddered at the bulky back brace she had to wear while she slept. As they sat in the garden, Armando brought a tray of *mojitos,* and Charlotte recounted her misadventures in the South Seas.

"Poor Jack," Jane sighed, lighting a *margarita.* "Did they ever find the fellow that did it?"

"I think it was some French sailors, but we had to leave in bit of a hurry," recalled Charlotte. "You see, there were some complications with the *gendarmes.* There always are, aren't there? The American consul was most uncooperative. In fact, he was rather glad to see us go."

"Don't say I didn't warn you," said Jane, "but then, I'm hardly one to talk. It's really rather splendid to have gone through what I did, at least once. This poor little man tried to cure me in New York. I had a marvelous time making things up for him, and I think he nearly went over the edge himself! I'm the only patient he hasn't been able to help. Isn't that just the berries?"

"Oh, Jane."

"Honestly, everyone feels so sorry for you. It gives you rather a leg up, don't you think? No matter what you do, everyone is so glad that you're still in one piece. 'Buck up, old girl,' is what my dear husband says. I've become very good at bucking up."

"Don't talk like that," said Charlotte crossly. "I've known you far too long, so there's no need to take that fey tone with me. It really doesn't become you."

"Whatever would I do without you, Charlie?" said Jane, unfazed by the rebuke. "Do tell me more about Jack. He must look like King Kong with those teeth."

"Actually," said Charlotte, "they almost look real. He's grown a mustache, and it tends to cover them up. Do you want to know the latest? He wants to go hunting with Bror Blixen in Tanganyika. In fact, he wants to go this winter. As if bull-fighting weren't enough. Jack's never touched a gun in his life, mind you. He said he wants a kudu head like at the Harvard Club. 'Why Africa?' I asked him. Do you know what he said?"

Jane pursed her lips in a questioning moue.

"He said, and this is a direct quote, 'It's damn fine country.' Do you think he's mad, Jane?"

"I should think so, but it does sound like great fun. Perhaps I'll go, too."

"I have no reason to encourage him. Whatever happens, *I'm* not going on safari. Not after Tahiti."

"Where's your sense of adventure?" teased Jane. "By the way, there's something I've been meaning to show you."

Jane tinkled the silver bell at her side, and Armando soon returned with a photo album. Handing it to Charlotte, she opened it to a clipping from the society page of the *Diario de la Marina*. Charlotte saw that it was the wedding announcement of Javier López Angulo and Adelaida Heydrich.

"All's well that ends well," said Jane.

"The poor boy was in love with you," said Charlotte.

"Actually, I rather hoped he would fall in love with you."

"You were very bad to lead him on."

"Don't be silly. Men fall in love all by themselves, don't you think? We usually have nothing to do with it."

"I'm not being silly. It's not as though you needed to sharpen your claws. Or were you simply trying to make Ernest jealous?"

Jane smiled at the thought of Javier, and sucked on the mint leaves floating in her *mojito*. Charlotte stormed up to her room and pouted for the rest of the afternoon.

By the time Grant got home, the two were on speaking terms once more. They joined Harry and Francine Dobbs for cocktails at their new house overlooking the Havana Country Club, and then had dinner at Sans Souci and played the roulette wheel. A handsome young officer asked Charlotte to dance, and thereafter he accompanied them on their excursions in Havana, often providing a military escort while they went from nightclub to nightclub in Marianao. Grant was quite taken with Major Jimenez, and one night at the Chateau Madrid, he told Harry:

"I say, sport. You've got to admit that they've put an end to all the nonsense. Say what you will about him, Colonel Batista is running a very tight ship."

"Colonel? I didn't know he'd promoted himself. Have you met him?"

"Heavens, no. I'm afraid he doesn't leave Camp Columbia much. He looks like the fellow that used to trim our hedges, dark as a Red Indian. The first time he had lunch at the embassy, I was told he had to learn how to hold his knife and fork. Can you imagine that? He was a stenographer, so at least he can read and write. There's a rumor he wasn't even born here. But maybe that's what Cuba needs, a strong hand. Don't you agree?"

Harry was still new to Havana, and not yet ready to voice an opinion on the subject.

"Let's see how long he lasts," he said diplomatically.

One morning, near the end of Charlotte's stay, Jane received a letter from Pauline Hemingway. Charlotte was miserably hung over and drank another cup of scalding hot coffee as her friend ripped it open. Jane's perkiness in the morning never failed to irritate her. No matter how much she smoked and drank the night before, after just a few hours sleep she was fresh and lovely as a rose. Charlotte had stumbled down to breakfast in her bathrobe, but Jane was in her crisply starched tennis whites, and read the letter between gooey bites of Eggs Benedict.

"Ernest is back from Africa," she said.

The thought of the Dark Continent was especially painful to Charlotte that morning.

"No doubt he shot everything in sight," she muttered.

"Pauline is such a trooper. She writes that he even shot a kudu on the last day."

"Can I borrow it for Jack?"

"Hush, there's more. He's bought a fishing boat of his own named the *Pilar,* and he's coming to Havana this summer. Isn't that topping?"

In response, Charlotte rolled her eyes and took another sip of coffee, wincing when it burned the roof of her mouth.

Javier and Adelaida arrived in France in June, 1934. Paris was chastened by riots that spring, but a warm, hazy fug had settled over the Seine and the chestnut trees sprouted precocious white blossoms.

They found a small apartment on the Rue de Tournon, a quiet street that funneled down from the Luxembourg Gardens to the Seine. It was near the Place de l'Odeon and around the corner from Shakespeare and Company, Hemingway's favorite bookstore. Adelaida promptly planted geraniums in the windowbox, and they bloomed in a profusion of red and white blossoms. There were many Cubans in Paris that year, but my grandparents saw no one, treasuring their anonymity. Their first few weeks in Paris, they strolled from one end of the city to another, from the cafés of Montparnasse to the Eiffel Tower, and across the Pont d'Iena to the Arch de Triomphe. From there, they traversed the broad Haussmanian boulevards to Montmartre, where the Sacre Coeur gleamed like a citadel on a hill, and followed the winding, cobblestoned streets of the Marais back to the river.

Javier's spoken French was enigmatic, at best. Until the end of his life, he was inordinately proud of it, but my grandmother told me he never learned to properly pronounce the *r's*. It was Adelaida who translated, having been taught by meticulous French nuns in Matanzas. Each afternoon, she did her shopping in the open air market of the Rue de Buci with a basket in the crook of her arm, pausing at the fruit stand to select the ripest melon, haggling with the butcher over the leanest cut of veal, and finally selecting a crusty *baguette* for dinner. Adelaida had never cooked before, much like her mother, who ventured into the kitchen only to reprimand the servants. Her first efforts may well have gone awry, but she soon became an accomplished cook. Many years later, in Havana, she was as likely to serve *fricassée de volaille* as *arroz con pollo*.

As he had dreamed in Havana, Javier found a café in Montparnasse to write in, but there were too many tourists and the waiter eyed him balefully. He resolved to rent a room where he could work undisturbed, and rented a tiny attic up four flights of stairs in the Rue Dauphine, just a few steps away from the Pont Neuf. There was barely room to move around in, and it was insufferably hot in summer, but against the sloping wall was a sturdy oak table. If he leaned out the narrow window to his left, he could see the Seine. For a few francs he bought a wicker chair from a café down the street, and he fashioned a bookcase from some planks he found in the courtyard. Alone with his books, he unwrapped a fresh ream of paper and carefully lined up his sharpened pencils in a row. It was then that he realized he had nothing to write.

Each morning, Javier left Adelaida and doggedly walked down the Rue de Tournon to cross the busy Boulevard St. Germain and enter the labyrinth of narrow streets that led to the Rue Dauphine. He climbed the uneven wooden steps to his office, as he jokingly called it, where the immaculately white sheets of paper awaited him on the table. After an hour of pacing back and forth, nearly bumping his head against the rafters, he went outside, and resumed his wanderings through Paris.

One afternoon, as he made his way back across the Pont Neuf, across from the verdigris statue of Henri IV astride a bronze horse, he leaned over the side and watched the water rush between the bleak stone arches of the bridge. Javier felt an almost imperceptible pull from the brackish current, as though he had cast his line and a huge marlin was tapping the bait. *Not yet,* he told himself. If he pulled too quickly, the fish would be gone, spooked by his impatience. If he waited too long, it might grow bored and swim away. He had to wait for exactly the right moment to set the hook.

The next morning, Javier awoke to the sound of voices not his own, like an echo from a half-remembered dream. He wanted to leap out of bed and write in the notepad he kept by his bed, but there was time. As Adelaida slept beside him, the voices growing louder, building up inside him until he was ready to burst. Only when he climbed the steps to his attic and sat down at the makeshift desk did he tell himself: *Now!*

The words came easily, as though he were merely copying down what he had heard, and he filled page after page. Only when he looked at his watch did he realize that several hours had passed, and he had not eaten. But he was not hungry, and the tumult in his brain continued. When he could no longer write, he walked until it grew dark, and ravenously consumed the *daube de boeuf* that Adelaida had been stewing all afternoon.

Javier feared that in the morning the dream would vanish, that the voices would dwindle into silence, and he would be unable to write another word. But as he neared the Rue Dauphine, he remembered the blanket of snow that covered Harvard Yard, and his icy breath in the morning air as he walked to class. He ran past the startled *concierge* in the courtyard and bolted upstairs in his haste to begin.

The hot, hazy mornings gave way to damp, dreary afternoons, and Javier heard the raindrops against the windowpane. He dispatched the first ream of paper, and began another. By then, Alejandro (a young man not unlike himself) had left Harvard and returned to Cuba. Javier didn't stop to read what he had written, but allowed the frenzied march of his handwriting across the page to continue. At the end of the day, he rushed outside to the Pont Neuf and felt the taut line that threatened to pull him under the murky water. It was there, he knew, several fathoms beneath the surface, a monster whose shape he could still only guess at.

Walking through Paris, Javier began to see Havana, the city he was now attempting to describe in his novel. The banks of the Seine became the waterfront, across the bay from the brooding walls of La Cabaña. The Boulevard St. Michel became the Prado, with Spanish laurels instead of plane trees, and the Pantheon became the Capitolio, its white marble dome gleaming beneath the faultless tropical sky. The *quais* along the Seine became the Malecón, the salty spray shooting over the seawall, and in the narrow streets around the Place de Contrescarpe he heard *pregoneros* hawking their wares. On the Rue de Buci he saw a chinaman pushing a three-wheeled cart full of pineapples, mangos, and papayas, stacked atop palm leaves. Javier wondered if he had gone mad, if the words had sucked the sense from him.

Javier completed another chapter, but noticed that his progress was more measured. Now, he often quit for the day after filling only a few pages. Hadn't Hemingway said that the most difficult thing about a novel was to finish it? But if he had come as far as he had, then surely he could go on. His protagonist could not decide whether to leave Havana, and roamed despondently through Habana Vieja. Soon, the torrent of words had run dry, and the more Javier struggled, the harder it became to write.

Adelaida grew worried when her husband came home moody and short-tempered. He brooded at the dinner table, picking at his food, but downing several glasses of red wine, followed by a glass or two of rum if he couldn't fall asleep. Yet in the morning, he trudged back to the Rue Dauphine through the thin rain, if only to stare for hours at the blank piece of paper before him.

As the endless winter cast a pall over Paris, Javier grew to dread the climb up the stairs. The attic was musty and cold, and he wore his overcoat as he crouched over the table. He no longer wrote, but merely attempted to fill the pages. He realized he no longer cared whether Alejandro left Havana and wrote his novel or not. As unexpectedly as they had come, the voices were gone.

For the last time, Javier walked to the Pont Neuf. The air was raw and the sky was grey with mottled clouds. The rain had flooded the city, and the brownish water of the Seine had risen above its embankments, nearly submerging the Square du Vert Galant, where Henri IV met his paramours. The rod was still bent, pulled down by the unbelievable power of his adversary, now only a few feet below the waves. Javier imagined bringing the line up hand over hand, so as to get a glimpse of the marlin, its long sword pointing straight up, its scythe-like tail churning the water, its stubby fins spread out like wings. He desperately peered into the swift current, pulling with all his strength, but he knew that it was gone. The line had come up empty.

For the next several days, Javier avoided the Rue Dauphine. He had no wish to write anything else. Finally, with trepidation, he returned to the attic began to read what he had written. After a few pages, Javier could go no further. He knew that no matter how many books he read, or how hard he tried, he would never write like Hemingway.

"I'll never be a writer," he confessed to Adelaida.

"It's not the end of the world, *mi amor*."

"But where will we go?"

"We've been gone a long time," replied Adelaida with a mysterious smile. "Maybe it's time to go home."

Her voice did not betray her secret as they passed arm in arm through the Luxembourg Gardens. In the chestnut trees were pigeons, plump from the long winter. The shiny brown chestnuts had fallen to the muddy ground, and the bare branches clawed the curdled sky.

Perhaps that was the day my grandfather burned his manuscript. He was ashamed of what he had written, but as he dropped the ashes in the Seine, he realized he could write a much better novel. He could not see more than a vague outline of it, like a shadow on the water, just beyond the horizon. But not yet. Not for a long time, yet.

"What will I do in Havana?" asked Javier.

"Cada uno de su chivo hace un tambor."

My grandmother had many sayings, and that was one of her favorites.

But what of Jack Halsey? I imagine that his marriage to Charlotte ended shortly after their ill-fated safari. For many years, he lived off a monthly check sent on the express condition that he not return to the United States.

This was fine by Jack, who grew easily bored with people and places, and had no intention of going back anytime soon, since he would only get locked up again. Hemingway was often in the newspapers, and it was relatively easy to follow his movements. Jack had grown quite expert in imitating his flat, midwestern accent, and he would belly up to a bar in Mexico City or Buenos Aires and demand a daiquiri. He rarely had to buy the second round, and by last call everyone was calling him Papa.

The collapse of his father's financial empire ended the remittance checks. It made no difference to Jack, whose tastes were frugal, and whose needs, though rather refined, could often be procured inexpensively. While Hemingway served as a war correspondent on the battlefields of Normandy, Jack kept a low profile, although he would occasionally autograph books, and was often asked to speak at garden clubs and ladies' luncheons.

Needless to say, there were several close calls. Jack was occasionally in New York and stayed under an assumed name at the Explorer's Club. Once, while he was having lunch at a delicatessen on Second Avenue, he looked up from his celery soda and saw that Hemingway himself had entered. By then, the writer had married a fourth time and lived on the outskirts of Havana. Jack ducked behind his copy of *The New York Times*, but he could not resist taking a peek at him. Hemingway was overweight, and wore a shabby tweed jacket. He had grown a scraggly beard, and his wire-rimmed spectacles appeared to be held together with tape. But in some ways, he hadn't changed at all.

Jack remembered the first time he saw him, that lemon-grey morning in Montparnasse so many years ago. He had not gone to bed the night before, and still in his top hat and tails, had stumbled into the Closerie de Lilas for a cup of coffee. Hemingway sat in the corner, writing his first novel, and Jack felt an odd shiver travel up his spine. He looked like a football player, not unlike many of the handsome young Americans that Jack befriended in Paris. But there was a hard-edged quality about him, like that of a stake charred in the fire. Jack asked him for a light, and Hemingway looked up with half-lidded eyes.

"Beat it, you goddam fairy," he said. "Can't you see I'm trying to work?"

He lit his own cigarette as Hemingway continued scribbling in his notebook with a pencil stub. For once, Jack was at a loss for words, and felt something beyond love, beyond hate, beyond any emotion he had yet experienced. Those were the only words they ever exchanged, but he was never the same again.

Like a jolt of electricity, this feeling assaulted him once more in New York as Hemingway sat a few tables away and ordered a turkey and tongue on rye. Jack debated whether he should simply introduce himself. Would Hemingway remember him, after all these years? Perhaps not, but they had many acquaintances in common. A surprising number, he thought. Would Hemingway understand that just as he himself had chosen to fashion art from words on paper, Jack had chosen as his canvas another man's life? Could he respect him as an artist?

Jack saw how such an encounter could lead to much unpleasantness, and decided against it.

He avoided Cuba altogether, where Hemingway was well-known, as well as places like Paris, Madrid, Venice, and Nairobi, where Hemingway could turn up unexpectedly. Instead, Jack was a frequent visitor to the Far East, where Hemingway never returned after the war, although he had a surprising number of fans. Jack lived for many years in Singapore. The steamy weather reminded him of Havana, and he became a fixture at the Long Bar of the Raffles Hotel. After much effort, he taught the Chinese bartender to make a passably good daiquiri.

Charlotte had remarried a number of times (as had her friend Jane) but Jack nonetheless kept in touch. Postcards would reach her from odd corners of the world. "Greetings, daughter!" said one card, from Sarawak. Many years later, Charlotte still shuddered at the thought of Jack's escapades on safari: Tying up their hapless white hunter, he had forced him to drink gimlets at gunpoint, and read aloud from *Death in the Afternoon*. When they returned home from Africa, she had him committed to an insane asylum, but Jack managed to escape by masquerading as a psychiatrist. Charlotte was terrified that he would reappear, but she never saw him again.

By then, there were other Hemingways about as well. In a bar in San Francisco, Jack saw a stout, white haired man with a beard pound his fist on the counter and demand a martooni from the bemused bartender. Jack shadowed him around the city for several days, and decided to kill him. In a pawn-shop, he bought a twelve-gauge shotgun and a box of shells, although since the safari he detested firearms. One night, Jack followed the ersatz Hemingway down a dark alley and shoved him against the wall with the barrel of the shotgun. The man was drunk, and gazed at him with watery brown eyes that had seen far too much. It was a fair imitation, Jack had to admit. He was wearing a thick turtleneck sweater and his soiled khaki trousers were held up by an old German army belt with the inscription *Gott mit uns*. Would he beg for his life, Jack wondered, or die with dignity?

At first, the man thought it was a stick-up and he fumbled for his wallet. Then he got a better look at Jack and rubbed his eyes uncomprehendingly.

"Who the hell are you?" he asked.

"Never mind who I am," Jack hissed, with every nuance of contempt he could muster. "You're a goddam phony!"

"But so are you!"

Jack swung the barrel against his jaw, and watched the imposter crumple. With the toe of his moccasin, he rolled the body into a pile of old newspapers. The man was still alive, breathing in ragged gasps.

"How do you like it now, gentlemen?" said Jack, and hid the shotgun under his raincoat before walking off.

During the next few months, Jack hunted down a number of other Hemingway impersonators, including a librarian in Seattle who liked to dress up as a matador, and a professor in Santa Fe who claimed that Hemingway was impersonating *him*. Jack gained the latter's confidence by offering to return the suitcase lost by the writer's first wife, Hadley, at the Gare de Lyon.

Jack was in Miami Beach when he heard the news that Hemingway had killed himself. At first, he refused to believe it. It was a few weeks after the Bay of Pigs, and the city was a seething cauldron of wild conspiracies. This was obviously a ploy of the FBI to lure him out into the open. Jack appeared in a bookstore on Lincoln Road and offered to sign a copy of *To Have and Have Not*, but received a very strange look from the clerk behind the counter. He knew at once what he had to do.

Jack returned to the boarding house where he was staying and removed the shotgun from its case. He kept it meticulously oiled in case he should unexpectedly encounter any imposters, and it gleamed malevolently beneath the bare light bulb in his tiny room. His dentures clicked against the cold steel of the barrel, and he winced at the taste of gun oil. Jack was not afraid of death, and if there was indeed a God, he hoped He had a sense of humor. Unlike Hemingway, his arms were not long enough to reach the trigger, and he had to take off his moccasin to press it with his toe.

"*Adiós*, Papa," he said.

Dos patrias tengo yo: Cuba y la noche. ¿O son una las dos?

José Martí

My grandmother had told me about Lula Montero, but it wasn't easy to find her.

The Moorish-style lobby of the Hotel Nacional was full of Mexican tourists: balding, middle-aged men in loud shirts. Sitting on the terrace beneath the royal palms, I sipped a daiquiri and watched them flirt with their gorgeous young Cuban girlfriends. When I asked the bartender if the old movie star was still alive, he merely shrugged—hunching his shoulders, pursing his lips, and raising his eyebrows. Then I slipped him a few dollars, and the next day he produced her telephone number. Each time I called, there was no answer, only the same anonymous beep. Once, a female voice answered, and my heartbeat quickened, but I quickly realized it wasn't her. With my high school Spanish I could barely make myself understood, but I mentioned my grandfather's name, and left the number of the hotel. Perhaps she would call back, I thought.

In Havana, I had doggedly followed Hemingway's trail, having climbed to the top of La Cabaña, where the cannon was still fired at nine o'clock each night, and walked up Obispo Street from the Ambos Mundos to the Floridita, where there was a bronze statue of Hemingway in his favorite corner. I visited the Plaza de San Francisco and the pier where the *Anita* had docked, and even went to Hemingway's house outside of Havana, now populated by his tribe of six-toed cats. No one was allowed inside, although together with a busload of Japanese tourists, I peered in through the windows at the stuffed kudu heads on the wall. But I could not find out if he ever saw Javier again. Then in a bookstall on the Plaza de Armas I found a yellowed copy of the *Havana Post* which described that morning of August 12, 1933 when the *abecedarios* slaked their awful thirst for vengeance. I realized that both Hemingway and Javier witnessed the dire events of that long-forgotten revolution.

Since I was leaving the next morning, I could no longer put it off and visited the tomb of my grandfather. From the Hotel Nacional, I took a cab to the cemetery of Colón, the grandiose necropolis on the edge of the Vedado. It was walled off and divided into quadrants, like a Roman camp, and many of the tombs were built during the "dance of the millions," containing fanciful marble pyramids and windows of Lalique glass. Constante Ribailagua was buried there, as was José Raúl Capablanca and Kid Chocolate—the best bartender, chess player, and boxer ever.

Abuela had forgotten where the gravestone was, but she remembered the day her husband passed away: September 3, 1953. In the office, I gave the date to the clerk, an old man in a crumpled *guayabera* and horn-rimmed spectacles. With a weary shrug he climbed a creaky step ladder to where the leather-bound registers were kept. Leafing through the dusty pages with practiced fingers, he soon discovered the entry, and carefully wrote down the location on a scrap of brown wrapping paper.

I found it beneath an old banyan tree, a somber burial vault with LÓPEZ chiseled on the weathered marble. Javier was buried beside his grandfather, his parents, and his infant son, who was conceived in Paris but died a few days after he was born. The names carved on the tombstone were worn but still legible. Stupidly, I didn't bring any flowers, or even a camera to take a picture for my mother. There were a few dried leaves atop the grave, and I brushed them away with my hand.

Abuela had told me that my grandfather died prematurely at the age of 44. One afternoon, his secretary found him slumped over his desk at the advertising agency that he started with Freddy Huggins after his return from Paris. Javier's death of a cerebral hemorrhage shocked all who knew him since he was in the prime of health, an athlete who once rowed in the regatta of the Havana Yacht Club. He was also said to be a good boxer.

The firm of López & Huggins had been launched with a series of clever promotions to increase the circulation of *Bohemia,* including a Shirley Temple look-alike contest, and a radio program featuring Zoila Martínez and the *Mulatas de Oro.* It quickly grew to become one of the most successful advertising agencies in Cuba, with a splendid office on the Prado, from which one could look over the laurel trees to the lighthouse of El Morro. It was only a few blocks from the old Teatro Alhambra, which was finally torn down in the late 1930s. By then, my uncles were born, and my mother. My grandparents moved out of the house in the Vedado (which became Miguel's after the death of Don Ramón) and lived in the penthouse of the López Serrano Building, high above the Malecón.

In the turbulent years that followed, my great uncle became an intimate of Batista's, who ruled Cuba until 1959. The business which had begun in an old *almacén* on Muralla Street continued to grow, although it was nationalized after the Revolution. Miguel managed to get some money out, but after a series of bad investments, he died nearly penniless in Miami.

But Javier was not interested in politics. His sister Lydia had married a young man she met while at Smith, and lived in Boston. My mother remembered that each summer, the two families vacationed on the rocky coast of Maine, and Javier never failed to complain how cold the water was. Ironically, as the advertising agency grew, my grandfather took less and less interest, and left the details to Freddy and Adelaida. Did he dream of writing the novel that he caught a fleeting glimpse of in Paris? Unaware of the shadow that crept up behind him, Javier bided his time, listening for the voices that he once heard so clearly.

Perhaps he saw Hemingway again at the Floridita, where they first met and nearly came to blows. The writer continued his quest for the great black marlin, crossing over from Key West on his fishing boat the *Pilar*. After his marriage to Pauline broke up, he moved to Cuba, and lived there until his suicide in 1961. I picture Hemingway at my grandfather's funeral, standing at the edge of the crowd at the cemetery of Colón, a bearish, bearded figure in a *guayabera* and khaki pants, old before his time. But he was in Africa that year, once again on safari.

When I returned to the Hotel Nacional, I found a message at the desk. It was from Lula Montero, the stage name Nely Chen adopted when she left Cuba. She lived on the edge of the Vedado, in a crumbling mansion on the banks of the Almendares River. Her door was opened by the girl I spoke to on the telephone, her great-granddaughter. She was tall and willowy, with caramel skin and jet black hair falling to her shoulders. Only fifteen, she had an achingly lovely smile and a mocking expression in her feline eyes. Was that how Nely looked when she met Hemingway?

I followed her into the living room, which had a damp, musty odor mixed with the scent of frangipani blossoms. The wall was full of photographs, and I eagerly scanned them to see if I could find Hemingway. I saw Nely with the roguish actor Adolfo Ibarra, whom she married in Mexico City after she left Cuba. This turbulent marriage lasted only briefly, and I soon spotted a more *soignée* Nely, wearing a sparkling tiara, on the arm of Nelson Echevarria, the wealthy Venezuelan polo player. By then, Lula Montero was a well-known actress in Latin America, and even landed a few Latina spitfire roles in Hollywood in the 1940s. I didn't recognize her other husbands, although they grew progressively younger and better-looking, if poorer.

But after the Revolution, Nely returned to Cuba. Her son, who was raised by the *babalao* in Santiago de Cuba, was a warrior like Changó, and joined the guerillas in the mountains of the Sierra Maestra. There was a photograph of him in army fatigues, taken in 1959, when he was in his twenties, a rifle carelessly slung over his shoulder, an unmistakeably wolfish grin on his broad, handsome face.

Nely entered the room clutching the slender arm of her great-granddaughter. She was nearly 90 but there was still a lilting grace to her step. She wore a loose, orange-yellow robe that swirled about her legs, and her head was covered by a turban of the same fabric, although a few white hairs peeked out along the curve of her unwrinkled neck. Despite the garish makeup she wore for my benefit (white powder, dark green eyeshadow, and purple lipstick) she was still a beautiful woman, her skin a pale cinnamon, almost as smooth as her great-granddaughter's. Nely's eyes were a clear, translucent green, slanted upwards like a cat's, and the mischief in her glance hadn't changed from the photographs on the wall. Leaning towards me, she ran her fingertips down my face. Her touch was light and feathery, and her long, lacquered red nails were cool against my cheek. She nodded slowly, as though recognizing me, although we had never met. Nely's voice was unexpectedly husky:

"Don't be shy like your grandfather," she said, and exchanged a secret smile with the girl.

They laughed slyly, and I felt the blood rushing to my face, but soon I couldn't help but smile myself. When her great-granddaughter went to make coffee, Nely proudly remarked:

"She is also a daughter of Oshún."

Her English was no better than my Spanish, but we somehow made ourselves understood. This time, I came prepared, and she seemed amused that I wanted to tape record our conversation. But Nely was delighted to have an audience once again, and she told me how she arrived in Havana from Santiago de Cuba and danced in the chorus line at the Alhambra. Nely smiled at the thought of Freddy Huggins, whose father was the president of the Havana Trust, sitting in the audience, night after night. Many years later, she saw him in Mexico City after his scandalous divorce from Mirta Rivero forced him to leave Havana. She described Captain Segura as the most handsome man she ever met, even more so than Tyrone Power, although he had a terrible temper, like most Cuban men. She told me little about her affair with the famous novelist, leaving it to my imagination. Perhaps she was still a bit jealous of the blond *americana* whose name she pretended to have forgotten.

Then her memory failed her, as it had been many years since anyone asked her about the terrible days of the *Machadato*. When the Alhambra was shut down by the police after the shooting on the Prado, she was afraid to leave the *solar*. Then Sergeant Crespo—the one known as El Zurdo—came and told her that Chief of Police Ainciart had ordered him to follow her, thinking she would reveal Captain Segura's killers. He warned that Ainciart would soon order her arrest, so she left Havana that very morning. Nely had never forgotten the grim scar on his face and the terrible hurt in his dark eyes, and was sad when she found out what happened to him. When Machado fled, the *abecedarios* caught him trying to leave Atarés and hung his butchered body from a streetlight in the Prado. By then, Nely was back in Santiago de Cuba. In the house of the *babalao*, she had her baby, a son of Changó.

"It was so long ago," she sighed.

I feared that she was tiring, but there was much more she wanted to tell me, of her glamorous life in Hollywood and her affair with Orson Welles, and the heady days of the Revolution, when her son came down from the mountains with Fidel. When she realized I was only interested in her life before she left Cuba, Nely fried an egg and said that like my grandfather, I was stubborn as a mule. Once more she exchanged a joke at my expense with her great-granddaughter, and then turned to me.

"You remind me of him," Nely said softly, recalling the distant night that Freddy brought Javier to the Alhambra.

I explained that I never knew my grandfather, although I was named after him. But I still needed to ask about Jane Mason, having read that she inspired the character of the wife in Hemingway's story *The Short Happy Life of Francis Macomber*.

"Was Hemingway in love with her?"

Once more, Nely pretended not to remember her, the proud daughter of Oyá, goddess of storms, whom Changó preferred to all other women. Her eyes turned opaque, and she slowly shook her head and said:

"He never loved anyone. It was the price he paid, I suppose. I would see him from time to time, sitting alone in the Floridita, drinking himself blind. I've never seen a man so alone."

Then Nely remembered, and she whispered:

"It was Javier who loved her."

There was much more I wanted to ask her, but it had already grown dark. I told her that I would surely return to Cuba someday, and leaned over to kiss her papery cheek. She had grown melancholy, or else was tired of dredging up useless old memories. But Nely summoned one last smile, as sad and beautiful as Havana herself, as I said goodbye.

I walked out into the pale, ominous night. The shabby houses of the Vedado seemed abandoned, many with boarded windows, but a woman eyed me suspiciously from her porch. I turned at the sound of footsteps behind me and was relieved to see a policeman making his rounds. Somehow, I found my way to the Havana Riviera, the garish hotel built by Meyer Lansky in the 1950s. But there were no cabs, and I decided to walk back to the Hotel Nacional. As I set out along the Malecón, the sky was clear and the purplish waves glinted in the moonlight. The long, sweeping boulevard was deserted except for an occasional passing car, but a salty breeze swept in from the water. Soon, I could see the lighthouse of El Morro, far across the bay, its beacon sweeping over the great blue river.

I remembered the article I was to write about Hemingway. With a bit of luck, I could hash it out on the plane to New York and get it to my editor by next week. I knew there was something else I wanted to write, and I thought I heard the echo of a distant voice, still too faint to be heard clearly.

But it was only two *jineteras*, pretty young girls on the prowl for tourists, their musical laughter blending with the murmur of the waves, their high heels clattering on the pavement. Mistaking me for a Cuban, they contemptuously walked past, on their way to the Hotel Nacional.

AUTHOR'S NOTE

A number of other books conspired to bring this one about. There are far too many biographies of Ernest Hemingway, but the best place to start is still *Hemingway: A Life Story*, by Carlos Baker. His early days in Cuba are often ignored but are covered in *Hemingway: The 1930s*, by Michael Reynolds and *Hemingway in Cuba*, by Norberto Fuentes. Hemingway was indeed a witness to the fall of Machado and described this period in *To Have and Have Not*. For marlin fishing, I relied upon his articles for *Esquire* such as "Marlin off the Morro." His ambiguous relationship with Jane Kendall Mason, the real-life model for Margot Macomber, is explored in *Hemingway*, by Jeffrey Meyers and *The Hemingway Women*, by Bernice Kemp. The logbooks of the *Anita* at the Hemingway Collection of the John F. Kennedy Library in Boston also proved invaluable.

The abortive revolution of 1933 is a seminal episode in Cuban history which is largely forgotten today. It set the stage for all that was to follow and led to the unexpected rise of Fulgencio Batista, who would effectively rule the island until 1959. A good overview is provided by *Cuba: The Pursuit of Freedom*, by Hugh Thomas. Remarkably little has been written about the ABC. The *abecedarios* have been unfairly derided as fascists but they were largely responsible for overthrowing Machado. For my description of the violence which swept through Havana on August 12, 1933, I relied upon contemporary accounts in the *Havana Post* and *Bohemia*.

I am also indebted to *Cuban Santería*, by Raúl Canizares for an introduction to the world of the *orishas* and to *Nationalizing Blackness*, by Robin Moore for a look at the music and theater of the time.

If my characters are fictional, the city they inhabit is as real as I could make it. Hemingway's room in the Hotel Ambos Mundos is now a museum and a statue of him guards his favorite stool at the Floridita. The Plaza de San Francisco and the dock where the *Anita* was moored have changed little, but unfortunately the Café de la Perla has disappeared. For descriptions of this long-lost Havana, I relied upon the delightful *We Remember Cuba*, by John Parker, and Cuban writers such as Alejo Carpentier. Any inconsistencies are my fault, not theirs.

My thanks to Mary for being the first to read it, to my parents for their recollections, and to my friends for their support, particularly Gustavo for driving me to Cabañas, Peter for his patience, and Mao for his pisco sours. *Gracias*.